MW01700781

Leslie -

My latest work. hope you enjoy it!

Love -

Colleen

River of Grace

Colleen K. Snyder

CROSSBOOKS
PUBLISHING

CrossBooks™
A Division of LifeWay
1663 Liberty Drive
Bloomington, IN 47403
www.crossbooks.com
Phone: 1-866-879-0502

First published by CrossBooks 4/23/2013

ISBN: 978-1-4627-2639-4 (sc)
ISBN: 978-1-4627-2641-7 (hc)
ISBN: 978-1-4627-2640-0 (e)

Library of Congress Control Number: 2013904805

Printed in the United States of America.

This book is printed on acid-free paper.

Dedication

"My story for his Glory"

All glory be to the Father
And to the Son
And to the Holy Spirit
Through Jesus Christ our Lord,

Amen.

Acknowledgments

Deepest thanks to:

The men who are teaching me freedom: Kondo Simfukwe, Keith Minier, Drew Waggoner.
The women who believe in me: Mom, Sue (my sisser, my matey!)
The friend who encouraged and edited this: Jan O'Daniel

FRIDAY

As soon as Collin Walker's feet hit the bottom step of the tour bus exit she heard it: that low, pounding, distinctive rumble of a river. A river somewhere nearby. Somewhere very nearby. She froze, overwhelmed by the panicked impulse to fight her way back upstream through the departing campers, dive under the back bench seat and not come out until the week was over and she was safely back home. A thought, useless but a thought, kept circling through her head: *"A river. Dear God in heaven, there's a river. A river. Dear God in heaven, there's a river."*

Her mental breakdown was interrupted by a young hand on her shoulder and a rather sarcastic, "Hey, case worker lady. You getting off this bus or what? They's some of us what wants to visit the facilities, you know? Been a long trip. Move it."

Life returned to Collin's feet at least and she stepped off the bus, moving aside to let the remainder of the 40 odd campers—and their vastly odder counselors—disembark. *"Odder? That's not a word." "Odder—you know: those cute little furry things that swim in the water? Odders in the wadders." "And wadders make rivers." "And rivers make Collin crazy."*

Collin shut down the internal tormentors. Sane. She was sane. She would be sane the remainder of this trip. Sane, you hear me? It would sure be easier to pull off without the cursed cackling in her head, but she'd deal with that later. The twenty-six year old Children's Services counselor leaned against the side of the bus to get her bearings and her breath. She slowly brought herself back under the rigid control she had developed over the years. The many years. The too many years . . .

Collin shook her head angrily to still the jaybirds. That same juvenile voice from the bus asked curiously, "Who you fightin' with in there, huh?"

Robbie Siders, her fourteen year-old ward for the week, stood in front of her trying to look cool and disinterested, all the while sounding exactly the opposite. Collin drew in a silent—but much needed—calming breath. "I'm working on a plan to beat your sorry anatomy in hoops, that's what."

Robbie offered half a grin. "No wonder you having a tough time of it."

Collin threatened, "Watch it, bro. You know the old saying, 'He who laughs last . . .'"

Robbie interrupted her with his own rendition of the axiom, "'. . . Didn't get the joke the first time.' I ain't afraid of you or any plan you got."

"Don't get cocky, my man. I nearly tied the score on you the last time we played."

"Nearly don't 'mount to nothing."

"Yeah, well, tell you what. This looks like good neutral territory. What say you and me meet on the back court tonight about nine and see if this plan I got works?"

"Back court? What back court?"

Collin sighed. "Rob, if this place has more than one court it has to have a back court. If it has a front court, it has a back court. I'll meet you at nine on the back court and we'll see if you're as good as your mouth on foreign soil."

Robbie grinned evilly. "My mouth got nothing to do with it. Be my feet an' my hands do the talking. You ain't never beat me yet, and you ain't never gonna."

"Never's a long time, my friend."

Robbie took two sliding steps back, then quipped, "You'd be the one to know 'bout long times!" He took off running for the lodge apparently assured in his own mind that whatever might have been wrong, Collin was back to her old self.

She looked around the entrance to Camp Grace, forcing herself to suppress the ominous and omnipresent sound of the river. Ignore the water and the place was gorgeous. High in the mountains of West Virginia, planets away from the streets of Oakton where she worked and lived and fought and died . . . The sun was lowering itself behind the towering trees that sheltered the lodge. Even though it was only seven, the valley they were in would soon be pitched in darkness. Vibrant green grass grew natural and wild in meadows and patches where the trees relented to allow sunshine. Flowering vines trailed up and around stumps, fence posts, and down spouts. Birds darted in and out of sight; fat crows cawed their superiority and then fled from kamikaze sparrows defending their territory. This was paradise. At least for the week, if she could handle it.

For Robbie she'd handle it. For Robbie she'd handle anything. Almost. She'd been his case worker for ten months. But she had never fallen as deeply for a "case" before. Without question she loved all her kids and treated them with the same intensity. But there was something familiar in Robbie, something that struck a chord in her past. Whatever it took, she was going to see he got the chance out of his past without the heartache and pain that continued to mark her life.

Collin cast off the shadows. This trip wasn't about her, it was about Robbie. A "challenge camp" the flyer said. A sports challenge camp offering both traditional and extreme sports in an effort to draw hardened and jaded youngsters. It was state approved—but not sponsored—which meant the cost had to be borne by the parent/s or the counselor. Yet no cost had been listed, which had made Collin suspicious. The flyer stated that financial aid or grants were available on request. But when Collin had called to request, the cost had been so ridiculously low she wondered if the camp was even real. Yet the state had approved it so she sent off the registration and fees, only to have both returned. The registration was approved; the fees waived. Interesting. Quiet and careful inquiries to other attendees revealed that they, too, were attending gratis. Collin determined to find out all she could about this camp: who owned it, and why he/she/they would be so interested in street kids that they would foot the bill to bring them here. And although the others might be simply pleased and grateful, Collin couldn't help but maintain a jaundiced eye. Paradise had its snakes, too.

A mental shot to the head brought her up short. *"Look around you, fool!!! Look around you!! You stand in God's glory, here by God's grace, and you're looking for corruption? Do you stand in the Taj Mahal and look only at the cracks? Walk through the gardens of Versailles and look for the weeds? Or, on your travel budget, go to Cedar Point and see only the gull droppings? Wake up!! Lighten up!! You're here to have fun. Remember fun? No? Then learn. It might come in handy someday. You teach it to your kids. Now learn it yourself."*

Properly chastised, Collin grit her teeth and headed for the lodge. She dodged a lone maintenance man unloading and carting the luggage. He may have smiled at her. He may have even spoken to her but Collin didn't notice. She would have *fun* She *would* have fun. She would *have* fun if it killed her. Internal consensus was that her "wise as serpents" act was good, but her "harmless as doves" needed tremendous work. This would be as good a place as any to relearn what she'd never learned to begin with. Or something like that. Collin growled under her breath and kept walking.

Once inside, Collin followed the escort down the corridors to the female side of the building. She noted Robbie's room number and the name of the counselor overseeing him. Only one was assigned to a room unless otherwise requested. Collin knew that some of these kids would be sleeping alone—not just in the room, but in the bed—for the first time. She envisioned a few sleepless nights for some of them. Hopefully it would work itself out. Collin found herself in charge of two ten year-old girls, Jill and Chenille, rooming together. Both were of the giggly sort; not ones you would suspect of being in trouble or on the verge of being declared incorrigible. But Collin knew their jackets—and their counselors—well. Which was why the girls were here, and the counselors weren't.

Collin showed them how to work the push-button locks on the doors (no keys to lose,) how to call her room if they needed anything during the night (no phones, intercoms only, and only to her room,) how to set the (built-in) alarm clock provided for each room. The rooms also came equipped with a night light (also built in,) rechargeable flashlight (the one mobile concession to pilferage,) and plenty of places to store, stuff, or hang belongings.

A sign on the back of the door explained the basics for existence at Camp Grace. Collin reviewed the salient features for her charges: breakfast was from seven to eight, no exceptions. Latecomers went hungry. Timing for lunch was predicated on the day's activities, as was dinner. Healthy snacks of carrots, celery, apples, raisins, and assorted power foods were freely available at the health bar below the main concourse.

The notice went on to inform new campers that on arrival they should stow their gear then report back to the great room at the head of the corridor for an overview of the camp, including its rules, regulations, and opportunities. Because of the lateness of the hour of their arrival, a full tour would be conducted tomorrow starting one-half hour after breakfast. Tonight they would meet the Camp Director, the staff, and the maintenance crew.

Collin left Jill and Chenille and wandered back to her own room. She shut the door and listened for a moment. Yep, it was still there. Even though the windows were closed and fastened, and the black-out drapes came down below the jams, she could still hear the tormentor of her dreams. Collin bit her lip then drew herself up again. It didn't matter. Sound couldn't hurt you. As long as she stayed away from the river it couldn't hurt her.

And where was it written she had to go any closer than she already was? Nowhere. Get over it.

Collin looked at the camp directions again. The edict to stow gear and meet back at the hall interested her. Did all buses arrive this late? These were standard signs, posted, it seemed, permanently. There must be some logic behind it but Collin was a little too travel-weary to figure it out. Maybe that was the reason right there. Let weary people rest before subjecting them to the temptations of all the fun and excitement. Made sense. Collin escorted the girls to the great room then looked for Robbie.

She found him sitting by the window staring up at the heavens. Outside, pine trees soared to vast heights reaching 100, 200, 300 feet high. Towering canyon walls marched away out of view to either side, their craggy peaks barely visible to human eyes. Robbie did not stop staring but acknowledged Collin's presence by whispering, "I never seen anything this big before. Never been anywhere this big."

Collin sat down beside him and said softly, "Now you get an idea of what awesome really means."

Robbie turned and looked at her for a moment, then nodded. "I guess so." He looked back out the window. "Can we go out there?"

"I'm sure that's on the agenda. But probably not yet. My guess is the next order of business will be the introductions, a list of rules to remember, question and answer sessions, and then dinner. After that, free time then bed. Tomorrow we hit it hard."

Robbie gave her a curious look. "You been to these camps before?"

Collin grinned. "A few." She motioned towards the crowd gathering in the center of the room. "Let's join the circle and see if I'm right."

Robbie reluctantly followed Collin to where the campers and counselors were congregating. The camp director was speaking, ". . . so if everyone could close in just enough to hear and be heard, I would appreciate it." He waited as the crowd moved in ever so slightly, then continued. "Good. Welcome to Camp Grace. I am Steve Parks, Camp Director. I won't bore you with our history; if you're really interested, we have literature at the office. If you're not, we'll save a few trees. Our mission is simple and is directly for you young people." Most of the campers looked up, curious. Robbie kept his eyes fixed on the floor, feigning non-interest. The director continued, "Our goal is to teach you one thing: you can. That's it. That's all."

A girl spoke up. "Can what?" General murmurs echoed the question.

"You can. Can do anything you set yourself to do."

An older boy snorted. "Yeah, right. Like I can jump like Michael Jordan."

Mr. Parks smiled. "Maybe. Have you tried?"

"Sure, man. I can't do it."

"Have you studied how he gets his lift? Have you practiced the steps he takes? Have you exercised and worked out and jogged and sweated like he does?"

The boy snorted again. "No."

"Then you won't jump like he does. Doing isn't something magic that just happens. It's something you make happen using all the resources and talents and abilities you have. Anyone here know who Muggsy Bogues is?"

There was general silence. Then to Collin's amazement Robbie said quietly, "The shortest player in NBA history."

The director nodded. "Good. Know how tall he is?"

Robbie answered, "Five foot three."

"Exactly right. About as tall as . . ." Mr. Parks looked for a target then chose a woman counselor as his example, ". . . about as tall as this. Your name, please?"

"Sherry Gerald."

"How tall are you, madam?"

She said, "Five one when I stretch."

The director smiled. "I see. Would you mind standing next to Mr. Lawler, please?" Mr. Lawler was well over six feet tall. The kids giggled and sneered as Ms. Gerald stood back to back with Mr. Lawler. It was as good a visual demonstration as they were going to get. The director asked, "Think it would be any match? Who is going to win here?"

"Mr. Lawler." The group was unanimous.

"So would Muggsy have any chance in the NBA?"

"No."

Mr. Parks turned to Robbie. "How did he do out there?"

Robbie kept his head down but said loud enough to be heard, "Played for Wake Forest in college. It's in the ACC. He was the all-time leader in assists and steals on his team."

Someone sniped, "No jive. He so close to the floor, ain't no one gonna see him coming."

Robbie glared in the direction of the speaker then continued, "Senior year he led his team in scoring. Finished as the ACC's all-time leader in assist and steals."

Someone from the opposite side of the room asked a buddy, "ACC? Ain't that Duke and Carolina? Those teams?"

"Yeah. He must have been good."

Robbie nodded. "He was. Was number two in the NBA in assists in 93-94 season and led the Charlotte Hornets in assists in 96-97. He played for the Warriors and he then played for the Raptors. He was old, but he was still hustling." Robbie looked sidelong at Collin, a sly grin on his face. Collin shook her head slightly but added nothing to the tale.

There was silence as the attentive audience tried to comprehend what was being told. When Robbie finished the director asked, "Okay, what did he have, magic? Or the want and the will to work to make a dream come true?" The silence deepened. Mr. Parks continued, "This week is to show you that you can. We're going to give you opportunities to do and try things you've thought about, dreamed about, had nightmares about, or just wanted to see." A nightmare or two flashed through Collin's mind but she shook them off instantly. Not now. The director continued, "None of them will be simple. All will require thought, sweat, practice, and in some cases teamwork. In the morning a tour of the camp will be provided for all those who can greet the daylight without a snarl. Snarlers can go in the afternoon. You'll have the opportunity to sample some of our offerings, weather permitting. There is a partial list of activities on the board at the end of the hall just to give you—I started to say 'fodder to chew on,' but three quarters of you would have no idea what I meant. So let's put it this way: it will give you something to think about."

He looked around and said, "A word to you counselors: your students have free rein to choose whatever they want. Their medical records have been reviewed and there is no physical reason anyone should be restricted from participating. Don't fall into the trap of thinking you know your children better than we do, or better than they know themselves." He smiled slightly. "It would do you all some good to participate as well. Show your kids you believe, too. Show them it works."

As a means of closing he said, "There are a few important people you will get to know. The first we hope you never see: our camp physician, Dr. Wallace." A thirty-something, casual-looking gentleman in blue jeans, khaki shirt and knee-high cowboy boots, with sandy-blonde shoulder length hair pulled back in a ponytail waved from his seat on the front desk. The director continued, "My assistant, Leeann Baker, will make any arrangements in case of emergencies either here or at home." An older woman, fifty something, slightly overweight, wearing a red business dress waved from her position against the wall. "Ted Johnson is our activities director." Another wave from another strategically placed employee. Collin noted that they seemed to be surrounding the group. Maybe sizing up the kids? Or maybe just getting a feel for the group dynamics? Mr. Parks continued, "Our maintenance staff is manned by Jeff Farrell, who appears to be missing." He looked at the activities director, who shrugged then mouthed, "Generators." Mr. Parks nodded slightly then finished with, "Our chief cook, Chef Michael, is downstairs preparing dinner. He will introduce himself to you there. Enjoy your meal. Afterwards you may walk around outside, or use the ball courts and recreation rooms. There is an indoor pool or you can sample the library. Relax and have fun. Enjoy your weekend because come Monday, you're mine." He grinned evilly, rubbing his hands together. "Any questions?"

If there had been, no one felt inclined to offer them. The director smiled and said, "You may consider yourselves dismissed, then."

The crowd moved off towards the dining hall. Collin caught Robbie's sleeve, slowing him down. She said, "That was real good work, Rob. You did study up on him."

Robbie shrugged it off. "I was bored. I figured I could get you off my back if you brought him up again."

"It was still good work." As they tromped down the steps to the dining hall Collin warned, "Just remember we've got an appointment tonight. Don't eat too much."

Robbie sneered, "Case worker lady, I could eat everything they got and still beat you."

As they turned the corner and entered the hall, Collin and Robbie stopped short. Ahead of them was the largest buffet either of them had ever seen. There was literally something for everyone. The pickiest eater would have no excuse to starve here. Meat, chicken, fish, casseroles, vegetables, (including French fries,) salads, pasta dishes, Mexican cuisine, desserts . . . all lay stretched out before them. Collin looked at the spread then asked, "You want to retract that statement?"

"You mean take it back? Yeah. I ain't never seen so much food."

"Neither have I, Rob. Neither have I." Collin wondered at the expanse. This couldn't all be for just them. No one in their right mind would prepare a meal like this for forty kids and a handful of counselors. The waste must be incredible. The thought nagged at Collin as she filled her plate then went to sit down. Robbie had headed off to a corner with some friends. The cafeteria was by no means packed and many of the tables were unoccupied.

Uncharacteristically, Collin didn't feel like dining alone. She would have to choose a dinner date. She could go join the kids, but having spent the better part of the afternoon and evening with them, she preferred a quieter companion. She looked around the room then noticed a young man sitting alone towards the back of the room. He was by no means . . . well, maybe by some means . . . okay, some might call him handsome. Sandy brown—bordering on red-hair, maybe late twenties, early thirties . . . honest features. Though as she stood there examining the man, she couldn't figure out what that expression really meant. How could a nose be dishonest?

Eyes, now, those could tell a tale. Except he was reading and hadn't noticed her. Yet. Good thing. He might think she was staring. Which she was. Sort of. A little.

The unfortunate object of her guarded scrutiny wore the uniform of a maintenance worker. Collin vaguely remembered passing by someone in just such a uniform earlier this evening . . . the bus. He was unloading the bus. Oh, great. And she'd walked right past him. Maybe he wouldn't remember. Maybe he wouldn't remember her. Maybe . . .

The man had a book propped up in front of his tray, reading as he ate. Collin felt extremely brazen at the thought of just walking up and saying, "Hi. I'm the rude idiot that ignored you earlier. Can I join you now?" Hussy. Brazen hussy. Maybe he wouldn't want company. Maybe he wouldn't want her company. Maybe . . .

Collin growled at herself, *"Shut up!"* This was ridiculous. She straightened her back and walked purposefully across the room, only to slow to a stop again as she neared his table. She couldn't walk up to a perfect stranger and force herself on him, could she? Could she?

The man looked up at her and smiled. The eyes did indeed tell a story. All reservations vanished as Collin rebuked the coward inside, *"You bet I can."* She smiled, feeling shy and awkward, and asked, "Mind if I sit down?"

The man waved gallantly, moving his books aside. "Of course not. It took you long enough to make up your mind, though."

So he'd been watching her? Did he remember the bus? Collin demurred slightly at the challenge but said only, "I promise I won't disturb you."

"That's good. People tell me I'm disturbed enough as it is." He grinned at her.

Collin sat down, feeling like she needed to take charge of this situation and quickly. She extended her hand. "I'm Collin Walker."

The man started to extend his hand then drew it back slightly. Collin noted that his hands were clean but stained from oil, grease, and other lubricants of his trade. She reached out further, took his hand firmly, and said, "Hi, I'm Collin Walker."

He shook her hand (a good strong handshake,) and said, "Jeff Farrell." He pointed to the name on his shirt. "That's to remind me."

"Wish I had something like that. But I need something to remind me where I am not who I am." There were too many whos anyhow. But she refused to discuss that right now.

Jeff asked, "Do you travel a lot then?"

"More than I'd like but probably less than I should." She let him chew on that one while she bowed her head and gave thanks for her food. When she looked up there was a different kind of look on Jeff's face, a look Collin couldn't read. Had she offended him? Put him off? Better to find out now than later.

The man smiled, finally, and said, "A woman who's not afraid to practice what she believes even in a crowd. You are a rare find."

Collin shrugged, a little uncomfortable. She deflected the subject and said, "I'm not even sure what I've got here. What's good?"

"Everything Chef Michael fixes. He's a great cook. And he knows kids. Your kids will go home fat and happy—well, they will if we don't run the fat off of them first."

Collin grinned. "That's what we came for." She looked at his books and asked, "What are you studying? Why are you studying? It's Friday night."

"Electrical wiring. So I can make sure we have power Saturday morning." He looked at her and asked, "You know anything about electrical wiring?"

"I know enough to call an electrician when I have a problem. Does that count?"

Jeff stared at her as if floored. He closed his eyes, shook his head in disbelief then slammed the book shut. A grin appeared and he let out a satisfied, "Yes!" He nodded to Collin and said, "Thank you. Thank you very much." Lastly he looked skyward and said, "And thank you!" Jeff must have noted the look of concern that shadowed Collin's face briefly, for he said, "No, I'm not nuts. Well, yes I am, but not about this. I've been fighting for two days trying to solve this problem and it's not mine. I need to call an expert. I get so wrapped up in these things trying to do it on my own." He stopped then said soberly, "I'm sure you've never had that problem. You wouldn't know."

Collin shook her head. "Of course not. Never. Not even once." She looked at the ceiling and asked, "You have lightning rods on your roof?"

Jeff grinned. "No. Are we going to need them?"

"Maybe. If I don't quit lying you will. What kind of problem are you having?"

Jeff looked surprised. "You really want to know?"

"I really want to know."

"Okay, it started Wednesday when we lost power to the horse barn. We thought it was a breaker but they all tested good. The power came back on while we were testing the lines themselves, which was a great shock to all of us."

Collin smiled at the joke and began sampling her food. She tried the tuna casserole first. It smelled and tasted just like her mom's.

Smell can be a powerful memory stimulus, and a surge of memories came flooding back. The thought of her mom cracked open the door on a gaping black hole, one she thought she had closed years ago. Collin stared into its depths, feeling the once familiar death grip on her awareness. With desperate effort she slammed the door, stomping it closed for emphasis.

Her satisfaction was short-lived as she slowly realized Jeff was still talking. She heard him say, ". . . and that's why we use the elephants instead of generators."

Collin knew she'd been caught, but tried to cover anyhow. "Fascinating. I thought you used kangaroos."

Jeff asked softly, "Where did you go? I don't think I've ever seen someone zone out so completely. I didn't mean to bore you, but you did ask."

"I'm sorry, Jeff. It wasn't personal believe me. I . . ." Collin fumbled for an answer—or an explanation—but could find none.

Jeff bailed her out. "Don't apologize. Teach me how to do that. I've got some professors I'd like to try that on. It would make their lectures a lot less boring. Or at least tolerable."

Collin smiled slightly, appreciating what he was doing. She followed his rabbit trail. "So you're in school? Where? What are you studying?"

Jeff shrugged. "Grad school actually. And I'm studying electrical engineering. But I think it's hopeless." He smiled. "And useless. All I need to know is to call the expert, right?"

"Right." Collin shook off the shadows and asked, "Are you from around here?"

"Unfortunately, no. I commute from Oakton. I work the challenge camps. I love to watch what this place can do for a kid."

"So Camp Grace isn't just for kids?"

"Again, unfortunately no. Well, I shouldn't say unfortunately. It's the way it's been allowed to develop so far. We have trouble convincing state agencies that we're legitimate. We do about four challenge camps for the inner city crowd in the summer and two or three in the spring. We also do two handicapped camps, but that requires a lot of modification so we have to schedule those carefully. The rest of the season we're a regular for hire camp. Winter, we're a ski resort."

"It must keep you busy."

"It does. But it's only part time. I just work the challenge camps, and set up and tear down for the handicap sessions." He pointed to her tray and said, "You stopped eating."

In truth Collin's appetite had vanished. Not wishing to prompt the return of any other "old business," she pushed her tray away. "I'm done."

Jeff shook his head. "You can't be done, you never even started."

Collin ignored him, though his concern touched her. She changed the subject. "What do you do when you're not at camp and you're not in school? It must be kind of tough on your family with you being gone all the time."

A bemused look crossed Jeff's face. "You mean like a wife-and-child-kind of family? Is that what you're asking?"

Collin tried to look innocent. "Not exactly. But are you?"

"Am I what?"

"Married?"

"Would it make a difference if I was?"

Collin said sharply—more sharply than she intended, "Yes."

"Good. It should. No, I'm not. No children, either. And I hope that makes a difference, too."

Collin had never felt less in control, more aggravated, and yet not nearly as intrigued as she was with this man. She couldn't read him at all unless it was in his eyes. And she dare not look there too long, nor too deep. She responded, "It does. It makes all the difference." She looked up at him and challenged, "It means you at least have the decency to consider someone else's feelings before subjecting them to your harebrained lifestyle."

Jeff grinned. "Touché. It won't always be like this. One day I hope to work here full time. But right now economics plays a big part in it. I have commitments in Oakton to care for."

"Like what?"

Jeff grinned again. "You are nosy aren't you?"

Collin nodded. "I'm a counselor. That's what we do. We ask questions, dig around in people's heads, make them tell us their deep dark secrets." Warning bells began to go off in her head. Too much truth for this weekend. Collin sat up straighter, trying to lighten the intensity of the moment.

Jeff shook his head slightly. "My turn to ask questions. I know you're a counselor. I know you're a very dedicated counselor because you're using your vacation time to be here, or taking the week off without pay, which means you're a very wealthy counselor and you wouldn't be in this line of work if you were, unless you really, really, loved kids. And then you'd be the one bankrolling this trip. Do you have any family? Meaning besides the obligatory mother, father, siblings, and yes, I'm asking specifically are you married? I see no ring, or ring shadow, but that doesn't mean what it used to. Married women don't wear rings and unmarried women have them on every finger. How's a guy supposed to know the difference?"

Collin shook her head in amusement. "Was there a question in all that?"

Jeff said seriously, "Several. One, are you married? Two, do you have family? Three, what do you do to enjoy yourself?"

Collin said, "One, no. Two, no. Three . . . um . . . I am enjoying myself."

Jeff seemed a little surprised. "You are?"

Collin nodded, a little surprised herself. "Yeah, I am. It's been a long time since I've had time to sit and talk to someone older than 18. At least not on this level."

Jeff looked around. "What, down in the basement?"

Collin said firmly, "Stop before you hurt yourself. You know what I mean."

Jeff grinned but said evenly, "Yes, I do. And I'm glad you're enjoying yourself. You strike me as a lady with far too little play in her life."

"And you're not?"

"A lady? I hoped that was obvious."

She frowned at him. "Stop that. Can you be serious?"

"For more than five seconds? Yes. And no, I am not without play in my life."

"So when you're not in school and you're not up here, you do what for fun?"

"I'm a paramedic."

Collin studied him a long while then said quietly, "So this is the fun stuff."

He smiled a bit sadly at her understanding. "This is the fun stuff. It's not always intense, and I love what I do. But coming here gives me a break." He stretched and added, "It also gives me a break from my dad. I manage some properties for him and he's death on detail."

Collin stomped the door to the black hole, lest anything even try to slip out. She said, her voice tighter than she intended, "I see. How long . . ."

She was spared from further self-revelation by the sudden appearance of Robbie. He came sauntering up to the table with his "I be cool" affect, but Collin could read the excitement under the surface. At least him she could still read. Robbie said, "A bunch of us is gonna walk to the canyon floor to see the river. You want to come, case worker lady?"

Collin shook her head. "No, Rob. You go. I'd slow you down, seeing as you're always telling me I'm 'old folk' you know."

Jeff jumped to Rob's support. "It's beautiful. You ought to go."

Collin continued to refuse. "Maybe later."

Rob protested, "Aw, come on, lady. I promise, ain't none of us gonna fall in."

Jeff added, "The trail's well marked and there's a turn out with benches. We keep it lit in the evenings. It's a great spot."

Collin looked at him, a little confused. Was he dismissing her? Had enough already? Seen what he wanted and she'd failed the test? What had she said this time?

As if sensing her thoughts Jeff said, "I'll be here all week. I'd like it if we could talk again." He grinned and asked, "Maybe you can explain about the kangaroos."

Still unsure, Collin nodded. "I hope so." She looked at Robbie and said, "Okay, man. Do you know how to get there? More important, do you know how to get back?"

Robbie laughed. "Lady, have I ever got lost?"

"That's not the question. You've gotten me lost plenty of times telling me how to get someplace to pick you up or drop you off. I refuse to be a den mate with some grizzly because you can't remember which tree we turned at."

Robbie chuckled. "Ain't no grizzlies in West Virginia."

"How do you know?"

"I learnt it in school."

Collin acted shocked. "You learned it in school? You mean they actually taught you something you can use? Will wonders never cease?"

Robbie pulled her to her feet and said, "Yeah, yeah, I know. So maybe it wasn't all a waste of time. Maybe there was some stuff that stuck. Let's go."

Collin waved at Jeff as Robbie dragged her off. "I hope I see you around, Jeff."

As Collin was pulled out of earshot Jeff said softly, "You will. You will."

As the ten kids—and one counselor—hiked ever downward towards the river bank, the excitement of the group was enough to drive most of Collin's growing fear into submission. Most of it. The balance she had to try to bury on her own. But finally she reached her breaking (and braking) point. Collin stopped as they neared the look out. They were still maybe a hundred yards from where the river would be; close enough to feel the throbbing pulse in her being, but not close enough to actually see the water. Or feel the spray in her face. On her face. Over her face . . .

Collin told Rob, "You guys go on. I'll wait here."

Rob looked at her, confused. "What? Why?"

Collin shook her head. "I got my reasons. You young guns forget what goes down easy goes back up exponentially harder. I'll rest up here and beat you all up the hill. Go on."

She read the instant of disappointment in his eyes before his cool facade kicked in. "Suit yourself. We be back later."

Collin sighed slightly as he turned and followed the crowd. This was going to be difficult. She would have to come up with an explanation. One near enough to the truth that she wasn't lying but dull enough to keep anyone from asking questions. Collin sat back against a tree, set her mind on reviewing praise hymns she knew. It would occupy the time—and her brain—until the kids returned.

It was a rather silent and subdued group that returned. Collin guessed the reasons but decided to make them put it in words to help crystallize the experience. She asked quietly, "How was it, Luke?"

The ten year old shook his head. His voice was low as he said, "I never seen anything like it. Nothing. It's so . . . so . . ."

Jeshua bailed him out. "So powerful. So big. The only running water I've ever seen comes out in the tub at home. I didn't know there could be something so . . ."

As the young teen ran out of words, twelve year old Awana picked up the torch and ran with it. Well, she walked with it, anyhow. "Yeah, I know what you mean. I mean, I seen rivers on TV before, on all those nature shows my folks make me watch." She grimaced, then continued, "But seeing it on a little screen doesn't give you any idea how . . ."

No one filled in the blank. No one had to. Collin understood exactly their feelings. She nodded and said quietly, "And this is only the first night. What else do you think they have out here?"

Silence met her, as ten teens and teen wannabes considered the possibilities ahead. Finally, someone—Collin couldn't be sure who—whispered softly, "Wow."

Suddenly someone else, equally anonymous, quipped, "Hey, I can say that backwards! Wowww." He dragged the word out for emphasis.

There was the sound of several someones slugging the jokester, who started running off, jeering at his jury. Swift pursuit followed him and just as swiftly halted, as the steepness of the hill overcame even their youthful exuberance. A mid-range walk became the gait of choice and talking gave way to simply breathing. And although the walk down had taken maybe fifteen minutes, the walk back took nearly twice as long. To their credit everyone made it without whining audibly, and no one had to be carried. Good thing, too. Most all the group outweighed her and, with the exception of Robbie, all the young males were taller than she was. Robbie, of mixed and unknown heritage, was coming into his growth spurt late. Very late. It was a source of injured pride and pain to him, and drove him to work hard to be taken seriously. Unfortunately not all the avenues he chose to work in were positive.

As the group returned to the lodge Robbie asked quietly, "Case worker lady, you mind not getting whopped in hoops tonight? It ain't gonna spoil your day or nothing will it?"

"Why, Rob?"

"I don't know." Collin rarely saw Robbie this subdued or contemplative. "I think I want to be alone for a while. Be alone and jus' think. Something 'bout the river jus' make me wanna think."

Collin nodded. "I understand." She let out a somewhat shaky breath then said, "Tomorrow night." They came to the parting of the sexes: boys' rooms to the left, girls' rooms to the right, with a staffed entry hall between them. Collin stopped, turned to face Robbie and asked, "You okay, bro?"

He nodded. "Yeah. It's just that everything out there is so . . . so . . ." Collin waited for him to get his thought out. He apparently couldn't find the words any more than the other teens had, so finished lamely, ". . . so big, I guess. I mean, city buildings is big but man made them. I could build one of them. But the trees and the river, all of it . . . it's huge, and it got that way without me being here; without no man being here helping it or telling it what to do. Like we don't even matter or nothing."

Collin ached to hug the boy but knew that was forbidden territory. She said quietly, "You matter, Rob. More than you know, you matter. If you think this is good, wait. It gets better."

"What?" Robbie wasn't following her.

Collin shook her head. "Never mind. We'll talk about it later. Good night, Rob. Get some sleep." She thought, *"At least one of us should."*

"Night, case worker lady." The two parted company, and went to their respective rooms. Collin checked on her two charges, who were contentedly positioned in the same bed. She set an 11 pm curfew on giggling, and a 12 am cutoff on talking. Probably a waste of time; the girls would be asleep within the hour anyhow. Collin went back to her room. She debated whether to shower now or in the morning. That 6 am breakfast call was awfully early. But the thought of running water cascading over her head was more fuel to an already-glowing ember she was trying hard to extinguish. Collin changed into her nightshirt, took her Bible from her backpack and settled into bed to read. She muttered, "Numbers. Genealogy. If that can't put me to sleep, nothing can." She opened the book, then added, "Either that or the tabernacle. The gifts those princes brought for the dedication. Trying to memorize that would be almost as good." She looked at the first page of the chapter and whispered, "I hope."

Outside the windows, the heartbeat of the river pulsed on.

SATURDAY

Morning tends to sneak up on Camp Grace. Nestled between the cliffs and the trees, it stays in shadow longer than expected. The sun hides just long enough to come to full strength and brilliance before popping up on the unfortunate inhabitants of the east wing of the lodge. Collin, however, welcomed the sunshine as a respite from the interminable night. She had drifted in and out of fitful sleep, never allowing herself to fall deeply enough to dream. She ached as she rose from the bed. Stretching only alerted her to more places that ached. After that walk last night she was going to be in wonderful shape she could tell. Today would be a thrill a minute.

Collin knocked on the door of her charges; there was no answer. She popped her head in and saw the two girls still asleep: one in the bed and one on the floor. Collin went in quietly and shook one camper carefully. "Come on, Jill. Rise and shine." She shook the girl in the bed. "Let's go, Chenille. It's your first day at camp. Up and at 'em. Move 'em out."

A voice from the floor groaned, "I can't move!"

Collin smiled. "I know the feeling. But if you want breakfast you've only got half an hour left to get it."

The sleeping bag on the mattress launched itself into the air. "Breakfast? Half an hour? No way, man!"

Collin nodded, "Find a way, man. I don't think these guys are joking about sending people away hungry. Unless you have a taste for apples and granola bars." Both girls began making gagging noises. "That's what I thought. You'll have to give up looking beautiful and settle for looking full. Now move it!"

She closed the door and retreated to her own room. There was no way she would make it to breakfast, either, but an apple and juice would be fine. It would. A niggle in the back of her conscience nudged her. Collin dismissed it. She was eating. She was. An apple was eating. After that spread last night there would be plenty of opportunity to fill up. She wasn't trying to control anything, here. She was just . . . she was just eating light this first morning. Besides, she really wanted to make the morning tour and find out just where she and Robbie had landed themselves. Steve Parks, the Camp director, had said last night that the tour started after breakfast. Which could be any time after eight. She should have checked last night for a definitive time. She knew the place: the front of the lodge. Collin opened her window, drew in a deep breath of clean air, and immediately shivered. Even though it was early August and probably sweltering back home, it was crisp up here. Dress accordingly. She washed quickly in the sink, promising the world a full shower later. She chose her jeans rather than shorts and picked a short sleeve pullover with a zip up sweatshirt. Collin ran the brush through her shoulder length hair, pulled her hat on, stuffed her Bible in her satchel and headed out the door. She banged on Jill and Chenille's door as she went by, "Ten minutes," and grinned at the resulting cries of anguish. Ah, lesson one compliments of Camp Grace.

The foyer was empty as Collin arrived. She took a quick look outside but nothing and no one was stirring yet. Collin risked a trip to the health bar, picked up an apple then returned it in favor of a banana. Less mess. The granola bars looked tempting but Collin decided to pass. She grabbed a bottle of grape juice then went to the counter to pay for it. The woman behind the counter handed her a bag. Collin shook her head. "I don't need that."

"It's for the trash, honey, in case you're not near a can when you're done." She eyed Collin sternly, "You aren't one of those who just drop things on the ground, are you?"

Collin raised her right hand. "Never. At least not intentionally."

The woman smiled. "Good. That's what I like to hear. Like to see it even more." She shook her head as Collin reached for her wallet. "No charge. Food at the bar is free, same as in the cafeteria. We want to encourage healthy living."

Collin looked around then said with a small sigh, "I suppose that means no coffee, right?"

"Welllll . . . we do make some concessions. But people have to ask. If they do, they're probably desperate. Are you desperate?"

Collin grinned, "I will be if I don't get some. With sugar, please."

The woman filled a Styrofoam cup full of steaming black gold, handed her the coffee, then directed her to the counter where the sugar and creamer were hidden. Real spoons were provided for stirring rather than those impossible sticks that never get anything properly mixed. Again, someone had thought of everything. Except donuts. Healthy food, right? Sorry, wrong department.

Collin went out sipping her coffee, then realized she should have asked what time the morning tour would leave. Or had left? She doubted it. Collin had yet to see more than three bodies moving about. Still, it paid to be early. She went out the front of the lodge and found an unoccupied bench. The fact they were all unoccupied made it easier. Maybe one in the sunshine? That narrowed it down by half. How about within eye and earshot of the front door? Good enough. Satisfied, Collin sat down. She pulled her Bible out of her satchel, pulled her hat down over her eyes and began reading.

At about 8:20 a tractor-tram combination pulled into the front parking area. Collin watched with mild interest as the driver circled the lot, straightened the rig out, and then pulled to a stop. As the man stepped off the tractor Collin realized that it was Jeff in "civilian" clothes. He didn't see her as he strode purposefully towards a shiny black jeep, whistling.

Suddenly Steve Parks came bursting out of the lodge. He spotted the retreating maintenance man and shouted, "Jeff! Jeff!"

Jeff stopped, turned, then walked back to meet the director. Collin was in position to hear the conversation without trying to eavesdrop. She tried to concentrate on her Bible reading but finally gave it up. Steve was asking, his tone friendly, "So, what have you got planned for today? Or specifically this morning?"

Jeff grinned. "I've got an appointment out at Shafter's pond. There's this big old bass with my name on it just waiting for me."

Steve nodded. "I see." He hesitated then drawled, "You know, Jeff, if it has your name on it, won't it be there tonight? Or Monday?"

Jeff eyed Steve carefully. "I don't like the sound of this."

Steve continued, "I know you've put in a lot of hours getting ready for this camp."

Jeff nodded. "Two weeks straight, Mr. Director."

Steve nodded. "And I know you haven't so much as left the grounds in those two weeks except to run for supplies. If anyone deserves time off it's you."

"Thank you. You calling me back to tell me this warms my heart." It wasn't sarcasm but a light hearted jibe. "What do you need, Mr. Director?"

"You know Gerald's out with laryngitis."

"Yeah and Nash has the flu."

Steve hesitated then said, "Orlon called off this morning; said his wife was in labor."

Jeff threw his hands in the air in frustration. "It's false labor! After four kids you'd think he'd know the difference."

Steve said slowly, "I hate to ask you, Jeff . . ."

"Then don't."

". . . and I wouldn't if I thought there was anyone else qualified."

"So send someone unqualified. It'll be a new experience for them. Cross training, you know?"

"Jeff . . ."

"Don't say it. Please. Don't say it."

"Would you take the tour this morning?"

"I've been on the tour. I don't need a tour."

"Jeff, please?"

"Mr. Director, you don't understand. This bass is over seven pounds. Think of it. Seven pounds. It told me itself in a vision last night. It said, 'I'm over seven pounds and I'm waiting for you. But you only get one chance and that's tomorrow morning. After that I'm history.'"

Steve's voice was skeptical. "It said all that, did it?"

Jeff nodded solemnly. "All of it. Every word. Except maybe the history part. I don't think fish understand the concept of history. Underwater physics, maybe, and trigonometry. But not history. Then again, this fish is old enough, it might know history."

Steve shook his head then said slowly, "I know I can't order you to go."

"Sure you can." Jeff's voice was even, as if instructing Steve on some point of order. "You are the Director and I am the maintenance man. Your job is to tell me what to do; my job is to do it. If it comes right down to it I'd much rather you told me. Then I don't have to berate myself for being an idiot giving up this fish."

Steve shook his head, bemused. "If you're sure about this."

"I'm sure. Tell me I have to take this group. Just say, 'Jeff, you have to take this group.' I'll take it, no problem."

Steve looked at him and said slowly, "All I have to do is say, "Jeff, you have to take this group.' and that makes it better?"

"Absolutely."

Steve nodded again then said solemnly, "Jeff, would you please take this group?"

Jeff groaned audibly then straightened up and said, "Sure, boss. It'll give me the chance to get to know some of the faces better."

Steve slapped him warmly on the shoulder and said, "Thanks, Jeff. I won't forget this."

Jeff muttered, "Neither will I. But I will forgive you." He grinned at Steve and asked, "You want me to go change into uniform?"

Steve shook his head. "Not necessary. I think we can tell you from the campers without too much trouble."

The two men left the parking lot: Steve back to the lodge, Jeff back to the tractor. Collin shook her head slightly. There was something definitely different about the man. Something well worth investigating. She put her Bible away and joined the small throng of brave and conscious souls out at this hour of the morning. Maybe a third of the campers gathered by the tram. Jill and Chenille were not among them. Surprisingly neither was Robbie. Collin looked around, trying to see if maybe he was wandering in from the outlying areas, but saw no one. She took a seat in the back so she could keep the entire group in focus. While a third of the campers might have been present only Collin and the diminutive Sherry Gerald represented the counselors. It should be enough in the event of trouble. Though Collin could not imagine what kind of trouble could happen on a tour tram. Quit looking for the snakes! She shook her head, looked up front, and saw Jeff's eyes in the mirror studying her. He grinned at her; she smiled back with what she hoped was a polite, dignified, not too eager but not uninterested smile . . . feeling like a total fool all the while. This was ridiculous. She was twenty-six for heaven's sake. Stop acting like a love sick thirteen year old. She growled at the inner demons who mocked her, then looked around for something to distract them.

Jeff waited for the last two youths to get on board then started the motor on the tractor. He was wired for sound, evidently, as his voice came out clearly over the tram speakers. "Good morning and welcome to the first and only morning tour of Camp Grace offered today. Your regularly scheduled guide is absent today with an excuse about his wife having a baby. Personally, I prefer being here. Anyone with me on that?" There were several shouts of "Yes!!" Collin raised her hand as well just to keep in the spirit.

Jeff continued, "We will cover approximately thirty miles on this trip which is why it's not a walking tour. We could use the horses, but their union said we couldn't go more than ten miles in a day and no uphill climbs. We couldn't promise that so we use the tractor. This is a two-way radio system so if you—meaning anyone back there—have a question go ahead and ask it. But one at a time, please. While our system's good enough to pick up all the voices my hearing's not so good that it can separate them. Got it?"

The kids nodded and generally complied with Jeff's request. A couple of them began looking for the microphones, trying to figure out how he could hear them. Jeff said easily, "Okay, then." He slipped the tractor into gear and they were off. "On your right is Highway 135, the only route through town, passing the only McDonalds between here and the state line." Shouts and cheers and cries of "Let me out!" followed. Jeff continued, "On your left is the barn, home to our fleet of milk producers. They work day and night to provide you with fresh milk for your breakfast, lunch and dinner consumption." A herd of cows lounged lazily over their hay mounds. "The ladies love it if you wave while we go by."

Collin watched closely to see who took the bait and was pleased to see at least three of the younger campers waved secretively as they passed the herd. As if on command, two Bossies lowed in return. Jeff commented, "They're saying thank you. Up ahead we have our version of the 100 acre wood, complete with bears, rabbits, owls and a very occasional lost piglet. But no tiggers or kangaroos." Only his eyes could be seen in the mirror and they were smiling.

One girl giggled and whispered to her seat mate, "He be talking 'bout Winnie the Pooh! How he be knowin' 'bout Pooh?" Her partner shook her head and giggled, too. Collin's heart ached; these kids were still babies. Inside the street-wise shell they were just babies.

Jeff continued his travelogue, pointing out various features of the vast campgrounds and the surrounding country side. The path meandered through woods, past streams, over hill and under dale (whatever that is) until it reached its zenith an hour and a half later on a small rise overlooking the entire county. Or at least the eastern half of it. Jeff pulled the tractor to a stop at a picnic area then announced, "Break time. Everyone out, stretch your legs and restore circulation to the feet. There are two coolers in back of the tram underneath the seat of the lady with the mysterious smile." Collin shook her head and grinned at him, embarrassed. His eyes danced and he said, "Sorry, with the beautiful grin. She's the one in the back. Ask her politely to move and unload the coolers. You'll find some drinks and snacks in there; enough to keep anyone from dropping dead due to lack of nourishment but probably not enough to spoil your lunch. We'll take about half an hour if you want."

Jeff removed the headphones and climbed down from the tractor. Collin didn't wait to be asked to move; she went ahead and vacated the premises on her own. She made her way over to where Jeff was surrounded by kids asking him questions, asking to ride on the tractor, asking to drive the tractor, etc. etc. She waited until the din died down and the crowd left (to check out the contents of the cooler) then said lightly, "Good morning."

Jeff grinned. "Morning. Why doesn't it surprise me to see you on this trip?"

Collin shrugged. "I'm the eager, get a jump on the day kind of person, I guess. Why are you out this early?"

Jeff grinned. "It's my job."

"That's it? That's the only reason you're here?"

Jeff shrugged. "It'll do for a start. What do you think so far?"

"It's huge, Jeff. I never realized how big this camp was." She looked out over the expanse and asked, "You own all this?"

"Camp Grace owns all this, yes."

Collin laughed. "Of course that's what I meant." She looked at him and asked, "But who owns Camp Grace? I looked through the literature last night and it never said."

Jeff said carefully, "It's a joint venture. God owns it and has a silent partner on the side. A very silent partner."

Collin cocked her head, curious. "Oh? How so?"

"He learned long ago to let God speak first. He says it makes things much easier that way."

Collin nodded. "He must be an older man, then."

Jeff gave her a quizzical look. "Why would you say that?"

"You don't gain that kind of wisdom this early in life."

"I see your point. Well, he's not what I'd call old."

"You know him?"

"We've talked."

Jeff's answers seemed a little guarded, as if this was not a subject he was terribly comfortable talking about. Collin decided their relationship was not solid enough to risk pushing him on it so turned the subject to other matters. She turned and said, "So tell me what I'm looking at. The camp I recognize. What's off to the left, there?"

Jeff looked where she was pointing then said, "That's the town of Hillsboro, population 1300, mostly related to one another." He continued describing the layout, moving in a clockwise direction. "That stand of trees marks the beginning of Shafter's pond, home to one of the biggest bass I've ever seen." He did not elaborate, and sighed only slightly. Collin swallowed a grin. "Depending on your eyesight you might be able to make out Cotter's windmill. He had it put up there so he could give people directions to his house. You know, 'Turn at the wind mill. You can't miss it.' And you can't except at night. Unless the wind is blowing, then you can hear it creaking for five miles."

While Jeff continued to describe the county, its occupants and their quirks, Collin listened with growing admiration. He seemed to know something about everywhere and everyone. None of it was harsh or critical. It all seemed in good-natured spirit. She could tell he had a great deal of affection for the land and its tenants. He must have spent a good deal of time here to know it so well. As he finished his panoramic overview she said quietly, "You must love this place very much."

Jeff shrugged. "I guess. I spent most every summer up here while I was growing up. It got to feel like home, I suppose." He looked at her and asked, "You have any place like that? That feels like home?"

"No." It came out flat and hard which was not her intention at all. She covered quickly, "I mean, no, no place special. We didn't get out much as kids."

"You said, 'We.' That would seem to indicate there were more of you?"

Collin cursed herself for the slip then said with extreme caution, "I just meant our family."

Jeff said smoothly, as if not entirely believing her, "I understand. How do you think the tour is going so far? Are the kids staying with me, or am I boring them?"

"No, you're doing great. You don't talk down to them and you don't talk over their heads. You seem to understand them at their level. That's important. You have to start where they are in order to bring them where you know they should be." She stopped abruptly, embarrassed. "But you already know that. That's what Grace is all about, isn't it? Stop me when I start babbling, will you? I've only had one cup of coffee this morning. My brain doesn't kick in 'til the third cup."

Jeff motioned towards the tractor. "I've got a thermos full of coffee if you and your friend want some. There are cups up there, too, if you need them. Kids may have to eat and drink healthy but we adults don't have to suffer." He grinned. "It's under the seat."

Collin did a half-kneel before him and said gratefully, "Bless you, kind sir. Bless you!" She looked over at Sherry and asked, "Coffee?" The woman nodded eagerly. Collin looked at Jeff and asked, "Can I bring you a cup?"

Jeff nodded. "Put some coffee in it too, please. Black."

Collin grimaced at him but went and found the thermos. She gave coffee to Sherry and Jeff then filled her own cup. It was fun standing around, sipping coffee, watching the kids explore the "picnic" area. Some were climbing trees; a first in their young lives. Some were seeing trees big enough to climb; also a first. The birds, the squirrels, the chipmunks, the myriad of bugs: all served to chip away at the crust the city had begun to form around the hearts, minds and souls of these kids. And as they played it was evident that none yet was too hard to be touched, too old in street wisdom that innocence could not still be experienced. Collin looked at Sherry and her voice was tight as she said, "This makes it worthwhile. Every penny they spend couldn't be enough to buy this."

Sherry nodded her voice equally tight. "Look at Molly." She pointed out a tall lanky girl of fourteen kneeling in the dirt with two other children looking at the bugs. "She's talking to kids her own age. She's down on her knees actually touching dirt like a real kid. She's playing. She's actually playing." Tears streamed down Sherry's face.

Collin hugged the woman, knowing the joy she was feeling along with the pain it elicited. Jeff looked at Collin in concerned confusion. Collin continued to hug Sherry but explained quietly, "Molly started walking the street three months ago. When she's made up she looks every bit of twenty. Getting her to associate with kids of any age is a major miracle."

Jeff prayed a whispered, "Dear God." He looked away then looked back and asked, "I suppose it's stupid to ask, but where are her parents? Don't they care?"

Sherry pulled away from Collin, wiping her eyes. "Her mother is the one that sent her to the streets. Her father is gone; missing in action from the home front."

Jeff nodded as if he'd expected the answer. Collin noticed his voice was somewhat tight as he answered, "I see."

There was silence between the adults for several moments then Collin cleared her throat and said, "Well, at least she's here, now. We've got one week to teach her what life's really like and the true meaning of the words, 'down and dirty.' I think she's getting a good handle on the dirty part." The bug watching had disintegrated into a dirt-throwing contest with the participants trying to see who could convey the greatest amount of the landscape back to camp. Collin and Sherry shouted, "All right, all right! Enough already! Brush it off, load it up, and let's move out!"

Sherry added, "We've still got maybe 15 miles to go and a lot of territory to cover."

Jeff nodded. "And the river to explore."

Collin echoed his words, "And the river . . ." She trailed off, life draining from her. The river? They were going down to the river? Today? Now?

Her face must have revealed more than she thought for Jeff looked at her with deep concern and asked, "Are you okay? What's wrong?"

She shook it off, or tried to, anyhow. Everything and everyone in her was screaming in protest and alarm, demanding to be let out and off this trip, now! Collin silenced them all then tried to smile at Jeff. It was a dismal failure, she knew, but she did it anyhow. "I'm fine." She saw disbelief in his eyes, so added, "It's personal, and I'll deal with it. Thank you." That wasn't what she meant to say nor even what she wanted to say, but it's all that came out. Jeff would have to deal with that on his own.

He studied her intently for a long time then said slowly and quietly, "Okay, if that's the way you want it. I'm up front if you need me."

Collin nodded. "I know you are. And I appreciate that. This is just old business that pops up now and again. I'm fine. Really."

Jeff was far from convinced but said only, "Uh huh," and walked back to the tractor. He waited until the last camper was seated, all the coolers were repacked and everyone was settled before saying, "Ready to go back?" A chorus of no's and two yes's followed. Jeff grinned, "Well then, we'll take the long way home." He looked up in the mirror and the grin faded as his eyes met Collin's. Collin tried to grin back. The look in his eyes said she was only partially successful in convincing him she was fine. Deal with it. She had to.

The remainder of the trip descended into a waking nightmare for Collin. As the roar of the river increased, reality constantly attempted to recede into shadow and only sheer force of will kept the darkness at bay. She was aware that Jeff had increased his banter, both in volume and frequency, but to limited effect. She sat pale and wan fighting back the memories that threatened to drown her. She clenched her teeth then bit her lip so hard the blood trickled inside her mouth. But it felt good. It gave her a physical foothold in the now to counteract the then that was trying to overwhelm her.

She felt the tram stop, heard Jeff commanding the campers, "Stay on the footpath. The slopes are covered with poison ivy and oak. If you don't know what that means, it means ugly red welts all over your body that itch like fire, burn like fire, and prevent you from doing anything fun because you're so miserable. And they last at least a week so you'll have come all this way to do nothing more than play in the weeds and watch everyone else having a good time. Stay on the footpath."

One camper piped up, "I ain't afraid a no plant."

Another warned, "I is. I got poison one time. I's never so bad off in all my life. Couldn't eat, couldn't sleep, couldn't do nothin'. You couldn't pay me enough to go down there."

The first camper was suddenly cautious. "For real? You ain't jiving?"

"No jive, man. Driver ain't jiving, neither. It's some nasty stuff. Stay away from me if you go down there."

The kids moved off, still discussing the merits of abstinence from contact. The roar of the river was a power that pulsed through Collin, singing to her that resistance was futile and she should give in to the siren song of the past. With thunderous tones it commanded her presence and her obedience. It was not taking no for an answer, either.

Suddenly a calm, quiet voice said, "I've seen fear before, and lady, it's all over you." A strong hand was laid on her shoulder as Jeff sat down on the bench beside her. He asked, "The river, right?"

She dared not respond but nodded shortly. She opened her eyes expecting to see mirth or ridicule. There was neither, only compassion and pity. He asked softly, "Bad experience?" Again she only nodded. He said, "We'll leave."

Collin said quickly, "No." Jeff looked puzzled. Collin said shakily, "I don't want the kids to miss out on anything because I can't handle the past. I'll be fine. Really, I'm fine." She did her best to reassure him that all was well but saw the disbelief in his eyes. Collin let out a slow breath, let out another, then repeated, "I'm fine. Really." She tried a smile. "See? No problem." She let out another slow breath. "I wasn't ready, that's all. I'm fine." She shuddered then tried unsuccessfully to smile. Collin touched Jeff's hand lightly and said, "Thanks. But I really am okay." She saw the look in his eyes and said quickly, "Okay, I'm not okay. But I will be. Give me a few minutes to pull it together, and I'll be fine. I promise. Really." She shuddered again.

Jeff reached up and wiped the blood from her lip. He studied her a minute then nodded silently and stood up. He squeezed her shoulder then turned and walked off to follow the campers. Collin let out a shaky sigh, wrapped her arms around her knees, and dropped her head on her arms. Lord, why now? Why here, in front of him? Any hope of a relationship melted away into a pipe dream. Guys usually ran screaming from girls with mental problems. And wisely, she might add. Collin continued to force herself to breathe slowly and felt a semblance of control return to her. Years and years and did I mention years of training bounced back into action after having abandoned her during the initial attack. *"The river is not my enemy. The river is only water. We drink water, we bathe in water, we use water to feed our plants and our animals. Water is our friend. The river cannot hurt you as long as you stay away from it. Thunder can't hurt you. It's loud but has no substance. The rumble of the river is like thunder: loud, but without substance as long as you stay away from it. You don't touch it, it can't touch you. You're safe, you're dry, you're away from the river. No problem, right?"*

Collin whispered defiantly, "Right." She pulled her head up, uncurled her body, and stretched uncomfortably. She scrubbed her hands across her face forcing blood and color back to her cheeks. Jeff would see the old Collin back. Well, maybe not the <u>old</u> Collin, but the old 'new and improved' Collin. The confident, cocky, in charge Collin. The . . .

Oh, shut up. She climbed down out of the tram and debated going down the trail after the group. No, that was pushing things too far. She'd just explore around here mindful of the poison ivy etc. She had no trouble identifying it. The reasons would remain nameless, as Collin couldn't deal with another blast from the past at this point. She found a warm rock on which to perch and worked on her "lizard in the sunshine" impression. The sun felt wonderfully soothing and the remaining tensions began to melt away. By the time the tour group returned she was humming softly and even managed a real smile again. She called out, "Did everyone have a good time?"

One youngster yelled back, "Yeah, but Reeshard nearly fell in."

The boy in question, a lanky fourteen year-old, snapped back hotly, "No I didn't. Rory pushed me!"

Another boy, probably the aforementioned Rory, shoved him good-naturedly. "I ain't never touched you. You trip over you own big feet. You feet bigger 'n Michael Jordan's."

Reeshard shoved back but with less play and more malice. "No way."

Collin slid off the rock sensing that intervention was needed now. Sherry Gerald seemed disinclined to step in as the boys involved were considerably taller and heavier than she was. They were taller and heavier than Collin as well, but that had never stopped her before. She stepped between the boys and said calmly, "Anyone know what size MJ wears?" Several suggestions were offered from ten to fifteen to eighteen to the absurd. Collin looked at Reeshard and asked, "What size do you wear?" She noted out of the corner of her eye that Jeff had returned with the last of the campers. Nice to have back up but this was her jurisdiction now.

Reeshard said sullenly, "Thirteen."

Collin nodded. "Thirteen. I know for a fact that MJ wears a fifteen. So Rory, you owe the man an apology."

Rory, who hadn't been looking for a fight to begin with, said easily, "Hey man, no big deal. I wasn't dissing you. Jus' having some fun, you know?"

Collin said sternly, "Your turn, Reeshard. You forget to put all seven layers of your skin on this morning? We've talked before about being thin skinned haven't we? About letting the jibe go? It's only the ones you hang on to that hurt you. I'd consider myself lucky to have feet the size of MJ. If I were a dude, and could walk and chew gum at the same time. And wasn't five foot six."

Reeshard couldn't help it. He smiled slightly then said, "I seen you play hoops. You pretty tough for an old white woman." He looked at Rory and said, "Sorry, man."

Rory shrugged. "Ain't nothing."

The situation having resolved, Collin said, "Okay, then, let's get back to camp. Everyone on board." Collin noticed Jeff studying her and she didn't know whether there was approval or doubt in his face. The man was simply tough to read. That could be a problem.

Collin waited until the last camper was on board then climbed into her perch. She saluted Jeff to let him know the tram was good to go; he saluted her in return. Collin shut the wheels inside her brain down before they could begin reading anything into his gesture. He was just signaling her back, for heaven's sake. Don't make a federal case out of it.

Jeff announced, "Next stop on our agenda will be what we lovingly call our marina. Six months out of the year overflow from the river fills the area enough for swimming, boating and a few other aquatic sports in the early summer. In the winter it's our ice rink for hockey and skating. The rest of the time it's just mud. But because God really likes this group he has seen fit to keep the river running high all summer and we still have our 'lake.' It's a short hike from there to the lodge and if we work this right, you'll have about half an hour to kill before lunch. Unless you want to take another swing around the camp?" Cries and groans of, "No!" "No way!" "Help!" filled the tram.

Collin caught Jeff's eyes; the man was smiling again. Good. No permanent damage done. Maybe there was hope. He said, "Guess not. I do hope someone got something out of this trip besides poison ivy. And a word of strictest caution: even if you don't think you touched anything, don't be stupid. Wash your hands, your arms and any exposed skin with warm water and soap as soon as you get back to your rooms. This is not a joke. And trust me, it will be quite obvious in the next day or two who listened and who didn't. We will know you by your rashes."

The rest of the trip was spent in silence, at least by Jeff. The campers continued to talk and battle and jibe as kids will do. Collin made it a point to listen to the drift and noticed somewhat uncomfortably that Reeshard continued to be the focus of attention. At least Rory wasn't part of the crowd. Yet. Collin watched, trying to decide the best way to defuse the situation permanently and distract the young vultures from their chosen target. She slid forward into the seat directly ahead of Reeshard—and currently inhabited by a chief aggressor. She looked at Reeshard and said lightly, "You never asked how I knew MJ's shoe size."

The boy beside her snickered and said, "Nike commercial."

Collin replied evenly, "Good guess. But wrong. He told me."

Reeshard was taken back. "He told you? When you see the man?"

Collin shrugged. "Summer camp a few years ago." "*Okay, so it was more than a few. Give me a break, here. This is a desperation maneuver.*"

"We were suiting up for a game and I asked him what size he wore. And he told me."

Her seatmate said sarcastically, "Yeah, right."

Reeshard was still in shock. "He told you? You played ball with him?"

Collin nodded as if it were no big deal. "Yeah. I brought the pictures with me, if you're interested in the truth." She stared at the boy beside her; he looked back defiantly. "Come ask to see them anytime. I love showing them."

She slipped back to her own seat and listened carefully to the dialogue that followed her exit. She knew of course how it would go: "She ain't for real."

"She is. You ain't been knowin' her like I is. She straight lady. She say she know MJ, she know MJ."

"Ain't no white lady never play ball with MJ."

"We go see the pictures then we know."

"Ain't gonna be no pictures. She blowin' smoke."

"You 'fraid to find out?"

"I'll go anytime."

Which was about what she'd expected. But at least this was an issue that could be resolved and as quickly as the boys wanted. If they wanted resolution and not just aggression. Which was also a possibility. She'd know soon enough.

The tram pulled into the parking area by the docks and everyone crowded to get off. Everyone except Reeshard and his three tormentors. They seemed determined to be the last ones off the bus. Collin sensed a confrontation. She noted that Jeff had gotten off the tractor but hadn't started up the slope with the others. He was hanging around discreetly as if waiting for someone. Or waiting for something to happen, more like it. He must know kids pretty well, too, then.

All four boys rose at once and there was some pushing and shoving to clear the aisle. Collin stood up and strode forward, determined to prevent a fracas. The shoving escalated; Collin caught the arm of the child closest to her. In her best gunnery sergeant voice she yelled, "Freeze! Everyone, now!"

The effect was instantaneous. The boys became statues. The only sound was of metal hitting metal, as a heavy, shiny object hit the floor. Collin had no idea whose pocket it had fallen from, nor did it matter. She retrieved the ornately engraved handle and held it up for all to see. If the sound of her voice hadn't been enough to keep them frozen, the sight of the knife was. Collin could see Jeff moving forward to intervene or maybe just act as back up. Back up she could handle; interference she didn't need. She kept her eyes firm and cold on the boys, nailing each one with a look that drilled right through them. She didn't even look at the handle but said angrily, "I've seen stupid in my time. But this—this is a winner. You got a free ride out of the hood to paradise, and instead you carry the hood with you. Stupid. Stupid, stupid, stupid. Look around you, dudes. You see any pimps here you need to worry 'bout? You see any pushers you got to defend your sisters against? What did you expect to find up here that you need to shed blood for? You gonna use a blade against a grizzly? What?"

Without even having to search she tripped the mechanism that released the blade. It slid out silently and engaged without even a hint of a click. Collin saw the horrified and stricken looks on the boys' faces, and knew its origin. She nodded and continued her monologue. "That's right, you got it. Blade's been exposed and blood has to be shed. Can't sheath it clean, can you? I crossed the line and now someone has to pay in blood." She saw Jeff moving forward as if he'd heard enough. She called out, "Just hold on, Fireman. The boys and I will be finished here in a minute." She looked around and said, "As soon as someone pays the price." She looked from boy to boy, from one panicked face to another. All machismo had disappeared from their manner; most were probably petrified wondering what this crazy woman was going to do next. Her voice softened slightly and she added, "Someone did pay the price, you know? You all stand there, guilty as sin, and someone had to pay the price. And pay it in blood." Collin reached over and in one smooth motion sliced the palm of her hand open. Blood began spurting freely, and the boys cringed. Collin continued, "But he didn't just bleed a little to satisfy some stupid ritual. He went all the way and died to save you." She held each boy in her steady gaze and said, "Want to know more? Come talk to me after lunch. Now get out of here." All four scrambled headlong up the hill.

Collin sank down on the nearest bench holding her hand. It wasn't quite what she intended but maybe it had made an impact.

It evidently made an impact on Jeff. He pounded into the tram, eyes blazing. Collin looked into his face and saw anger, disbelief, frustration, a tinge of disgust, maybe? He grabbed her hand and began trying to staunch the blood but said nothing. Collin decided to try to lighten the moment. She commented, "Knife was sharper than I thought."

Jeff glared at her and seethed, "Don't. Don't even try to make a joke out of this. You know how stupid that stunt was?"

Collin felt her hackles begin to rise. She said sharply, "I know what I'm doing. I've been working with kids for a while now. It's my job. It's what I do."

Jeff's tone matched her own. "Since when does being a case worker require self-mutilation?"

Collin jerked her hand away from him. "Listen, Mr. Fireman, I didn't ask for your help because I didn't need it. I still don't. I know these kids. I work with these kids. I live with these kids. I will deal with them the best way I know how without interference or judgment."

She started to brush past him but he caught her arm. His tone softened and he said, "You need stitches."

Collin shook her head. "No I don't. I'll heal just fine."

Jeff repeated more strongly, "You need stitches. It's my job to know that. It's what I do."

They locked eyes but once again Collin had to drop hers unable to withstand the intensity of his gaze. She looked down and nodded, acquiescing to his knowledge. But she had to salvage at least a modicum of pride. She insisted, "If you can do it, here, now, then fine. Otherwise we bandage it and forget it. I'm not going to the infirmary."

Jeff looked at her, disbelieving. "Are you crazy? Lady, this is not a hospital. It's a tourist train! Did you leave your brain behind somewhere or is our lofty elevation too much for you? Do you see an abundance of sutures and catgut lying around? Needles and anesthetics? What kind of condition is that?"

Collin silently pulled her arm away from him, climbed down out of the tram and walked away without looking back. Inside a voice was repeating, *"Dumb. Dumb. Wrong. Wrong. Stupid. Dumb. Wrong."* And while she might agree with the assessment, she could not force herself to turn around. As she mounted the steps to the lodge another little voice insisted, *"Best match you've ever had and you're going to blow it. Pride, Walker. Pride. Swallow it and turn around. Tell him you're sorry. He already knows it but tell him anyhow."* A third voice battled back, *"Never! Who does he think he is, telling you what to do? He doesn't know anything about kids. You do."*

The accusations would rage for hours, if not days. Collin let the voices argue unrestrained; observer rather than participant. Right or wrong it didn't really matter. She'd made a choice; she'd have to live with it. As she made her way to her room, still dabbing at the blood that would not cease and desist, she shook her head slowly. She really screwed up this time. Collin took a washcloth from the shelf, wrapped it tightly around her hand and lay down. She was tired. Between the river, the boys and Jeff, she was drained. Maybe a nap would help. Make the world go away for an hour and she would deal with it then. Collin lay down, closed her eyes and slept.

A light, hesitant tapping on the door woke her some two hours later. A young female camper called, "Ms. Walker, some of the guys want to see your pictures. I ain't sure what they talking about but they say as you'll be knowing."

Collin shook the fog from her brain and said, "I'll be there in a minute." The hand was still oozing; Collin rewrapped it, dug a small photo album from her bag and walked out. Not for the last time did she thank the Lord for not only the opportunity to attend that particular sports camp, but also the wisdom to invest the $100 for the pictures they offered. It had cost her dearly in pain and sweat at the camp earning the money for the photo album. But the experience and the pictures had proven invaluable many times over.

There was a group of about five young men: Reeshard, Rory, and the tormentors on the tram, waiting for her. Reeshard waited until she reached the group then said, "There's some as don't believe you, Ms. Walker. I said you'd have the pictures. Which one of us be talking truth?"

Collin motioned towards a small table in the foyer and said, "Over here. We'll settle this." The group gathered around the table and Collin opened the album. The very first picture was of MJ towering over a group of young girls, his arms surrounding the entire team at once.

Muted awes sounded. Collin pointed to a 16 year old girl standing beside "The Man" and said, "That's me."

Someone noted, "Don't say Walker. Say Winger."

Collin nodded. "I know. I changed my name when I turned 18."

"How come?"

"Personal reasons. I haven't changed that much. I'm still ugly as a mud fence. Anyone doubt that's me?"

One or two of the boys looked closely at the pictures then at Collin. Finally they nodded. "That you. Still wearing the same stupid hat, too."

"Thank you. I appreciate that." Collin led them through the album, through the week at camp in North Carolina. From breakfast, practice, drills, lunch, practice, scrimmages, practice, clinics, practice, dinner, practice . . . There were shots of MJ, Wade, Pippin and other NBA notables permeating the scene. And coaches from Duke, Carolina, NC State, Kentucky, even Dick Vitale. They were all there.

Rory looked at her with new respect and said slowly, "Dag, woman. You met 'em all."

Collin smiled. "Not all, but a bunch. The most important thing they taught us was respect. Respect for ourselves, respect for our teammates, and respect for our opponents. Cop an attitude, and you ride the pine. It was easily the best week of my life." She looked around and said softly, "I learned a lot. Maybe you can, too. You want to play the game? Respect. Treat people the way you want to be treated. Now get out of here."

But the boys seemed to hesitate, unready to depart. One of the tormentors looked down then looked back up and asked, "Who you be talkin' 'bout on the bus? That died for us? Alex figured you be talking 'bout some somebody back when you was little.

She said quietly, "Before me, Trace. Long before me. The man was Jesus."

Trace nodded. "That's what I figured but no one believed me."

Alex objected, "But he ain't real. He jus' some story in a book Gramma keep on her shelf."

"Wrong, dude. Way wrong. He lived, he died, and he's alive now. And he paid in blood—his own blood—for all the bad things you do, and I do, and Alex and Reeshard and anyone else you care to throw in." Collin stretched for a means of explaining the sublime. "What I did on the bus was first off, stupid. But God can use stupid, too, which is a good thing, 'cause that's what I have to offer most. But it's like that. When a blade's open blood has to be shed to make it right or else bad things happen. That's the street law, right?" Pensively the boys nodded. "When you do something that breaks God's law, more than just blood has to be shed to make it right. Someone has to die, to give all their blood."

Alex muttered, "That's vicious."

"So is breaking God's law, man. That's where murder, and rape, and drugs, and fights, and hate, and lying and stealing come from. It's a terrible thing to break God's law. Which is why the penalty is so bad. It's supposed to make you think before you do what's wrong." Collin watched the boys for effect, to see if anyone was getting it. The silence was hard to interpret so she continued, "God knew if he enforced his penalty on everyone, no one would ever make it. So he selected his son Jesus to die, to take the place of everyone in the world and pay their price. Jesus, the son of God, was born as a human, lived long enough to experience all of life, then gave it up for us miserable people. He was beaten, spit on, whipped, nailed to a tree, stuck with a spear in his side, and all because he loved you and didn't want you to suffer, too."

Timmons, one of the fourteen year olds yawned loudly. "I been hearin all this at home. Ain't no real count in it. May mean somethin' to some but don't mean nothin to me. I'm going to the game room. Anyone comin'?"

Reluctantly, almost embarrassed, the boys stood up to leave. Collin saw the look on Reeshard's face mirrored in Trace and Alex. All three wanted to stay but were too much under the sway of Timmons' leadership. Trace mumbled, "Thanks, Ms. Walker. Maybe we can talk some more later. You be in tonight?"

"Yeah. Ring the room or have one of the girls come get me. I'll be around all week, too, you know." The boys ducked their heads but said nothing more, hustling to catch up with Timmons.

Collin watched the boys leave, listening to the renewed discussion of the camp, and how cool it must have been, and why don't they do camps like that nowadays instead of just back then? Old folks got all the breaks.

Old folks. She felt like old folks. Her hand throbbed and the bleeding continued unabated. This was not good. But if she applied more pressure and didn't move it much, it should close up soon. Collin went back to her room, wrapped a second handtowel around it, and lay back down. Another hour. All she wanted was one more hour. Honest. Collin closed her eyes and drifted off to uneasy sleep.

The flashing of the message light over the door penetrated her brain. Collin sat up groggily and tried to get her bearings. She was in her room, her hand was still seeping blood, and it was a little after seven p.m. She'd missed not only lunch, but dinner as well. Oh, joy. She muttered quickly to ward off the accuser, "That wasn't by design. I didn't miss those meals on purpose. I'll make it up later."

The hand, however, needed attention now. Jeff had been right, of course. She needed stitches. Everyone else was always right. When was she going to learn that?

Collin pulled up short from the self-deprecation. While the taunt might be true it wasn't helping the situation. She knew the regular infirmary hours were over for the day, and really didn't want to go into a long explanation of her own stupidity, anyhow. She wondered if groveling carried any merit with a certain janitor/paramedic she knew. Or used to know. Or thought she knew, once. Or wanted . . .

Enough. Collin discarded the soaked wash cloth, secured a clean one around her palm and went to the message center. The woman at the desk smiled politely and asked the politically correct, "May I help you?"

"I'm Collin Walker. You have . . ."

The woman's smile broadened and she interrupted. "Oh, yes. I have a message for you." She turned around, bent down and pulled something from under the counter. She set a small Dixie cup with a single hand-picked daisy in it on the counter along with a Camp Grace business card. Collin turned the card over and read simply, "Sorry." Beneath it was a three digit number which Collin took to be an extension number or a pager code. If she could cry, this would have been as good a time as any. She bit her lip to stop the trembling then asked, "May I use the phone?"

The woman nodded. "Of course." She smiled as she discreetly vanished into the back office.

Collin's hands trembled only slightly as she punched in the code. There was a moment's clicking as one electronic device communicated with another and the call was transferred from here to there to who knows where. But finally a voice said, "This is Jeff. Tell me who you are, why you called, and how to find you and I'll call you back. Leaving out any of the requested details could delay my response. Especially the how to reach you part."

And while it was good to hear his voice, a recording was not what she needed right now. Collin contemplated hanging up but knew how much she hated it when someone did that to her. Even if it was a wrong number have the decency to say, "Sorry, wrong number." Please! Collin waited for the compulsory beep then said softly, "If I said, 'stupid and dumb,' would that be clue enough as to who this is? I'm sorry, Jeff. I . . ."

The line clicked and Jeff's voice said urgently, "Collin, don't hang up. Stay on the line a minute." There was a moment's silence, some clicking then Jeff came back on. "Okay, I think that's got it." A long shrill beep followed then broke off. Jeff grumbled, "I love technology. I just love it."

Collin grinned and said, "Ain't it great?"

Jeff asked, "Where are you?"

"At the message center." She hesitated then admitted, "I was coming up to find you to apologize for my behavior this morning."

Jeff asked, "Can we do this in person rather than long distance? I'm down in the game room and it's kind of loud."

Again Collin paused then asked, "Do you have keys to the infirmary?"

There was silence on the line then Jeff said, "I'll meet you there in fifteen minutes."

Collin asked, "It's not a problem, is it? You're not breaking any rules, going where you're not supposed to?"

Jeff assured her, "I have free run of the camp, lady. Other than the female wing. It's not a problem. I'll meet you there in fifteen minutes. Be there."

Collin nodded obediently, realized he couldn't hear a nod, and said, "Right." She hung up the phone, called "Thank-you" to the receptionist, picked up her daisy and her card and walked out of the lodge.

The long summer days meant it was still light as she reached the infirmary. It occurred to her that the two of them alone might look improper to any passerby or onlooker, but wasn't sure how to rectify that difficulty. They could, she supposed, go out on the porch and perform surgery. Or up on the rooftop, maybe. Or put it on camp-wide closed-circuit TV, if they still had such a critter. Maybe they could just video tape the whole thing, so they had proof of what they'd been doing. Or better yet . . .

Collin smacked herself mentally. Knock it off, you guys! Get a grip! Jeff would have the answer. Surely he'd have dealt with this problem before. She'd trust him to figure something out.

He had. Collin saw him walking up the path accompanied by Steve Parks' assistant, Leeann Baker. Ms. Baker smiled at Collin as they arrived and said, "Jeff told me you cut your hand and needed stitches, Ms. Walker. He asked me to chaperone you two young people just to keep things looking proper."

Collin nodded, relieved and disappointed at the same time. She wouldn't be able to have the conversation she wanted with other ears to hear. But at least she'd get her hand fixed.

If Jeff was reading her thoughts, he couldn't have read them any more clearly. He said, "We'll get the hand sutured then we can take a short walk." He looked at Leeann and said, "You've been to Potter's ridge haven't you?"

She nodded. "Oh, yes. That's a beautiful place to watch a sunset. Mr. Baker and I used to go up there at least once a week until he got too sick to walk. Then I'd push his chair. He really did love our spot. It's where he proposed to me." Her eyes twinkled with the memory. "And I turned him down. Three times."

Jeff laughed, "At least he was persistent."

Leeann shook her head. "Not persistent. Bull headed."

Jeff unlocked the door and the threesome entered the small suite. It was divided into three small areas: waiting room, office, and examining room. Off to either side were small confinement/convalescent rooms for patients awaiting transport either to the county hospital or ready for return to camp life. Jeff led Collin to the examining room area. Ms. Baker did not follow, however, but made herself comfortable in the office area. Collin looked at Jeff quizzically. Jeff shrugged. "She hates the sight of blood and she can't hear to save her life. But she refuses to wear a hearing aide. Says it would make her look old. Pride. It'll kill you."

As Jeff began irrigating the wound Collin said, "Jeff, I'm really sorry for how I acted. I was way out of line; way over the line, in fact."

Jeff kept his eyes focused on her hand, and said, "This is going to hurt. I need to reopen the top of the cut." He looked up and asked, "You want a local, first?"

Collin shook her head. "I don't need it."

Jeff said quietly, "You don't need to impress me, Collin. I know you're tough."

Collin responded patiently, "I'm not trying to impress you." Okay, at least not about being tough. She continued, "I have a very high tolerance for pain. A very high tolerance."

Jeff eyed her a moment, then said, "Have it your way." He began working on the top of the incision, gently peeling the layers apart.

Collin could feel the tugging and the pressure but little else. She said, "I didn't plan that stunt, you know. Or maybe you don't know but I didn't. It just seemed to lend itself to the moment."

Jeff didn't look up but said sharply, "Lend itself? How does something like that just 'lend itself to the moment'?"

"I know the rituals these kids hold sacred. You put a knife back without drawing blood, it's your own blood it will shed next. They believe it so strongly it terrifies them."

"You don't help a child overcome a fear by participating in their blood rituals."

"You don't overcome it by telling them they don't exist, either." Collin's voice carried more heat than she had intended so she backed it down. This was, after all, supposed to be an apology. A mending of the waves, not a bid to restart the war. "I only wanted to scratch the palm not cut it in half. I really didn't know the knife would be that sharp."

Jeff straightened up and said, "You nearly nicked the bone and you practically severed one tendon. You'll need real surgery on that one when you get back to civilization. I can give you the name of a good surgeon if you want it."

Collin shrugged. "Thanks but I don't know. That kind of work gets pretty expensive and I have an idea that Workman's Comp is not going to cover this one."

Jeff grinned in spite of himself. "You're probably right on that. Call him anyhow, okay? Give him a chance. It might not be as expensive as you think."

"We'll see." She looked at the hand and asked, "Are you about done?"

"I still need to suture it. Let me get some Lidocaine."

Collin again stopped him. "Jeff, I don't need it. I can handle stitches."

Jeff said firmly, "Well I can't handle putting them in without it." He looked at her dead even and said firmly, "One of us is going to be anesthetized before I proceed and I don't think you want it to be me."

Collin eyed him closely and saw the rock solid determination in his eyes. She started to speak, stopped, breathed out slowly then nodded. "You win. Do it."

Jeff said quietly, "I didn't know we were in a competition. I thought the idea was to fix your hand the best way possible."

"It is."

"Good." As Jeff set about numbing her hand he said conversationally, "You know they've done some studies . . ." He stopped then said, "I just realized how busy 'they' must be. They're in to everything. Do you ever wonder who 'they' really are? Or maybe it's an 'is.' Oh well." He shrugged then continued as if he hadn't interrupted himself. "There were these series of studies done about minor surgery on people who don't experience pain" He began suturing, still talking easily. "Veterans with hysterical paralysis, comatose patients, even people with superior minds who could control the pain response in their bodies. And they all found that patients who could control or tolerate pain still recovered faster with anesthesia than without it. Seems the mind may not recognize the trauma but the muscles and nerve endings still do. They still tense up, get rigid, retract and have all the normal reactions that someone with no pain control experiences. If the body is relaxed it doesn't have to fight and can accept the procedure rather than reject it. I thought it was kind of interesting."

Collin swallowed hard, bit her lip, counted to ten, counted to twenty then said, "I see. And I get your point."

Jeff shook his head. "No point being made. Just sharing some information." He finished up then said, "That should hold it together. A few post-op instructions. One, keep it dry for 24 hours. Two, Monday, you have Dr. Wallace look at it."

"Why? You did a great job. I've seen plenty of stitches and you did fine. I don't . . ."

Jeff shook his head and cut her off. "My license to practice medicine is limited to the emergency variety, Collin. I'm always overseen by a physician. That's the rules. Dr. Wallace sees it Monday, understood?"

Again Collin swallowed the challenge she wanted to make. She nodded and said, "Dr. Wallace on Monday. Right."

"And if everything goes well you can take them out on Friday."

"I can take them out on Friday. Gotcha."

Jeff corrected himself quickly. "You can have them taken out on Friday."

Collin looked at him then asked, "Jeff, have you ever had stitches?"

Jeff nodded. "Once or twice. Maybe three times. Maybe more than that."

"Uh huh. Do you always have the doctor take them out?" She added quickly, "Or his nurse or his or her designated representative?"

Caught. Jeff thought, thought again, thought some more then finally sighed and admitted, "Okay, so you can take the stitches out if Dr. Wallace or I have looked at the wound to make sure it's healing properly."

Collin said quietly, "Jeff, I know when a wound is healed and when it isn't. I've seen enough of them to know what to look for: puffiness, discoloration, fever, drainage, tenderness, and contrary to popular opinion, I will be able to tell. Does that about cover it?"

Jeff eyed her then said slowly, "Okay, so you've had infection 101. Where does all this experience come from?"

"That's not important. Trust me that I know something about when stitches can come out or not. If they're ready I'll pull them. If they aren't I'll leave them in. Satisfied?"

Jeff hesitated then nodded. "Satisfied." He cleaned up the operating area, wrote a note for Dr. Wallace then said, "I guess you're free to go." He walked with her back to the waiting room and said loudly, "All finished, Leeann." Collin held up the hand to display the bandages.

Ms. Baker stood up and said, "My, that didn't take long at all. I thought somehow we'd be here for a while. Seems a shame that you had to drag me along for just these few minutes, Jeff. Everyone here knows you. There's not a soul around that would think you'd be doing anything improper."

As they walked out and Jeff locked the door he said, "And I'd like to keep it that way, Leeann. Avoid every appearance of evil, you know. And besides . . ." his eyes twinkled at Collin, ". . . not knowing Ms. Walker as well as I might like, yet, I thought she might feel safer with a witness present."

Leeann beamed. "That was considerate of you." She smiled at Collin and assured her, "He is quite harmless. A bit ornery but nothing a good woman couldn't tame."

Jeff groaned. "Leeann, please. I'll tell my own lies, thank you."

Collin snickered slightly. It was fun seeing him blush. At least he knew how. That set him apart from the majority of male-kind as Collin knew it. He had principles, he had morals, he had strength of character. He was definitely out of her league. Collin sighed slightly inside. Too good to be true and then some. Oh, well, it would be fun while it lasted. She promised herself she wouldn't fall too deep, nor let him fall at all.

They walked Ms. Baker back to the lodge where Jeff thanked her again for coming out. Collin added her thanks to his and Leeann went on inside.

Jeff looked at his watch and said, "We've got some time before curfew. You want to walk or sit?"

"Walk." That way she wouldn't have to face those eyes directly. The two began to meander along the trail around the camp; Jeff tended to lead which was fine by Collin. Jeff asked after a moment's silence, "What are you going to do about the knife?"

"What do camp directives say?"

"We don't have any. I guess we never thought it would be a problem."

Collin looked at him in surprise. "Were you in on the rules planning, too?"

Jeff said smoothly, "I told you it's a joint venture. Everyone's input was valued."

Collin was impressed. "Very democratic of the owner."

Jeff shrugged. "Sometimes he can come up with a good idea. Not often, but every now and then."

Collin looked at him. "Sometimes I can't tell whether you like him or not."

"Sometimes I have the same problem." He repeated, "What are you going to do?"

Collin said slowly, "Well . . . I don't know whose knife it is. I could find out, probably, without too much effort. Then the culprit should be shipped home, postage due, to learn there are severe consequences to stupidity. Everyone else's baggage should be searched to teach the kids that guilt by association is still a real element to deal with. Then . . ."

Jeff interrupted and said more strongly, "What are you going to do?"

She studied him a moment then said softly, "I'm going to pitch the thing in the deepest part of your river out there. Or, well, see if I can find someone who'll pitch it for me then wait and see if there's need for any more action. I don't know that anyone else brought a weapon to camp." She looked at Jeff and admitted, "I never thought it would be a problem. Guess I don't know kids very well, either. I can pass the word among the counselors to watch or to ask." She looked at him, suddenly puzzled. "What were you doing in the game room tonight? Weren't you off today? Or supposed to be off?"

Jeff shrugged. "They kept blowing breakers. I was trying to figure out what they were doing that was overloading the circuit."

"And?"

"Multiport extension cords with too many game pack rechargers on each one. I set a load limit and they'll either live and work with it or they'll play games without benefit of electricity. Their choice."

Collin grinned at him. "I like your style, Mr. Fireman."

Jeff said softly, "I hope so."

Collin let that one slide. Things were moving too fast and too erratically for her. She decided to look for a safer tack. "What do you think I should do? With the knife I mean." Let's have no confusion here, folks.

Jeff said slowly, "I've been trying to figure that out all day. 'Grace' is what we're all about, or what we say we're about. I can't see that irreparably punishing a child for stupidity helps him learn much. If we send him home what's he learned?"

Collin said quietly, "That he got punished because he got caught. No different than at home."

Jeff nodded. "Right. But if we let him stay and complete the course then he has the chance to learn there's a better way. Maybe he doesn't learn it but he has the chance."

Collin asked hopefully, "So you'd let him stay?"

Jeff nodded. "If it were up to me. It's not, Collin, you have to know that. Steve Parks has that prerogative not me. I'm just the maintenance man. But if you talk to him, say after lunch, before the assembly, I know you'll find him receptive. He's a good man—a godly man—and he'll want to do what's best for everyone."

Collin was a little surprised. "You haven't told him already?"

"No. I thought you would want to handle it first." He grinned slightly, "Figured you might want to address the matter of your hand in your own way. Steve expects kids to be unstable. I'm not so sure how he'll deal with counselors that are less than on the level."

"Thank you so much. I appreciate the vote of confidence." Collin frowned at him but then grinned. Jeff merely smiled in return.

They passed several counselors and campers all straggling along enjoying the cool air, the tall trees, and the peaceful silence. But the undertone of the river still rumbled along. Collin murmured softly, "You can hear it everywhere, can't you?"

Jeff nodded. "It does tend to dominate the area." He looked at her and asked carefully, "Is that a problem?"

Collin hesitated then admitted, "Only when I sleep."

Jeff was silent for several moments then asked even more carefully, "Does talking help?"

Collin smiled sadly at him and said, "Distance helps. Beyond that, nothing."

"Prayer?"

They stopped walking. Collin stared out over the panoramic view, without speaking. She bit her lip, then said quietly, "Not yet. Let's leave it at that, okay?"

Jeff studied her a moment. His voice was gentle as he said, "Okay."

Collin looked at him, ducked her head, and said, "Thanks."

"No problem." His tone was still light as he added, "We probably ought to head back. We're going to lose the light before long."

Collin nodded. "I don't suppose it would look proper to be out alone after dark."

"Not without a juvenile escort. I sometimes feel like this is Never, Never Land."

"And you're Peter?"

"No, Captain Hook." He looked at her as they walked. "Who would you be? Tinkerbell, right?"

She threatened him in mock anger, "Watch it, Mister. I'm no good fairy by anyone's standards. If I had to be someone I'd be the croc."

"Why?"

"People start bugging me, I'd eat them."

Jeff grinned. "Works for me." They walked on in silence but it was a comfortable silence that neither felt obligated to fill. Still, after a while Jeff ventured an observation. "We have a chapel service here in the morning if you're interested. We also provide transportation to local churches of various denominations. I personally have a problem transporting some of the cults to their places of worship but was informed we couldn't make that distinction. That's if you're interested, of course."

Collin smiled slightly. "Where do you go?"

"In town. It's a little independent, fundamental, Bible-believing church called Good Faith. About half the staff goes there."

"So does the church help sponsor the camp?"

"Only by prayer which is the best help we can get."

Collin nodded. "Amen to that."

Jeff looked at her curiously then shook his head. "You are a tough nut to figure, Walker."

"Why?" What had she said?

Jeff shook his head again. "Never mind." They reached the lodge; Jeff opened the door for her. Collin went in still trying to figure out what she'd said to elicit that comment from him. Jeff stopped at the message center, picked up a half dozen slips of paper, held them up and said, "Job security." He looked through them quickly then said, "And they can all wait until Monday. I love it."

Collin asked, "The kids are complaining? About what?"

"Not the kids. The animals." He held up one slip and read it. "Mavis doesn't want to stand next to Lucinda during milking anymore; she thinks their colors clash." Collin shook her head. He read another one, "Arnold, the pig, is complaining that the cats keep stealing his swill." He looked down again and continued, "I like this one. The sheep think the water in the trough is too warm and are insisting I rig the ice maker for them."

Collin had heard enough. She stared him dead in the eyes and said firmly, "Good night, Mr. Farrell."

Jeff looked at her in surprise. "Going so soon? I just started these."

Collin repeated, "Good night, Mr. Farrell."

Jeff grinned and said, "'Nite, Collin. I'll see you tomorrow sometime."

She turned and walked towards the female wing, a little puzzled. Sometime? What did that mean? Why didn't he ask her to meet him for lunch? Or breakfast? Toast, even. But sometime? He hadn't even invited her to his church. What was going on here?

Besides raging paranoia? Who was she kidding? And what was she doing? This trip wasn't about prospecting, it was for Robbie. Remember him? Maybe, just maybe, she should check in on him like a dutiful counselor would. Get to work, woman. Work, not play. Work.

Collin nodded internally. The voice was right. The voice was always right. This trip wasn't for her personal enjoyment it was to touch Robbie. Collin snagged one of the campers and asked him to check Rob's room to see if he was there. Nope. The game room was a possibility as was the gym. Collin debated then on a hunch went to the gym.

Pay dirt. Four lanky figures—okay, three lanky figures and one short figure—were in mortal combat on the pine. Collin watched for several minutes but was unable to determine who was on what side. It looked more like a free-for-all than a competition. She continued to watch and finally decided it was one-on-one squared. Every man for himself with no one keeping score. That was her favorite game. Every basket was a game in itself. Didn't matter how many times you scored before, when you brought the ball down the court it was always tied at nothing.

Collin waited until a basket was scored and the ball careened out of bounds. She called, "Time!", and gave the referee's hand signal. The boys looked over at her; Robbie broke into a grin and yelled, "Hey, case worker lady! What you been doing all day, huh? Get your shoes on and come learn how the game is really played."

Collin grinned and shook her head. "Not tonight. Come over here so I can talk without shouting."

Robbie left the ball and came over. He looked at the bandage on her hand and said solemnly, "Guess they wasn't lying, huh. You cut bad?"

Collin shook it off. "No." She was curious. "What is the word?"

"That you ain't playing with a full deck. I told 'em I knowed that long time ago. Didn't need to go slicing on your hand to prove it."

Collin felt her heart sink. That was all anyone had gotten from it? That she was crazy? Marvelous. She said in almost a whisper, "I see."

Robbie continued, his voice lower, "Got 'em askin' questions, though. Asking who this someone be you be talking about, why he be dying for them, that kind of stuff."

"What'd you tell them?"

"Told 'em go ask you."

"You think they will?"

Robbie shrugged. "Don't know. You ain't been where no one can find you."

Collin started to bristle but stopped. Circular logic this late at night was dangerous. If she hadn't had to go for stitches she would have been able to answer any queries. But if she hadn't cut her hand no one would be asking questions in the first place. Not tonight. She'd think about it tomorrow. After she and that someone had time to work this thing through properly: meaning he talked and she listened.

Collin nodded and said, "Well, if anyone is interested I'll be in my room. Guys can ring it, girls can just come on in. Hour doesn't matter, you know that. I'll be up. Or awake, anyhow."

Robbie motioned towards her hand. "Guess our match gotta wait, huh?"

Collin chuckled. "At least 'til Monday night."

"Ain't using pain as no excuse, now."

Collin stared at him dead even and asked, "Have I ever used pain as an excuse?"

Robbie was not intimidated. "Used everything else. Still ain't beat me."

"Swagger on, my man. Your day is coming. You go on and practice with your friends, there. You're gonna need all the help you can get."

Robbie chuckled. "I hear the wind blowing. 'Nite, case worker lady."

"Good night, Rob."

Collin made her way back to her room, closed the door and sank down gratefully on the bed. Her first full day at camp and what had she accomplished? Made a fool of herself in front of the campers, nearly alienated the neatest—and the word sounded lame, but there wasn't any other way to describe him—man she'd ever met, and endangered her ability to participate in half the activities she might want to join. She'd done herself proud to be sure. What could she possibly do for an encore?

Her hand throbbed. It wasn't that she didn't feel pain. She did. Quite frequently in fact. Like the shooting agony behind her eye that signaled the onset of another particularly nasty headache. It was precisely because she suffered so much that she had learned to control her response to pain, elevating it to such a degree that she could ignore it entirely. For a limited amount of time. And she'd reached her limit. Reluctantly she rose and got two of her migraine pills. Better to take them now than wait until they had no effect. Maybe it would help the hand as well. She hoped.

Collin swallowed the pills, chased them with water, then washed up, changed, and turned back the covers. But before she could crawl between their comfort, a timid knock sounded at the door. Collin called out, "Come in."

Jill stuck her head in the door and said, "Trace and Reeshard want to talk to you, if you ain't already in bed. You want me to tell them you done for the night?"

Collin said quickly, "No, that's okay. Tell them I'll be out in a minute."

As Jill left to carry the message, Collin shrugged back into her clothes, grabbed her Bible, then headed down the hall. She prayed silently, *"Lord, I know I've screwed today up royally. We can talk about that later I promise. But now, maybe, just maybe, there are two lost lambs out there that are looking for a shepherd. Give me wisdom and help me to say what you would have me to say. Nothing more, nothing less. Speak through me, Lord."*

The boys were waiting outside the door looking a little uncomfortable; tentative and unsure whether to stay or escape before being detected. Collin kept her tone even as she acknowledged their presence. "Trace, Reeshard. Can I help you?"

Trace looked at Reeshard, then cleared his throat and said, "Uh, Ms. Walker, we, uh, Reeshard and me and Alex, uh, we had some questions about what you was talking about earlier. Alex wanted to come, but, uh . . ."

Reeshard said quickly, ". . . he couldn't get away. He really does want to know, though. He said to tell you that."

Collin nodded, knowing more completely than either Reeshard or Trace what was holding Alex back. She said only, "That's fine. Let's go out into the lobby where it's quiet."

Collin led the boys to the bench seat by the panoramic windows, sat down with her back against the pane and said, "Okay, what do you want to know?"

Again, Trace took the lead. "I heard what you said about Jesus taking the rap for us. I kind of understand, since you put it the way you did. But I don't get what I'm supposed to do about it. I mean, he died a long, long time ago. How does that mean anything to me?"

Reeshard nodded. "Yeah, like, okay, he died for all the bad stuff people do. Maybe I do bad stuff now. But how does it make me any better?" He cocked his head and asked, "What he got to do with you, anyhow? How does he make a difference in your life?"

Collin prayed silently. Indeed, she hadn't stopped praying since leaving her room. She finally said, "Okay, you've got a couple of separate issues going on. Let's start with your first question. What does his death have to do with you? Nothing and everything." She didn't let the boys get lost on that one but asked Trace quickly, "Tell me what sin is."

Trace thought then said, "Doing bad stuff. Stuff the Bible tells us not to do."

"Reeshard?"

Reeshard nodded then added, "Doing stuff anyone tell you not to do."

Collin shrugged that one off. "Not exactly. Let's stick with what Trace said. Sin is doing what God says is wrong. God sits on this golden throne in his heaven and says, 'This is what's right. Do it, and you can come live with me. Don't do it, and the gates are closed and locked forever.' The trouble is, none of us can do what's right. We're all trouble makers, all set on doing things our way, not God's way. From the moment we draw breath we lock the door to heaven on ourselves."

Trace asked, "And Jesus dying opens it?"

Collin hesitated, then said, "Jesus' death didn't open the door, it destroyed the lock. When you ask him into your life, that's when he makes you his own child and you can enter in and live with him forever."

She let that sink in, hopefully. "You asked me how it makes me different. Ever watch Gwenneth? Watch what she says and does? Think about who she is for a moment."

Trace whistled low. "Tell me 'bout her. That is one wicked female."

Reeshard nodded. "She near cut my throat for dissing her shirt once."

Trace said, "She be needing the Lord that's for sure."

Collin said softly, "Truth. But so did I when I was her age. And I could make her look like a saint."

The shock in the boys' eyes was genuine. "No way!"

"Way. Very much way. That's what difference the Lord makes." Collin sensed that the fruit was not ripe unto harvest, yet, so asked, "You got any more questions?" If they did, it was only in their eyes but not on their lips. Collin suggested, "Then think about what I told you. If you think of anything else, or maybe want to get to know him, you know where I am. Better still, I figure you know where he is. Ask him to forgive you, ask him to come into your life. Then listen for him to welcome you home." Collin grinned slightly and added, "Then come tell me. But you can usually tell when someone's asked him in. They can't quit grinning for days. There's a joy that spreads all over you, and trust me, ain't no way to hide it." With her good hand she squeezed both boys' shoulders and said, "'Nite. I'll catch you both tomorrow."

Trace and Reeshard mumbled the street equivilent of, "Good-night" and headed back to their rooms. Collin watched them go, sighing only a tiny bit. Once the door to the male dorm closed she retreated to her own room and changed back into her pajamas once again. She turned off the lights but left the small nightlight glowing. Campers weren't the only ones who could use a little comfort in the middle of the night. Collin knelt beside the bed, closed her eyes and prayed softly, "Lord, I really messed up today, and I'm sorry. I thought I was doing something great and wonderful for you but that's not what it ended up. I was doing what I thought best, not what you would do. Take this mess and use it for your glory, Lord. Forgive me and show me how to serve you better. 'Speak, Lord, for your servant hears.' Or wants to, anyhow. Help Rob and Trace and Reeshard and Alex in spite of me." She hesitated then, since he knew it already, asked, "Lord, if it is at all your will, could you let Jeff and I become good friends? I know he's your child and I know I don't deserve anyone that special. But could we at least be friends? I like having someone to talk to; it's kind of fun. I know that's not why I'm here and I don't want to interfere with what you want me to do, but if it fits anywhere in your plans . . ." She trailed off then sighed and said, "Your will not mine, Lord. One last thing then I'll shut up and let you talk. I need to sleep tonight. But the nightmares are back and I can't shut them out. The scripture says you give sleep and that if I do what is pleasing to you, you will give me rest. I want to do what's right. Does that count? I'm trying, Father. I know how trying I can be, too. But I really am trying. You know that. You at least know that. Maybe not as hard as you think I should; or maybe not as hard as I think I can. Show me where I'm falling short, Lord. Show me where I'm failing. Tell me what you want and I'll do it." A very old sense of desperation began to creep over her, and the rumble of the river grew imperceptibly louder. While Collin might not be able to cry on the outside, inside a single tear trickled down, and her prayer became a mournful, whispered, "Please. Please." She sobbed softly once then crawled into bed. She offered, "I love you, Lord," then closed her eyes and against all odds slept.

SUNDAY

Morning came with the wake-up call she'd left at the message center while Jeff was getting his animal notes. Collin rose feeling strangely rested and almost refreshed. Almost, but for the dull ache that was the remnant of her headache. Which was preferable to the real thing, any day. Collin whispered gratefully, "Thank you! I love you, Lord. Now what are we doing this morning?" The camp literature had mentioned several church services. Collin looked to see if Jeff's church was listed and found it in alphabetical order like every other church. Sunday school was at the traditional 9:30, services began at 11:00. Also traditional. Did she feel like tradition today?

Tradition was nice. Tradition was safe, too. She'd stick with it. Collin knew that breakfast hours were extended on Sundays, from 7 to 9, so there was no reason why she should miss breakfast except by choice. And through the night the Lord had spoken to her of many things, among which was the reminder of the matter of eating. The recurring habit of denying herself food when she felt out of control of a situation needed to stop. Excuse it as she might, it was still an old defense mechanism that had to be renounced—again. And again. And again. She would eat. She would.

Of course the Lord hadn't said how much she had to eat . . .

No games! Collin shook off the tempter and headed for the showers. As luxurious as these rooms were, there were still communal showers at either end of the gender segregated halls. It was a bit difficult and awkward to shower while keeping one hand dry, but Collin breezed through it once she remembered all the tricks and techniques. Collin hummed lightly as she dressed for church, glad she'd thought to bring at least one more-than-casual, but less-than-work, outfit. Comfortable for walking, sitting, or anything else that was required. Collin brushed her hair out carefully, pulled it back to the side and headed out the door. She checked on Jill and Chenille, found they were both sleeping in, but had set their alarms so as not to miss breakfast. Collin left them snoozing and snoring, respectively, and went down for breakfast.

The same expansive spread was available for breakfast as had been at dinner the first night. She still could not get over the tremendous waste that had to be going on. It made no sense. Everything else Camp Grace did seemed well thought out and planned, using exceptional insight and forethought. Why would this be an area that went so unmanaged? She really did need to seek out Jeff on this. If anyone had an answer it would be Jeff. Whether you could understand it or not was a different story.

Collin ate, but lightly. A banana, half a whole wheat muffin with butter, a small bowl of oatmeal. It was more than she'd eaten in a couple of days, so felt it would satisfy the "eat!" mandate. A glass of milk and a cup of coffee rounded out the meal leaving Collin feeling ready to tackle anything: with one exception. Yet even the river wasn't going to get her down this morning.

As Collin passed the message center she noticed an announcement posted on the bulletin board declaring an all camper meeting for two pm this afternoon. The list of challenge courses would be posted at that time, after an explanation of conditions and requirements. The meeting would be at the pavilion opposite the marina. Come one, come all!

Collin felt a twisting in her stomach and just as quickly dismissed it. She hadn't even seen the list, yet. Absolutely no sense in worrying now. She could save that for after the meeting.

As Jeff indicated, all she had to do was ask and a car and driver were provided to deliver her to the church of her choice. She felt both extravagant and foolish to find the church was only about three miles from the camp: well within walking distance. She told the driver not to bother coming back, that she would walk after church was over. He did not argue with her.

It was just past nine as she walked in to find a small group of people milling around. Most were chatting, laughing and generally catching up on the week's events. One or two people smiled at her. One man with an "usher" tag stared at her: that "I think I've seen you here before but I'm not sure and if I ask if you're new and you're not I'm going to feel like a total idiot" look on his face. Collin resisted the temptation to let him suffer and stepped up to him. She said brightly, "Hi. This is my first time here, so I'm not sure where I'm supposed to go. Do you have an adult Sunday School class?"

From that point on, it was church standard operating procedure. One of the single women "adopted" Collin for the morning and led her to the class, then to the sanctuary for the morning service. Collin debated where to sit. She preferred the front row: less distraction. But people tend to have "their" places, and she would hate to upset anyone unnecessarily. Back rows usually were occupied by mothers with infants or toddlers, perfect for those rapid retreats. Fun to watch the babies, but harder to focus on the sermon. Maybe a couple of rows back from the front, on the outside aisle. That was usually safe, if awkward.

"Come off it, you're finding a place to sit, not making a lifetime commitment! Just grab a two by two area of pew and sit in it!" Collin shook off the rules of church seating etiquette, picked a place to sit and sat. She looked around and watched the congregation file in slowly, though not reluctantly. By eleven the room was about 2/3's full, meaning maybe 125 people not counting non-adults. The choir made its way in, filled the chairs designated for them, and began singing acapella even before the talking stopped. Which of course brought the talking to an immediate halt. Good way to do it. It was one of the old hymns, "Victory in Jesus," but done in a rhythm and tempo unlike any she had heard before. Soloists did point and counterpoint on successive phrases, with the body of the choir providing the background "ooo's." It was soulful. It was chilling. And it was beautiful. Collin closed her eyes and let the music wash over her, felt the Spirit sweep through her and loosen the dirt and cobwebs in her mind and soul. Loosen, not remove. That was still her job.

On the last verse the choir director turned and motioned for the congregation to rise and join the choir, still acapella. Harmonies sprang up from various quadrants of the sanctuary completing the sense of unity as a body of believers. For once the imagery of the last line of the chorus: "beneath the cleansing flood" did not cause that involuntary and annoying flutter in her gut.

Collin did a quick search, but couldn't spot Jeff anywhere. Of course, with her eyesight, unless he was within five pews front or back of her she couldn't see him anyhow. She really needed to do something about her vision. And her vanity. She had a perfectly good set of glasses at home. Or they would be good if she'd wear them. They were supposed to help her with her headaches but had failed of that purpose. Collin could deal with blurred vision but not the headaches so she had abandoned the glasses when they didn't help.

"So sue me for stupidity, okay? It's not the dumbest thing I've ever done." "No, but it ranks up there with the biggies. You'll have to work some to top the knife trick, though."

Collin shrugged off the accusation and turned her attention to the pastor. His sermon was directed at the problems we face: how we can know what is our part and what is God's part. Why aren't we seeing more results? Are we trying too hard, or not hard enough? Collin cringed. She prayed silently, *"This isn't fair, Lord. I am trying. I really, really am trying. But every time I think it's gone, you bring it back up. What do I have to do that I'm not doing?"* The pastor spoke of the peace and freedom that came from walking in total harmony with God, and how much fuller and sweeter life could be. Collin thought bitterly, *"I want that. I want that peace. I don't know how to get it, Lord. Show me what I have to do and I'll do it. Whatever it takes. Show me. I'll do it. I'll work harder, I swear. I will. You'll see. I can do this. I can."*

The service ended with an invitation for anyone interested in extended prayer time to remain and the rest to, politely, leave quickly and quietly. Those that stayed huddled near the front. Though Collin couldn't see or recognize faces across the room, she could identify voices in a crowd. Steve Parks asked prayer for the session just started at Camp Grace. He explained very briefly that these were special kids and really needed the Lord in their lives, as well as guidance for choices. Collin smiled slightly. It was nice to know someone besides herself was praying for her group.

The next voice was Jeff's and it startled her. "I've got some difficult decisions ahead. Okay, so they're not difficult for the Lord, they're just difficult for me." He paused then asked sincerely, "How do you choose between what's better and what's best? How do I know which is which? If the Lord has promised to bless both, how do I know the difference?"

Someone offered, "Sounds to me like you can't lose either way. Pick one and go for it."

Collin cringed. *"You don't understand, do you? There has to be a* right *one. Even if both are right, one is 'righter' than the other. It matters."* The pastor said simply, "We'll pray God will make His will clear to you, Jeff." He looked around and said, "If there are no more requests we'll go to the Lord. For you visitors, I generally lead out in prayer and then if anyone wants to add anything, that's fine. We do limit ourselves to short prayers. One or two lines only." Nods followed; the pastor said quietly, "Let's pray."

Collin listened to the prayers that were being offered then began praying on her own. Whatever it was that Jeff was fighting, she prayed that God would help him find that "perfect" will he wanted. She left her own struggles unvoiced, not willing to raise the dead here and now. All she would do is confirm her willingness to do whatever it took to settle the issue and move on. Make sure her life was on God's track and move on.

The group prayed for about twenty minutes then the pastor closed in a final prayer. As they broke up the pastor came over to her and smiled. "We appreciate your support, Miss. I'm Adam Douglas."

Collin shook his hand. "Collin Walker. I'm one of the counselors with the group at Camp Grace."

Pastor Douglas smiled. "Welcome even more, then. How long will this group be here?"

Jeff was suddenly behind her. "They're supposed to ship out next Saturday morning. Though from what I've seen, a few of them could really benefit from staying longer."

Collin took that silently, not wanting to start a fight or make an issue in church. She'd at least wait until they got outside. She nodded to Pastor Douglas and said, "There are some of them I'd like to move up here permanently. Hide them on the mountaintop away from the evils of the world." She smiled at Jeff and said, "But only until they're as old as Peter, James and John. Then they can come down."

Jeff said, "As long as you stay with them to supervise."

Collin let that one go as well. She addressed the pastor, "That was a tough sermon, Pastor. It sounds so simple. The fact you pastors have to preach it so often tells me we're not getting the message."

A wry look came over Pastor Douglas' face. "Maybe we're trying to convince ourselves." He held up his Bible and said, "The answers are in here. We simply need to read it and do it."

Jeff said quietly, "Read it, understand it, and do it. Some of us can be a little slow in the understanding part." Collin wondered fleetingly if that was directed at her until Jeff continued, "I don't know how many times I've bulled ahead doing something I thought the Lord was telling me to do, only to find out later that I had misunderstood his command. Maybe I'm the only one that dense."

Douglas laughed. "Not even close, Jeff. Not even close." He looked at the clock on the wall and said, "If you'll excuse me, I have a lunch commitment. My wife expects me home at precisely one o'clock and after twenty-five years I have learned not to disappoint her." He shook Collin's hand again and said, "Pleasure to have you, Miss. Walker." He looked pointedly at Jeff and asked, "See you tonight?"

Jeff shook his head. "I don't know yet. Have to see how the afternoon goes."

"I understand. We'll pray the Lord makes a way for you to be here."

Douglas walked off. Collin and Jeff slowly wandered towards the door following the rest of those who were finally leaving. One or two called out to Jeff or simply waved. Seems he was fairly well known in these parts. A good sign. Collin sighed internally as several old adages began to repeat themselves in her head: *"If you find something that's too good to be true, it probably is.""Nothing messes up a good fantasy more than reality."* Collin thought sadly, *"I'm really going to miss you, Jeff."* For both their sakes she should break and run now. Not wait until the inevitable happens, just go while they were friends, sort of.

Jeff's voice broke into her thoughts. "Walker, which way are you going?"

She looked up and realized they were standing at the corner of the church lot and that Jeff had been asking her a question. She looked at him, embarrassed, and said, "Oh. Were you talking to me?"

Jeff grinned. "Apparently not. I asked you how you were getting back to camp. Is the driver coming back for you or what?"

Collin shook her head. "I'm walking."

Jeff looked at her suspiciously. "Walking?"

She pointed to her feet. "Walking. They work. It's not that far and I can use the exercise. Besides, it gives me the chance to ponder the pastor's sermon."

Jeff looked at her and said, "The way you get lost in thought you're liable to end up in the middle of someone's corn field and never find your way out."

She acted highly offended. "I resemble that remark."

Jeff nodded shortly. "Deserved it, too." He hesitated then asked slowly, "Without being forward or pushy or a nuisance, you want some company?"

Collin grinned. "I won't get lost, Jeff. I go down ten blocks and turn left at the tracks. Follow that road to the abandoned grist mill, turn right and the camp is on the left whenever I come to it. Take me about an hour to make it."

Jeff nodded. "You could do it that way. I could show you a shorter way, one that has less traffic, sidewalks most of the way and trees. If you're interested."

Two natures rose in Collin: the street survival nature screamed *"NO!"* while the quieter, gentler nature whispered, *"That sounds like fun. Go for it."* Jeff must have read the indecision in her and said quickly, "Bad idea. I'm sorry, Collin. I shouldn't have suggested it."

Collin shook her head. "It's okay, Jeff. I'm so used to living in the 'hood, I forget that people can make offers without ulterior motives. Someone reminded me on the way up here that I needed to work on my suspicious nature."

"What, to make it more suspicious?" Jeff grinned. "Am I helping?"

She laughed. "No." It occurred to her she hadn't seen the black jeep in the parking lot. She asked, "Just curious, but how did you get here?"

"I walked. Planned on walking home, too. And I know this great shortcut back to camp: not much traffic, sidewalk almost the whole way, and trees." He looked innocently at her and asked, "Interested?"

Collin nodded. "Very. Which way do we go from here?"

Jeff took her church bulletin and drew a rather uncomplicated map complete with street names. He handed it to her and said, "Now you can tell if I'm deviating from the path."

Collin said, "If the path is correct to begin with."

Jeff looked as if that thought hadn't occurred to him. He shrugged haplessly and said, "Oh, well. I'm sorry."

Collin laughed. "Don't be. Let's get going or you're going to miss lunch."

"And you aren't?" Jeff led off down the street.

"No. I don't miss meals. I skip meals. There's a difference."

"Either way you don't eat. What's the difference?"

"Whose choice it was. Missing a meal happens by accident. Skipping a meal is a choice."

Jeff shook his head. "You're a control freak, aren't you?"

"You better believe it." *"And you better learn it now."*

Jeff digested that one then changed the subject. "What did you think of the sermon? No, first, what did you think of the whole service?"

"I love your church, Jeff. It's very traditional. If that's not insulting."

Jeff shrugged. "No insult. We are what we are without apologies. I am what I am with apologies only to my parents and my maker." He chuckled. "And my parents are used to me so I quit apologizing to them years ago."

Collin decided not to explore the area of his parents lest he reciprocate. She asked, "What did you think of the message?"

"I asked you first."

"Yeah, but you know your pastor. Was he trying to say we shouldn't have problems, that if we 'really' trusted the Lord we could simply lay the problem down and not concern ourselves with it any longer? It would just be gone?" Collin could not hide the edge of frustration in her voice.

Jeff said slowly, "I think that was the point he was driving at. You disagree?"

Collin said more sharply than she intended, "I think it's hard to accept. I've heard it over and over before and I've never been able to do it. I don't buy the simplistic 'you're just not trusting' excuse because I know I am. At least I'm trying. It's simply not that easy to do." Again her frustration was evident for all listeners. She backed off, took a couple of slow breaths then said in a calm voice, "Other than that, I think he's a good preacher. I enjoyed it." She smiled at him. "Okay?"

He grinned. "Okay. Just thought I'd ask." He hesitated then asked, "What did you think of the choir?"

"I thought it was wonderful. The harmonies were fantastic. They must practice all the time."

Jeff shrugged. "Most of them do. The bass section tends to be more sporadic."

"It didn't show. You couldn't tell it. I thought they sounded great."

"They'll appreciate hearing that."

"How many people are in the bass section?"

"Two."

"And in the choir itself?"

"Couldn't you tell?" Jeff's voice hinted his amusement.

Collin paused, said, "Welllll . . . no. From where I was sitting the choir was one solid indistinguishable mass."

Jeff laughed. "What?"

Collin shrugged, embarrassed. "I'm pretty well blind beyond four rows. That's one reason I don't drive much at night. And I walk a lot."

Jeff continued to laugh. "Why don't you get glasses, lady? They do make them you know."

"I know. And I have glasses. I just don't wear glasses."

"Oh that makes sense."

"It does. Somehow."

Jeff shook his head and grinned. "Now I understand."

"Understand what?"

"I saw you but you kept looking right past me. I thought you were upset with me or pretending not to know me or something."

"Why would I do that?"

"Why would you look past me?"

"Did you wave?"

"Not from where I was sitting."

"Where were you sitting?"

"In front of you. In front of the church. In the bass section."

Collin shook her head. All this, and he sings in the choir, too. Unbelievable. Unbelievable. She would definitely miss him.

The remainder of the trip they talked about nothing more substantive than life at the camp. Jeff filled in details about the history that the literature left out. But he continued to skip around questions about the owner. Which of course made Collin more curious and determined to unearth the mystery. The walk was pleasant though Collin found herself more winded than she should have been after walking little more than half an hour. She really did need to get out of the office more often. Especially if she was going to continue challenging Robbie. And speaking of . . . maybe Monday night they could finally get in that game. The hand should be healed enough. And if it wasn't, well, she'd worry about that later.

As they arrived at the camp it was just past one o'clock. Jeff headed off for the maintenance shack. Collin headed straight for the administrative offices. First thing first: she needed to talk to Steve Parks. This could be tough.

Collin decided not to change clothes but to go in her most presentable, professional attire: or at least of what she'd brought to camp. Maybe she could lessen the impact of her stupidity. As she approached the director's office she rehearsed several possible explanations and scenarios for her actions, all of which sounded frightfully inane. The truth, woman. Stick with the truth. However condemning it might sound.

The door to Steve Parks' office was open and Collin could see the director sitting at a desk mulling over some papers. She bit her lip slightly then tapped on the door. Steve looked up and said, "Come in."

Collin stepped inside the office and said hesitantly, "Mr. Parks, I'm Collin Walker, one of the counselors." She paused then added, "I need to speak to you but if now isn't a good time I can come back later."

Steve stood up quickly, "No, no. Come in. Glad to have you." He escorted her to a chair then sat down opposite her. "How can I help you?"

Collin searched for words then said, "Jeff Farrell said I should talk to you about an incident yesterday in which a knife was . . . found. Dropped by one of the campers."

Steve looked grave and said, "Yes, I heard rumors to that effect. I refuse to act on rumors, Miss Walker. I choose to wait until the facts are revealed."

Collin breathed out slowly then admitted, "The facts are a knife—a switch blade—a highly illegal switch blade—was dropped during a scuffle between four campers after the tour. I don't know for sure which camper it belonged to, and I didn't pursue the matter at the time."

"You were there when it happened." It was more a statement than a question.

"Yes, sir, I was."

"Please dispense with the 'sir.' It makes me think I'm my father."

Collin did not smile but pushed ahead. "I decided to deal with the matter in my own way, much as I would at home. I know these kids; I know their motives and their fears. I believe I handled the situation correctly." The shouts of derision in her brain led her to qualify her statement, "Most of it, anyhow." She held up her bandaged hand and admitted, "This part was questionable."

Steve studied her a moment then asked softly, "What was that about? Those were a major part of the rumors I heard."

Collin shrugged, more than a little embarrassed. "It sounded brilliant at the time. The streets have their own legends and myths, Mr. Parks." She couldn't bring herself to "Steve," yet. "One of those is that if you expose a blade you cannot sheathe it again without drawing blood, even if it has to be your own. I was trying to demonstrate that because of their hatred, someone's innocent blood had to be shed. Not that I was claiming to be innocent, of course, but I wanted to give them something to think about." She gave him a half, hapless smile and said, "My intentions were good; my execution stunk."

Steve pondered everything for a moment then said, "You would have handled this the same way back home? Not turned the knife in? Not tried to find the owner?"

Collin nodded firmly. "I would have done exactly the same. I'm trying to turn these kids around not condemn them. Any edge I can use, I will."

"And you don't believe there is any risk or danger to anyone else at the camp from the owner?"

"No, I don't. He's a scared kid. The knife probably belonged to an older brother and the boy will get the snot beat of him for taking it when he gets home. I won't give it back to him, though, whoever it belongs to."

Steve thought some more then said, "I'd like to take some time to pray about this. I noticed you were in the after service prayer group so I believe I won't offend you if I ask you to pray with me."

Collin smiled. "Absolutely you will not offend me."

"Good." The director bowed his head, and began silently praying. Collin followed his lead, closed her eyes and prayed, *"Lord, I didn't ask before but I'm asking now. Please help us know what to do about all this. And let your will be done, not mine."*

After several moments of intense silence, Steve Parks began to pray aloud. "Lord God, Father, you gave us this camp and all that's in it. You gave us the skills we have, the wisdom we have, the experience we have. But Lord, nothing in my experience covers this situation except your son and how he taught us to treat one another. I can think of no other scripture that even comes close to this. If there is, or if there is something you mean for me to learn about dealing with these children, please let me know. Every life matters, Lord. Miss Walker believes she knows the best way to handle this. If it's her wisdom I'm to follow, make that clear, too. Help me do it right, Lord. This camp exists for one purpose: to bring you glory and do your will. Help me know what that will is. In Jesus' name, amen."

Collin echoed softly, "Amen." She looked up at the director and said quietly, "Thank you."

"You're welcome. I want time to let him present his answer before I make my decision. I'll have an answer for you by this evening."

"That's fair. That's more than fair. I appreciate you being so understanding."

"I'm not understanding any of this I'm afraid. But I'm trying to learn." He stood up and extended his hand. "Thank you for coming, Miss Walker. I hope you enjoy our camp."

Collin grinned. "I already do. Thank you." She shook his hand then left the office as quickly as was proper.

Collin hustled to her room, changed into jean shorts and a T-shirt and headed back to the pavilion. The notice she'd been anticipating—or dreading, depending on how you look at it—was prominently displayed on the bulletin board. The directions said that choice of activity could be made after the meeting. A sampling of classes would be available throughout the afternoon for those still undecided. All selections must be made before dinnertime or campers and counselors would sit the week out as an observer. Collin scanned the list looking for what she might do. More important, what she thought Robbie might do. The obvious was the basketball sessions but Collin had the gut feeling Robbie would pass. He could play all the hoops he wanted to at home. Some of the extreme sports, now, might interest him. Downhill roller blading, maybe. Or street luge. Collin prayed quickly, "Not that, please. I'll follow him on anything but not that." She continued to read: horseback riding, canoeing, white water rafting, wilderness survival training, cooking, fishing, tree climbing, tree identification (look, Dad, it's a tree!) animal observation, avian tagging . . . it was endless. Collin wondered how all this would be tied to the real world. What was there about survival in the wilderness that a child could apply to living on the streets of Oakton? Climbing trees? Fishing? She shook her head slightly.

"Negative thinking on a Sunday afternoon? That's not allowed up here. It's in our constitution." Jeff smiled as he approached the pavilion, broom and dustpan in hand. His eyes twinkled slightly.

Collin had to look down. Drat him! She recovered herself, however, and asked, "What are you doing?"

"Sweeping out the grand hall before your meeting. Which, by the way, isn't for another half hour."

Collin shrugged. "I like to get a jump on things."

"Uh huh." Jeff wasn't impressed. "Classic evidence of type A personalities. Control freaks. Can't stand to be late can you?"

Collin said defensively, "It's been known to happen."

"Maybe. But not often. I know people like you. You'd rather miss an entire movie than walk in ten minutes late."

"But if you miss the first ten minutes you might never figure out what's going on."

Jeff shook his head, mumbled something about control and began to sweep down the benches. Collin watched him a moment then asked, "Can I give you a hand?"

Jeff looked down then said, "Nope, already got two. And you don't have one to spare."

Collin grimaced at him then tried again. "Okay, may I help you then?"

"Why?"

"Because I'm standing here doing nothing and . . ."

Jeff interrupted, ". . . and someone paid good money so you could have the privilege of doing nothing this week. This is my job."

Collin protested, "But I don't like doing nothing."

"Live with it. It might do you some good." Jeff continued to work as if enjoying her discomfort.

Collin scowled at him and said, "You're selfish, you know that?"

"Yep."

"Can you talk while you work or is that verboten?"

"If you mean does the employee handbook allow it, the answer's yes. If you mean can I walk and chew gum, that's questionable. But I'm usually up for a challenge."

Collin ignored the foregoing and asked, "If you could choose one of these courses which would you take?"

"Are you going to take a class? Actually go with your kids?"

Collin shrugged. "I think so. Depends on what Rob chooses I guess."

"What won't you do?"

Collin objected, "Wait a minute, I asked you first."

"Oh, yeah. I forgot about that. Let's see. What would I do? Probably hang gliding. I haven't got to try it, yet, but I've always dreamed of soaring with eagles."

"Then why don't you?"

"Time. There's not enough time to do it during the day and they won't let me go at night. Something about lack of thermals and falling like a rock. I don't understand it. What about you? What out there scares you enough to want to challenge it?"

Collin shrugged again. "I don't know for sure." Which was a lie but she wasn't about to bring it up. "It depends on Robbie—Rob, I mean." She noticed the hint of confusion on Jeff's face and explained, "I promised him I would never call him Robbie to his face. I try to make it a habit not to refer to him that way any other time, either."

"What's his real name, Robert?"

"No, Robbie. That's what his mother named him. And he hates it."

Jeff nodded in sympathy. "I can see how it would be tough on the streets with a name like 'Robbie.' Tough to be taken seriously."

"You got it. And with his lack of height, too. We're not joined at the hip but we do tend to challenge each other to go further. Whatever he takes I'll probably tag along."

Jeff warned, "You don't 'tag along' on any of these classes. You're either in or out."

"Oh, I intend to be in all right. That is not a problem." It surprised Collin that Jeff didn't ask her whether she had met with Steve Parks or not. Probably felt it was none of his business at this point. Not that that usually stopped people from inquiring anyhow. But it added to the list of special things that impressed her about this man.

Campers and counselors began to arrive, and you could tell who had gotten whom out of bed. The campers gathered around the notice and began reading the list. An assortment of emotions were expressed by the assortment of "yeahs," "ooohs," "way cool, mans" and the ultimate, "dude." Spelled phonetically it would look more like "dooode." In any event the campers seemed pleased with the offerings.

Collin searched for Robbie and noticed him standing a little off by himself. She studied him a minute then walked over to him. "Hey, my man. What's shaking?" Out of the corner of her eye she noticed Jeff finish his task, gather his things and slip away.

Rob said sullenly, "Nothing."

"Got your game face on or what? Today's the day, little brother." Collin tried to get him going but Robbie wasn't buying it.

"What day? What they gonna let a little kid like me do? I can't hardly ride the coasters at the Point. How'm I gonna steer a canoe?"

Ted Johnson, activities director, approached at that moment and said, "You don't steer a canoe. You pilot one. And there are no weight or height restrictions at this camp."

Robbie looked at him suspiciously. "They ain't?"

"No, there aren't. If you want to take canoeing then that's what you take. But let's share this information with everyone, shall we?" He walked to the center of the pavilion, raised his voice and said, "If you will all take a seat there will be just a few things to cover before we start." He waited until everyone was settled—or as settled as excited young people can be. He smiled at everyone then promised, "No long speeches. The choices are on the board. Choose whatever you want to try but understand this: every field up there will require hard work, sweat, and extreme concentration. Even the cooking." Someone snickered but the director said, "Don't laugh. This isn't cooking for one or for friends. This is banquet cooking, serving between 250-500 people every day." Ted looked around and said, "Some of you may have noticed we cook a lot of food here. Did anyone wonder where it all goes?" Collin's hand shot up quickly, as did a few other mostly adult hands. Only one youngster raised hers. Ted said, "As a means of community service we supply meals for shut ins, homeless shelters, battered women and children's shelters, the local community hospital and the like. They deserve nothing but the best and that's what we promise to deliver. So the pressure is on all the time, every day." He looked around and said, "Not that you can't have fun along the way. Otherwise we're a slave labor camp and that is not our prime directive. So pick something that looks fun, looks challenging, looks like something you've never tried before and may never try again. There are no size restrictions other than Mr. Lawler, here. I'd have a hard time finding a horse tall enough for him." The kids laughed; Mr. Lawler merely doffed his hat and waved it. Ted finished with, "One last promise. One person in class or fifty, it doesn't matter. No one gets shut out. If you already know what you want to do, hike up to the barn and register. Being first on the list gets you no special privileges. If you want to wander around and examine the equipment, the animals, the teachers—and yes, I'll be available to point out which is which—or the site locations, go ahead. You have until dinner to make your choice"

Voices buzzed slightly as possibilities were imagined. Ted continued, "But a word of caution: these classes are consecutive. What you learn on day one you will use the next day. There is no room for changing your mind. Once a class has started you can drop out, but you can't join another class. Those who don't last can still enjoy the run of the camp, swim, hike, fish, whatever. Anyone who doesn't want to attend a class may sit out as well. But you were all selected to come because someone knew you had the right stuff to make it through. Someone believed in you. Believe in yourself as well. Have a good time." The director smiled then walked off, leaving the crowd to dissipate on its own.

Kids and counselors alike drifted back to the bulletin board to study the list with new respect. Collin watched Robbie's face for any hint of what he was thinking. He stared at the board then let his eyes drift off down the canyon. A chill ran over Collin's spine. She asked quietly, "What are you going to pick, Rob?"

Robbie looked at her then asked, "You coming with me?"

Collin hesitated then answered truthfully, "Depends on what you pick. I know my limitations, Rob. I'm not a kid like you. There are some things I can't do."

Robbie asked, "You gonna let me say that?"

"Not until you try."

"You saying you done tried all this stuff?"

"Some of it, yeah, I've tried. Not all of it."

"What?"

Collin's frustration began to increase ever so slightly. "Rob, just pick something you want to do, man. Don't worry about me. I'll either come or I won't. Don't base your life on what I do or don't do."

"I ain't." Robbie seemed hesitant to continue then said, "But you're kind of fun to have around, when you ain't being annoying or stupid."

Collin laughed. "I'm never stupid. Annoying, I'll buy."

Robbie shook his head. "Case worker lady, you something else." He looked back down the canyon then said, "I want to ride it, lady. I want to ride the river."

Collin nodded. It was exactly what she feared. She said softly, "I think that's a good choice for you. You'll do well."

Robbie looked at her. "You coming along?"

"I can't, Rob."

"Why not?"

Collin shook her head, her heart threatening to hammer its way out of her chest. "I promise you one day I will explain it. But I need you to trust me that I can't." She looked at him, her eyes begging his understanding.

Robbie studied her a minute then said slowly, "I'll hold you to that, lady. I'll let it slide this time, but you better have a good excuse."

"I will." She'd make one if the truth couldn't be told. She managed to quiet the shaking in her hands and gut and said, "So, you want to look at the equipment?"

"Naw, I want to know what you gonna choose."

Collin shrugged then said, "I thought about cooking . . ." Robbie grabbed his throat and began making choking sounds. Collin continued, shoving him lightly, ". . . but considering how I cook at home I figured I wouldn't poison anyone while I'm here. I have always wanted to ride horses, though."

Robbie looked surprised. "For real? Why?"

"I don't know. They're so big and powerful. I've been fascinated with them for years. Scared of them, too."

"You? Scared? Of a dumb animal?"

"Yes, me, scared of a dumb animal. They're so powerful, so majestic. Do you realize that if horses had thumbs they could rule this planet? There's nothing that could stand in their way."

Robbie looked skeptical. "Thumbs?"

"Yeah. Without thumbs they can't operate the remotes."

Robbie gave her a disgusted look. "You ain't real, you know that? You ain't for real."

Collin grinned. "Yeah, but you gotta love me." She rumpled his hair then shoved him. "Go on up to the shelter and get signed up so you'll know where to go. I'll be along shortly." Robbie grinned then headed up the hill towards the sign up room.

Collin walked back to the bulletin board to stare at the list again. Most of the campers had drifted off either debating their choices, or hustling to register in case the director wasn't right about everyone being allowed in the classes. Before long Collin was left alone, still staring at the board. It wouldn't go away. Rationalize all she could, it still wouldn't go away. But she couldn't do it. She couldn't. What had Jeff said, "What scares you enough to want to try it?" And Robbie wanted to know if he could use her excuse. They didn't understand. They couldn't. She whispered, "But you do, don't you? You know what it's about."

The Voice inside whispered, *"It's about trust. Do you trust me?"*

Collin felt the blood drain from her face and her knees grow weak. She sat down on a nearby bench and asked, "Why? I'm perfectly happy not going near rivers. I can live my entire life in your service and never have to come within miles of a river. Please don't ask." Collin looked up at the cathedral sky above her and repeated, "Please, please don't ask."

And the Voice didn't. He merely repeated the question, *"Do you trust me?"*

Collin grit her teeth. She felt like a four year old about to have a tantrum, but didn't care. She protested, "It's not fair, Lord. That's not what I came up here for. We came here for Robbie, remember? He's the one you're supposed to be working on." Silence. "I don't want to go on the river, Lord." More silence. "I can't go on the river."

Scripture echoed in her mind; *"I can do all things through Christ who gives me strength."* Collin ground her teeth in anger and said, "That's a cheap shot. That's not what that means." Her defiance faded as quickly as it came. She sat back against the bench, totally defeated. "Father, please don't ask. Please."

She sat in silence for several minutes unable to choose or move. The bulletin board remained impassive, neither suggesting nor eliminating options. The world seemed incredibly still as if waiting for an answer. There really was only one and Collin knew it. He knew it, too. Chastised and defeated she said brokenly, "You know I'll go. I do trust you. But can you please take away the fear? Or at least the nightmares?"

No answer came, and she didn't really expect one. Silently she got up, dusted herself off, and turned reluctantly around to head for the barn for sign up. Her feet felt like lead as she moved, unwilling to hurry along the inevitable. As she rounded a corner she practically ran into Jeff who was standing quietly in the path. Collin wondered how long he'd been standing there and how much he had heard. It only added to the pain and frustration. Collin refused to meet his eyes, determined to pass him without speaking. But she stopped as he said softly, his voice almost tender, "Collin . . ."

She would not face him and did not lift her eyes. Jeff continued carefully, "I wasn't trying to listen and I'm not prying. I know a private conversation when I hear one. I just want you to know if there is anything at all I can do to help, I will." He laid a hand on her shoulder; she turned at last to face him. He smiled sadly and added, "I can't change his mind, though. I've tried enough times but it doesn't work. And I think you know that, too."

Collin ducked her head slightly, not willing to admit nor deny his appraisal. She looked into his eyes and saw nothing but compassion. Her walls began to crumble slightly and she whispered, "But I can't do it. He knows that. Why can't he just leave things alone?"

"Probably because he won't leave you alone, either." Jeff faced her dead on. "Collin, I have no idea what you and he are fighting about, and I don't need to know unless you want to tell me. But I do know he loves you. Everything he does is out of love for you. And it's always for the best."

Collin studied him a moment then asked with sarcasm born of fear, "And what Seminary have you been to?"

"The University of Life, milady." Jeff swept his arm around in a grand circle. "Everywhere, everything. It's all from living. I've been where you are, Collin. You've been where you are before, and you know it. What happened the last time he challenged you? You got through it, right? And it made you stronger."

Collin could feel the frustration rise in her as she listened to him talk. Yes, she knew what he was saying. But this was different. This was . . . this was *this*. God could bring her through everything else but this . . . this was . . .

Her mind snapped back into focus. This was no different to God than any other experience he'd led her through. He either loved her or he didn't. She either trusted him or she didn't. Had he ever given her cause to doubt either his love or his faithfulness?

Unexpectedly Collin laughed and it surprised her. Jeff's eyes sparkled. On impulse Collin reached up and hugged him. Equally as fast she let him go and said, "I've got to get signed up or all this will have been academic. Thanks, Jeff." She turned and hustled up the hill to the barn.

Jeff stood alone, watching her go. He grinned, pleased, and said softly, "No problem. No problem at all."

Robbie finally caught up with Collin in the dining hall after dinner. He grabbed her playfully from behind as she sat silently staring at a mostly uneaten plate of meatloaf. The first bites had tasted wonderful. But the knots in her gut were posting "No admittance" notices on her stomach. Robbie asked boisterously, "Hey, case worker lady, where you been all afternoon? I looked everywhere for you. And I looked at all the lists. Your name ain't on none of them what I saw. You gonna wimp out on me?"

Collin faced him slowly, putting on her tough-guy face. "No, I am not going to wimp out on you. You obviously weren't looking at the right list."

"I looked at all the indoor stuff; made sure you wasn't cooking nothing." Collin sneered at him; Robbie ignored her. "Then I looked at the hoops list figuring maybe you might finally want to learn the game." Collin swatted at him this time but he ducked and moved out of arm's reach. "You didn't even sign up for your horse stuff. I figured at least you'd want to do that seeing as how you sure can't drive them horses you got at home."

Collin said archly, "If you are referring to my car and my driving abilities, I know very well how to handle them. And I did sign up." The play in her began to dissolve as Activities Director Ted came forward to announce the classes. Collin motioned for Robbie to sit down beside her. As if sensing something was coming, he pulled a chair up next to her and sat down. His face was quizzical as he watched her but she merely indicated the director was waiting for everyone's attention.

When it got quiet Ted began, "I'm very, very pleased with the choices that have been made today. I believe we have the broadest selection of interests that I've ever seen. Which means some of you are going to get one-on-one attention in your chosen field. Others of you will benefit from additional staff help as we fill the requirements for the class." He stopped then said, "Let me put that another way. If what you wanted to do was play football but only two other campers signed up, you will still play football. But it will be against staff or any local students that we can recruit. I promised no one would get closed out of a class and I meant it." The campers cheered and certain worried and downcast faces began to glow again. Collin wondered briefly if maybe her class could be under-filled and they would have several professionals with them. It didn't hurt to hope, did it? Or to ask? She sent up a silent prayer, all the while feeling like a cowardly traitor.

Ted looked around the room at the counselors and added, "I was pleased to see some of you adults getting in the spirit of the camp." He looked specifically at Collin and then at two male counselors. "I wish more of you had, however. Perhaps we can count on you to participate in other ways. Say, as taste testers. Or tackling dummies." The campers roared with laughter, pointing to varied individuals as likely candidates. Ted motioned to the crowd for quiet, then continued, "Be that as it may, we will see how the week progresses. Let me give you the daily schedule. All classes begin tomorrow at 8 a.m. sharp. Your instructor will designate the meeting place; look for it on the board after 9 p.m. tonight. Be it up on the mountain, down in the valley, or under the river that's where you will meet the rest of the week."

Collin shivered slightly. She felt her jaws clench but resolutely forced them to relax. The director was moving on. "The most we have in any class is seven. Surprisingly, it's one of the tougher classes we offer." Collin grimaced. Her prayer had obviously been answered with a resounding, "No!" She was not going to get off easy it seemed. Okay, have it your way.

Ted brought his instructions to a halt. "So that's all I have. Meet your team where I told you and have a great time. Remember, you can."

Collin looked around, confused. She'd obviously missed some directions. She looked at Robbie who was studying her quizzically. She asked, "What?"

"Where you been? You kept zoning out, lady. What you thinking about?"

Collin shrugged. "What comes next I guess. What are you supposed to be doing?"

"Meeting the team by the back doors just to know who they is. Supposed to help us with 'bonding' or some such stuff." Robbie looked at her again and asked, "You got any idea what you supposed to be doing?"

"I do now." She stood up, took a deep breath and said, "Let's go. Let's do it."

Robbie jumped up. "Go where? What did you sign up for?"

"White water, what else? You think I'm going to let you have all the fun and glory?"

Robbie protested, "But you said . . ."

Collin cut him off. "I know what I said. But things change. I changed my mind, okay? I found a mind and changed it for my old one. It has a better warranty: thirty minutes or thirty questions, whichever comes first. So don't use them all up at once."

They hustled to the back door and Robbie shook his head. "You ain't real, lady. You know that? You ain't for real."

"That's what you keep telling me."

The team was comprised of six campers and Collin. Three males and three females, ranging in age from ten to fourteen. Collin recognized the brother-sister twins Niles and Nyla, a gang in themselves. Although she had not dealt with them directly, their tough-guy attitudes preceded them. Collin had seen the physical after-effects of some of their handiwork on the bodies of her own kids. Frankly speaking, they were not nice people. But someone thought them capable of change. Or else just wanted a break from dealing with them.

That was unworthy of her. They were kids, that's all. They had souls. Or so it was believed. There were times it might be questionable but at the very least the Lord loved them, so Collin would, too. Also along for the fun and excitement were Chonnell Rice and Lynn Pardner. The epitome of giggly preteens, Collin could not imagine why they had signed up for this class. Must be more inside than she thought. At least she hoped there was. The thought of going out to sea with the two of them was daunting. The thought of going out to sea itself was terrifying enough.

The remaining male contingent consisted of Robbie and Ta'waan, a tall, gangly thirteen year-old who Collin would have sworn was at least sixteen. He had polished his "cool" image to a high luster and wasn't shy about letting people know it. What a crew. What a crew. Collin felt her heart sinking even as she talked with the group. With this they were going to challenge the river? She could only hope—and pray—that the instructor was very good. And that they, as a team, were very lucky.

The meeting broke up just after nine with an agreement that they would all meet for breakfast at seven, sharp. The kids went off, excited but cool, trying to act as if tomorrow would be nothing special. Collin hung around the porch until they were gone then walked over to the seats provided for guests, placed to afford the maximum view of the sunset.

It would have been gorgeous if Collin had had the heart to look at it. As it was, she curled up in a tight ball, pulled her knees into her chest, dropped her head down to her knees and let out a very long, slow, shaky breath. It was not going to work. It wasn't. There was no way. Merely talking about the river was giving her fits. What was she going to do when they actually got out there? Could she even get in the boat? There were no guarantees on that one, even. What was the Lord thinking? Collin snarled internally, *"I know, I know. I don't need to know what he's thinking. I just need to obey. Okay? I'm, obeying. It doesn't make it easy. I'm scared. I admit it."*

One of the internal accusers jeered at her. *"You got no faith. You got no trust. You got nothing but talk and it means nothing. You're gonna freak out and then how do you explain it to Rob? What does your faith do for you then??"*

Collin groaned inside. Possibly outside, too, though she hadn't intended it. A strong warm hand was laid on her shoulder, and the getting-to-be-familiar voice asked with concern, "Are you okay, Collin?"

Collin lifted her head and said, "Go away. You're not supposed to see me when I'm like this."

Jeff sat down on the bench across from her. "Like what? Curled up like a beach ball? Which you know, if you get stuck like that, it would take eight surgeons working 24 hours straight at least 10 days to fix?" His eyes were twinkling but his voice was gentle.

Collin stared at him then nodded. "Right. Exactly." She uncurled slightly but kept her arms wrapped around her knees. "What are you doing out here this late? Don't you ever get to go off duty?"

Jeff shrugged. "Technically I'm on call 24 hours. We had a little plumbing problem over in the men's wing and I had to fix it. Took a little longer than I anticipated but I got it finished. I was on my way out, saw this rather contorted figure out here and thought I'd investigate." He hesitated then said softly, "What am I investigating? Is this some form of meditation I'm interrupting? Or a new prayer position I've yet to come across in scripture?"

Collin looked away from him and said quietly, "It's the Collin Walker method of telling the world to go away and leave me alone."

"Does it work?"

She looked at him and asked, "Is the river still there?"

Jeff looked out to be sure then said, "Uh huh."

"No." She stretched out a little more. "But I keep hoping."

Jeff said carefully, "You don't have to go on the river, you know. I'm afraid of fire but that doesn't mean I'm going to go running through every burning building I see until I conquer it."

Collin said, "But you're a fireman. You should be afraid of fire."

"And for some reason you're afraid of the river. Maybe there's a good reason."

Collin barely whispered, "There is." She looked at Jeff and said, "But the Lord seems to want me out there. I don't know why, and yes, I've prayed and asked him. He's a little short on 'why' answers right now. Just kept asking me if I trust him. What kind of question is that?"

Jeff chuckled, and she knew he knew where she was coming from. "He's usually short on those 'why' answers. I hear, 'Because I love you,' a lot, though." Jeff paused then admitted, "Of course sometimes there is the, 'because I said so' response. I think God must have learned it from my dad. Dad is the master of that phrase." Collin shuddered involuntarily; Jeff asked with concern, "Are you cold?"

Collin nodded. "Yes but not like that." She left it hanging, determined not to tell all at this early stage of their—dare she say—relationship? Why scare him off so soon? Collin breathed out a slow sigh then said, "I suppose I should get back to my room and try to get some sleep. The crew wants to sit together for breakfast and storm the classroom early. They want to see if they can keep the book time to a minimum and the river time to the max."

"That will suit Mitch fine. He'd much rather be on the water, anyhow." Jeff gave Collin a somewhat enigmatic look and said softly, "I hope you have a good time tomorrow. I mean that. Mitch can be . . . a lot of fun they tell me."

Collin remembered something and said, "Jeff, are you going to be busy tomorrow night?" Lest he think she was being forward she asked, "Did you play hoops in school?"

Jeff looked confused. "Yeah, I played some in college. Why?"

"Ever ref a one-on-one game? No time outs, no time limits, first one to 100 wins?"

Jeff whistled low but said, "I suppose I could hold my own. Why?"

"Rob and I are in a competition and I promised to beat him while we're here. Tomorrow night looks promising if the good doctor will release me to play."

"Is Rob any good?"

"He's very good."

Jeff asked wryly, "Are you any good?"

Collin said archly, "I can hold my own. I haven't beaten him yet, but I'm getting there."

"By choice?"

"Trust me he doesn't need my help to win. I always play him hard and fair." She hesitated then admitted, "Okay, sometimes it's not always fair. I have been known to practice a diversionary tactic or two." She paused then said, "The Salamon twins. Mark Riley on his Harley. The night Coach Leonard cruised by in his Viper. Not that any of it worked but it was worth a shot."

Jeff said, "You want me to ref. That means you actually have rules?"

"Mostly in bounds kind of things. I'm trying to reinforce the 'within the lines' kind of mentality."

"I thought thinking and playing 'outside the lines' was all the psychological rage."

"Maybe it is in some circles. But to survive in the real world you've got to know where the lines are, and that there are lines in the first place. You have to know the limits before you challenge them."

Jeff nodded his approval. "Good thought."

Collin acted surprised. "You mean I had one? Someone mark that down!" Jeff shook his head at her; Collin sobered up and asked, "Can you come and ref?" She stopped then said, "Will you come is a better question. I mean, if you want to. Maybe you've already got plans or something." Suddenly Collin felt awkward and shy for having asked the man.

Jeff shook his head. "No, I think it would be fun. I could use the exercise." He studied Collin a moment then added, "I can see where you would be a formidable opponent."

Collin deliberately ignored the comment and said, "We get competitive, yes. We haven't drawn blood, yet, but it's not for lack of trying. I promised him I would beat him one of these days. But beat him clean. And it has to be clean, Jeff. No tipping the scales one way or the other."

Jeff said evenly, "Absolutely. I wouldn't do it any other way. How is Rob going to feel about having a third party observer?"

"We've had refs before. Rob knows a win by anything other than pure ability or dumb luck isn't a win. If you gotta cheat you ain't a winner. We both want to win. We just want to do it right."

"What time and where?"

"Nine o'clock, on the back court."

"We don't have a back court."

Collin sighed. "Details, details." She asked in measured tones, "Is there a court with lights?"

"Yes."

"Which one?"

"Court number two."

"Then that's where we will meet. Understand?"

"Understood, yes Captain."

Collin shook her head, chuckled and stood up. Jeff rose also, smiling at her. Collin said, "I'm going to my room now. You can carry on doing whatever it is you were doing before I interrupted you and I'm sure I will see you in the morning."

Jeff saluted. "Thank you, Captain. Have a pleasant evening. Good night, sir."

Collin smiled at him; Jeff dropped the military bearing and said, "Sleep peaceful, Collin."

"Thanks, I will." Collin walked back to her room. There was a note posted on her door from Director Parks. Collin opened it slowly, almost fearfully. As she read it she began to breathe again, then to smile, and finally to whisper, "Thank-you, Father. Thank-you." She kissed the note quickly, stuffed it in her pocket and walked inside. This was going to be a great week.

MONDAY

But while sleep she did, peaceful would not be the word to describe it. Harrowed, maybe. Nightmarish, definitely. But not peaceful. She was flying. She was falling. She was drowning. Faces peered at her through the water. Some lifted her up. Some held her under. There was fear, there was terror, there was panic, but overall there was incredible disbelief coupled with sorrow. Collin tossed, groaned, and moaned through the night, unable to break the cycle. She drifted from dream state to dream state, always on the edge of consciousness but never allowed to cross the line. By five in the morning. she was never more grateful to hear an alarm clock. She sat up, feeling battered and beaten, more exhausted than when she had gone to bed. The initial spasms of a monster headache reared its ugly face and Collin groaned. Not now. Not today. Please. A little help and a lot of relief, please. Collin prayed softly, *"I'm doing this for you, you know. Please, help me. And be with me."*

"I am with you always. And I am doing this for you, you know. Because I love you."

The answer was some comfort; enough to get her out of bed, anyhow. She dressed slowly, wishing to forgo the breakfast ordeal all together. She couldn't eat had she wanted to. Suck it up, woman. Quit being a cry baby, quit feeling sorry for yourself and do the deed. You'd think you were the only one out there who had problems! Straighten up, get your game face on, and go. You are Collin, the giant killer. Kill him and get it over with. Now move!!

Collin accepted her marching orders, straightened her shirt and strode purposefully out the door. Right. Time to finish this thing. Time to slay the beast, vanquish the dragon, and reclaim her sanity . . . Well, maybe the last was a bit much to strive for, but she could at least defeat one enemy. Right? Right? Was anyone in there listening? I said . . .

Collin shook off the mental musings and entered the cafeteria. She was about fifteen minutes early, but knew that the coffee was always ready half an hour before breakfast for those who like to slide into the day rather than greet it full force. They thought of everything here. She really did need to find the owner and thank him/her/them/it. Collin poured out a cup of coffee then looked, in what she hoped was a non-obvious way, around for Jeff. Alas, nowhere to be seen. Deep sigh. She grinned at herself then shook her head. He really was incredible. She hadn't felt this . . . what? What was she feeling? Infatuated? Thrilled? Moved? Who knew? Who cared? She was having fun and it felt good. Not since before . . .

The mental protective walls crashed down hard. "*Don't. Don't even go there. Not today, not ever. Over. Done. Leave it.*"

The grin left her face and Collin went to a table and sat down. She faced the door so she could see when her crew came in and sipped at the warm black brew in front of her. It was going to be a long day.

"I think I know what your problem is. You have too much time alone. You spend all your time thinking and it leaves you miserable."

Collin turned to face Jeff and asked, "First off, how did you get in here, and second, what are you talking about?"

Jeff sat down, toolbox in one hand, coffee in the other. "I saw you come in. I was in the kitchen fixing one of the microwaves. You were smiling for a while but then you stopped. Now you look sad. You think too much."

Collin eyed him. "Right. And you don't think?"

"That's what people tell me. 'Jeff, boy, you just don't think.' Usually they're right."

Collin laughed then said, "I doubt that very much." She stretched a little then asked, "You have a full day ahead?"

He shrugged. "Not too bad. Why?"

"Just wondered." Collin hesitated then said, "Thought maybe if you weren't too busy you could come . . . with . . . our class." Some of the steam went out of what was meant to be a jest as she realized how true it was. But she finished lamely, "I don't think as much when you're around."

Jeff's eyes told her he knew exactly what she meant but he said lightly, "So I make you brainless? Is that it? I'm not sure how to take that." Jeff reached across and touched her hand. "You'll be fine. I talked it over with the Lord and he assured me that he's doing all of this for your good and that I could tell you that. And I could tell you that he's got it all in control and everything will be fine. Okay?"

Collin nodded sadly. "I know. He told me the same thing." She took a long swig of coffee then said, "Thanks, Jeff."

He smiled. "Just relaying a message."

Collin cocked her head. "God's messengers were always angels. Does that mean you're an angel?"

Jeff laughed, "No one has ever called me one of those, before!"

Collin shrugged. "Just a thought."

The door banged open and a crowd of campers came pouring into the cafeteria, Rob among them. He yelled and waved, "Hey, case worker lady! You did get out of bed!"

Jeff finished his coffee in a gulp and said, "That's my cue to leave. See you after class? Unless Mitch makes you brainless, too, I guess." He appeared slightly unsure.

Collin shook her head. "What are you babbling about?"

Jeff shrugged. "You'll see. I'll talk to you later. I'll be praying for you, Collin." In a rush, he was gone

Collin stared after his fleeing form and wondered what in the world all that had meant. He'd said something about Mitch the night before, too. It made no sense. But then, there was a lot about Jeff that could be called senseless. And all of it was good. Very good. She was really going to miss him.

Within five minutes Collin was inundated with crew members with voracious appetites. Pancakes, sausage, French toast, donuts, cereal, eggs, toast, bagels . . . and that was just on Ta'waan's plate. The others were all overloaded as well. The exception was Pardner, who was eating light. She limited herself to only one of everything. Collin looked around and asked, "You guys eat like this before going to the Point?" The Point was an amusement park infamous for its killer coasters.

Rob said quickly, "Don't get this kind of stuff at home, case worker lady. Gotta eat it while we can." Nods and muffled, "Mmphs" voiced agreement.

Collin said, "I understand and I agree. But you don't have to try to eat it all in one morning. There's going to be some sick puppies out there if we hit the water."

"Naw!" "No way!" "Never happen" cries of protest met her statement. Collin shook her head and said warningly, "I hope you're right. I have a feeling barf bags are not standard equipment. Just think about it."

Nyla sneered, "That why you ain't eating? Too scared?"

Collin looked the girl dead in the eyes and said, "Too smart. I know my limitations. Can you say the same?"

Nyla laughed harshly. "I ain't got none. Isn't that what they teaching us? I can do anything I set my mind to."

"Set your mind and train your body, Nyla. Don't forget that last part. It takes time to train a body to obey your will." She should know. It had taken her years to learn how to ignore pain. How to restrain emotion. How not to cry.

Rob said, "Case worker lady be cool. She be knowing what it be like. She say chill out on the feast, we maybe should chill out."

Collin smiled slightly. "You're probably safe today. I don't think we'll be hitting the river first thing. But keep it in mind." From the gestures that followed Collin gathered that Niles, Nyla and Ta'waan disagreed with her most vehemently. Pardner and Chonnell were less sure, torn between the image of the three and the sense of the one. So they did what most girls their age would do: they compromised. They only ate about half of what was on their plates. Which was probably a good deal more than they should have even then, but was less than they could have. So call it a half a victory. Collin would take it.

The crowd finished up, bussed up, and headed for the docks to meet the mysterious Mitch. They found him sitting on a stump seat lazily kicking his heels in the sunshine. He smiled pleasantly as the six campers and Collin gathered in. His eyes seemed to linger slightly longer on Collin but she brushed it off. He was maybe thirty, maybe younger, tan, well-muscled, and yes, what you would call drop dead gorgeous. Collin smiled back just to let him know she was alive. He motioned towards the ground and said, "Sit. You will come to appreciate the feel of solid ground under you before this week is over." He waited until the group was seated then said, "My name is Mitch and I will be your teacher." He stopped then said, "Actually that is a misnomer. I will be your guide. It is the river that will do the teaching. I'm just here to show you how to get started."

He looked slowly over the class, measuring the faces. He said, "Three girls, three boys . . ." he looked at Collin and said, ". . . and you. This will work out fine. Most of our water craft were designed for eight so we won't have to modify anything." He had the class stand up then said with concern, "This could be a problem." The height variance again. As always Robbie was the shortest of the bunch. Collin could see the pain in the boy's face as he prepared to be singled out once again.

But Mitch was better than that. He continued, "No problem with who has the helm: that has to be you, my man." He slapped a hand on Robbie's shoulder. The boy looked at him in surprise. Mitch nodded. "Yeah, you. You look strong enough. What's your name? Do you know what the helm does?"

"Rob. And he steers the boat."

"I'll buy that. You will stand in the back and take instructions from the lookout up front. Are you good at taking and following instructions?"

Robbie looked quickly at Collin then said, "Yeah, I am."

Mitch saw Robbie's glance at Collin and asked quickly, "What is she to you, helmsman?"

"She's my case worker. She's the one what brought me up here."

Mitch stared at Collin a moment then asked, still addressing Robbie, "Do you really want her here with you? You don't have to, you know. That's the rules of the game up here."

Collin began begging silently but fervently, *"Say no. Please, please, please say no. Please."*

Robbie hesitated then said, "Naw, she can stay. She's pretty cool for an old white lady." He grinned at her. Collin formed her hands into a circle a little smaller than the size of a fourteen year-old's neck. Robbie got the picture in record time and added, "But she's cool, you know? Crazy, vicious, but cool."

Collin relaxed her fingers and smiled. She just wished she could relax the knot in her gut as easily. She said to Mitch, "I didn't take class just because Rob was taking it. He's a free agent, answerable for himself. We made a deal that for this trip we're independent individuals. And I will say he's living up to the independent part quite nicely."

Mitch nodded. "Okay by me. Just wanted to make sure we all know what's coming down." He turned his attention to the remainder of the crew issuing them their assignments. As he did, Collin breathed in slowly. She had a feeling there would be lots of slow breathing going on for the next week. Suck it up, woman. Robbie came back to where she was standing, eyeing her for approval. Collin said quietly, "Thanks for letting me stay, Rob. I appreciate it."

Robbie shrugged. "I figured that way down you really wanted to do this. I didn't want to get in your way."

Collin promised, "Believe me, I won't get in yours. I'm nothing more to you than Chonnell up there is. Crew mates and that's all. Mitch is the boss."

Mitch evidently overheard the comment and said quickly, "The river is the boss. Always remember that. The river is the one entity you must never, ever overlook. She'll talk to you, sing to you, show you beauty you can't even dream of. She'll forgive you all your little mistakes but the one thing she won't forgive is being ignored. Never, never, never take her for granted."

Collin paled noticeably as Mitch talked. She could see in his eyes that he noticed though he said nothing. Ta'waan took up the challenge and said with disdain, "Man, you talk like it's alive or something. It's just a river."

Mitch studied Ta'waan a moment. "What's your name?"

"Ta'waan."

"How old are you?"

"Thirteen."

Mitch asked, "You want to live to see fourteen?"

Ta'waan stared back defiantly. "Yeah."

"Then trust me. The river is alive. She moves, she breathes, she changes constantly. You have to know that to be able to ride her. Otherwise she'll pitch you out and swallow you up in a heartbeat."

Collin paled even further and started the slow breathing she'd taught herself years ago. In, out, in, out . . . As long as you're breathing you're living. Mitch looked around and again Collin caught his eye lingering slightly on her face. She forced a smile but probably should have refrained.

Mitch finished his survey of the class and asked, "How many of you are scared?" Collin's hand was first in the air. Chonnell looked at Pardner; the two girls giggled then raised their hands. Rob looked at Niles and Nyla, then at Ta'waan, then at Collin. Finally he must have looked inside, for at last he raised his hand slowly as well. Mitch said, "Good. Good. That means I have something to work with, with you four." He turned to the remaining three and said, "You, though, have a long way to go to be river men. The first thing you learn in any venture is to respect the power and the will of your opponent. Perhaps if we take a walk down to the water you'll begin to understand."

As Mitch directed the class down a foot path towards the roaring rapids Collin gave up slow breathing for controlled panting. Not on the first day. Not all at once. Please, please, not all at once. They rounded the final curve and the river lay open before them. Surging rapids threw foam balls to the trees and rocks below. Waves mounted three, four, five feet high, and raced by with tremendous speed and power, twisting into convoluted shapes and dimensions. Collin closed her eyes and backed up against the small fence, curling into as small a ball as she could manage. Life drained from her as the shadows and specters danced between her and reality. She could hear Mitch yelling over the thunder of the rapids explaining what this series of turns was called; how you navigated that turn, how many boats had lost their crews at each point. She didn't try to follow the lecture but let it wash over her, becoming part of the flood that threatened to drown her.

Collin had no idea how long she sat there, her fingernails digging trenches in the fence rail. But at length someone broke the spell by taking her arm, lifting her up and leading her away from the sight of the river. She was finally able to open her eyes and acknowledge that Mitch was directing her steps. A deep scowl was on his face as he looked at her. As they arrived back at their initial meeting spot Mitch hissed, "What was that all about?"

Collin drew a shaky breath and said, "It's from Macbeth. Act seven scene four. I like to practice it now and then just to stay on top of it."

Mitch lost his scowl to be replaced by a look of confusion and uncertainty. He drawled slowly, "Okay." The remainder of the class filed past, with looks of curiosity, disdain, and outright disgust at Collin. Mitch directed them, "In the shed there is all the equipment we'll be using. Find a helmet, a life vest and a paddle that fits you. I need a word with our counselor, here, then I'll be right with you." As the crew began digging out the equipment, Mitch pulled Collin to the side and demanded, "Explain."

Collin said simply, "I have a problem with rivers."

Mitch said snidely, "Psycho therapy sessions are next month. This isn't some carnival ride, counselor. I need people out here I can count on, who won't wig out on me at the first sign of a bubble. I can't have you endangering the lives of these kids because you're trying to exorcise some personal demons. I'll throw you out of the boat before I let that happen."

Collin said evenly, "I came to learn to raft. That's why I'm here, and the only reason I'm here." Somehow she instinctively knew telling Mitch that God wanted her to be here would not get the same response as it did from Jeff. Best to leave that part out. She continued, "You don't have to worry about me putting anyone's life at risk, including your own. You won't have to throw me out. I'll jump overboard long before that could happen."

Mitch relaxed slightly and asked, "What was it, some sort of boating accident?"

Collin kept the shudder out of her voice and said evenly, "Not exactly. Let's just leave it there, please?"

Mitch's voice softened even more. He rubbed her arms gently and said, "No problem. If I can help let me know. You're too fine a woman to be troubled like this."

Collin hesitated then said, "There is one thing."

Mitch smiled, his eyes dancing. "Name it."

Collin resisted the growing urge to push Mitch across the clearing and said, "Rob doesn't know about this. He knows I'm scared but that's about all. I'd like to keep it that way."

Mitch began massaging her shoulders. "You are really hung up on this, aren't you? It really terrifies you. You need to relax."

Collin finally could handle it no longer, but carefully took Mitch's hands off her shoulders. She smiled at him and said, "I'm fine. I think some of the class needs a little help with sizing." She motioned to where Pardner stood in a life vest that reached below her knees.

Mitch laughed and said, "You're right. But one last thing. Macbeth doesn't have seven acts."

"My school version did. But when I saw the play at the downtown theatre three years ago all the cheer leaders and belly dancers were missing. Go figure."

Mitch stared at her, unsure. Finally he asked, "Is that what Rob means by crazy?"

Collin shrugged. "You'll have to ask him. I'm sure he'd love to tell you some stories."

Mitch nodded. "I'll do that. I will indeed." They walked over to join the crew.

The remainder of the day was an emotional blur for Collin. They marched as a group to lunch and at Mitch's insistence sat together. It was his way of "reinforcing teamwork." Collin wasn't sure so much togetherness wouldn't reinforce disharmony. But Mitch was confident he knew how to build a crew so Collin acquiesced. This time. She saw Jeff sitting by himself studying intently at a table piled with books. She wished she could catch his eye but he didn't look up from his research. She sighed slightly and turned, only to realize Mitch was staring at her. She arched a brow and asked, "Is there a problem?"

Mitch shook his head. "Have you met our janitor?"

"Jeff? Yes. Do you know him?"

"Not really. We don't share much in the way of interests. I'm more of a people person. I like to get out, have a good time. The town may not have any real night life but there are a few places worth going. Maybe I could show them to you if you're interested."

Collin smiled politely and said, "I appreciate the offer but I think I'll pass. This is more of a working vacation for me."

"Well, don't say no yet. Think about it. Maybe by the end of the week you'll feel different. It'll give you time to get to know me." He smiled a winning smile and touched her hand lightly.

Collin smiled back. "We'll see." She noticed Jeff getting up and leaving suddenly. Probably being paged. Poor man. She caught Mitch's face out of the corner of her eye and a look of deep disapproval had come over it. Collin shook her head internally. Live with it, mister.

After lunch there were drills in proper boarding and disembarking procedures, practice throwing life ropes, instruction on the correct way to grab a drowning victim, how and how not to tow an unconscious person, and the required CPR. All of it was fast moving and intense. Collin had to admit Mitch did know how to relate to the kids. He even shook the dynamics of the group by pairing Collin with Nyla as rowing partners. Which prompted the first revolt of the day as Nyla snarled, "I ain't being partners with no white lady." If she had spit in Collin's face, she couldn't have made the phrase more insulting.

Rob jumped in immediately. "She ain't no white lady. She cool. She be one of the brothers."

Niles hooted, "Eastside brothers! All they got is ladies. Ain't a real man . . ."

Mitch thundered, "Enough! There will be no dissension on this crew!! I said you row together and you will row together."

Nyla continued to protest, "She ain't near strong enough to pull with me! We be rowing in circles and I be carrying all her load."

Collin offered evenly, "Nyla, I think we can settle this."

She sneeered, "Yeah, you row with Ta'waan. He more your speed."

Before Ta'waan could join the fray Collin repeated, "We can settle this, no problem." She looked at Mitch and asked, "Can I propose a challenge?"

Mitch looked both annoyed and intrigued but said only, "What?"

"Paddles at arms length. We can judge our pairings from that."

Now the look was one of respect, understanding, and a glint of irony. Mitch nodded in approval and said, "That should do it very nicely."

Nyla's voice carried an edge of uncertainty. "What you talking about?"

Mitch took back control of the class and said evenly, "A simple test of strength, endurance, and focus. Each of you will take your assigned paddle; hold it out in front of you vertical to the ground above the surface. If you are right handed use your left hand. Left handed do the opposite. That way we can see who has the kind of strength we need." There was a twinkle in the man's eye and he fairly winked at Collin.

The group spread out in a semi-circle. Mitch ordered, "Chonnell, Pardner, you two need to stand on the bench. Otherwise your paddles are going to touch the ground to start with."

Robbie didn't wait to be told but jumped up on the bench between them. He quipped, "I'll stay up here and keep an eye on them." He glared fiercely at the two girls who both went into fits of giggles.

Mitch instructed, "We'll stay 'til the last man—or woman—falls. Once your paddle touches the ground lay it down and have a seat."

Nyla laughed harshly. "We be here all day. Me an' Niles, we be the last two here."

Ta'waan asked heatedly, "You want to place a bet on that?"

Mitch interrupted strongly. "No betting. No mouth. Now's the time to prove yourselves." He looked at his watch and said, "Ready . . . now. Paddles up."

Obediently, eagerly, and yes, defiantly seven paddles rose into the air. Collin expended a small amount of energy in watching the way the others gripped their paddles. Niles, Nyla and Ta'waan all throttled theirs tightly, a sure sign of an early exit. Robbie held his with a more tender grip, reflecting at least a part of her teachings. He was learning. There was hope.

The two girls were hard to see but from the rock steady manner in which Pardner's paddle hung, Collin guessed she, too, had some training in stamina. Must be more to the child than Collin initially thought. Good thing.

Having scouted the competition and finding it as she expected Collin closed her eyes and retreated to her inner circle, to the island kingdom she and Erin had created years ago for this very purpose. It was their hideaway, their mental refuge from present trials. Collin had added a few features since Erin . . . since Erin. She'd begun building another wing on the castle, mostly to house all the books she'd been reading. The lower third of the foundation was to be of cashews each individually placed and cemented with fudge . . .

Mitch's voice called, "One minute."

Collin registered it as a fact and let it go. She had an uncooperative nut to deal with, one that preferred the white chocolate to the dark. Collin fought with it for several moments then simply chose to eat it rather than continue the disagreement. Amazingly there were no more protests over which fudge was used.

"Three minutes."

Collin finished the cashew foundation then poured the marshmallow layer. It might have been easier to form if the confections hadn't melted in the sunshine. But you do what you can with what you've got.

"Five minutes."

Collin wondered if she should check in and see who was still up. A quick peek wouldn't hurt. The woman opened her eyes and looked around. Yep, Niles and Ta'waan were down. Nyla looked to be going soon. The fierce grimace on her face, the sweat dripping down her cheeks, the rather violent shaking of the paddle . . . Stick a fork in her, she's done.

As if in reaction to Collin's thought, Nyla slammed the paddle into the ground and let out a grunt of pure frustration and disgust. She stomped over to where her brother was parked, flopped down beside him and sat steaming.

Another paddle dropped, followed almost immediately by a second. Chonnell and Robbie were out, too, though with less fanfare and far less grief. That left only Collin and Pardner. The youngster looked at Collin and called, "No gimmies 'cuz I'm youngest."

Collin nodded but grinned. The child certainly did have more than Collin expected. Maybe her crew mates would take another look, too. Collin called, "No gimmies. You got it." Without looking at Mitch she retreated again to her kingdom and her marshmallow shaping.

"Ten minutes."

Caramel followed the marshmallows.

"Twelve minutes."

Another layer of fudge, the white this time. She wasn't particularly fond of white but hey, it was chocolate.

"Fifteen minutes."

Hmmm . . . what goes good with white chocolate? Almonds to be sure. What else? Candy cherries? Naw, too slippery.

"Seventeen minutes."

Collin reached to open the cabinet and see what was left inside but became aware of a slight catch in her left shoulder. Interesting. Wonder what that was from? Oh, well, it didn't matter. She'd stretch it out later. For now . . .

"Walker, snap out of it, woman. Game's over. Wake up!"

Collin regretfully bid the island goodbye then opened her eyes to see Mitch standing in front of her, a strange look on his face. Collin read too many emotions in his eyes to even try to decipher whether they were positive or negative. She bypassed the riverboat captain and looked over to Pardner. The girl was beaming and crowed, "Eighteen minutes! Longest I ever held out like that. You good, lady. You real good."

Collin grinned, stepped around Mitch and crossed over to where Pardner was still standing on her bench, minus her paddle. Collin slapped hands with the girl then risked a hug. Pardner returned it happily. Collin pointed to the child and said, "You are good. Get a little older, get a little muscle on you and there's no one gonna beat you, you know that? But you know what? You put that mind of yours to use on something real, something that matters, girlfriend, and there's nothing you won't be able to accomplish."

Pardner ducked her head slightly, probably having heard the same speech before. But this time it was coming from an equal, from one who understood. And that could make all the difference. Maybe.

Again Mitch resumed his authority. He drawled, "If there are no further objections I'm going to assign rowing partners. Strength is not the only criteria, you obviously don't know." He smiled sweetly at Nyla who merely gave him an icy stare in return. Mitch ignored it, at least on the surface. Collin hoped it was only on the surface. She'd hate to think he was that much of a fool.

Mitch continued, "The length of the stroke of each partner is equally important to the balance of the pull. That's why Nyla, you and Walker will be pulling together, as will Pardner and Chonnell. Niles and Ta'waan are closer to being the same size than Ta'waan and Walker. And why Rob, here, is on helm. He's his own man, without equal." He slapped hands enthusiastically with Robbie but there seemed to be less excitement on Rob's part. Again, if Mitch noticed it, it didn't show. He smiled annoyingly at the group and rubbed his hands. "And now that I've settled that rather minor disagreement we can get on with the important business at hand."

As Mitch turned to continue his instructions Collin shook her head in disgust. She looked over to see how Nyla was reacting and found a look of equal distaste on the young woman's face. Nyla turned from glaring at Mitch to glare at Collin. But Collin held her eyes in a long, steady gaze, neither mocking nor condescending. After several moments Nyla's gaze lost its fierceness and took on a measure of, if not respect, at least mutual understanding. It might not be peace but it was a truce. And that was always preferable to war, cold or otherwise.

Eventually five pm came and the class was dismissed for the day. Mitch encouraged everyone to sit together at dinner and to spend as much time with one another as possible. But the crew scattered upon arrival at the lodge. Before everyone got away Collin grabbed Robbie and reminded him, "Nine o'clock, my man. Court two. Come with your crying towel, 'cause you're gonna need it, mister."

"Yeah, yeah. I hear the wind blowing. I be there and have you whipped by nine thirty."

Collin grinned. "Talk is cheap, my man. You just be there."

Robbie waved her off as he headed for his room, laughing. Collin chuckled then headed for her own sanctuary. She sighed deeply as she collapsed on the bed, too tired to move further. She could stay here all night . . . if she wasn't so stupid as to challenge someone half her age to a young person's game. She could tell people she did it for Robbie, but the truth was otherwise if she'd admit it. Which she wouldn't. Robbie learned from competing. And he loved the game. So did Collin. What more could you ask? Collin decided she should be on the court at eight thirty just to warm up, get the feel of the asphalt, check the resilience of the back boards . . . any edge she could come up with. Preparation was critical.

So was renewing her energy levels. Food would be a good idea. Food would be a great idea. She should eat. She should. Eating might take her mind off the throbbing in her hand.

Her hand. The doctor. Collin slapped herself mentally. She'd promised Jeff she'd have the doctor look at it. But the infirmary was closed by now. Drat. Drat, drat, and double drat. Would he believe her that she had forgotten, or would he think she was just being hardheaded and defiant? Granted, she was hardheaded but she wasn't trying to be defiant. This time. Well, there wasn't much to be done about it now except face him and suffer the consequences. Whatever they might be. Collin muttered, "I would have gone. Really I would have, if I'd remembered sooner." Or had a brain to remember with.

Stupid woman. Collin shook her head, pulled out her Bible and opened it to Psalms. She needed to refresh her spirit more than her body. Reading would help. Reading always helped. She would feed on God's word and that would be enough. Collin shut down the voice inside that intimated this was *not* what the Lord meant when He said, "Man shall not live by bread alone, but by every word of God . . ." She would eat. Later. Now shut up.

At eight-thirty she rose, dressed for the game, slipped a sweat shirt and jogging pants on over her outfit, took her basketball and headed for the health bar. She debated whether to go for endurance or the sugar high; settled for two bananas, a granola bar and a can of juice. As she walked out the door that magical voice said, "Now why did I know you'd miss . . . excuse me, skip dinner and come here instead?"

Collin leveled the bananas at him and said, "Don't move, mister, I've got you covered."

Jeff shook his head and grinned. "You're in a good mood. What's the secret?"

They walked over to one of the picnic tables so Collin could eat. Collin noted that Jeff was wearing a Carolina-blue warm-up suit with the number thirty seven on it. Interesting. She sat down, and said. "I survived my first day."

"Congratulations."

Collin looked at him and repeated, "I survived, Jeff. We went down to the water and I survived. I never thought that could happen." She turned her vision inwards, considering the monumental impact of the occasion.

Jeff smiled and said gently, "That's great, Collin. Does that . . ."

She looked up at him and said quickly, "No, it doesn't take care of the problem. It just means I survived being near it. Sort of."

"Sort of near or sort of survived?"

"Both. I'd probably still be standing there if Mitch hadn't pulled me away. But I was still breathing and that's all that matters."

Jeff asked slowly, "How did Mitch get on with the kids?"

Collin shrugged. "No serious problems. He seems to relate well with them. A bit antagonistic, maybe a bit too much know-it-all, but they know how to handle that. I think the class will do fine." She eyed him then asked, "Why?"

"Just curious that's all. People react to Mitch in different ways."

Collin studied Jeff and thought about pursuing this vein, but decided against it. Let Jeff have his foibles, too. She cleared her throat then said, "Jeff, I have a confession to make. I didn't make it over to see the doctor today about my hand." He looked up at her; she rushed ahead, "It wasn't that I wasn't going to go. I just forgot. It didn't bother me at all and it never crossed my mind that I needed to have it looked at. I wasn't trying to be rebellious or hardheaded, I just forgot. Class started and then there wasn't time for anything else and we didn't finish up until five and by then the infirmary is closed, and the doctor's gone, and it was too late. I'll go tomorrow I swear. No, I won't swear. I promise I'll try, okay? Okay?" She put on her best little girl face and said, "Please?"

Jeff shook his head at her, laughing. "Okay, okay. I'll forgive you. I'm not sure you should be playing ball tonight, though."

Collin said quickly, "It will be fine, Jeff. You really do great work. Trust me, I've had stitches in about every place you can have stitches so I know craftsmanship when I see it. And your technique is good." She placed special emphasis on the word *good* to make her point. "And I'm not trying to influence your decision, either. If you say I can't play, I won't play. But I don't think it's a problem."

Jeff looked at her a little confused. "Are you saying that if I told you that you couldn't play you'd actually listen to me? And do what I said?"

Collin hesitated then nodded. "We're told to obey the authorities over us. On this trip, that means you as far as the hand is concerned. I'm not told I have to like what you say and I can't find anywhere where it says I can't rant and rave and cry in protest. But I would have to obey you."

Jeff thought a moment, then said, "'Do everything without murmuring or complaining.' How about that one?"

"Cute, cute. You want a sword drill?"

Jeff laughed. "Who can quote Scripture better? I don't think so. I know too many verses in the Revised Farrell Version."

Collin nodded, "Companion to the Walker Version I believe. It's the thought translation."

"Right." Jeff nodded as well then smiled and said, "Let me see the hand."

Collin stripped the bandage off of it and said, "It's already starting to heal down at the bottom. That's where the ball slaps my hand the most."

As Jeff examined her hand he said, "I'm familiar with the dynamics of the game. You're still going to take a beating on that palm."

Collin suggested, "Compromise. We'll take a half time break and you can look at it again. If it's broken open or looks like it's going to, you can call the game and I'll quit, I promise. I may not speak to you again if I happen to be winning but I will quit. Deal?"

Jeff studied her a moment then shook his head in defeat. "All right. You got one half."

Collin grinned widely, threw her arms around him on impulse and hugged him repeating, "Thank you, thank you, thank you!" She as quickly dropped her arms, aware that she was being excessive in her exuberance.

Jeff looked at her with a strange half smile and asked, "You always get like this before a competition?"

Collin tried to appear prim and proper as she peeled her banana. "Like what?"

"Goofy. You're goofy."

Collin shrugged. "It's part of the package. You got one part of me you get the whole shooting match, lock, stock and rusty barrel."

Jeff said quietly, "I see." He did not expound on what it was he saw, however.

Collin finished her bananas and her juice, dumped her trash and said, "I'm going to the court, now, to warm up. Are you still working or are you free?"

Jeff bowed deeply and said, "Madam, I am yours to command." He waited for her to rise, then they headed to court number two.

Once there Collin stripped down to shorts and shirt and began to dribble slowly, sort of getting the feel of the ball on her hand. Not bad. A little twinge now and then but not bad. Jeff looked at her questioning. Collin shrugged. "It's fine. No problem." She looked at him and asked, "Warm up with me?"

Jeff shucked his sweat shirt revealing a Tarheels jersey underneath. Collin studied the name and number closely. Farrell. 37. What was it? She tried to make a connection that niggled at her mind but would not stand up and be counted. Jeff noticed her scrutiny and asked, "What?"

Collin shook her head dismissing for the moment the unformed thought. "Nothing. I was just trying to remember something." She grinned and said, "'Old data. Pay it no mind.'"

Jeff was not convinced. "Uh huh." He took the ball from Collin and began up the court at an easy jog. Collin followed him; he passed her the ball, she passed it back. He picked the pace up slightly; Collin matched him. He passed the ball back, again she returned it. At mid-court he fired the ball to her and broke for the basket. Collin hit him with a near-perfect strike. He caught it mid-stride, bounced it once, then executed one of the prettiest lay-ups Collin had seen in years. The ball made nary a sound as it slipped through the basket dropping home for the two. He caught it and waited for Collin to finish her jog down the court.

Collin reached him and with respect said, "Nice. Very nice. You've played more than a few hoops in your time, Mr. Maintenance Man."

Jeff did not comment but tossed her the ball. "Your turn. Let's see what you've got."

Collin shot up the court, taking him slightly by surprise. She crossed the court diagonally then threw the ball back across the court to Jeff. He caught it, pirouetted, threw it back. Collin did a touch pass back; Jeff lobbed it high above the rim. Collin leaped high, brought the ball down gently and swooshed it through the basket. It felt so good to be active again! To be moving and not thinking. She dribbled the ball slowly until Jeff arrived. He cruised up nodding, "Not bad for an office worker. You've worked the pine some yourself."

Collin shrugged. "Unrealized passion. I just can't let it go." She motioned to his jersey. "I used to follow the ACC, especially the Tarheels. Knew all the players, all the stats . . ." The bell went off in her brain again, the "I know that I know something but I don't know what it is" bell. She studied Jeff again trying to figure out what it was.

Jeff saw her scrutinizing look and asked, "What? Is my shirt on backwards? What is it?"

Collin shook her head as if to clear the cobwebs. "I'm sorry, Jeff. It's one of those fragments of memory that won't connect to anything else."

Jeff rubbed his chin, and his voice mimicked a German cartoon psychiatrist. "I see, I see. Fragmented memory connections. Very interesting. And how long have you had this problem, frauhlein?"

"Since before I was born I think. Is that significant?"

"It could be. It could be."

Collin jumped in the game. "Is there any hope, Doctor?"

Jeff shook his head solemnly. "I do not know for certain. We must dig deep for the answers. Tell me how do you feel about your father?"

It was an innocent question and quite in keeping with the spirit of their tomfoolery. But it hit Collin like a brick and she blanched. She looked away quickly, shielding her glance from those penetrating eyes and breathed out slowly. She was still trying to form a response when Jeff said gently, "That's a dumb game. And a stupid question. How about another lap around the court?"

Collin smiled weakly at him and said gratefully, "I think that is a great idea."

Before they could complete it, however, Robbie came running on the court. Collin looked at him sternly and stated the obvious. "You're late. I could have scored ten points by now."

Robbie pulled off his sweatshirt and retorted, "Yeah, and I'd still beat you."

Collin warned him off. "Don't get cocky, dude. Just because you ain't been beat yet don't mean it won't happen." She began dribbling slowly trying to plan her attack. She had been studying Robbie as he played on the courts behind where she lived and she was getting a feel for the young man's rhythm and style. But could she put it into use? Information without application was dead, so she'd been told. Well, time for some real world application. Collin feinted to her right then quickly reversed field, spun once and broke towards the basket.

Rob was a shadow with her, not caught at all by her juking. Which was typical; it was Collin's opening move in every game they played. Robbie could follow her in his sleep. Which was what Collin was counting on. She took the usual two steps toward the basket as if to hit the lay-up. Robbie was waiting for her, timing his leap to her motion. But at the last possible second Collin pulled the ball back in, whirled, reversed direction and came up behind Rob, lightly kissing the ball off the backboard and into the cylinder. She dropped down, drew her elbow back sharply in exultation and hissed, "Yes!!"

Robbie stared at her dumbfounded. "What was that? You ain't never made a move like that before."

Collin grinned evilly. "Yeah, and I never drew first blood before, either. Live with it." She looked over at Jeff standing on the sidelines. He merely shook his head. Collin looked back at Robbie and said, "I warned you I've been practicing. Never take an opponent lightly, my man. He just might jump up and bite you."

Robbie was neither intimidated nor impressed. He dribbled the ball to half-court saying, "Yeah, yeah, yeah. I hear the wind blowing. You talk good. But one shot don't make no game. Just get ready, case worker lady."

Robbie turned at the midline and blasted back towards the basket. Collin waited, bouncing on the balls of her feet. Rob's typical move would be to spin at the top of the key if his opponent came out to meet him. But if the man—or woman—held back, he would just shoot it from there. If she came out half way, however, maybe she could alter the trajectory of his shot causing a misfire. Better still, fake . . . Collin shook her head sharply. Too much thinking, not enough acting. She stepped forward to intercept. Robbie dribbled twice then started to slide around her to the right. Collin refused to take the bait, instead standing her ground as he rotated back to his left. Robbie hadn't anticipated her countermove and left the ball dangerously exposed. Collin slapped the ball away; they both raced after it. Robbie got there first but was unable to press the advantage as Collin was all over him, refusing to let him advance. He realized he was close to stepping on the out-of-bounds line and that Jeff was silently waiting to make any call necessary. In near desperation Robbie slammed the ball at Collin's foot hoping for a rebound.

The ploy worked and the ball careened off her shoe out-of-bounds. Jeff blew the whistle. Collin glared at him. "It never touched me!"

Robbie ran after the ball. Jeff warned, "Arguing with the ref will get you thrown out, you know." He looked down at the whistle and said, "I've always wanted one of these. I've had enough of them blown at me, that's for sure."

Collin continued to pout. "It never touched me. It didn't."

Jeff quipped, "Would you like a little cheese with that whine?"

She glared at him. "Cute. Real cute. Who invited you to this party?"

Jeff thought a moment then said, "I believe it was you. Something about fair play and learning where the lines are."

Collin grumbled, "Yeah, yeah, yeah. Just throw the ball in." She smiled at him and his eyes were shining.

Robbie returned with the ball. He accepted the throw-in from Jeff and brought the ball up the court with deliberate steps. Collin shut the brain down and began to let her training, instincts, and most recent practices control the motion of her body. For every action, an equal and opposite reaction. For every reaction properly executed: two points scored, or a defensive victory won. Spin, block, shoot, run . . . An hour flew by. The lights dimmed. Jeff blew his whistle and called, "Half-time; take a break. I've got to reset the timers."

As he jogged to the far end of the court, Collin and Robbie took the opportunity to double over and try to breathe. They were both puffing hard, harder than they should be. But between gasps for air Collin declared, "Tie score, my man. Mark it down in history."

Robbie waved her off. "I hear you. Ain't worried."

Jeff made his way back and asked, "Don't you two think you might want to call it a night?"

Collin was aghast. "Quit, now? When the score is tied? Are you crazy? I'm not about to let this man off the hook."

Robbie was equally defiant. "No way, man. Have her telling everybody how she tied me to end a game? Ain't happening, dude."

Jeff listened then said, "Let me see the hand."

Collin hesitated only a millisecond then extended the left hand. "It doesn't hurt at all, Doc. It really doesn't."

Jeff muttered, "You're so high you couldn't feel it if it did."

Collin said jokingly, "Come on, Jeff. We're having fun. We don't get to have fun all the time. Please? Just for a little while longer. Just until I beat him." Robbie snorted. Collin rephrased her supplication. "Until one of us wins or one more hour, I promise. Please? Please? No pain, no gain, you know."

Jeff re-bandaged the hand and said archly, "I believe the correct rendering of that is 'no pain, no brain.'"

Collin stuck her tongue out at him then instantly regretted it. Well, almost instantly. She was out of control and she knew it, but she was having fun. She did temper her enthusiasm long enough to take a long look at Robbie to see how he was doing. Ah, youth. He looked fine. Winded but fine. She asked him, "You good to go, my man? I mean that seriously. Just because I'm acting the fool doesn't mean you have to."

Jeff added, "Amen."

Collin glared at him but asked Robbie again, "You want to call it a night?"

Rob shook his head. "I ain't tired. And no old white lady gonna tie me in hoops."

Jeff cautioned, "One last warning. Do you know what altitude means?"

Collin laughed, "Yeah, it's how high above the rim my man Rob gets when he's trying to block one of my shots. Now give me the ball." She snatched it from Jeff, her eyes laughing and dancing as she stepped across the end line. The look in his eyes was unreadable: intense, but unreadable. Collin decided she would have to learn to decipher those eyes and soon. But not tonight. Tonight was for Robbie's education and enlightenment. Old case workers could still compete. Robbie headed in from the baseline and then they were back at it.

They played yet another hour with no clear winner. Spin, block, shoot, run . . . argue with the ref . . . run, run, run. Collin regretted the "no time out" rule more than she ever had before. Her lungs burned from lack of oxygen for reasons she couldn't fathom. Robbie, too, was having trouble. He was leaning over, clutching the bottom of his shorts, waiting for Collin to bring the ball in. Exhaustion was everywhere over him as Collin knew it was on herself as well. Only Jeff seemed untouched by all the exertion, though he had run up and down the court all night with them. Superman in the flesh, maybe? Collin stood on the sidelines dribbling the ball. Rob was standing halfway between the midcourt line and the top of the key panting. Collin stopped, picked up her dribble and said, "I can't breathe. Let's finish this tomorrow."

To Collin's everlasting relief Robbie gave no argument. "Right, lady. I'm there with you." He looked at Jeff and asked, "Okay, ref, what's the score?"

Jeff looked surprised. "You didn't tell me I was supposed to keep score. I thought you two were doing that yourselves."

Collin groaned loudly in dismay. "Don't tell me we've done all this for nothing!"

Rob joined the protest. "An' I was beating you good, lady."

Collin reacted with shock. "You were not! The score was at least tied if I wasn't ahead."

"You ahead? In your dreams, case worker!"

The three collected their belongings and walked back towards the lodge. Collin continued the debate. "Well I would have been if the ref had been doing his job instead of watching the cheerleaders."

Jeff said haughtily, "I call them like I see them."

Collin bumped him from the side and said, "You didn't tell me you couldn't see them worth a nickel."

"May I inform you, madam, that I am held in the greatest regard by many of my peers?"

"Oh, really?"

Jeff nodded. "That is quite correct. I've been told there is no other referee quite like me. In fact, I've been assured that after God made me he destroyed the mold."

Rob looked from Jeff to Collin then asked, "You two related? You both weird."

Collin grinned. "Aw, Rob, you know you love me."

Rob threw up both hands as if to ward off evil and ran off screaming. Collin looked at Jeff and asked innocently, "Was it something I said?"

Jeff shrugged. "Kids. Who knows these days?" His pace slowed considerably. Collin noticed, and found it nice to stroll along rather than driving with purpose. Jeff seemed hesitant, as if wanting to say something but not finding the right words. Collin waited patiently. At length Jeff said, "You're good, you know that? At hoops, I mean." He added the last almost as an afterthought.

Collin shrugged. "Thanks. I used to love the game. I wanted to go to Duke and play for Coach K. so bad I ached."

"Why didn't you?"

"I wasn't a guy. Technicality, maybe, but it was enough to keep me on the sidelines."

Jeff grinned. "I see. Why didn't you play women's ball?"

Collin looked shocked and offended. "Play hoops with a bunch of females? Are you out of your mind? Only guys play real hoops. Girls just pretend."

Jeff repeated, "I see. And where did this bit of intellectual garbage come from?"

Collin shrugged, dropping the subject. "Here and there. It doesn't matter. I missed the chance to do something I really enjoyed and . . ." She stopped, looked at him and asked, "Why am I boring you with all of this? Why are you so confounded easy to talk to anyhow?"

Jeff shrugged. "I don't know. I guess I'm non-threatening." He gave her a sad puppy dog look and said, "Would you ever feel threatened by this face?"

Collin shoved him laughing. "Yes! It's you innocent types that get me in trouble."

Jeff straightened up. "You mean you have others?"

"No I mean I've met others. And I refuse to say anything else." They reached the door of the lodge but neither made as if to go in. Collin leaned against the wall and took a deep breath. "That hurts."

"It's supposed to hurt to let you know when you've pushed too far."

Collin shook her head. "But I've played with Rob a dozen times for a lot longer than this."

Jeff looked at her and there was frustration in his voice. "Collin, look around you. Where are you?"

Collin did the perfunctory round-the-world glance then said, "At Camp Grace."

"Which is in the middle of the mountains, right?"

Unsure where he was going with this, Collin nodded. "Uh huh."

Jeff said slowly, "Try and stay with me here. You live in Oakton, elevation between minus ten and a hundred feet, depending on where you're standing. This is Camp Grace, elevation 4000 feet at the bottom of the canyon."

Collin began to see the light. "Ahhhh."

"Uh huh. Ahhh is right. Thin air, lack of oxygen, lungs burn . . ."

Collin finished the sentence for him, ". . . brain cells go dead if there were any to start with. I'm sorry, Jeff. You were trying to tell me that earlier and I ignored you. How could I be so stupid?"

Jeff grinned slightly. "Practice maybe?" Collin scowled at him but didn't say anything more. Jeff let her off the hook. "It's easy to get caught up with things here. And you looked like you were enjoying yourself."

Collin continued to frown but at herself. "Maybe too much. I forgot what I'm here for."

"A chance to unwind right? That's what this is all about for you. The camp will take care of Rob. That's what we're here for."

Collin looked at him. "How come you're so smart?"

"It's a mystery. A great mystery."

Collin shook her head. "The mystery will be if I can get out of bed in the morning. Getting up to face the river is not enough incentive, believe me."

Jeff hesitated then suggested, "How about breakfast with a friend?"

Collin studied him a moment then said softly, "I'd like that. I'd like that very much."

"So would I. Is six too early? I can get us a special dispensation to get in then. I have to be at work at seven."

Collin groaned. "You're not making this easy you know. But then," she hesitated, then continued, "nothing good comes easy, right?"

Jeff shrugged. "I don't know. Sleeping comes easy."

Collin wasn't sure if he was reversing his field and giving her an out or what. She said, "Six it is. I'll see you then." Jeff held the door for her; she smiled and said softly, "Good night, Jeff. Thanks for putting up with me tonight."

Jeff smiled sweetly. "Nite, Collin." The door closed and he was gone.

TUESDAY

When Collin's alarm went off at five she was actually asleep and enjoying it. It took her several moments to remember who she was, what she was, when she was, where she was, and why she was. She didn't bother with the how she was, that seemed immaterial. When all the pieces came back together she rose, showered, dressed and went to the chow hall. It was still early; probably ten minutes to six or so. She didn't care; she liked watching Jeff arrive, the way his face lit up when he saw her. As she was sure hers did when the vice was versa. Somehow she had never learned to control that bodily reaction when approached by someone she loved . . . or thought she loved . . . or wanted to love . . . or hoped loved her . . . or . . . Collin shook it off. Stop that! As she rounded the last corner she saw Jeff standing in the hallway leaning against the wall looking at his watch. He had that ornery, catbird grin on his face and he shook his head as she walked up. "Yep. Early."

She grimaced and asked, "Would you rather I was 'fashionably late' to everything? Though why being late is considered fashionable is beyond me."

Jeff shrugged. "No. I just find your enthusiasm for punishment delightful." He pushed off the wall and said, "The cook has consented to fixing short order breakfast for us. I'm the apple of her eye, and she has three daughters of marriageable age." He stage whispered, "None of whom

I'd consider if they were the last females on earth, but I haven't got the heart to tell her." Jeff led Collin down the corridor and into the dining hall. "Besides which, she knows I'm the only one that can keep her beloved coffee urn going. It's at least fifty years old and you can't find parts for it anymore, but she insists it's the only one that will make decent coffee."

"If you can't find parts how do you keep it going?"

"Charm and good looks." Collin scowled; Jeff grinned and added, "When that fails me, as it most often does, I resort to salvage, spit and glue, and magic. Since she still offers me breakfast it must still be working. How was the coffee yesterday? I assume you had some since I know you didn't have anything else other than that banana."

Collin picked up a tray and silverware from the line, slid it down the rails and asked, "How do you know that? And it was two bananas."

"Oh, excuse me, two bananas. And I have my sources."

Collin eyed him closely. "Are you spying on me, Mr. Farrell?"

"Nope. Just keeping an eye on a friend." He looked at her and asked softly, "I can say that can't I?"

Collin smiled, suddenly a little shy. "I thought that was why I was here: breakfast with a friend."

"I didn't want to be . . . presumptuous. Forward. Pushy. Overbearing." He looked at her and said, "Stop me anytime. I'm running out of synonyms and my thesaurus won't fit in my pocket."

Collin grinned, her eyes shining. "I like a man with an expanded vocabulary. It's a refreshing change from those whose entire linguistic repertoire is 'yo.'"

Cook was waiting on them, smiling at Jeff. "Jeffrey! You didn't tell me your friend was a girl friend. I'd have put out the good linen."

Collin blushed slightly. She noticed a little color in Jeff's cheeks as well. A good sign. It meant he didn't do this on a regular basis. Jeff said, "Mom O'Brien, this is Collin Walker, one of the counselors with this session. An exceedingly dedicated counselor. To a fault, even." Collin glared at him; Jeff ignored her. He continued, "She bleeds for these kids she's so . . ."

Collin dropped her tray on the rails for effect, extended her hand and said, "Hi. I'm Collin Walker. He's an idiot, if you hadn't already figured it out."

Mom O'Brien laughed. "Oh, I've known that for years. Our camp idiot. But we love our Jeffrey. Nice to meet you, Ms. Walker. I don't think I've seen you here before."

Jeff sniped, "Good eye, Mom."

Collin glared at Jeff but said, "I've been in the dining room several times. But with all the fresh air and the excitement and the change in altitude . . ." She scowled at Jeff who merely whistled softly and looked over and up and around the room. Collin looked back to the cook and continued, ". . . I haven't had much of an appetite. But everything always looks and smells delightful."

Ms. O'Brien said, "Well it's a team effort. Chef Michael plans the meals and I fix them. But this morning you get to choose your poison."

Collin hesitated then said, "I'll have whatever Jeff has but less of it. A lot less of it. A whole lot less of it."

Cook laughed. "She knows you, Jeffrey. She's seen you eat."

Jeff sniffed. "I'm a growing boy."

Cook snorted. "Growing fat on my good cooking."

Jeff smiled winningly, "And you know you do it so well, Mom."

"Enough with the charm. What do you want to eat?"

Surprisingly to Collin, Jeff ordered a fairly light and sensible breakfast: wheat toast and eggs, fruit, juice, and coffee. Collin added a glass of milk to her order. It took only a few minutes before they received their food then went and sat down. Collin noticed that two or three other camp workers were already in attendance. So the cafeteria must open early for the early shift. That was a nice touch. Depending on what it cost, of course. As they sat down Collin asked, "I know this can't be part of the regular camp service. It has to cost extra. Who do I pay for it?"

Jeff shook his head. "Don't worry about it. It's covered."

"No, Jeff. I want to pay for my own breakfast. You shouldn't . . ."

Jeff repeated evenly, "Collin, it's taken care of. We don't charge extra for early morning meals. No employee is charged for the meals they eat. They can eat anywhere they like, of course, but meals here are free. Even to the campers meals are free. I can't see the fairness in inviting someone to come visit, putting them off someplace without transportation, then charging them for food. You wouldn't do that to a guest at home; we won't do that to our guests here."

Collin smiled and said softly, "I love the way you say 'we' and 'our.' You really feel like you're part of this camp don't you?"

Jeff grinned and said, "I couldn't love it more if it were my own."

"It shows. It really does."

Collin bowed her head but Jeff said quickly, "Wait." Collin looked up, puzzled. Jeff seemed to be struggling with a thought then asked hesitantly, "Can I pray for us?"

Collin smiled. "I'd like that."

In a move so forward it surprised her, Collin reached out and took hold of his hand. Jeff smiled slightly then closed his eyes, as did Collin, and began to pray, "Father God, thank you so much for today, for this day you made. You've given me so much that is beautiful and wonderful, that gives me joy and makes me happy. Nothing gets by you, Lord. You love me and care for me and watch over me. Help me to walk like I'm supposed to today, to do what's right. And Father, if I can, help me to make it easier for someone to live. Put this good food to your use and put us to your work. In Jesus' holy name, amen."

Jeff squeezed Collin's hand lightly then let it go. She smiled at him and said, "Thank you, Jeff."

He shrugged. "I was reminding myself."

"Thank you anyhow." She looked down at the table and said very softly, "I know you've already made my day easier." Jeff was silent; Collin looked up and his eyes were on her, but gentle. He shrugged again but said nothing. After a moment he attacked his breakfast. Collin cleared her throat and asked, "How come you're eating so light this morning? And what is it you have to do that requires such an early start?"

Jeff said archly, "I don't always eat like a horse. I couldn't keep this slim, trim physique if I did."

Collin grinned but since it was still early and her rapier wit was still encased in foam rubber she returned instead to her question, "So what are you doing this morning?"

"Our dairyman's wife had emergency surgery yesterday so I'm filling in as the milk machine."

"Are you everyone's back up here?"

"Only in a pinch. There's a 'real' man starting this afternoon. I'm just covering the morning shift."

Collin shook her head slightly. "They expect too much out of you, I think."

Jeff said evenly, "No more than I'm willing to give. I could always say no."

"Have you?"

"On occasion. I do know my limits, Collin. And the Lord has creative ways of reminding me if I forget."

Collin said wryly, "So I've experienced." She hesitated then asked carefully, "How'd you come to know the Lord, if that's not too personal a question?"

Jeff said firmly, "That should never be too personal to ask. I was raised in the Lord. My folks are staunch believers so I was carried to church from the time I was a week old. All the nursery rhymes I remember were Bible verses. Mom didn't sing lullabies; she sang hymns and praise choruses. I accepted him as savior when I was about five. But then I did the customary rebellious thing for a couple of years in my teens. I got far enough away from God to know that wasn't where I wanted to be, and made him lord of my life at about sixteen. I've been walking with him—or as close to it as I can—ever since." Jeff shrugged slightly. "Not very dramatic I'm afraid. But it's a path I hope my own children take someday. With the exception of the rebellious part. I'd love to see my kids go straight from cradle to grave loving and serving Jesus. Am I selfish or what?" He grinned to show her he knew better.

Collin said quietly, "Why is that selfish? I think it would be great if that could happen to a child. Isn't that what the Lord desires anyhow?"

"Wants, yes. Gets, no. Or at least not that I've ever heard. Unless you're the exception?"

It was the perfect lead in for Collin to tell her story but she hesitated. How much could she tell without having to go into all the bloody details? Would Jeff follow up with questions she didn't want to answer yet? Questions she would one day answer—or tell, if he didn't ask—but not now? Collin realized Jeff was waiting and the silence was becoming an answer in itself, but the wrong answer. She said slowly, "No, I'm not any exception. My . . . parents didn't know the Lord. I think my mom was just starting to learn when her influence . . . um . . . stopped . . . when we were about five. I didn't really hear anything else about the Lord until I was . . . fifteen?" She thought a moment then nodded. "Yeah, just after my fifteenth birthday. I . . . got involved, I guess you'd say, with a street mission in Oakton. I heard the message that God loved me right where I was, had forgiven me everything and still loved me. I couldn't pass up that kind of love and still live, so I gave him my life. I asked him to use me wherever he could, and we've been together—mostly—since then." She smiled, relieved she'd gotten through it, and echoed his, "Also not very dramatic."

Jeff studied her a moment then said very softly, "Maybe not. Someday maybe you can fill in the details for me." He hesitated, looked down, then looked back and asked, "Can I ask just one question? You said 'when we were five.' Can you tell me who 'we' is?"

Collin said quietly, "My twin brother, Erin." And rather than have him agonize over whether to ask or not she said, "He died when we were fourteen." She paused then added, "He broke his neck." More than that she would not offer.

Jeff again studied her face, then said carefully, "I'm sorry." He finished eating, looked at the food still left on Collin's plate and said, "At least eat the eggs, so Mom O'Brien won't think it's her cooking you don't like. She's very sensitive about stuff like that."

Collin nodded obediently. "Yes, Mother." Later she would thank him for not digging deeper, though from the look in his eyes he wanted to. He at least had the sensitivity to know that the last fifteen minutes of breakfast was not time enough for a thorough examination of the subject. Especially with a horde full of campers ready to descend on the room. She smiled shyly and said in a small voice, "Thanks."

Jeff shrugged self-consciously and said, "No problem. One of these days, if you want, you can tell me. But only if you want."

Collin nodded but did not answer. She finished off her eggs; smiled at him, childlike, and said, "See? I finished them."

"You certainly did. Now finish the fruit and the toast and you'll have actually eaten something."

Collin stuck her tongue out at him then said, "You are pushy you know that?"

"What are friends for?"

Before she could answer two strong hands rested on her shoulders from behind and Mitch's voice said, "Well, surprise, surprise." His voice was smooth and friendly though Collin could sense something else in it. She couldn't interpret it, but there was something more in the tone than just friendliness. Mitch continued, "The counselor and the janitor. How democratic." He began massaging her shoulders lightly.

Collin said lightly, "Jeff and I are old friends. Ever since Friday night, right?"

Jeff nodded. "I believe you're right."

Mitch said archly, "So is that what you've been doing the last couple of days instead of working? Hitting on the clients?"

Jeff grinned, not intimidated in the least. "Something like that. What did you need?"

"The moorings on dock seven that you 'fixed' last week have come loose. Again." There was a tinge of sarcasm and ice in the boating instructor's voice.

Jeff seemed surprised. "Again? That's a problem. Are you using that dock this session?"

Mitch said angrily, "That's not the point. The point is you were supposed to fix it last week and you didn't. Whether I'm using it or not doesn't matter."

Jeff said patiently, "If you're using it I'll tighten the moorings down this morning and keep them tightened down through the week. If you're not using it I'll close it down, tear the moorings out and replace them. It'll take a couple of days to get the parts in but it would be ready for next session. It depends on what is most convenient for you."

Mitch seemed slightly mollified. "I see. I suppose I could use one of the other docks until you get it fixed right." He looked dead at Jeff and said, "Assuming you know what you're doing."

Collin bristled but the look in Jeff's eyes was enough to silence her protest. He said simply, "If you don't find it safe we'll bring in someone who does know." Jeff rose from the table and said, "I'll go check it right now." He smiled at Collin and said, "Thanks for breakfast, Collin. I'll see you later." He picked up both their trays and walked off humming quietly.

Mitch let go of Collin's shoulders and sat down quickly opposite her. He smiled his winning smile and said, "So, breakfast with the janitor. How noble of you to condescend to the little people."

Collin patterned her response after Jeff's and said simply, "He's good people. I like him. What can I do for you this morning?"

Mitch chuckled, "That could be a loaded question. I have so many needs."

Collin smiled and said, "Well, let's start with any that have to do with our classes."

Mitch laughed. "Okay." He became more serious. "I thought I encouraged you to eat as a crew. Why would you come down by yourself?"

Collin said evenly, "Jeff and I arranged to meet for breakfast. I'm here for the crew when they come in and I'll sit with them then."

"But you won't be eating."

Collin said, "They really don't care. The bonding idea is wonderful, Mitch, but as essential as you think it is, these are street kids. Independence is a very hallowed concept to them."

"But what about the gang idea? Gangs hang together."

"Gangs are built or grown by careful selection. You don't throw a bunch of strangers together and call it a gang and expect gang loyalty or interrelatedness to just appear overnight. It takes longer than a week to form a gang, Mitch."

Mitch said dryly, "And I suppose you would know all of this."

Collin kept her tone even. "It's my job, Mitch. It's what I do all day, every day. You've got at least three different gangs on your crew, maybe four. And then you and I are outsiders trying to fit in. When the kids come in see if you can pick them out."

Mitch snorted. "I know my crew, Collin. I know what they are. It's not the kids I worry about it's you. You're the one that's not fitting in yet." Mitch picked up her right hand and said earnestly, "Your fear can bring this whole crew down. You need to tell me what it's all about." He gave her a look of intense sympathy and empathy and said, "You can trust me, Collin. For the good of the crew, tell me."

Collin studied his face, bit her lip then said, "No, Mitch. Not here and not now. My fear will not impact the rest of the crew. No one knows about it but you, and unless it bothers you personally, it's not going to be a problem."

Mitch continued to hold her hand, twisting it this way and that, admiring it. He said softly, "You have beautiful hands, you know that?"

Collin pulled it away carefully and laughed lightly. "Thanks. It's a matched set. Had them all my life." To distract him she said, "Are we going on the water today?"

"Not out on the river, no. Not yet. Crew needs to learn to paddle together first. Why?"

"I'm going to prove to you that there will be no problem. I can do this, Mitch."

He looked at her curiously. "It means that much to you? You fear it that much that you'll put up with all this?"

Collin drew a deep breath, unsure how to answer. Finally she said, "I do and I don't. Let's just leave it there, okay? If there comes a time that I need to tell someone I'll consider your offer."

Mitch patted her hands in a tender manner and said, "I'll hold you to that, Collin."

To Collin's relief the doors opened and ravenous campers came pouring in, intent on the destruction of as much food as they could consume in one hour's time. Nyla, Niles and Ta'waan descended on Mitch and Collin hooting and laughing. Snide giggles of, "Oooo . . . teacher's pet" and, "Trying to score brownie points?" and a few other comments were offered. Collin watched Mitch's face closely and noted the satisfied look in his eyes. She debated whether to deflate his ego all at once, or let him continue in his delusion. They were kids, let it go. God would uphold her honor if ever it came to that. As for Mitch, well, as long as she gave him nothing to feed on she wouldn't worry. She wouldn't rub his nose in her relationship with Jeff, either, though the thought was sorely tempting. Tempting, yes, but wise, no. Collin rose and moved to a larger table so the campers could join them. She looked for Robbie and spotted him among those already in line, his tray filled even though he hadn't reached the "good stuff" yet. She smiled. This was fun, watching him get the "good goods" in life for a change. He was relaxing, unwinding and just having fun.

Mitch's voice buzzed in her ear. "What makes you smile so much?"

Collin moved away from him reflexively and said brightly, "Rob. He is really enjoying this camp." Mitch sat down close beside her; Collin slid her chair away a few inches to give him room. This was going to get real annoying. She'd have to come up with a plan and soon. Other than laying him out. Maybe she should report him. Maybe she could end up ruining the week for everyone, too. Maybe she should ask Jeff for help.

Yeah, right. As democratic as Camp Grace seemed to be, Jeff was still just maintenance and Mitch was a teacher. There had to be some insulation of layers there. No, she would handle it her way. For now. If he crossed the line she'd lay him out, and *then* tell someone.

Again the kids saved her from further advances as Chonnell and Pardner came to the table and sat down. Chonnell looked around to see if anyone was watching, dropped her head slightly and briefly, prayed quickly, then looked up again to check that no one had caught her. Collin smiled sadly. Poor kid. But bless her for trying to keep faith. *"She's not ashamed of you, Father, she's just scared. And you know that, too, better than I do. Help me help her if you want me to. Otherwise help me keep my mouth shut and not interfere with what you are doing,"* Collin prayed silently.

Chonnell's devotions apparently went unnoticed and she began to ply Mitch with questions, all the time shoveling food into her mouth. "We going on the river today?"

"Not yet."

"We going in a boat today? How we gonna learn to tackle the river if we don't get in the water?"

Pardner quipped, "We don't want to be in the water, moron. We want the boat to be in the water and we're in the boat. Ain't that right, Mr. Mitch?"

Mitch laughed. "Well, that is the general idea."

Chonnell was undeterred. "Okay, smartie. When we gonna get in a boat? We ain't even seen no boat yet." She swallowed a tremendous mouthful of food then continued, "We got all this stuff assigned to us and no place to use it. When we gonna get our rowers wet?"

Mitch grinned. "Paddles, Chonnell. They're called paddles. And I hope today."

Chonnell snapped, "You hope? You the teacher, you supposed to know this stuff. How come you don't know what we gonna do?"

Collin stifled the giggles that threatened to escape. This was fun. Mitch stared at his pint sized tormentor somehow not comprehending how this tiny figure could challenge him so brazenly. Collin thought, *"Deal with it, Mr. Mitch. They're going to be like this with you all week long. These aren't your usual Boy or Girl Scouts. These are my kids. Be sharp or go home, man."* Collin kept a straight face and said, "Chon, it probably depends on how quickly we learn what we need to, so we don't end up in the water or look like total idiots in the process." She looked at Mitch and said, "Is that about it?"

She saw a combination of rage and resentment, but also relief in the man's eyes. What she couldn't determine was who it was directed at:

Chonnell for questioning his abilities or herself for trying to rescue him? Either way she didn't like the implication. But Mitch merely laughed and said brightly, "You got it! Chonnell, I love your spunk."

Chonnell eyed him suspiciously. "What you talking about, spunk? What's that?"

"Courage. Determination. You aren't afraid of anything, are you?"

Chonnell hesitated then said fiercely, "No, I ain't. Got no reason to be."

Niles, Nyla and Ta'waan had arrived followed by Robbie. With the four new arrivals the questions of their day's activities were repeated, readdressed, rehearsed, rehashed and re'd to death. The campers soon cleaned their plates, cleaned the table, and cleaned out of the dining hall. Mitch took them to the clearing behind the boat docks where an eight-man raft had been set up. There they practiced entering and exiting the boat, falling out of the boat, reboarding the craft, paddling positions, moving around from position to position, exchanging positions, etc. etc. etc. They worked hard at it until after lunch, but Mitch provided sandwiches, chips and drinks for everyone.

Collin took the proffered fruit juice, but declined the sandwich. She was too tired to eat, anyhow. Plus she had a promise to fulfill. She asked Mitch for time out to go up to the infirmary to have her hand checked.

Mitch asked, curious, "What did you do?"

Collin shrugged. "I cut it Saturday. It's no big deal. I got stitches put in and I need to have them checked."

Niles hooted. "No big deal? Ain't what I heard."

Collin looked at him and said evenly, "Stories get exaggerated, Niles. Don't believe everything you hear on the street. Isn't that the Macon code?"

Niles looked at her, suddenly unsure. Her invocation of his gang's code was warning that she knew it, was in effect an insider, and was cautioning him off of something. He said slowly, still eyeing Collin, "Yeah, I guess. Could of just been someone's story."

Mitch was fascinated. Collin knew he hadn't missed the interplay between herself and Niles, and it only served to heighten his interest. "No, Niles, tell me what you heard. Even if it's just a story it's got to be a good one."

Robbie stepped in to the rescue. "Niles heard the same story I did. Case worker lady here was trying to impress one of the teachers how she knows this way-cool game she call mumble logs or something like that."

Collin offered, "Mumbly peg, Rob."

Robbie acted totally bored. "Yeah, whatever. Had something to do with throwing knives around or something stupid. She a white woman; she got no business playing with knives. Went to pick it up out of the ground and sliced her hand open like the fool she be." For effect he turned and looked at her with almost disgust. "Ain't that about what they saying happened?"

Niles chimed in, "That's the way I heard it."

Collin sighed and said, "Look, it wasn't quite like that. But I suppose that's as close to the truth as we're going to get today."

Mitch looked at her, shocked. "You cut yourself playing games with a knife? In order to impress someone?" His eyes narrowed slightly, "Like Jeff maybe?"

Finally something she could answer with absolute honesty. "I was not trying to impress Jeff at all. I was merely making a demonstration and the knife went deeper than I intended."

Mitch shook his head slowly. "You are something else, Walker. I don't know what, yet, but you are something else."

Collin asked quickly, "Does that mean I can go up and have it checked?"

"No. Infirmary is closed for lunch. But I'll get you back tonight in time to go in and get it looked at. Doc stays around late on Tuesday nights for special cases. You'll have plenty of time."

Collin had an uneasy feeling and said, "Please, Mitch, I'd really like to try and go up now. The hours he has posted don't say anything about being closed for lunch."

Mitch acted surprised. "You doubt me? I know Doc. He's closed, Collin. As your instructor you need to trust me on these things. You'll get there this afternoon, I promise. I can look at them if you want. I've had some training in first aid."

Collin shook her head. "That's fine. I think they're okay but I was told to come back and have the Doctor look at them." Collin sensed she should not push the issue lest Mitch begin to ask questions she had no desire to answer. She said, "This afternoon will work. He closes at six, right?"

Mitch nodded. "Yes, but like I said he's there late on Tuesdays. He'll be there until eight or nine at least. We'll get you taken care of, Walker. Chill out. It's just stitches."

Collin tried to laugh. "I'm cool, I'm cool. It's no big deal I know. So what do we do now, Coach?"

Mitch looked around at the crew, and said, "Let's try all these exercises one last time then put this boat in the water."

Six campers began cheering. Collin grinned as she realized even the laid-back older ones were yelling approval. They were as tired as she was of climbing in and out of that blasted rubber bowl. She looked at Mitch, smiled and said, "I think you've got a winner."

Mitch smiled back at her. Collin shuddered involuntarily as he said, "I know I do." Somehow Collin had the bad feeling his meaning was something other than face value.

And so the afternoon progressed. The group did all their multitude of position changes, shifts and etcetera's until Mitch was satisfied no one would capsize the boat. Then they carried their gear to the docks where a second identical craft was waiting for them in the water. With all the skill one morning's training could impart they climbed aboard, got settled and situated and pushed away from the dock. With some measure of difficulty they paddled out onto the "lake" area then spent the remainder of the day circumnavigating its perimeter.

But if Magellan had had to circumnavigate the world with this crew, he never would have made it, much less been remembered fondly in the history books. Whatever truce Collin thought may have existed with Nyla did not extend to Niles or Ta'waan. Ta'waan was woefully ignorant of the proper way to recover a paddle from the water without splashing bladefuls of water on the crewmember behind him: namely Collin. The first time it happened he was most apologetic. "Hey, lady worker, sorry! I didn't mean to get you all wet. Jus' can't get the hang of this paddling stuff. Never done it before, you know?"

Collin merely smiled and called forward, "No problem, Ta'waan. We've all got a learning curve to master." She chose to ignore the smirk on Niles' face and the swallowed giggle from the young woman beside her.

Three strokes later Collin caught another faceful of water. Ta'waan looked around at her and said weakly, "Sorry, ma'am."

Collin grinned. "You're getting better. You're catching more water with each stroke."

Nyla sniggered then said, "So's you."

Collin laughed. "You could say that. Though I don't think I'd say it too loud. Brothers are notorious for treachery and deceit."

Nyla looked at Collin curiously. "You got brothers?"

Collin bit her lip then admitted softly, "One."

Nyla snorted, "Yeah, well, having a brother don't let you know nothing 'bout having a twin brother. Niles wouldn't never turn on me."

"Never's a very long time, Nyla."

Nyla laughed harshly again. "See what you know." She yelled forward, "Hey, Niles! Tell this know-it-all white woman that you . . ."

She never got to finish the sentence. A faceful of water hit her between her sneer and her gloat, putting a definite punctuation on the discussion.

Nyla spit and spluttered and rained curses on Niles' precedents and descendants for generations on either side. She eschewed the water and went after him with her paddle, jumping up to get better aim.

And of course jumping up in a boat is number one on the list of "Never, never, nevers" that are issued with the owner's manual. Mitch thundered, "Sit down!" as Nyla lost her footing and pitched over the side. Niles screamed in pure panic; Collin started over the side to bring Nyla back. Mitch thundered again, "Sit down, everyone!!"

All eyes fastened on the river boat captain. Mitch ordered, "Everyone look out to your right."

Which everyone did, to see Nyla calmly dog paddling in place, letting the life jacket carry her weight. Mitch instructed sternly, "Nyla has it perfectly figured. No panic, no floundering around, just quietly waiting to be rescued. Right, Nyla?"

Nyla said snidely, "No, I'm waiting for someone to throw that fool of a brother of mine over so he can join me."

If no one else saw, Collin did. The interplay between the twins was powerfully reminiscent of many she and Erin had shared. Niles' eyes were tinged with fear, doubt and regret. Nyla's burned with anger, malice, but behind it all, forgiveness. There was a secret being shared here, one Collin could deduce with only a little effort.

But Mitch couldn't deduce his own face in front of him. He smiled evilly and said, "Maybe we should. Teach him a lesson in life saving."

Collin stood up abruptly and jumped into the water. Diving makes a much more dramatic statement but is terribly awkward in a life jacket. She swam up to within a few feet behind Nyla and, ignoring the mask of anger on Mitch's face, called, "Always approach from behind." She waved the crew into a chorus and together they chanted the instructions for rescuing swimmers (conscious or un,) towing said same to shore or safety (whichever was closest,) and then recovering them from the water.

Only after Nyla and Collin were back in the boat did Collin look at Mitch with her most winning smile and say, "Did we get it right, Cap'n? Huh? Did we? Did we get it the way you taught us? Miss anything? We definitely want to make you proud of us. Are you proud of us? Huh? Are you??"

She refused to take his scowl as a final answer. Collin knew she was on the edge of total insubordination and that, by rights, he ought to throw her out of class. Hmmm . . . now there was a thought. Maybe she could agitate him enough . . .

But finally Mitch laughed. (Drat!) He nodded and included the entire crew in his accolades. "Yes, you all did it right. You all did it perfect. I'm very proud of you." He shook his head then said, "You've proved you can rescue each other. Now let's get back to learning how to paddle so we don't have to."

With that everyone resumed their proper positions and the circumnavigation resumed. After a few quiet minutes Nyla leaned towards Collin slightly and asked, "Why you jump in? I know how to swim."

Collin debated then said carefully, "You do. Niles doesn't."

Nyla stared hard at Collin, shocked. When she finally found her voice she asked, "How you know?"

"I read his eyes. Read yours, too. Your suggestion that the crew throw him over was a cover. You never thought Mitch would take you serious, did you?"

Nyla continued to stare at Collin, unsure whether to trust her or not. Finally she said, "Never." She hesitated then asked uncertainly, "You going to tell Mitch?"

Collin snorted a little. "Tell him what? That Niles needs to wear a life jacket?" She fanned her own vest and said, "Gee, no. I don't think so. If Niles falls over he floats like the rest of us. If he can kick his feet and wave his arms he'll be fine. We just won't put his name first on the life-saving roster. Deal?"

Nyla gave Collin one last long look then shook her head. "Why? Why you do this?"

Collin shrugged. "I had a brother. I know what it's like."

Nyla shook her head but said nothing else. She returned to concentrating on her stroke, working slightly harder to match her pull to Collin's. She did, however, seem to be having a little extra difficulty on the forward recovery: she kept flipping water on her brother's back. Collin noticed that her own paddle seemed to be possessed of an additional zing at the end, one that caused plentiful droplets of water to fly off the end and land in a shower on Ta'waan's neck. The boys turned and glared at their tormentors; Collin and Nyla looked at each other, grinned, then in unison chorused, "Sorry."

By the end of the day the crew could have paddled the lake in their sleep. In fact Chonnell and Pardner were. Collin noticed even Nyla and the boys were getting tired. The kids had been pushed hard. So had she but she felt surprisingly energized. The thought of seeing Jeff tonight for her rematch with Robbie was invigorating in and of itself. Not that she'd be able to play worth squat but at least she'd see him.

Mitch finally directed the boat back to the docks, looked at his watch and said, "Good job, crew. Good job. I'm proud of each and every one of you. Great technique. It's six-thirty. Go up, get your showers. Chow hall is open an extra 1/2 an hour for you." Moans and groans greeted him but the thought of food roused most the campers. As everyone filed out of the boat Mitch called out, "Walker, would you stay behind, please? I want to work on your stroke a little more."

Collin was facing away from him so he couldn't see the expression of dismay that crossed her face. But someone did. Robbie stepped back between Mitch and Collin and said, "Hey, man, case worker lady and I got an appointment an' I really need her. Can she do what she got to do with you tomorrow? This is important stuff we gotta do, real important."

Collin picked up the ball and raced down the court. "Mitch, the kids aren't just up here for fun. We're still working with them as counselors, too. Rob and I scheduled this time quite a while ago. I'll work twice as hard tomorrow if you say I need to. But I need this time with Rob."

Mitch stared hard at both of them then said almost sullenly, "Go on. Get out of here. I'll see you early in the morning. Crew eats together, remember."

Collin nodded. "Right. Together."

"Seven am. Dining hall. Be there. Crew only."

"I understand." She understood a lot more than he thought, maybe. Collin said, "Let's go, Rob." As they rounded the corner away from the docks she said in a low voice, "Thanks, my man. Nice job."

Robbie was proud of himself. "An' I weren't lying, neither. We got an appointment. I got to finish whipping your sorry butt in hoops tonight."

Collin smiled, "After what you just did I should just let you win." She paused then said, "Should. But I won't. Some things you just don't do. And giving you a win in hoops is one of them." She wanted so badly to reach out and hug him but knew it was absolutely forbidden. Forbidden not by company directive but by Robbie's parameters for their relationship. Some day. Some day she would give him the hug he needed and deserved and wanted. But not yet.

Robbie was silent a moment then asked, "Why you ain't put him in his place?"

"He's in his place, Rob. He's the teacher. I bring him down, what does that do for the rest of the crew? If I try to bring him down and for some reason fail, he takes vengeance on everyone. I can ride it out. We only got three more days. I've dealt with worse than him, believe me."

"Montgomery?" Collin nodded. "That guy was a dirt bag."

Collin chuckled. "I should disagree with you on principle's sake. But I can't. You're right." She hesitated then said, "It would help if you kind of kept an eye out, you know? Like you did just now. I'll do everything I can not to get left alone with him. But if I get in trouble I can use all the backup I can get."

"You got it, case worker lady. I don't want to be breaking in no new counselor. I just getting you trained."

Collin laughed and shoved him lightly. "Get out of here. Go wash up and eat. I'll be in later."

Robbie warned, "You better be eating some power food yourself. You're gonna need it tonight."

"Yeah, yeah, yeah. I hear you." She headed up the hill towards the infirmary. If Mitch was correct the Doc should still be there, and she was in good shape with her promise to Jeff.

But the "lights out, no one home" appearance of the office left her with a sinking feeling. She went up to the door and knocked anyhow, just to satisfy her already shredded honor. No answer. There were no notes of any kind indicating that the doctor had been called away suddenly. More unsettling was the fact that there were no notices of extended hours, either. What kind of game was Mitch playing? Honest mistake or deliberate power trip? Time would tell. Jeff would have to understand.

Well, actually, he didn't have to understand. She only hoped he'd understand. She sighed, then headed back down to the lodge. She debated to eat or not to eat, bandied the question, and decided finally to eat. And get the nag in her head off her back. At least another banana, a protein bar and an apple for a change of pace. She really needed to go back to her room and stretch out her muscles, not as in stretching out to sleep. Though that was sorely tempting, too. She ate as she walked, pitched the peels and cores at the can by the dining hall and went to her room. A good, hot shower loosened up most of the knots she would re-inflict on them later. Maybe she would go to the gym to finish the job. Safer than going to her room and listening to her pillow's siren song. Much safer.

Collin changed clothes, took another change with her and headed for the gym. Mr. Lawler and another male counselor whose name escaped Collin were already there working out. Good. Safety in numbers. Not that she had anything to worry about. Guys like Mitch usually worked only during daylight hours and primarily at the office. They were opportunity takers not seekers. Collin selected a mild series of isometric pulls and stretches on the universal gym, something to ease the muscles, not stretch them beyond comfort levels. She kept one eye on the clock, however, to make sure she didn't risk missing her deadline and showing up late on the court. When one is trying to teach responsibility to a child it behooves one not to be a bad example oneself. No matter how good one's intentions or excuses may be. Right, one? Right.

Collin worked until just after eight, changed into her hoops duds, grabbed a final banana from the snack bar and trotted to the ball court.

Jeff had already arrived and had brought a five gallon cooler with ice water, hauling it up on a small wagon. Collin noticed some plastic cups lying beside the cooler. She grinned at him and said, "You think of everything, don't you?"

Jeff bowed low. "We aim to please, madam." He straightened up and asked, "How was your day?"

Collin shrugged. "It was." Not wishing to sound negative she added, "We got to paddle around the lake a few times. That was fun. But mostly it was a lot of work." She grinned. "I swear, though, if Mitch had ordered one more boarding drill he was going to have a mutiny on his hands. And I'd have led the charge."

Jeff grinned, "Oh my, rebellion in the camp? Maybe I ought to warn Mitch."

Collin shook her head. "Naw, let him learn on his own. He needs to learn a few things." Oops, she hadn't meant to add that. Collin looked at Jeff and saw him studying her, trying to interpret her comment. Collin added quickly, "That's not what I meant to say. Or at least not how I meant it to sound. Or I meant . . ." Collin stomped a foot in frustration. It was bad enough to stutter mentally. Did she have to do it out loud, too? Collin pulled herself together, smiled and said, "Disregard all that. How was your day?"

Jeff continued to study her a moment longer then said, "It was . . . busy. Full. I got the dock taken care of. I hope. Someone has been tampering with the moorings, though why they would is a mystery to me. It's not like it hurts anything at the camp. We're not in full operation so we can switch docks with no problem. It's more an irritation than a problem. But I'm going to keep an eye on it for the next week or so just to make sure. Other than that, the ladies and I had a terrific milking session this morning. I found out they appreciate the old hymns, aren't much for Southern Gospel, and pour their hearts—and their milk—out over praise choruses. They told me it was the best milking they'd had in a long time. The fact I have warm hands probably helped some. A little quirk of theirs, I guess. They hate cold hands."

Collin shook her head. "You're a nut."

"Pecan or cashew?"

"Filbert."

"Filbert?" Jeff acted surprised. "Filbert? What's a filbert?"

"I have no idea. Which is why it reminds me of you. I have no idea about you sometimes."

"I hope that's not a bad thing."

"Not at all. It makes you intriguing."

Jeff looked a little concerned. "So to keep you interested I have to be crazy? This could be tough."

Collin said carefully, "No, you just have to be you." She hesitated then added, "And you don't have to 'keep' me interested. I . . . uh, I . . ." Words failed her as did every other mental process. She fought valiantly for some intelligent way to finish the thought. Failing intelligence, she searched for any way she could find to close out the sentence. That too, failed. Finally she looked at Jeff, shrugged haplessly and said, "I like you."

Jeff grinned but it was a little shy. "I think you're a special lady, Collin. A little demented, maybe, but that's something we can work with."

Jeff was saved—or barred—from further disclosure as Robbie came running up the hill yelling, "Case worker lady! Case worker lady! Where you been all night? Me and the crew been looking for you all over. Mitch called us all together after dinner. He got a bonfire going down by the docks and he be telling stories about the river and how he ridden it. It's sweet, lady. Really sweet. You gotta come down and listen. You gotta. Mitch was real disappointed when you didn't show up."

Collin said dryly, "I'll bet."

Rob shrugged. "Whatever. I told him you was probably up here and he said he come get you but I told him I'd be there faster. He really want you to come."

Collin shuddered involuntarily, keenly aware that Jeff was missing none of this. Not commenting or questioning, but not missing it, either. She said evenly, "You did good, my man. Why don't you go on and listen for both of us? You can fill me in later."

Robbie shook his head. "We got a game to finish."

"We can finish it any time, Rob. Go listen to Mitch. You'll have a good time I'm sure. Hang with the crew."

"You sure you don't want to come? Man may be a weasel but he tell a good story."

"I'm sure he does." Boy was she sure.

"Ain't gonna upset you, me not having to beat you again?"

Collin ordered in mock anger, "Out. Go. Vanish. Disappear. Take your sorry self and be gone."

Rob laughed and ran off shouting, "Later, Jeff! Bye, case worker lady."

Collin turned to Jeff and said, "I'm sorry I messed up your evening for nothing."

Jeff shrugged. "I didn't have any plans, anyhow. Are you sure you don't want to go down with him?"

"I am absolutely sure I don't want to go down with Rob."

Jeff asked carefully, "If it wasn't down by the river?"

Collin tried to keep her voice even. "I don't care where it was. I do not want to spend this evening, or any evening for that matter, with Mitch. Can we let it go at that?" She was getting irritated and that was not what she wanted.

But Jeff couldn't seem to let it go. He asked, still being careful, "Is there a problem?"

Collin said firmly, "I can handle it. It's personal and I'll deal with it. Okay? Let it go, Jeff." And to lighten the moment she placed both hands on his shoulders, looked him straight in the eyes and said, "I would much rather spend my time with the janitor than with a blowhard ship's captain."

Whatever levity she had intended disappeared in the depths of those eyes. And the longer she looked and read the emotions there the less of a jest her statement became. Finally, as her own emotions began to jumble and swirl, she dropped her eyes and turned away. She cleared her throat and said a little weakly, "I really did want to play ball tonight."

Apparently Jeff found something in his own throat as well. He coughed slightly then said, "You know, to tell the truth, I was kind of hoping to play, too. Some two on one, maybe."

Collin looked at him in surprise. "Really?"

"Yeah. It gets a little boring playing by myself. You always know who's going to win."

Collin shook her head. "Not when I play alone. There are too many personalities out there with me."

Jeff grinned. "Case worker lady, you are something else." He stopped then asked, "Why does he call you that?"

"Because that's who I am: his case worker. Rob's had so many workers in his life he vowed three workers ago not to learn anyone else's name until they'd been with him at least a year. I've got about two months to go."

"Tough kid."

"Good kid, tough upbringing."

"You care a lot about him, don't you?"

"I'd adopt him if I could."

"Why don't you?"

"His mother won't give him up. She'd lose some of her support money. And I can't give him the one thing he really needs: a strong male influence. If he had one male role model that would show him you can be strong and still love, win without cheating, and succeed in life without all the bells and whistles, I think he could make it. I can show him that, but he only says, 'yeah, but you a woman. Ain't like that for us dudes.'"

Jeff said quietly, "Sounds like he needs a father."

Collin said angrily, "He needs someone that will care about him."

Jeff looked at her a moment then said easily, "I think we've established that the river and fathers are problem areas. Are there any other topics I should know not to bring up?"

Collin slapped at him in frustration; Jeff ducked. She threw the basketball at him and said through clenched teeth, "Yes. My weight and the way I dress. Are we done with our analysis, yet?"

Jeff backed up, baiting her but his eyes shining. "What's the matter, case worker lady? You can handle everyone else's problems but no one better touch one of yours?" He threw the ball back to her and there was a sting on it.

Collin's eyes glinted. "You don't get it, do you? I make the rules. I call the shots. I'm in control. That's how it works." She fired the ball back to him.

Jeff trotted towards half court. "So what are the rules, lady?" Again he passed her the ball.

Collin joined him. She enumerated tersely, "One: first man to 100 wins." She passed the ball back to him, hard.

"How high does the woman have to score?" Jeff fired the ball back.

Collin ignored him. "Two: no time outs. First one to walk off the court loses." Ball.

"Anything else?" Ball.

"Just one more rule." Ball.

"What's that?" Ball.

"I win." Collin broke for the basket catching Jeff flatfooted. He raced after her but was unable to catch her before she had laid the ball in cleanly. As the ball dropped through she yanked her sweatshirt off, threw it violently to the ground, and stood ready for Jeff's first assault on offense.

Jeff cruised to the endline staring at Collin, trying to read her. Let him try. She stared back defiantly. Jeff took the ball and said slowly, "So that's how it's played, is it?"

Collin nodded curtly. "That's how it's played."

Jeff challenged, "Then lady, give it your best shot." He dribbled slowly and deliberately back to the midline, then turned, pointed at her, and started back up. Collin watched him for a moment then went out to battle. The war was on.

But the next six points belonged to Jeff as Collin had a hard time picking up his rhythm. After his second bucket she began to see a pattern, however. Just before shooting he faded to the right as if favoring the left knee ever so slightly. Not that it slowed him down any. Collin had to stretch to stay up with him. His crack the other night about the office worker was not far off the mark. She really did need to get serious about staying in shape. As his third basket in a row sank Collin nodded. She had him now. Collin brought the ball to mid-court and dribbled up slowly, studying him. What was it her coach said: the eyes. Always watch the eyes.

Jeff's eyes were dancing, taunting her. He jibed, "Study long, study wrong, they always say."

Collin asked coolly, "And who would they be?" She faked to her left; Jeff mirrored her. Spinning around she moved right, then came back to her left. As Jeff moved back she slapped the ball over his head, bouncing it high enough to dodge around him, catch it, then break away for an easy two points. She let the ball fall and retreated to mid court.

Jeff retrieved the ball and nodded with respect. "Very creative. Don't think I've seen that move in the NCAA." He dribbled past her. "Wonder what the Dean would have thought of it?" Jeff crossed the half court line, turned around and started back up, intending to shoot by her as in past engagements. But Collin was ready for him this time, sliding to her left, blocking his path. Jeff dodged left but she had anticipated him and was already there. Ducking and weaving he fought his way up the court but was unable to elude Collin's defense. He gave her a shake-and-bake move and drove towards the basket firing the ball at the last moment. But Collin timed her leap perfectly, catching the ball at its apogee, and smashed it away with a carnal pleasure that surprised her.

Jeff eyed her with new respect and said, "You been sand bagging, lady."

Collin retrieved the ball and fired it to him. "You gonna talk or you gonna play?"

Jeff's eyes narrowed slightly and his voice held a trace of an edge as he said, "Play."

With that they were back at it.

And at it hard. Neither kept time, neither kept score. Each basket was a mini-game all in and of itself. Collin was stretched again and again to her limit and beyond, fighting to keep up, stay even, and sometimes even pull ahead. She had a ragged idea that the score was close but would never swear by it. She desperately wanted a break, but seeing as how she'd made the rules, couldn't bring herself to admit she wanted one. The fire inside had burned down to glowing embers, ready to be re-ignited if required, but just as ready to die if allowed. She was tired but would die before admitting it to Jeff. Not that he was faring much better than she was. Number thirty-seven hadn't had the opportunity to strip down out of his warm-up suit and was sweating profusely. He was also breathing hard and had developed an increasingly apparent limp. What wasn't he telling her?

He waited at mid-court, slowly dribbling the ball. As she set herself on defense once again he asked, "No time outs, right?"

Collin hesitated then stiffened her game face. "No time outs." No mercy. Not yet.

Jeff eyed her closely then said evenly, "Have it your way, lady." He broke up the court; Collin stumbled then had to chase him, always a step behind. Jeff put in the lay up, caught the ball as it fell through the net then heaved it as far down the court and out of bounds as he could.

Collin yelled angrily, "Hey!" and went after the ball. Out of the corner of her eye she saw him quickly shuck the warm up suit and stand ready for her return. The weasel. Well planned, but still a weasel. He'd pay for that one.

Or maybe he already had, once. Jeff was limping in earnest but smiled at her as he met her at mid court. "Sorry."

"You certainly are." Her eyes were drawn to his knee and its web of surgical scars. She looked up at him. "Blow out?"

Jeff shrugged, "Ancient history," then asked, "You gonna talk or play?"

Collin stood dribbling the ball slowly, deliberating. She waited as the voices in her head lined up pro and con: *"Beat him while he's down. Take full advantage of the opportunity handed to you and crush the vermin. Let him know right now who's the strong one, here."* Or: *"Let him know who's the strong one, yes. Strong in mercy. Strong in kindness. Strong in not having to prove your prowess through another's pain." "What would Jesus . . ."* Collin laid the ball down and said firmly, "Talk. You're hurting."

Jeff said sharply, "What, you find what you think is a weakness and suddenly it's time for analysis?"

Collin said, "No. I just . . ."

Jeff said impatiently, "Let's play ball, woman. You were ready to beat my brains out just two minutes ago. I'm the same man I was then. These scars don't change anything." In frustration he picked up the ball and launched it in a high rainbow arch that swished silently through the net.

Vanna White turned over the last consonant on the board, and the answer became clear. I'd like to solve that puzzle, Pat. Collin whispered softly, "Jeff Farrell. Number thirty-seven. North Carolina. You were going to be the next MJ."

Jeff shook his head in disgust. "That was press hype."

"I watched you play. You were that good."

Jeff retrieved the ball and said darkly. "Were. Past tense."

"You still are that good, Jeff."

"Against shadows in the street maybe."

Collin sensed the game was over, or at least on hold. Side by side they walked over to the water jug. Collin asked, "What happened? The doctors were talking about a full recovery."

Jeff snorted. "The doctors' ideas of recovery and the Coach's ideas of recovery weren't quite the same. He knew I wasn't listening to the therapist. He knew I wasn't going to listen. I wanted to play ball, period. So he protected me against myself. Didn't cut me from the team, just didn't let me play until he was convinced I was 100%. Which I never got back to." Jeff sighed slightly then shrugged. He smiled sadly at Collin. "But God knows I love the game." Collin found her throat tight, unable to speak. Jeff touched her cheek lightly; she looked at him. He said softly, "I guess we've all got a few demons yet to master."

Collin poured a cup of water for Jeff then one for herself. Both chugged them greedily and went for refills. Collin poured a second cup for Jeff and one more for herself. Jeff drank his, but Collin dumped hers over her head, splashing the remainder on her face. It felt deliciously cool.

Jeff watched her, grinning. "What's that all about?"

Collin smiled. "It feels great." She poured another cup and said, "You ought to try it." She raised the cup as if to repeat the shower but at the last second dumped it over Jeff's head.

Jeff jumped back in surprise sputtering, "You!"

Collin grabbed another cupful of water and threw it at him before he could recover, then took off running. Jeff grabbed the water jug, disdaining the cups, and chased after her. Collin headed for the grass figuring there was less chance of irreparable harm to either of them if this game went awry. She ducked and dodged but with the slippery footing could not shake him. Even with a limp the man was fast. Think, think. Element of surprise, maybe? Collin slowed enough for him to almost catch her then spun on her heels and doubled back. She guessed Jeff would empty the contents of the jug at her as she passed. She might get a little wet but she could live with that.

What she wasn't prepared for was his counter attack. As Collin sped past him Jeff dropped the jug, reached out and tackled her. In a flash he reached back, grabbed the jug and emptied the remainder of its five gallons over her. Collin spit water and yelled, "Foul! Technical foul! You can't do that!!"

Jeff stood over her laughing. "Another one of your rules?"

Collin said determinedly, "Yes." She reached out and tripped the unsuspecting maintenance man, dragging him to the grass with her.

Jeff was caught by surprise and landed with a thud. He started laughing and couldn't stop. Collin lay beside him, laughing with him. Jeff finally gained control of himself and rolled up on his side, looking down at Collin. She looked up at him and smiled gently. Again she stared into those oh, so expressive eyes, and was drawn in by their emotions. Jeff hesitated then reached out and very tenderly kissed her, tentatively, as if not sure how she would respond. Collin put her arms around his neck and kissed him in return.

It was long. It was intense. It was everything Collin had ever thought a kiss should be. And it scared her. Collin broke off suddenly and sat up straight. She looked at Jeff and there was a stricken, guilty look on his face. He said quickly, "Collin, I'm sorry. I . . ."

Collin grabbed him, hugging him hard, burying her head in his shoulder. Jeff cradled her in his arms and rested his head lightly on hers. She whispered, "You big dummy, don't apologize. Don't ever apologize." Sitting there felt very warm, very natural, very right. Like she could sit there forever . . .

Suddenly the court lights went out and they were in total darkness. Collin gasped, Jeff chuckled. "Timer. That's supposed to mean time's up and everyone goes home. We probably ought to take that hint."

Collin nodded. "I think you're right. It's been a long evening."

Jeff stood up, helped Collin to her feet, but did not release her hand. They gathered up the ball, their assortment of sweat shirts, and the remains of the water jug. Hand in hand they walked back to the lodge. As there was a crowd of campers at the door there was no good night kiss, only a gentle squeeze of the hand, a smile, and a whispered, "See you tomorrow." Then he was gone. Collin entered the lodge alone but, for the first time in many years, not lonely. And yes she smiled all the way to bed.

WEDNESDAY

Seven a.m., however, found Collin sitting in the dining room, off by herself, as alone as she could manage in a room bustling with campers. She clutched a cup of coffee, swirling it more than drinking it, lost deep in thought. Last night was the first night since they'd been here—the first night in years, actually—she hadn't dreamed of the river. Not that dreaming of Jeff was any less disturbing, but at least with him she wasn't drowning. At least not in the literal sense. Or at least not . . .

A voice startled her, commanding sharply, "Stop it!" Collin turned around quickly; Jeff stood there with a tray of food and a stern look on his face. He set the tray down on the table and said again, "Stop. Stop analyzing, bisecting, dissecting, or whatever way you're trying to take apart what happened last night and accept it for what it was. I had a great time. Every muscle in my body aches but I had fun. Did you?"

Collin nodded, feeling properly chastened. "Yes I did. And yes, I ache too. I need to get out of the office more often."

Jeff grinned. "I need to do a lot of things more often. Here." He set a toasted bagel with cream cheese in front of her and commanded, "Eat. It's good for you."

Collin said reproachfully, "Jeff . . ."

He mimicked her tone and said, "Collin . . . you have to eat to stay healthy. And you need to get your strength up if you ever hope to beat anyone at basketball."

Collin glared at him. "What do you mean 'hope to beat'? I was whipping you pretty handily last night."

Jeff shook his head sadly. "You really have to do something about these delusions, milady."

Collin started to protest but Jeff silenced her. He took her hand, bowed his head and again asked the Lord to bless the food and their day. Collin added some silent thanks of her own, then looked up at Jeff's "amen" and smiled at him. She said, "Okay, maybe I wasn't ahead but I didn't lose."

Jeff started in on his breakfast and asked conversationally, "Who walked off the court first?"

Collin stared at him in disbelief. "What?"

Jeff shrugged. "You made the rules, lady. I was just following them."

Collin looked for something to throw but had only her coffee and the bagel at hand. Her personal religion forbade the wasting of a good cup of coffee and she feared doing Jeff serious bodily harm if she hit him with the bagel. She was left with no recourse other than to steam silently and threaten, "You wait. You wait."

Jeff smiled that catbird smile of his then got serious and said, "Listen, I've got to tell you something and I don't want you to take it for anything other than face value, okay?"

Collin felt a too-familiar twisting in her gut and the defensive walls began to rise. Her voice got quiet and she asked, "What?"

Jeff shook his head and said, "See, you're doing it already and you don't even know what I'm going to say. If this relationship is going to go anywhere you have got to learn to trust me better than that." His tone was light, almost as if he'd anticipated her reaction.

But Collin's defensives were coming up to full steam. She asked evenly, "Does one kiss make a relationship?"

Jeff reached out, took her hand and said softly, "Actually, it was two. And I hope so."

Those eyes. Those cursedly intense eyes . . . Collin softened and asked, "What's wrong?"

"I have to leave this morning. I'm flying out in about an hour. Dad called me last night and some deal he's been working on for the last six months has suddenly been accelerated to this afternoon. He needs my help."

Fireworks went off in Collin's brain and she wanted to scream "I need your help!" But with supreme maturity and restraint she said only, "It's good you two are close."

Jeff shrugged. "We're business associates. He runs the business and I get to associate with him. Works for me." Jeff must have noticed that the levity wasn't scoring points so changed his tactic. He squeezed her hand tightly and said, "Collin, if for any reason you need me, or maybe just want someone to talk to, I left my numbers on your dresser." Collin looked up at him sharply; Jeff continued smoothly, "I was in there to fix the vent screen. Someone complained about it rattling at night."

Collin relaxed slightly. Of course he wouldn't have been in her room without a legitimate reason. She was the one who lodged the maintenance request in the first place. She said, "I didn't complain. I just mentioned." She gave him a small smile and said, "Thanks."

"Collin, I'm coming back. Thursday evening or Friday morning at the very latest. I promise."

Collin held up her free hand to stop him. "Unless you've become God since last night don't promise me anything." She continued softly, "Just tell me you'll try, okay? That'll be good enough."

Jeff squeezed her hand again, then, in a unique gesture Collin had not seen before but found immensely touching, he placed his palm upright against hers and said solemnly, "I promise I will try to the very best of the ability God gives me to be back here before you take the river ride. And I also promise to try to call you every evening and every morning until I do get back." He stopped, hesitated, then said, "If you want me to."

Collin needed time and space to sort out the emotions that were boiling inside her. She said simply, "That would be nice. If you have the time. I imagine you're pretty busy while you're home."

Jeff snorted, dropping his palm from hers. "Busy? Let me detail a day in Oakton for you. I'll get there around eleven. Dad will pick me up at the airport, take me to lunch somewhere that he dislikes but knows my mom will approve of, then we'll go to the property site. I'll do as thorough an inspection as I can get access to, which is never thorough enough, but it's the best we can do. Then we go back to the office, spend the next couple of hours hashing out whether his plans for the site are feasible, logical, practical, economical or profitable. Last hour there we spend praying about what the Lord wants us to do with all of this. We'll get home and Mom will have forgotten I was coming home so she hasn't fixed enough to eat and we'll all go out to dinner." Jeff probably noticed the concerned look that crossed Collin's face and said softly, "Mom had a stroke about two years ago and she hasn't been herself since. She's regained all of her functionings but something in the brain just never made it all the way back. It's tough to explain. She's just not all Mom."

"Jeff, I'm sorry."

"We all are. But the Lord has His time and purpose. Everyone loves the new Mom."

Collin asked carefully, "But misses the old?"

Jeff nodded without speaking. He picked up his tale and continued, "After dinner I'll help Mom with some of the housework, listen to Dad rehash the decision of the day, feed the dog, water the cat, feed the cat to the dog . . ."

Collin slapped his arm. "You're so bad."

"Wanted to see if you were listening. Actually we don't have any pets. Let's see, what else? Dad will end his evening watching a little television, usually some documentary about alligators or the mob or something educational. Mom will sew or needlepoint or do something creative with sharp objects until Dad finally decides it's time for bed. He informs Mom, she puts everything away in specific places and order, which takes about half an hour then they go to bed."

"And what about you? What do you do in the midst of all this excitement?"

"I spend most of my evening helping Leesa with her homework."

"Leesa. Is that a younger sister?"

Jeff's voice softened and there was a look of pride in his eyes. "Actually, she's older than me. About three years older."

Collin was a little confused. "Is she in college?"

"No. Leesa has Down Syndrome. She's a senior in high school this year." His eyes beamed as he said, "I'm so proud of her determination. She told me she didn't care how long it took, she was going to graduate. And she'll do it, too."

Collin was silent, trying to think of what to say. The more the man talked, the more incredible he became. She found her throat inexplicably tight but managed to say, "I think it sounds like a very full day. And a good one. I envy you."

Jeff shrugged. "It's family. It's my family, anyhow." He took a deep breath, let it out then said, "I'd better get going. I've still got chores to do before I leave." He handed a piece of folded up paper to her and asked, "Would you give this to Rob? I told him last night I was leaving; told him I'd give him my number if he got stuck on anything. He'll know what I'm talking about." He grinned. "That's one great kid."

Collin nodded. "Yeah, I know." She hesitated then said, "I'm going to miss you, Jeff." Both ways.

Jeff touched her hand and said, "I'll miss you, Collin." He paused then said, his tone serious, "This 'personal' thing between you and Mitch. I know you can handle it all by yourself. But if by some minuscule chance you do need help—not that you ever would, mind you, but just on that one in a million chance it happens—Steve Parks is always on call. And trust me he will listen to anything you have to say. Day or night, it doesn't matter."

Collin nodded quietly but offered nothing more. Jeff studied her as if expecting some response he wasn't getting. Finally he said, "Take care of yourself, milady. I'll see you soon."

Collin gathered in all her runaway emotions and said simply, "Bye, Jeff. I'll be here." Jeff disappeared out the door.

On cue the crew came jamming over to the table hip hopping and be-bopping to someone's singing at a table across the way. Robbie slid his tray across the table and chimed, "Hey, case worker lady. Heard you got beat at hoops last night, and I wasn't even there to do it."

Collin was astonished. "What? Who told you such a despicable lie?"

"My man Jeff. Ain't he telling it straight?"

Collin sighed angrily and said, "In his own twisted logic I suppose you could say that was true. When did you see Jeff?"

"Last night after we got back from the bonfire. And Mitch is still upset you didn't come down. Anyhow, Jeff was down in the game room fixing one of the units. I got talking with him then we got playing around. He showed me fifteen different ways to beat WOW. He cool."

"You think so, huh?"

"Yeah. He told me you had him beat but you walked off the court so he won." Robbie looked at her curiously and asked, "You going soft on me, lady? You ain't never walked off the court."

"Call it a mental lapse. Call it stupidity. Call it a one-time event that will never, repeat never ever happen again." Collin wasn't sure whether to be flattered or annoyed. Was Jeff using Rob to get information about her? She asked nonchalantly, "So what else did you talk about?"

Rob answered between bites of pancake, "Me mostly. Where I was from, things I like to do, what I thought about school, that kind of stuff. He asked me why I chose white water."

"And you told him . . ." Collin prompted.

Robbie chewed thoughtfully then said, "Power. Man that can ride that can do anything."

Ta'waan added, "He ain't lying. You should have heard the stories Mitch was telling last night 'bout all the rivers he's rode, all the places he been. It was sweet, man."

Collin pushed the untouched bagel aside and said calmly, "That's great, guys." She looked at the diminutive duo and asked, "So why did you two choose the river?"

Chonnell said excitedly, "I seen this show 'Reading Rainbow' and this guy, LeVar Burton, went down a river in a boat. It looked so cool I had to try it. It looked like fun, like the rides at the Point."

"Did Mitch tell you it was going to be all fun?"

Pardner shook her head. "Course not. I know it be hard work. I ain't afraid of working. I been toting Mama's laundry baskets full of people's wet clothes since I was old enough not to fall in 'em. Washer's in the basement and we live on the third floor. I can pull my own weight."

Niles cracked, "Yeah but you don't weigh nothing so it don't count for much."

Collin interceded before blood could be drawn. "What about you two? Was this a joint decision or someone lose the draw?"

Niles' eyes narrowed slightly, "How you know 'bout that?"

Collin smiled a little sadly and said, "I had brother. I know how these things work." She noted the curious look on Nyla's face but let it go and looked at Niles. "I'm guessing you won the draw. Why white water?"

"Like the dudes said: power, man. It's all about power."

Ta'waan asked unexpectedly, "Why little old white lady like you sign up, huh? You working for the Man so you got all the power you want. Why you out here? My counselor didn't sign up for nothing."

Nyla added roughly, "Can you see Mrs. Pelfry doing any this?"

Niles chuckled. "Like to see her on the luge, man. She be doing barrel rolls down the mountain."

Collin started to intercede, stopped, thought about it again, started again, stopped again . . . all in the matter of less than a second. Her final decision was to say nothing and let her silence speak. That and a look of stern disapproval. If that carried no weight, well, too bad. This was crew talk, not school talk. Let the counselors' lives speak for themselves.

Pardner said, "I think Mr. Tremont is doing the rappelling. Saw him yesterday an' his hands is all torn up and bandaged. He laughed like it was no big deal; say he was havin' fun."

Chonnell shook her head. "Ms. Peacock brought a ton of books with her. She say she got no intention of getting dirty, wet or otherwise 'inconvenienced' by this. She come to babysit, that's all."

Collin corrected the girl, "It's Ms. Petcock isn't it?"

"Not the way she go strutting. She too high class for this. Told me over an' over that if she could find a job somewhere else that'd pay her what she worth, she be long gone."

Collin ached inside. Role models. What role models were she and her kind really presenting to the kids? What was she presenting to Rob? When all else was said and done did he see anything worth following? Worth imitating? Did he see Christ in her?

Nyla brought Collin out of her soul searching and repeated the question. "So why you choose rafting?"

Collin hesitated then debated how to answer. To speak or not to speak? Reveal her secret fear, or dissemble and pay the consequences later? Where was the coin when she needed it? What would Jesus . . . Collin looked around the group then said honestly, "I signed up because it scares me."

Niles said, "Say what??"

Collin looked in Robbie's eyes as she explained, "I had a bad experience on a river when I was a little kid and I've been afraid of going in, or even on one, ever since."

Rob studied her eyes as if trying to discern fact from fiction. He asked slowly, as if trying to understand, "You been scared? Ever since you was a kid? Of a river?" His voice was almost incredulous. The two little girls giggled. Ta'waan and Niles laughed harshly. Only Nyla was silent. Collin answered Robbie, "Yeah. Of a river."

Robbie snorted. "I ain't believing that. Not you. You ain't afraid of nothing. I seen you out on the streets, lady. I seen you face down Jigger's lieutenant. I seen you standing 'tween the Snakes and the Skins when they was ready to rumble. You ain't telling me you afraid of water."

"You don't think I was scared those times? Come on, Rob. I was terrified. But I had to go out there. And I knew I wasn't alone, either."

Rob muttered, "Look like it to me."

She smiled slightly. "That's because you could only see on the outside. It's who's on the inside that counts."

"Yeah, well, ain't he still on the inside? What be the difference 'tween now and then?"

Collin had to think that one over a moment then admitted, "Nothing I guess. I've just never had to try to face it before." She nailed him with a glance. "Oakton is not exactly blessed with raging rivers, you know."

Niles began mocking to Ta'waan, "How anyone be scared of a river?"

Ta'waan's voice took on a falsetto, "Oh, my, the river's gonna get me."

Collin saw the blood rising in Robbie's face. She laid a hand on his arm in warning, then said quietly to Niles and Ta'waan, "I hope you never have to find out. I hope you never run across anything that scares you." She chose to forgo nailing Niles with a knowing look; he'd figure it out soon enough. Collin looked around instead and said, "You better finish up. Mitch will leave without us if we're late." Ah, but at least they would be late as a whole crew. He couldn't complain on that count!

Frivolity was put aside as food was crammed in mouths, half-chewed, then washed down with colas as is the manner of teens and teen wannabes. Not five minutes passed before the table was cleared, trays and seat backs returned to their full upright position, and everyone headed for the door. Robbie held back slightly, enough to drop him and Collin out of earshot of the others. He said lowly, "You ain't afraid, lady. You just think you are. I be knowing you. You can't quit. You can't."

"I'm trying, Rob. I really am trying. But this is big, man."

Robbie shook his head. "You bigger. Or the one you always be telling me about be, ain't he?"

"Yes, Rob, he is."

"Then you can do it. I know you can."

Collin stopped, put both hands on Robbie's shoulders and said, "If you can pilot the boat, I'll stay in it."

"Your word?"

"My word."

Robbie grinned wide, slapped her fist and said, "You got it. Let's catch up." He raced off to join the others.

Collin closed her eyes and prayed softly, "Don't let me let him down, Lord. Please, don't let me let him down." She walked on towards the dock but there was little joy in her steps.

Mitch waited patiently, the camp van behind him. His eyes narrowed slightly as Collin approached and he said, "You did come. We missed you last night. Thought you might have bailed on us. It was supposed to be a crew thing, you know."

Collin said evenly, "I had already made other plans. But I hear you're a great story teller."

Mitch refused to let it go. "Plans with who, the janitor?"

Collin kept her tone even. "Plans with Rob and Jeff, yes. When Rob canceled I saw no reason to cancel on Jeff, too." She went back to her diversionary tactic. "Rob was quite impressed with your style, though. He did a great deal of bragging on you."

Appeals to ego are usually great mollifiers and this was no exception. Mitch said with satisfaction, "Oh, I don't know. You'd have to hear me in person to really judge. How about tonight?"

Collin shook her head. "I don't know, Mitch. We'll have to see how today goes. Yesterday was pretty full." *"But you were able to put in over an hour on the court anyhow." "Let's not mention that shall we? Mitch doesn't need to know everything we do."*

Mitch said snidely, "I suppose it depends on what Jeff is doing, too."

Collin answered truthfully, "No, it doesn't." She didn't add that he was out of town.

Mitch was surprised and delighted. "It doesn't? You mean the fling is over and a real man has a chance to turn your head?"

Collin said patiently, "Mitch, you've got six bored campers getting antsy. Where we come from that's asking for trouble. You better get these kids directed towards something or they're liable to practice dismantling the engine just to keep up their skills."

Mitch turned around and saw that, with the exception of Pardner and Chonnell, all the teens were poring over the van's motor like vultures. He shouted, "Okay! Let's go. Everyone in the van. Adults up front." He smiled at Collin, a man in whom hope had been reborn. His comment was general but Collin had the uneasy feeling it was meant for her alone as he declared, "This is going to be a great day."

The group piled in the van with the usual amount of heffing and heefing over who had to sit where and with who. But once they were settled and the van was in motion Robbie called hey, "Hey, Mitch? Where we going anyhow?"

A chorus of seemingly disinterested but curious voices echoed his sentiment. Mitch said jovially, "Oh, I thought we'd go for a ride up in the mountains."

Pardner called, "We in the mountains now. How far up we gonna go?"

"Up to where our river was born."

That set off a buzz of discussion. "Rivers don't get born do they?"

"Naw. Ain't no such thing as a baby river."

"Sure they is. Ain't you never heard nobody talkin' 'bout 'The Mother of all Rivers'?"

"Yeah, an' Mama use to tell me 'bout 'Ole Man River.' Some song they use to sing an' play back when she knew Moses."

"Yo mama never knew Moses."

"Did too. Daddy say she older 'n Moses an' meaner than Satan. Then he laugh."

"Be laughing while he runnin', he be my daddy an' call my mama that."

Mitch decided to refocus the attention of the group. "In order to get to know a river it's important to understand where she came from, where her roots are."

Nyla slapped Collin lightly on the shoulder and said, "First this river born, now it got roots. I don't think the man know what he talking about."

Collin saw a twinkle of . . . rage? hostility? irritation? How many synonyms for "anger" did she know? However many there were, they were there in Mitch's eyes. She'd seen it before when Pardner challenged him at breakfast the morning before. Maybe this class needed to come with a warning label: "No negative personal comments about the teacher." Actually for these kids it should read, "No dissing the man." Either way this could be trouble.

But Mitch managed to bury his wounded pride and told Nyla, "Oh, you'll be surprised all the things I know." Collin exchanged confused looks with Nyla; they both settled back in their seats leaving Mitch to himself.

The remainder of the two hour trek was spent in relative silence. Twice Mitch managed to brush Collin's knee while changing gears. The first time she ignored it; the second she debated, then suggested, "You know, it's pretty tight quarters up here. Can we move this water jug to the back? It would give me more space for my feet and you wouldn't be fighting my knees for fourth gear."

Mitch shook his head. "Sorry, Walker. Jug's full and there's no way to shift it while we're moving. Maybe after the rest stop up at the top of the ridge. It's only another ten miles or so."

Collin swung her knees as far to the right as she could manage, twisting them around and under. No possible chance encounter could be excused now. Mitch looked at her and shook his head, "Lady, you can't be comfortable like that."

Collin smiled. "I feel no pain, Mitch. Trust me."

The flash of excitement in his eyes was almost terrifying. He smiled and said, "No? None at all?"

Collin grinned without mirth. "When you're dead from the neck up you feel no pain."

From the back Niles called, "Yeah, but they say fear be all in your head. How that be, huh?" He nudged Ta'waan, and both boys began laughing.

In the mirror Collin saw Nyla's eyes boil. But before the girl could mount her attack Collin said softly, "Nyla, let it go. It doesn't bother me."

Nyla stared at Collin, studying her. After a few moments she nodded and settled back.

Mitch lay his hand on Collin's arm. There was concern in his voice as he asked, "Does he know how afraid of the river you are?"

Did anyone know how afraid of the river she was? Other than the Lord? Maybe one person and he was gone. Collin shook her head. "No. He knows I'm afraid; they all do. I told them."

"Did you tell them why?"

Collin thought, *"Afraid I told them something I haven't told you?"* Aloud she said, "No, I didn't. I have enough dreams about it without bringing it up voluntarily. I simply said I had a bad experience. That's all anyone needs to know." *"And more than I want to remember."*

Mitch rubbed her arm lightly. "I really could help you with that, Collin."

She disengaged his hand politely, patted it then said firmly but in a friendly manner, "No, Mitch. It will be fine, I'm telling you."

Mitch put his hand on her shoulder. "It'll destroy you, you know. Hiding fear inside. It will kill you."

Again Collin repositioned the errant hand and said, "I guess I'll have to take my chances. It's been a lot of years and I'm still breathing. Between the Lord and I, I think we've got it covered."

Bingo! The magic Word that stops most advances. Mitch turned away from her, looked in the mirror and called, "Another hour and we're there. Or we're at the parking lot. Then we've got a short climb and we'll be at the birthplace of our river and all its nightmare secrets." He grinned at Collin but said nothing further.

Collin repeated well-loved scriptures to herself, *"The Lord is on my side, I will not be afraid. What can a man do to me? The Lord is on my side as my helper."* Being away from the river made a difference. Being away from Jeff made a difference, too, but she refused to entertain that thought more than she had to. Content. Content. She was content.

The last distance was covered with only one final disruption. Ta'waan and Niles were jabbing each other in the ribs, whispering and laughing. Collin knew something was coming and could only guess whether she or Mitch was the target. Most likely herself. When their plans were finalized Ta'waan called out, "Hey, Mitch, you know the lady here afraid of the river?"

Mitch nodded. "Yeah, I knew. So what? Everyone's afraid of something."

Nyla drawled snidely, "Yeah, bro. Everyone 'fraid of something. Ask Niles. He know 'bout being afraid."

Niles said bitterly, "I ain't afraid of nothing. You be knowing that, sister. Of course I ain't saying you got nothing you 'fraid of." It was a threat, or as much of one as he could mount.

Collin started to intervene but Mitch cut her off. "No, that's where you're wrong. It's a proven fact. Everyone has fear of some kind." He looked in the mirror and called, "Hey, Chonnell what scares you? Things that go bump in the night? Monsters under your bed?"

Chon called back, "It's the monsters in the 'hood get me nervous. Pusher down on the corner: I seen how he got my sister hooked an' how he got her walking the street. I wonder if I got what I need not to get taken, too. That's the monster I worry 'bout."

Collin said softly, "That's not fear, Chon. That's good sense."

Pardner chimed in with a fear less intense but more communal. "I still don't like it when it get dark outside an' Mama done left the window shades open. Ain't never sure what be lookin' in."

Nyla nodded. "Yeah, I hate that, too."

Collin offered, "Open closet doors at night. Let's the bogey man out."

Niles hooted. "Bogey man?"

Nyla said dryly, "Yeah, you know. Kin to the ghost in the attic."

Ta'waan started to howl but Collin cut him short. "Be a real man, Ta'waan. Admit it. You've got things that scare you. Maybe it's your aunt Thelma's spinach pie. Or those bottlebrush kisses from Uncle Mo. 'Fess up, bro."

Ta'waan looked shocked. "How you know 'bout Aunt Thelma's spinach?" He remained staunch however. "Ain't scared of nothin'. Real man ain't scared of nothin'."

Mitch drawled, "Snakes? Ever been locked in a room with handful of hissing, slithering, agitated snakes?"

"Ain't gonna bother me. I'd stomp 'em."

"Ever seen a rat up close? Those beady little eyes staring you in the face?"

"I'd pitch him cross the room." There was the slightest decrease in Ta'waan's machismo level, however.

Despite the cries of "Yuk!" and "Stop!" from the junior contingent Mitch pressed forward. "What about pain? You afraid of a little pain?"

"That ain't being afraid. That being smart."

"Really? You telling me that holding your hand in the fire until the flesh starts to melt, and the skin crackles and the . . ."

Collin said sharply, "We get the picture, Mitch. Vividly." This game was getting decidedly ugly. And Mitch was enjoying it far too much. There was an unhealthy light in his eyes that Collin distrusted. Time to shift gears. Even if it meant sacrificing her knees. She stretched out slightly, drawing Mitch's attention from his imagery and asked in little girl plaint, "Are we there yet?"

Now *there* was a universal unknown they could all share. All seven crew members, regardless of age, race, or gender began to raise the calls of the parents'/bus drivers' worst nightmare: "We there yet?" "How long 'til we be there?" "I gotta go!" "He's touching me!" I wanna sit by the window!" "Aren't we ever going to be there?"

Collin kept a close eye on Mitch's face, especially on his eyes and the muscles of his jaw. But the catcalls seemed to bother him not at all. Indeed, he was humming to himself, smiling and chuckling. He looked happy and that bothered Collin. Not that she wanted him unhappy; an unhappy Mitch was hard enough to deal with. But a happy Mitch? Couldn't we have an in-between Mitch? A not too morose, not too sunny river boat captain? A . . .

The van jerked to a stop as Mitch yelled, "We're here!"

Collin looked around and asked, "Where?"

They were stopped in an abandoned parking lot, or "panoramic turnout", more likely. Mitch said, "From here we go on foot." He pointed to a ridge maybe two miles down and away from their present position. "Our river starts just over there. There's a fairly smooth trail so no one should have to work too hard getting there or back."

Mitch led out accompanied by Chonnell and Pardner. Ta'waan, Niles and Robbie held the middle ground while Collin and Nyla brought up the rear. Collin sensed the younger woman had something on her mind, but Collin wasn't going to begin to try to guess what it might be. They walked along in silence for several moments before Nyla broached the subject. "Lady, twice now when you talk about your brother you say you 'had' a brother. Like he gone or something. And you look sad when you say it. Your brother, is he dead?"

Collin took her time getting herself together then said quietly, "Yes."

Nyla refrained from the customary, but meaningless, "I'm sorry." After a moment she asked, "He been gone long?"

Collin smiled sadly, realized she was doing it then said, "Somewhere between twelve years ago and just yesterday."

"He older or younger?"

Collin hesitated then said softly, "Younger. By fifteen minutes. He was my twin, Nyla." Nyla stared at her, speechless, unable to process the information or the horror.

They were lagging behind slightly and from the head of the pack Mitch yelled, "Walker! Nyla!! Pick it up! Let's go!!"

Nyla snapped out of her nightmare then growled, "Someone need to shorten that dude."

Collin grinned. "You do, I'll watch."

Nyla's eyes took on a mischievious twinkle and she said slyly, "Yeah, I know how you is with a knife."

Collin swatted at her accuser but Nyla ducked out of range and trotted to catch up with her brother. Collin shook her head then followed suit, joining up with Robbie and Ta'waan. Collin noticed that Ta'waan's face looked a little pale, a little strained, a little, dare she say—fearful?—as he looked out and down the sheer cliffs. He was marching on the outside of the three abreast formation and was thus closest to the edge. To be sure there was a rock barrier wall, but it was slightly less than waist high and did nothing to obscure the view of how far down it was to the base of the ridge. Collin debated letting the boy suffer for his arrogance earlier. But an internal remembered rumble of her own fear put her in action. She called carefully, "Ta'waan, can I have the outside? I can't see over you. Tall people need to be in the middle."

Ta'waan looked at her and his face was a mixture of shame, gratitude and relief. But he said only, "Yeah, no problem."

Robbie looked at Collin, question in his eyes. After ten months, he'd learned to read both her eyes and her actions and would know there was purpose in her request. She held his eyes only momentarily: long enough to tell, not long enough to show. He nodded imperceptibly and she knew he knew.

The three walked on in silence for a few moments then Robbie said, his tone conversational, "You know, case worker lady, I been thinking 'bout all that fear stuff Mitch was throwin' 'round in the van. I figured out it's pretty easy to say you ain't scared of something you ain't never had to face, ain't it? When he asked Ta'waan 'bout them snakes I thought the same thing. I ain't afraid of no snakes. Ain't never seen one 'cept in the zoo and it was behind glass. How'm I gonna know what I's afraid of 'til it actually happens?"

Collin nodded. "Good point, little brother." It pleased her to watch Robbie's teaching technique. Pleased her more that Ta'waan was actually listening. Now if he actually learned from it, well . . .

Robbie continued almost as if Ta'waan weren't even there, "You afraid of the river but you got a reason. You been in the river, somethin' bad happened, an' now you afraid. That make sense." He stopped then admitted, "I use to be afraid Tulle's daddy would come back and finish what he promised." He looked at Ta'waan and said, "Tulle be my half brother. His daddy killed him and tried to kill my mama before the police killed him." Collin knew the history; knew that Robbie was leaving a great deal of the horror of that night out. She wondered that he would even bring it up. But he had his motives and Collin wasn't about to interfere.

Robbie sighed slightly, "Fact is I knowed he was dead, knowed he couldn't hurt me but I was still scared. Still am scared sometimes. Is that stupid?"

Collin kept her voice as gentle as she could without letting her voice crack. "No, Rob. That's not stupid at all. Whether you're afraid or not doesn't make you more or less of a man. It's what you do with the fear that makes the difference. I'm afraid of being stung. When a wasp or any other flying critter comes in the office do I run for the woman's room and hide until it's gone? Or do I kill it and get on with my day?"

Robbie grinned. "Don't know. What do you do?"

Life was returning to Ta'waan and he decided to jump in on this one. "She little white lady. She hide in the bathroom."

Collin smiled sweetly at Ta;waan and said, "Wrong! I get out the longest flyswatter I can find, or the bug spray, or Marne's hair spray and I kill the bugger. Scared or not I got work to do and I have to do it. I can't be ducking shadows all day long." She glared at them both and said, "Can't hide in the bathroom, either. If everyone that was scared was hiding in there it'd get mighty crowded."

They walked on some more then Ta'waan asked slowly, "So what if it's not something you can kill?"

Collin hesitated then said, "There was this summer, once, when I went out barefoot. There was this bank of flat rocks that had been baking in the sun all day. Didn't hurt when I started out walking on them, but by the time I got to the middle, I realized my feet were burning. There wasn't any place to get relief and no grown up in sight." *"Except the one that put you out there to begin with. But let's stick to the important part of the story."* Collin ignored the reminder and continued, "I had two choices that I knew of. The first was to flop down, cry, and wait to be rescued. And in the meantime even more of me would be getting burned and I'd be even more miserable. The second choice was to suck it up, keep walking, and no matter how it hurt, get it over with. The solution to fear is to face what you have to, avoid what you can, and get through it. I've been afraid of rivers, but since I haven't had to go on or near one, it hasn't been a problem. People that are afraid of heights shouldn't look down from tall buildings. But if they are ever in a place where they have to be up high someplace then they need to take a deep breath, let it out slowly, and keep doing whatever it is that brought them there."

The trio walked on in silence for a few moments until Ta'waan asked, "How old was you when you walked them rocks?"

"Ten."

"An' you walk on out?"

"Didn't see much choice."

"Where was your mama an' Daddy? Why couldn't you just call for them?"

Collin bit her lip then said, "My mom was dead by then. My father . . . my father was a whole different story. One which I'd rather not dig up." She smiled wanly and said, "Sort of like avoiding those fears if you can."

But Ta'waan couldn't let it go. "He mean to you?"

Collin closed her eyes as a series of descriptive flashbacks rolled past her consciousness. When the videos were finished Collin said, "You might say that."

And now Robbie jumped in, apparently realizing his case worker lady was opening up—or falling down, one of the two. In any event he asked, "You afraid of him?"

To which there was only one answer. One honest answer. "All the time. Every moment of my life I lived with him." *"Not living with him is no picnic, either. Knowing he's still out there, still trying to hurt us . . ."*

"How you live like that?"

"I wouldn't let him win. I wouldn't let the fear stop me from living, from going on, from trying. I would not give him that satisfaction." Collin shut down anything internal, refusing to debate, remember or otherwise continue the discussion. She looked pointedly at both boys and said firmly, "You make up your mind that whatever it is won't beat you and you go on."

"WALKER!!" Mitch thundered from his point position. "What is the matter with you, woman? This is only the head of the river not the river itself! If you're going to lag behind, at least let the kids get past you! I'd like to get back sometime tonight! Move it!!"

Collin smiled, waved, and under her breath muttered, "I'm gonna feed him to the grizzlies. So help me, before this trip is over, I'm going to feed him to the grizzlies."

Robbie said, "Uh, case worker lady, ain't no grizzlies . . ."

Collin cut him off. "I'll find some. I'll hire some. I'll buy some if I have to. I don't care if it's Smokey Bear, I will feed him to the bears."

Ta'waan grinned, "That I'd like to see."

Robbie slapped hands with him. "I'm with you, bro."

Collin grinned widely but only on the inside. A Southsider and an Eastender agreeing on something. Would the wonders of this camp never cease? Well, they would if the group didn't catch up to Mitch in short order. The mostly perverse side of her nature wanted to link arms with the boys and skip forward singing, *"We're off to see the Wizard . . ."* And while it might be fun, she was afraid a) the boys would fail to know what she was talking about, b) the choreography would fail and they would end up falling the remainder of the way to land at Mitch's feet or c) Mitch would fail to see the humor in any of the forgoing and would throw them all off the boat. No, she should play it straight. Collin smiled with genuine pleasure and said, "Let's go boys. We've got a river to birth."

With a little extra effort the front trio caught up to Mitch, followed almost immediately by the back duo. Mitch sneered, "Nice you could join us."

Collin smiled at Mitch and said, "It's too beautiful up here to walk fast, Mitch. We don't get to see mountains, much less be in them. Tallest thing out my window is a telephone pole. Or a billboard."

There was a chorus of general assent. Mitch sighed slightly then relented. "Okay, I forgot. It is beautiful up here. After we get our lesson in river origins you can climb around or look around if you like. But let's do what we came for first."

He led them to a point on the side of the hill where a small stream bubbled happily from between two boulders. Mitch explained, "This is an outlet for an underground lake somewhere deep inside the mountain. Water flows out but no faster than it is replenished." He pointed down the hillside and said, "You can follow the path down the hill as it curves to the left, there. It's pretty tame up here but it gathers speed as it goes down, picking up rocks and pebbles along the way. They scour out the creek bed and let the waters flow faster." He continued his lesson, "When the snows melt they not only feed the undergound lake but feed the stream as well, giving it volume. Smaller feeder streams join it near the bottom . . ." He pointed to the south end of the valley, ". . . over at Three Forks.

"From there it gathers steam with each thunderstorm that smashes through here. And we can have some storms, believe me." He smiled with fiendish pleasure and said, "And then is when you really want to be on the water. Spring is best for rafting but only for the experienced. This time of year the levels are down and the current slows considerably. Which is why you, my crew, are here now instead of then." He smiled then clapped his hands and said, "Okay, so much for the outside view. Now I want to take you to see that underground lake. There are caverns just over the point there where we can investigate a little. You should enjoy this. I know I do."

Something in his eyes bothered Collin. Of course there wasn't much about Mitch that didn't bother Collin but that was beside the point. The idea of actually walking underground, in the dark, with him behind her was a daunting thought. And one which she absolutely was not going to allow. As the group tramped back up the hill, over the hill, and back down the other side, Collin slipped forward to walk with Chonnell and Pardner. After further consideration she called back, "Nyla, come join the female contingent. Girls against the guys." Which was the story of a lifetime.

Nyla skipped forward happily, put an arm around Collin's waist and murmured, "Safety in numbers?"

Collin murmured back, "You got it, girlfriend."

If Nyla objected to the term she didn't show it. Instead she tousled Chonnell's hair and said, "We teach you two how it be. Us women got to stick together."

Collin grinned and added, "Until we find a man of our own, and then it's every woman for herself."

Nyla laughed out loud, then repeated, her eyes shining, "You got it, girlfriend."

They reached the entrance to the caverns and Collin found to her relief that it wasn't the hole she had been anticipating. It was a state run "tourist site," for want of a better expression. Mitch went to the head of the line, showed his Camp Grace ID and the group was passed through without comment. Other than the customary "Welcome," of course.

The tour itself was professionally guided. The group walked along narrow, but roped, passageways, squeezed through even more narrow passageways between massive boulders, slid under boulders, around boulders, between boulders . . . all to reach a limestone cavern somewhere near the heart of the hill. Lights along the way bounced crystal reflections of light off the ceilings and floors, reflecting in small pools of silent mineral waters.

When the group was fully assembled, and as the guide was describing the difference between stalactites and stalagmites, Collin's mind began to wander, again. As usual. As always.

The guide recited, "Stalactites are formed first, by water laden with lime and salt dripping from the ceilings of the cavern. Stalagmites form from stalactites, and are on the floors of the cavern. When the two grow together we call it a column."

"Hey! Hey, everybody!!! I got it! I got it!! Stalactites come first. And they come first in the alphabet. Now we can remember which is which! I got it!"

Internally Collin sighed. Okay, so it wasn't of earth shaking significance. But it solved a problem she'd always wondered about. You take your pleasures where you can.

The guide was still talking, pointing out the beauty of the caverns, the salt formations, the cascading waterfalls. He looked around and smiled. "Yes, it's one of the remarkable wonders in this area. But remember, this is not what the explorers saw when they discovered this place. Their first glimpse was far different."

With that he plunged the cavern into utter darkness; darkness you can touch and feel. There were several screams and Collin felt several small arms grab her from all sides. She whispered, "Close your eyes. Just close your eyes. It'll be over in a minute."

The guide chuckled and just as quickly the lights returned. He said, "Until they were able to light up the cave all this beauty was wasted on the night. It took man to open it up for all to enjoy."

Chonnell whispered to Collin, "Bet God enjoyed it 'fore man got here. He don't need no lights."

Collin hugged the child quickly and whispered, "Bet you're right."

The tour concluded with a walk around the underground lake, large enough to row across, or maybe even float their raft. It was impressive. Collin decided much—not all, but much—of Mitch's sins could be forgiven for bringing them here. Here again was something the city-dwelling campers and their counselor might otherwise never experience. For that, Mitch was to be thanked. Of course, maybe she would wait until the trip was over. Or maybe the week was over. Maybe she'd send him a letter after she got back to Oakton. Maybe . . .

"WALKER!!" Collin snapped out of it, to find herself the loose caboose on the train and the rest of it had left the station. Mitch berated her angrily, "What is it with you? Are we boring you? Not good enough for your company? Not interesting enough to merit your attention? Explain yourself!!"

Collin shook her head to clear the cobwebs then said evenly, "I can't explain, Mitch. It's a character defect. I lose touch with reality sometimes."

"Sometimes?? Walker, you haven't been in touch with reality since you got off the bus! I swear I ought to slap you on permanent shore duty and relieve the crew of your influence!"

Collin studied Mitch a moment trying to read the man's eyes. There was an almost hysterical light in them, far out of proportion to the crime. Did he want her to grovel for forgiveness? Expect her to beg to be allowed to stay? Was this a bid to regain power in the kids' eyes? Collin debated, then said slowly, "I apologize for my lack of attentiveness, Mitch. I don't deliberately tune out. Being near the river has me unbalanced and it's a defense mechanism my brain uses."

Mitch looked fascinated. "Defense mechanism? Defense against what?"

Collin shrugged. "Pain. Fear. Memories. It's sort of an all-purpose tool." She hesitated then said evenly, "I promise I will do all I can to stay with the class, mentally and physically. I admit I've been a little worse today than before . . ." *"A little??"* ". . . but I'll pull it together. I promise. Write today off as an aberration. I'll be better tomorrow." She adopted a sober, solemn, sincere affect and waited for Mitch's decision. The man glared at her angrily. Collin guessed that wasn't the response he expected or wanted. But there it was, and he would have to deal with it.

After a moment the glare disappeared, to be replaced by an expression of measured interest. He said faintly, "Defense mechanism, huh? Maybe we can test it some more sometime before the week is over. See just how good it really is."

Collin sensed the challenge, or maybe more correctly put, the threat. Two worlds collided in her brain: *"Take him. You know you can. Take him." "Don't be a fool. Sure, you can take him but what do you prove? You can hold out in a test of stamina? He already knows that. You don't show pain? You know how that game ends up. Just smile, say, 'Maybe.' and leave it at that. Be smart. Be sane. Be anything but stupid. For once. Please."*

Collin smiled at Mitch and said demurely, "Maybe." And without further comment she hustled to join her crew.

The trip home went without event. As they pulled into the camp parking lot at the end of the day Mitch instructed everyone, "We meet early tomorrow. Six a.m. at the boat house."

Rob groaned; Ta'waan protested, "What about breakfast? Cafeteria don't even open until then!"

Pardner and Chonnell joined the chorus, "Yeah! What about breakfast? When we gonna eat?"

Before mutiny could ensue Mitch said quickly, "It will be open! I promise you. I'll get special permission for you to go in early. Would I let my crew starve? Come on, people. You've got to learn to trust me."

Pacified, the crew grumbled and mumbled out of the van back to the lodge. Collin had the distinct feeling there would be an attempt to double up on dinner in case Mitch failed of his word. Hope the cooks were ready! Collin climbed out of the van and said, "Thanks, Mitch. I enjoyed today."

Mitch swung out of the van and said, "Hold up a minute." Collin had a feeling what was coming next and took a slow, deep breath, letting it out equally slowly. Patience and tact. Patience and tact. "*Lord, provide the tact, please, and I know better than to pray for patience."*

Mitch waited until the kids had cleared off a respectable distance then said, "It really was a good idea telling the crew you were afraid. I'm a firm believer in getting everything out in the open. No secrets."

Collin nodded. "Right. No secrets."

"Then you'll share why you're so afraid. You don't have to tell the crew and I certainly won't say anything. But we need to get this out in the open."

Inwardly Collin sighed. This was definitely getting old. Maybe she should make up something. Something sufficiently horrid that would keep him happy. Instead she said firmly, "Mitch, what it was really doesn't matter. What matters is that I'm here. Against all odds I'm still here. And with your help I intend to stay here."

Mitch's face brightened. "So you're really going to stick it out?"

"As long as I can. Rob really seems to want me to stay, so I'm going to give it my best shot."

Mitch smiled broadly. "That's great. That's wonderful. That means you get the chance to get to know me better. You'll find out I'm not a bad guy after all." Again his hand was on her shoulder.

Collin slipped out from under it and said, "I already know what kind of guy you are, Mitch." She kept her tone light and friendly. "You're a terrific person and you're great with the kids."

"So you'll have dinner with me? I'll take you somewhere in town, away from all the distractions. It'll do you good to get away from all the kids."

She shook her head. "I can't, Mitch. Not at night. The kids are why I'm here. They're my job, my responsibility."

"Other counselors leave. I think you're the only one that hasn't left for at least a few hours."

Collin knew that to be untrue but didn't make an issue of it. "I can't speak for anyone but myself, Mitch. I have a duty to uphold."

Mitch scoffed. "Oh, right. Duty. Give me a break, woman."

Collin shrugged. "It's who I am."

Mitch argued, "No, it's not. I've watched you. I've seen you clowning around with these kids. You know how to play, how to have a good time. That's all I'm offering you, Collin. The chance to have a good time. To relax, get away and have a good time the way adults do. We really could have a good time together, you know."

Mitch's voice was dropping lower and softer and Collin decided enough was enough. She said evenly, "Mitch, I like you. But that's as far as it goes. I'm not up for anything but friendship with you or anyone else. My life is too complicated as it is."

Mitch wasn't listening. He moved closer to Collin and whispered, "Even friends can have a good time, Collin."

He reached out for her; Collin side stepped him and said sternly, "Not like that. The answer is no, Mitch."

It stopped him cold. He looked at her, uncomprehending. "No?" He repeated it for clarification. "No?"

Collin wanted to turn and run but experience told her to wait on resolution if possible. Otherwise they come after you when you're not looking for them. At least here he was standing in front of her where she could see him. She repeated, "If we can be friends, great. You're my teacher and I enjoy sitting in your class. I enjoy listening to your stories. You're a great guy, Mitch. You'll be a great guy for someone else. But not me. You deserve better."

Mitch stared at her then said slowly, "You're probably right. I do deserve better than you."

Collin nodded, not about to argue to the contrary for ego's sake. "And I hope you find her soon."

Mitch nodded. "I'm sure I will. I'm sure I will." He looked at Collin and actually smiled. "Thank you, lady. Thank you."

Collin distrusted the voice and the eyes but said, "Glad I could help. I'll see you in the morning, Mitch." She turned and walked off towards the lodge, half expecting Mitch to come running after her. But the man evidently had better things to do . . . or other irons in the fire . . . or other fish to fry . . . or other eggs . . . Collin shook her head violently to derail the running commentary. She hated when her brain went off like that. Maybe she could find a maintenance man to fix it. Maybe she could find a maintenance man to fix a lot of things that were wrong in her life. Maybe she had already found a maintenance man . . . Collin shook her head, pounded it sharply and muttered, "Quit that!!" She pulled open the door to the lodge and stepped inside.

Dinner over, what there was of it considering her lack of appetite, Collin found she couldn't get settled. Like a dog with an itch it can't scratch, or a bear with a bee in its bonnet, or a . . . Collin smacked her head lightly. "Quit that!" Neither the verandah, nor the library, nor the comfort of her own quarters seemed to satisfy her. She knew what it was she wanted but couldn't have. Well, maybe Rob could help her out. She went down to the game room and found Rob noisily playing video games with a mob of campers. He was the center of focus as he revealed move after move designed to beat the enemy in pompous fashion. She heard one camper say, his voice incredulous, "Jeff taught you that? The janitor taught you that? Janitors ain't cool, man."

Rob said hotly, "Don't matter what a man do on the outside, dude, long as it's honest. It's what he got on the inside makes him cool. And Jeff is one cool dude. Watch this."

Collin slipped quietly back out of the room. Rob was better off here. Somehow he was learning. And now even passing it on to others. That was cool. Too cool. Way cool.

Collin sighed. Which cool though it was, it didn't solve her restlessness problem. Maybe a walk. Maybe a run. Maybe not. There were no lighted paths outside. Only the lodge had perimeter lights and walking around and around the lodge was not Collin's idea of relaxing. The only other outside lighted area she knew of was the basketball court. She could go up there, shoot a few hoops, practice a few moves, maybe dream a little . . .

Collin didn't waste time finishing the thought but headed back to her room. She changed into her sweats, grabbed her ball and headed towards the court. Physical exercise, that's what she needed. Yeah, right.

The glow from the lodge provided enough illumination to reach the court without difficulty. Collin snapped on the court lights, set the timer and slowly began dribbling up and down the court. Somehow it wasn't nearly as satisfying as she had hoped it would be. Nor nearly as reminiscent of yesterday. Maybe she should work a little harder. Harder, that was the answer. That was always the answer. Don't understand a problem? Work harder. Can't get the hang of something? Work harder. Falling behind? Work harder. Don't ask for help, don't look for excuses, don't try to analyze the situation, just work harder. The old familiar demons began whispering in her mind, *"Harder. Work harder. You're only afraid because you're not working hard enough. You should have stayed at work. You never work hard enough. You're out here playing. You should be back at home working harder. How will you ever please anyone if you don't work harder? Work harder. Work harder."*

Collin began to pound the ball against the blacktop as anger and frustration built in her. She began jogging around the court, running laps as she dribbled. The demons continued to hound her, echoes of her father's voice. *"Harder. Work harder. You're a girl, a worthless girl. You want to win? You want to be as good as your brother? Work harder. Harder. Harder. You can't cry. You don't have time to cry. You have to work harder."*

The laps were going faster now, the ball rising and falling with each step. And still the demons mocked, *"You'll never be anything. You're a girl. A worthless girl. Girls don't know how to work hard. Your brother would have worked hard. Your brother would have made something of himself. Something to be proud of. But not you. You don't know anything about working hard. You want love? You want respect? Work hard. Harder. Harder. And know that no matter how hard you work it will never be hard enough. Never be hard enough. Never . . . ."*

Collin made no sound as she ran. Her teeth were clenched, her face devoid of emotion. Run. Run. Don't stop or they'll catch you. Run. Run. Harder. Harder. Run. Run . . .

Collin pulled up abruptly and shouted, "No! I will not run anymore." She began moving again at a slow jog, trying to cool down. The voices in her head continued to jeer and mock but she ignored them. Couldn't silence or block them out completely, but could ignore them. She bounced the ball slowly, keeping pace with her steps. She whispered, "I did work hard. I did everything you asked me to do. I just couldn't be Erin. Erin couldn't even be Erin for you." Her paced slowed to a walk, then to a halt. She turned and faced to the west, looking in the direction of the lodge but seeing a distant mile beyond it. The lights on the timer went out but Collin didn't move. Darkness did not bother her. The glow of the lodge was sufficient to navigate home. She stood on the hill and said tightly, "I wanted to love you, Dad. But you wouldn't let me. I tried, I really tried." *"But did you try hard enough?"* Collin looked up at the stars and asked, for neither the first nor the last time, "What else could I do?" She wanted to cry, needed to cry. But no tears came; there were none left and she'd been forbidden their comfort long years ago. The deep silence of the heavens was her only answer. Collin dropped her head in defeat, acknowledging once again the futility of the inquiry. She closed her eyes and stood motionless.

From nowhere an explosion went off in her brain as someone or something struck her from behind. She dropped to her knees, unable to react or respond. Another blow hit her in the back and she curled to the ground. A frantic voice in her head urged her, *"Roll right! Roll right!!"* Collin responded out of instinct, barely dodging the kick aimed for her head. The dust settled in Collin's mind; she forced herself to think. While she ducked blows, of course. Her assailant was dressed all in black—gee, really?—was taller than herself and outweighed her by a lot. She would stop and assess his dimensions later; for now, survival dictated ignoring the minutiae. Collin rolled to her feet, keeping the attacker between herself and the lodge in order to see him. Easier said than done: the man was determined to remain incognito. He grabbed her arms; she grabbed his. They grappled together for a moment then in one smooth motion Collin twisted, stepped back, ducked and threw the man over her head. She was rewarded with a sharp "crack" as his head hit the pavement, and a loud "oof" as the oxygen exited his lungs.

Collin didn't hang around to pat herself on the back. She crouched low and ran, knowing that the light ahead was both worst enemy and best friend. At the hill's crest she slid flat to the left, knowing better than to make a straight run for cover. She listened for the thud of her assailant's feet but heard nothing. Collin risked a very quick look over her shoulder and saw the man outlined against the sky. His step was light, nimble even. A chill ran through her as Collin realized with that inside/outside other sense that this was not a first-time venture for the man. She left all further contemplation for a later date and continued moving as silently as possible to her left, angling away from the lights of the lodge. The hill bottomed out then rose gently again, forming a narrow creek bed. Collin knew if she could gain the far shoulder she would be invisible to the menace above her. But to cross was to risk detection by sound. The "I can't see you, so you can't see me" theory of defense was tempting, but not an option. Did muggers carry flashlights? The idea seemed highly incongruous with a man dressed in black pants, black shirt, wearing a black mask and gloves. The man hesitated at the top of the hill as if unsure how or if to proceed. Collin wished on him all the mental confusion and uncertainty she could. Maybe he could take some of her own.

As she took stock of the situation she realized that the lodge doors were still open. Well and fine and good for her. But not good for the young campers she could hear laughing and talking. Sound carried far in thin air. If she broke for the lodge, what would prevent Master Monster from abandoning her as prey and choosing someone less feisty? Not acceptable. She wished desperately to know what time it was. The doors would be locked at 10:30 with all campers accounted for. Counselors were exempt from head counts. Too bad.

Collin looked back up the hill and realized she'd lost track of her opponent. Great. She carefully picked up a handful of stones and prepared to throw them as a diversionary tactic. But where to throw them? Was he stupid enough to fall for the oldest trick in the book or would he head the opposite direction, knowing it was a ruse? Did she really have time for a prolonged debate? She strained her senses to pick up any sign of the man but received nothing. He could be gone for all she knew. Except for the prickling of the hair on the back of her neck, and the twisting of her gut. Collin drew in a silent breath then threw the stones as hard and in as wide a pattern as she could. At the same time she leaped across the creek and began running hard to the right.

The stones made effective sonar. The thuds off the grass were muted and gentle. It was the thuds off a padded object a mere two feet or so away that caused her heart to surge. Any pretense at strategy disappeared and Collin headed for a line of trees. She could still hear the voices of campers, clearly indicating roll call had not yet been enforced. How many were out there? Enough to be a deterrent or just enough to be an invitation? Could she risk it? Could she live with herself if she were wrong? Could she live if she didn't?

Too many questions and no time to answer them. Collin dashed between the trees seeking cover in the brush. She made herself as small as possible then waited. Her lungs burned but she couldn't risk the gasp for air that might reveal her position. Slow, small breaths weren't getting it, though. As silently as she could she drew in a deep breath, willing herself to exhale slowly, quietly, ever so slowly, ever so quietly . . .

But not quietly enough. A strong hand slammed down on her shoulder, jerked her to her feet then swung her hard into the nearest tree. Collin felt the rough bark tear at her cheek and tasted blood. Now for it. She grabbed the tree, arresting his swing with a whiplash stop that tore her free of his grasp. Before he could react she ducked back past him, sliding through the trees and back out into the open. It was "tag" with a vengeance; a "catch me if you can" dance that Collin wasn't sure she could sustain. She could hear the man crashing out of the trees, discarding all pretense of stealth. Okay, cat and mouse was officially over. Time for scared bunny rabbit and big bad grizzly bear. Speed was Collin's only hope, and that was slim to none. But with fear came added adrenaline and Collin began drawing on it now. She managed to stay far enough ahead of her attacker to be out of reach, but not let him lose interest and look for an easier target. Collin prayed frantically, "Ring the bell, please. Ring the bell. Get those kids inside."

Finally, blessedly, the bell rang. Collin stumbled in relief, dropped to her knees and reversed her field. All she could think of now was getting to the safety of the lodge. But even as she reached the courtyard, again a rock hard fist pounded into her back. Stunned, she sank to the ground, unable to offer any semblance of resistance. Several sharp kicks connected with her ribs, her jaw, her chest. Collin closed her eyes and prayed softly, "Oh, dear Lord, help me." She waited for the finishing blow, hearing the man's labored breathing as he loomed over her.

But instead of striking her the man picked up her right hand. He held it gently, almost tenderly, petting and stroking it. Collin opened her eyes to watch in fascination as the man kissed each finger, one at a time, kissed the palm of her hand, then wrapped his hand around hers. He squeezed her hand lightly, as between friends, then lay her hand at her side, palm down. He patted it gently, stood up, then in one vicious movement drove his heel full force into her hand, grinding it into the pavement for effect. Collin groaned slightly but did not cry out. In silence the attacker turned and walked away, disappearing back into the blackness.

Collin was stunned, grasping for reason in a world gone insane. What under God's heaven had that been all about? Collin gasped for air, trying to clear her head. Who was that? Did she really want to know? Did she need to know? Did she care? The answer to that one was easy: yes. Was he just an opportunist, a vulture waiting on available prey? Or was he some kind of stalker who had somehow selected her as his target? Collin pulled herself painfully to her feet cradling her crushed hand against her waist. She aimed for the side door nearest her room to avoid detection. She didn't want to answer questions until she had time to think. If she could. She was weak, her head was swimming and she felt nauseous. She stopped twice to let her head and stomach settle before gaining the entrance. Gratefully it was unlocked.

The lights were still on in the corridor but it was presently deserted. Collin could hear the hum of the music from the campers' rooms, meaning everyone was home but not asleep. She used the wall for support and managed to reach her room without incident. Opening the door was another matter, however. As she lowered the injured right hand it began to throb wickedly. She quickly raised it back up again and went with the left hand. She had trouble keying the lock but was eventually able to reverse her thinking enough to open the door. Collin stepped inside, closed the door behind her, leaned against it and slowly slid to the floor. It felt good just to sit and rest. Maybe she could sit here the rest of the night. Or the rest of the week.

Three pieces of paper were scattered on the floor beside her: phone messages that had been slipped under the door. All three from Jeff, she noted. She looked at the times idly; saw that one had been placed around noon. The second had been received around 6 pm and the third less than half an hour ago. However good the man was at everything else, his timing was lousy. Where had she been half an hour ago?

Fighting the mystery monster. Collin drew in a sharp breath. Oh, yeah. Him. Something had to be done about him. But without endangering the kids or causing a panic. There was too much good going on here to want it shut down by some psycho with a finger fetish. As long as he left the kids alone she could deal with him on her own and no one need be bothered. But was that the answer? How did she know he wouldn't pick a different target tomorrow night? Or tonight? No, Collin felt certain the man was done for the day. Whatever sick pleasure he got from his attacks he'd accomplished already.

She had to think. If she went to the police they might shut the camp down. Worse, how would the kids react to a police presence? It would be no different than home, and that's what they were trying to change. All the good they were striving for could vanish. Look at Rob. He was turning into an actual leader out there. She couldn't take a chance on blowing this for him.

But could she take the chance that the monster might choose another victim? What if she didn't report it, and the next time he did more than just play patty cake? Could she live with herself then?

The argument kept running in circles, getting nowhere. She needed a neutral, outside source to help her. Which left Jeff out even had he been here. But the Camp Director: Steve Parks. Jeff had said he was a godly man: objective, unbiased. He wouldn't want negative publicity for his camp, to be sure, but publicity over a mugger was far less damning than over a murderer or child molester. He'd know what to do if anyone did. Question was, how did she contact him? While having his number was all well and good, what she didn't have was a phone. Camp Grace, in its infinite knowledge, had seen fit not to put phones in the rooms, and cell phones had to be left at home or surrendered on arrival. Wise move on their part she might add. Which was also well and good, but left Collin with the question, how do I contact Steve Parks? Hoping he would merely drop by was tempting but hardly in the realm of reality. Teleportation was also not a viable option. Could win her fame and fortune if she pulled it off . . . She was getting punchy she could tell. The only true answer was to walk to the message center and use the phone there. Painful as it might be, she had to get up, clean up and walk to the message center.

Collin grit her teeth, clenched her jaws, sucked it in, held her breath . . . and still didn't move. This was going to hurt. Slowly and carefully Collin began inching up the door, rising almost to a standing position. She maneuvered her way to the sink, looked in the mirror and felt her stomach lurch. She hadn't realized one tree could do so much damage. If he'd have picked a birch tree it wouldn't be so bad. Or an aspen, even. Did they have aspen trees in West Virginia? Did it really matter?

Collin grabbed a hand towel, soaked it in warm water then applied it to her face. She groaned in pain and felt her knees shake. Steady there, mates. Hang on to it. Again her stomach lurched, but as she knew there was nothing in there to lose, she ignored it. Collin pulled the towel away without scrubbing, trying to peel away the dirt and debris without disturbing the rest of the damaged area. She rinsed the towel and reapplied it a second time, repeating the process twice more after that before she settled for what she got. The hand was going to be more difficult to deal with. It was going to take some professional help. She wrapped it as tightly as she could stand then fashioned a sling from a spare shirt. She brushed the dirt, dust, twigs and leaves out of her hair and off her clothing, gingerly pulled a hat over her head and straightened up slightly. This was as good as it got, folks. Anything internal would have to wait for attention. Collin headed out of the room, down the corridor, and away to the message center.

She stopped twice to simply lean against a wall and catch her breath, letting the waves of pain and nausea subside. Her head throbbed and her vision blurred constantly. What should have taken five minutes took nearly twenty but she made it. The phone was in a locked cabinet but counselors were privileged to receive the pushbutton combination. Collin pulled Steve Parks' phone number from her pocket, opened the cabinet then stopped. What could she say? How could she tell him there was a psycho loose in paradise without eliciting panic or worse yet, disbelief? Collin stared at the phone then prayed softly, "Help me do this your way, Lord. I'm convinced calling Director Parks is the right first step. Please help me know what to say from there. I don't want to ruin what you're doing with the kids or with me. I still don't want to ride the river but I still want to do your will in all of this. Help me make the right choices, please."

She felt the slightest modicum of peace rise in her, along with the slimmest sense that yes; she was on the right path. All this amid the cacophony of voices in her head that shrilled she was wrong, had been wrong, would always be wrong . . . Collin ignored the choir and dialed. She assumed at this hour of the night—the clock on the counter said it was after eleven—that she would get an answering machine or voice mail of some kind. She was wrong.

On the third ring a strong male voice said, "Parks residence. May I help you?"

Collin hesitated then said as evenly as possible, "Director Parks, this is Collin Walker, one of the counselors with the group at Camp Grace. I spoke to you on Sunday afternoon." Collin hoped he would remember her but not the reason for the talk. She pushed ahead, "I hate to call you this late but it's important that I speak to you." She managed to get that much out without breaking down. So far so good.

There was only the slightest pause then he said, "Collin Walker, right. I remember you. Didn't you sign up for the white water rafting? You're the one Jeff has been talking about. Quite highly, I might add."

Oh he has, has he? About what? Collin let that train whistle on down the tracks without stopping and said, "Is it possible to meet with you tonight?" She noted a tremble making an appearance in her voice and hoped he didn't.

His voice took on some concern as he asked, "Is it that critical?"

Collin admitted slowly, "I'm not sure and that's why I need to address it with you."

"Does it concern the safety of Camp Grace or its guests?"

How to answer that? Yes? No, except maybe for one? She hesitated then admitted shakily, her voice slipping out of her control, "I don't know. It could."

Parks asked carefully, "Ms. Walker, are you all right? Where are you?"

Collin took a few slow breaths, got her voice back under submission and said, "I will be. I'm at the message center."

"My office is directly across the hall. We can be there in twenty minutes. Do I need to call the police?"

Collin said quickly, "No." She tempered it, "Not yet. Not until I talk to you."

"Are you in danger?"

"No. Not now. Neither is anyone else, sir." Her knees began to quiver. Collin pulled as much of herself together as possible, then said, "Twenty minutes will be fine. I'll be waiting in front of your office."

"No, go on in. Combination is 6351. We'll be there as quick as we can."

The line went dead. Collin stared at it, trying to decide what she'd done. The man didn't sound panicked, just terribly concerned. Which was the effect Collin wanted. She hung up the phone, closed the cabinet and hobbled over to the Director's office. She keyed the combination then went inside. Collin bypassed the receptionist's office, decided against Leeann's area and went straight to the Director's inner sanctum. It was neither swanky nor austere but had the look of an office where someone actually worked. Sort of like hers, but larger and more organized. Much more organized. Extremely more . . .

Never mind. Collin tried to sink down in one of the leather chairs in the corner, but found the position uncomfortable, lacking in support for all the places that currently needed or wanted support. She went for the old reliable standby: she slipped to the floor and curled up in her tortured beach ball routine, the one Jeff had objected to two nights ago. Or maybe it was three. She couldn't sort out time. Whatever it was, she would straighten out before the Director and whoever his "we" was arrived. Collin dropped her head to her knees and decided to rest for a few precious minutes. As ragged as she felt, there was no danger of going to sleep and missing their arrival. She would hear them coming in, she knew.

Or thought she knew. Someone was shaking her gently, calling, "Ms. Walker, Ms. Walker. Steve, she's in here. On the floor. That's why you missed her." A woman's voice insisted, "Ms. Walker, Ms. Walker. Can you hear me?"

Collin woke groggily, raised her head slowly and looked into the face of a horrified woman. Middle aged, but one of those active, young at heart, doer-not-a-watcher kinds of people. Collin guessed she might be Mrs. Parks and that her expression was a reaction to Collin's face. Collin swallowed and said, "It looks worse than it is."

The woman said softly, "Child, have you seen how it looks?" She helped Collin to her feet and into one of the chairs then called sharply, "Steve, in here. And call for the squad."

Collin protested urgently, "No!! That's not necessary, really. I'll be fine."

Steve Parks walked in, took one look at Collin and started to dial. Collin insisted, "Please, not yet. Help me figure out what's going on, first. Please."

Steve looked at Collin, looked at his wife, looked back at Collin then laid his phone down on the desk. He pulled a chair up so he could sit in front of Collin, pulled one up for his wife beside of Collin, waited until she was seated then sat himself and said, "Tell us what happened."

Collin leaned back in the chair, pulled her feet up, closed her eyes and tried to relate without emotion the events of the past hours. It was tough not to let the pain and fear color the retelling, but she worked hard to be objective. As she finished, she looked up at the Parks' to see if they believed her.

Mrs. Parks' face was a dark mask of anger and revulsion. Steve's face was totally unreadable, impassive. He picked up his phone and without a word to Collin dialed a number. Someone answered; he said, "Maggy, Steve Parks. Let me speak to the Sheriff, honey. Get him out of bed. Yes, it's that critical. Yes, I'll wait." By way of answer to his wife's look of surprise Steve said, "Maggy came home from college yesterday just for a visit. Be here to the end of the week. I told Angel we'd be by tomorrow to see her."

Collin wanted to cry. Here we are transacting neighborhood business in the middle of a phone call about a monster loose in our midst. This place was not part of the real world.

Someone apparently came on the line. Steve looked back at the phone and said, "Bo. The Handyman's back . . . Yeah, I'm sure . . . No, this isn't a copycat. It's him. Too many details . . . yeah, I know. I have the victim. Shaken up, but she insists she's fine." Steve glanced at Collin and his gaze was firm. "I'm not buying it, so you might have a medic on hand." Collin sighed slightly. Steve finished up, "We'll be there in half an hour. Right. Bye." Steve hung up, and stood staring at the phone.

Collin asked carefully, "Will someone let me in on the secret?" She looked from Mr. to Mrs., neither of which would meet her gaze directly.

Steve finally ventured an explanation. "You've been the unfortunate recipient of the third attack by our local horror legend, the Handyman. Three years ago in June he attacked a college senior, a lovely young girl named Melissa Raimey. Two years ago July it was Laura Mars, a member of the local community who worked at the stables for the summer. Last year he gave us a break and we thought it was over. Now this."

"And all the attacks were the same?"

Steve nodded. "Identical. Locations were different but the end result was the same."

Collin asked, "Were the girls hurt? Did they give a description the police could use? Was anyone ever arrested?" She could feel frustration rising in her. "What happens next? Does he come back or is this it? Did either of the girls ever see him again?"

Both Steve and his wife exchanged meaningful glances Collin could read all too well and wished she hadn't. Steve cleared his throat and said, "No one is sure, Ms. Walker."

Collin interrupted, "Please, make it Collin."

Steve said, "Collin, then. And we should be going. Let me help you up."

Collin accepted his arm gladly and found herself putting more weight on him than she had intended. But between the two of them, she managed to rise. Walking was tough, but with Steve's help she managed a semblance of a normal gait. As they left the lodge Collin asked, "Why doesn't anyone know? Couldn't the girls tell anyone? What . . ."

Steve interrupted and said quietly, "The girls were badly shaken from the initial attack and weren't able to tell the police much. Melissa disappeared the next day. Sheriff's deputies found her body a week later, missing the right hand."

Collin swallowed hard trying to control the revulsion and fear that was threatening to turn itself into a massive fit of hysteria. She steadied her voice and asked, "Laura Mars?"

"She left a note saying she was going to her uncle's. She never arrived."

Collin closed her eyes. "They found her when?"

The trio reached the car. Collin and Mrs. Parks climbed in the back seat while Steve drove. Mrs. Parks draped a blanket around Collin's shoulders, tucking it in tightly around her. Collin repeated her question. "How long before they found her?"

Mrs. Parks said softly, "They never did. A hand was delivered by mail to her parents with her rings and bracelets still in place."

Collin opened her eyes, asked, her voice hollow, "Left hand?"

"I honestly don't know."

Collin sat frozen in place, feeling a sense of numbness, followed by an even stronger sense of outrage. This had to stop. Whoever the monster was he had to be stopped. Deadly calm rose in her, along with the complete certainty that this was why she was here. She asked, "What do we do now?"

Steve jerked around and looked quickly at her before refocusing on the road ahead of him. "There's no 'we' here, Ms . . . Collin. This is a matter for the Sheriff to handle. I don't believe you'll be involved beyond giving your statement to the authorities."

Collin started to shake her head but immediately decided against it. Rattle no brain cells unnecessarily, if you please. Instead she said firmly, "I am involved. He chose me for whatever twisted reason he has.

I've seen him. I know his type. And I'm not innocent and trusting like his other victims." She shivered slightly then shivered again with more force. The macho speech would go over better if she could stop shaking so violently.

Mrs. Parks tucked the blanket in more closely and said softly, "Let the men hunt this animal, dear. It's what they do."

Collin whispered, "I've got to try. He's killed two people. I won't let him make it three. I've got to help. I've got to." She had to stop shaking, too, but that wasn't happening either. Collin closed her eyes and willed her body to relax. Some of the parts complied; most laughed hysterically. Collin grit her teeth and tried again. "*Relax . . . relax . . . I said, relax!!!"*

The car swung into the Sheriff's station and pulled to a stop in front of the door. Steve got out, let his wife out then helped Collin exit the vehicle. She started to offer the blanket back to Mrs. Parks but the woman refused it. Instead she wrapped it around Collin's shoulders and said, "Keep it, dear. It can be chilly in there."

Collin didn't know if there was a double meaning in the woman's words but said gratefully, "Thanks." Steve assisted Collin up the ramp into the building. Collin noted with grim satisfaction that she was walking just a tad more under her own power. Maybe some of the shock was wearing off. Good.

A uniformed man in his early sixties met them in front of the check-in counter. Balding on top, bulging slightly in the middle, Sheriff Bo Lodi looked the epitome of the bumbling backwoods law enforcement caricature. But the hard eyes and the grim set of the mouth vanquished any such foolish misconceptions. Steve made the briefest of introductions: "Sheriff Bo, this is Collin Walker. Collin, Sheriff Bo Lodi."

Collin indicated her crushed hand and said, "Forgive me the amenities, Sheriff."

Bo eyed Collin up and down, measuring her for . . . what? Veracity? Stability? Sorry 'bout that, Chief. Courage? Collin wasn't sure what the measuring rod was for, nor what the standard of approval was. She held his gaze evenly, neither cowering nor attacking. After a moment he nodded a trace and Collin guessed she had passed the initial test, whatever it meant. Bo looked to Steve and asked, "So you really think it's him?"

Steve said, "Listen to the lady's story, Bo. Then you tell me."

Bo drawled slightly, "Fair enough." He led the way to his office where a young stenographer was waiting. He must have seen the look on Collin's face and said simply, "It's for your benefit, ma'am. This way you don't have to keep telling the same story over again."

Collin asked dryly, "In case it changes?" The Sheriff merely shrugged and smiled. Collin sensed mixed emotions in the man but couldn't define them. Maybe he couldn't define them, either.

Mrs. Parks said soothingly, "No one is doubting your story, dear."

Bo sniped, "Not until I've heard it."

Mrs. Parks glared at the Sheriff but Collin said evenly, "That's only fair."

Bo directed her to a seat then gave her a second chair to prop her feet up on. His adversarial tone softened slightly and he said, "We have Dr. Wallace standing by if you want to see him first."

Collin grimaced then said, "No. I want to catch this animal. I can heal later."

Bo snorted. "Tough lady."

"If I have to be." Collin drew in a slow breath, let it out then said shakily, "I was out on the lighted court, court number two, about nine."

Bo asked, "Alone? Why?"

"Yes, alone, and because I wanted some exercise. I love the view from up there so I figured that was as good a place as any to go at that time of night."

Bo asked, "Doesn't bother you to be out alone after dark?"

Collin realized this would be an interrogation as much as a deposition, so warned her brain to be prepared to shift gears mentally as often as necessary. There was some rumbling in dissension, but the boys in the back agreed they would try. Still, it was going to cost her dearly down the road. Collin answered, "I'm a social worker in Oakton, Sheriff. Most of my clients or their parents can't be found until after dark. You have your forest and its shadows; we have our streets and theirs. The dark doesn't bother me in the least." Until now. Collin swallowed slightly but did not add the thought.

Bo shrugged, less than impressed. "Then what?"

"I'd been jogging for a while and lost track of time. The lights went out and something hit me from behind."

"Hit you where?"

"On the shoulder. Like maybe he had his hands doubled in fists and swung them like a club." Collin closed her eyes, reliving the attack, trying to fill in details she might have missed in the panic of the moment. Bo did not interrupt again but let Collin flow through the ordeal. Collin tried to put herself back in the event, yet maintain an observer's detachment. She described the second blow and the desperate roll away from the man. She looked up; saw him silhouetted against the stars. He looked massive, well over six feet, maybe 200 pounds. But there was something not right in his shape. Collin voiced the doubts to her listeners as she continued the telling. She told of the desperate attempt at deception by throwing the rocks and of the different sounds made by the rocks hitting the ground, or hitting the padded figure in front of her.

Collin's eyes flew open. She looked at Bo and said, "Padding. That's it. That's what was wrong. He was wearing padding to make himself look bigger."

Bo and Steve exchanged looks. Steve said, "Didn't Laura mention . . ."

Bo nodded. "It was never released as one of the details, though." He looked at Collin with new interest and said, "Go on."

Collin closed her eyes again and continued through the remainder of the night's ordeal. When she was finished she remained motionless, drained. Bo put a hand on her shoulder lightly and said, "You did good, lady. Real good. It's over."

Collin looked at him and said, her voice hollow, "It's not over. He's still loose out there."

Bo nodded. "And we'll catch him. You can be sure of that."

Collin sat up a little straighter and said coldly, "You're right I'm going to be sure, 'cause I'm going to be there when you nail him."

Mrs. Parks rebuked her gently, "Dear, let the men handle this."

Collin's voice was ice. "I'm the best lead they've got." She looked at Bo and challenged, "I'm the only lead you've got, aren't I?"

Bo said sternly, "I don't put civilians in danger no matter how important they are to a case."

Collin argued, "I'm not a civilian; I'm a government worker."

Bo dismissed it. "State worker, and you're in the wrong state."

"Details. He wants me." The thought made her shudder from revulsion. She continued, "He's coming back after me, whatever you do. That gives me the edge. I'll be watching for him."

Bo drawled, "All that does is put you on edge and make you paranoid."

Collin said coldly, "You don't know me, Sheriff."

"I know your type. This isn't Hollywood cops and robbers, lady. This guy has killed two women. He won't care what you think you know." Bo's voice was hard.

Collin's voice was equal to his. "I won't be number three. I won't give him that satisfaction. And there won't be a number four."

Steve said, "Collin, be reasonable."

"Never. I've never been reasonable before and I'm not going to start now." She knew Bo was the one she had to convince, so directed her arguments towards him. "Sheriff, I'm not in this for glory or pride or to fill some power-mad ego trip or for any other reason you might be thinking. Yes, I'm scared. Yes, I know it's dangerous, and yes, I know I could get killed. Okay? I know all that. Walk my territory for a week, Sheriff. I'm familiar with hazards. I can live with them. I can't live with letting this animal go and having anyone else be hurt or killed, and I didn't do everything in my power to stop him." She took a deep breath before plunging on ahead. "He chose me and maybe that will be his downfall. It gives you something to work with." She chose her pronouns carefully. "You have a chance you never had before. You've got a jump on him. You know his patterns and you know his target. Let me help you nail this . . . this monster. I'll do exactly what you say, what you tell me to do, when you tell me to do it. All I want is for the camp to remain open and nobody knows what's going on." She hesitated, then added, "And nobody knows that I helped you."

Bo looked intrigued. "You hiding something I should know about?"

Collin shrugged, tried to look indifferent, but failed. "There are two people at camp I don't want to explain this to. One is Rob, my ward for the week. He'd think it was 'cool' or 'sweet' or something and want to help. I don't want him in any danger so he can't know about it. I'll tell him anything he needs to know. He wants to ride the river and I want that for him."

Bo said softly, "Sounds like the social worker has gotten involved here."

Collin glared at him. "I'm always involved with all my kids. But Rob's one of the best kids I've worked with and I will not have him robbed of his dream by some perverted . . ." A host of words crammed into her mind, all wanting to come out at once. Collin swallowed and said, "I'll not have him robbed."

Bo said, "You said two. Who's the other?"

Collin blushed and tried to look "cool." She failed as miserably at that as she did looking indifferent. After an awkward moment she admitted, "One of the camp employees. We've struck kind of a friendship and I think he might be a little upset with this." *"A little?"* Collin refused to entertain any internal debates at this point. She caught an exchange of bemused looks between Steve and his wife and wondered what that could mean.

Bo said with interest, "An employee? Has he been there long?"

Steve said, "Bo..." but Collin interrupted him. "He said he's been there since the camp was started." A cold chill settled in Collin's chest and her eyes opened wide in horror. Dear God in heaven, no.

Steve must have read the thought there, for he reached out and touched her hand gently. She looked at him; he smiled and said reassuringly, "Don't even think it. There's no way. Absolutely, without question no way." He looked up to Bo's narrowing gaze and said, "She and Jeff have been . . . talking."

"Farrell?" Bo's face broke into a wide grin and he laughed. He looked at Collin and said, "Lady, you've been on the streets way too long if you think for one moment it could be Jeff Farrell."

Collin said sharply, "I don't know what to think, Sheriff. I know how to survive." She backed it down a notch and said, "Will you allow me to help?"

Bo stopped laughing, finally, and said sternly, "You got conditions, I got conditions."

"Name them."

"Number one: when we're done here Dr. Wallace comes in and examines you. If he says you're okay to go, fine. If he says you need to go to the hospital, you go to the hospital. No questions asked and no arguments. Understood?"

Collin hesitated then nodded carefully. "Understood."

"Number two: you do nothing, repeat, nothing, and I say again, nothing without consulting me. There will be none of this flying by the seat of your pants, situational decision making. You got that?" Bo's voice was hard. "Not one finger gets lifted unless I say so."

Collin couldn't help it. She quipped, "Let's hope not." Bo glared at her; Collin instantly recanted. "I'm sorry. I'm punchy." She looked at the clock on Bo's desk and saw it was 1:30 a.m. She groaned and said, "And I'm supposed to be at the dock at 6:00."

Steve said slowly, "I'm not sure that's a good idea."

Collin looked at Bo and asked, "Shouldn't it be business as usual? Normal routines and all that?"

Bo drawled, "You plotting my strategy, Lady?"

Through clenched teeth she said, "First off, no, I am not plotting anything, I was asking a question. Second, the name is Collin, please."

"Very well, Collin . . ." Bo drew the name out just slightly, ". . . let's see what the doctor has to say before we make any decisions." He looked over to Steve and said, "Why don't you take the Mrs. and go on home. I'll make sure the lady here gets back to camp or to the hospital. Anything I need from you I can get in the morning. I appreciate your help, Steve."

Steve shrugged. "No problem, Sheriff. I want this monster off Grace's back." His voice softened and he said, "Not nearly as much as you do, I know." He clapped Bo on the arm, then escorted Mrs. Parks out of the office and gone.

Bo left with them, then returned with a young man that Collin recognized from the first night's staff introductions. Bo said, "Collin, this is Dr. Wallace.

Doc, here is your patient. Let me know what you find." He glared at Collin and added, "Especially if you find a brain in there."

Collin smiled sarcastically at him then wished she hadn't. Some muscles weren't responding favorably to being moved. Dr. Wallace asked, "Should there be a female officer in here as well?" He looked at Collin and questioned, "Do you want someone else in here?"

Collin started to shake her head, thought better of it then said, "No. I promise not to sue anyone for anything, okay? Let's just get this over with."

Bo said dryly, "I'm a witness you said that. I'll hold you to it."

"You do that." Bo grinned and left.

Wallace commented, "This is not much of an examining room. You'd do much better at my office."

"This is fine. You're not going to find anything anyhow. I'm bruised but not broken, except for the hand. It's a mess."

"How about if I be the judge of that? It will keep the sheriff happy."

"By all means."

Wallace started off by checking her eyes, checking them again, and checking them a third time. Maybe he was looking for the brain Bo had asked him to find. Good luck. Collin managed to control the pain enough to keep the groans to a minimum as Wallace poked and prodded the worst of the bruised areas. It called for a good deal of slow breathing but she managed. Okay, a great deal of slow breathing and an even greater deal of concentration. And she probably wore at least one layer of enamel off her teeth from all the gritting. But she managed. Mostly.

Finally Wallace completed his exam and said, as if grudgingly, "I may not like it but I have to agree, bruised but not broken. And yes, the hand is a mess. You're going to need a very good surgeon to put that back together properly." He looked at Collin curiously and asked, "Has it been broken before?"

Collin said levelly, "Most every bone in my body has been broken one time or another, Dr. Wallace. I know what broke feels like." She tried to appear nonchalant while asking "Does this mean I'm free to go? That I can go back to camp?"

Wallace eyed her critically. "Are you that anxious to face this guy again? You could stand to spend a few days in bed recovering, you know. Even not-broke wounds need time to heal."

"I'll rest when this is over. I promised myself I'd finish this and I intend to." Promises. Promises. Something about promises . . . Collin said suddenly, "Oh, while we're at it, would you mind checking some stitches? The person who put them in made me promise I'd have you look at them." She held out her hand, unable to remove the bandage herself.

Wallace snorted, "What? Some self-help wizard who thinks he knows medicine but now is afraid of a law suit?" He began unwrapping her hand.

Collin said softly, "Not exactly."

Wallace gently pulled back the bandage and checked the stitching silently. He carefully felt along the suture line, examining the new-forming scar. He looked at Collin and said, "That's quite a cut. How'd you manage that?"

"Long story. Short version: sharp knife."

"I guess." Wallace finished his appraisal and said, "If you see him before I do, tell Jeff the sewing is fine, as always. I really wish that man would consider med school."

Collin was a little surprised. "How did you know it was Jeff?"

"I've seen his workmanship before. He's good."

Collin asked dryly, "Is there anything he can't do?"

Wallace grinned. "Find a good wife. But I think he's given up trying on that one. He told me that he's going to wait for the Lord to bring him one, like some character in that book he's always reading. I told him even God needs a little help now and then. And the looking itself can be fun. Somehow he just doesn't see it that way. Go figure."

Collin decided the subject needed to be changed. She said, "So you'll tell Sheriff Lodi that I'm okay to go."

"Is that what you really want? You're not going to be able to suppress the pain forever, you know. I know what you were doing and you are hurting, lady."

Collin repeated her favorite litany. "I'm fine. I can handle it."

Wallace shrugged. "If that's the way you want to play it, so be it. I'll tell him."

Collin said quickly, "I'm sorry you had to come out here for nothing."

Wallace shook his head. "I was already here. Wednesday is poker night."

Collin was shocked. "Poker? In the sheriff's office?"

Wallace nodded. "You bet. And we play for high stakes, too. You have to bring a batch of homemade cookies to get in. You women have your cookie exchanges, we have ours. Loser gets to clean up the crumbs." He opened the door and looked outside, saying, "Come on in, Bo."

The sheriff walked in suspiciously. "Well?"

"She's not fine but she's functional. In my opinion you'll have more trouble if you don't let her go than if you try to confine her. Though confinement might not be a bad idea." His eyes narrowed as he looked at Collin but he was smiling as he said it. He looked back at Bo and asked, "You need me for anything else? Otherwise, I'm missing out on a hot batch of Aunt Hazel's brownies."

Bo shook his head. "Get out." Wallace grinned and ducked out of the office. Bo walked in, sat down, and simply stared at Collin. Collin waited for the man to make his decision. She sensed that there was nothing more to do or say that would influence him in her favor, but that the wrong word could swing him against her in a heartbeat. Bo's eyes narrowed and he asked, "Are you good at following directions? Or do you have to have every why explained minutely before you do what you're told?"

Collin said carefully, "A man with your experience knows what he's doing, Sheriff. I trust you to give orders based on what is best for the situation whether I understand them or not."

"Very flattering. But you didn't answer the question."

Collin tried again. "Yes, I can take orders. And follow them without questioning." The perverse part of her nature wanted to follow that up with "Why?" but she refrained. Now was not the time to be cute. Cute was for Jeff, not Bo.

Bo nodded curtly. "I'll hold you to that." He pulled two slim folders out from a file cabinet behind his desk and said, "Here. Look these over." He handed them to her and then asked, "You drink coffee? Strong coffee? Cop coffee?"

Collin grinned. "Oh, yeah. I spend a lot of time at police stations with my job. Espresso has nothing on the syrup at the bottom of the pot."

Bo's voice reflected approval for the first time that night. "You might be all right, lady." He exited the office.

Collin looked at the first folder, marked "M. Raimey," and said softly, "Let's hope so." She began reading.

By the time Bo returned with two vile looking cups of coffee. Collin had scanned both folders and was going back over them a second time, comparing notes. Bo set the coffee down in front of her and said, "Black, right?"

Collin nodded. "That's fine, thanks." Whatever it took. She sipped it then nodded to Bo. "Good stuff." It would definitely keep her awake.

Bo eyed her to see what her reaction to her reading material might be. He drawled, "Not much to go on is there?"

Collin said quietly, "No, there isn't. First question: why didn't either woman go to the hospital? From the description of their wounds, it was certainly warranted. And they would have been safe from the follow up attack."

Bo asked dryly, "Why aren't you going?"

"I have my reasons."

"So did they. Pride. Stubbornness. Too strong-willed to admit they had been victimized. Sound familiar?"

Bo's voice had a sharp edge to it that Collin had to defuse and quickly. She said, "Then that's another part of his pattern. It means he doesn't just pick someone at random. He selects his victims for their temperament. Which means he has to get to know them, first."

Bo eyed her carefully, as if listening. "Maybe."

Collin tread lightly, "Sheriff, the problem with serial killers, other than the fact they exist at all, is that they have to kill so many people before you can establish a pattern. Some escape for years by altering their M.O."

Again Bo's voice became hard. "You teaching Law Enforcement 101, now?"

Again she tread lightly. "No, Sheriff. The point is our animal hasn't altered his approach in any of the attacks. Which means he's not very bright, or just totally consumed in his passions. These files may be small but they do give enough of a hint of what to expect next. Both girls disappeared the next day following a call or a summons from a supposed relative. I can't be taken in that way."

"Why? You immune to being fooled? You smarter than everyone else?" There was heat in Bo's voice.

Collin continued to be patient though it was getting tougher. Her head was throbbing, her hand was throbbing, her sides were throbbing, the room was throbbing . . . She said, "I have no family, Sheriff. I'm a visitor so no one knows my friends."

"What about your boy you brought up here? Or any of those kids you're with? You're telling me that if someone handed you a note from your ward saying, 'come here, I need you' you would think twice before responding?"

"Rob and I have had to play this game before when he's been hiding from his mother's variety of live-ins. We've set up a system of codes and messages and we make it work. No one else is going to summon me anywhere."

"You're so sure about this you're willing to lay your life on the line. What if he changes patterns?"

"He won't."

"Why not?"

"He's showing himself to be a creature of habit. He only knows one way to do things. He'll follow his game plan."

Bo thought that one over then asked slowly, "Other than Mr. Jeffrey Farrell, who you have 'gotten to know' this past week," he smiled, but his eyes narrowed slightly, ". . . who would know you're a stubborn, strong-willed woman?"

Collin considered the question then said slowly, "I don't know. My boating instructor, Mitch Kellum."

Bo shook his head. "He's clear. Wasn't hired on until after the first murder had occurred and dismissed him as a suspect after the second. Physically he didn't fit the profile. Anyone else?"

Collin repeated, "I don't know, Sheriff. It doesn't have to be someone I know. It could be someone who's simply observing. Someone hunting a quarry." She pointed to the picture of Bo standing beside a large, recently shot black bear. "Did you walk up and introduce yourself to him before you shot him?"

Collin saw what she hoped was the shadow of a smile. Bo said slowly, "You're a tough woman, Walker."

"Let's hope our monster doesn't figure that out too soon."

Bo added, "Amen. I'll take you back to camp."

THURSDAY

It was close to three in the morning before Collin got to crawl into her bunk and try to sleep. Then morning come with a predawn wakeup call of the obnoxious kind. Fierce pounding on her door jarred her to wakefulness. Fiercer pounding in her head threatened to knock her out again. Collin had the distinct feeling she could stop the outer pounding much more rapidly than the inner so stumbled out of bed, hobbled to the door and hissed, "What?!"

Chonnell and Pardner sang in chorus, "Time to get up! Rob say stop moping and get moving. He say you missed breakfast, again, and now you gonna be late to practice. He say if you ain't woman enough to admit you don't want to go, least you could do . . ."

Collin seethed, "You tell Rob . . ." Flashes of reason returned to her brain before she could get herself in too much trouble. She looked at the clock: it was five forty. She told the door, "Tell Rob to meet me at dock one in ten minutes and we'll have a talk about being late. Ten minutes, dock one. Got it?" In response Collin heard giggles and grins, followed by scuffling, laughter, and then silence. Oh, to be young and foolish again. Okay, oh to be young again. Foolish, she'd never given up.

Changing clothes one-handed was a chore. Good thing she'd never been much on shoe laces. Avoid anything that tied or buttoned. Zippers were good, Velcro was better, pull-ons with no fasteners were best of all.

Collin slipped on her bathing suit, donned a pair of elastic top shorts, pulled on a pull-over then looked in the mirror.

The face was going to be a problem. Much of the swelling . . . okay, let's be honest, here, folks, some of the swelling had gone down. But the face was still very red, very scratched and very ugly. Okay, uglier than normal, she admitted it. What to do? She never wore make up so had none to use now. Zinc oxide? And look like a ghost? Maybe. Or she could look like she was trying not to get sunburned. Yeah, right. Get real. No, it could work . . . it could help, anyhow. Couldn't hurt for heaven's sake. Collin carefully applied two rather large dollops of the white cream to her cheeks, grabbed her seldom-used sunglasses and looked for a hat. She wished she had a wide-brimmed sun hat but knew her collection of chapeaus did not include such a creature. A sombrero would have been better, but tough to pack in a gym bag. She selected the widest visor she could find, pulled it low on her forehead, jammed the sunglasses on and headed out the door.

Another phone message was taped to her door. Collin felt her stomach drop as she realized that it, too, was from Jeff. He was going to think she was ignoring him or avoiding him. She would call him tonight, no questions asked. She could play the fool long enough to keep him from suspecting anything was wrong. She hoped. For now, there was the river and Mitch to contend with.

Walking was still painful, though less so than last night. How she was going to handle the paddle was a bit of an unsolved mystery. But being able to walk in the half-light of the almost morning, breathing in clean air and listening to the twitters, chirps and clicks of the creatures of the woods was almost a healing in itself. However evil the night, joy comes in the morning. God's creation went on oblivious to man's inhumanity to man. And although her world might seem out of control, God's world wasn't. And if her world was truly his, then hers wasn't, either. She might not understand it, but there was still reason and purpose.

And love. Scripture came unbidden to her mind; *"I have loved you with an everlasting love." "The steadfast love of the Lord never ceases; His mercies never come to an end; they are new every morning." "How precious is your steadfast love, O God."*

Collin began to breathe a little easier as she walked. She prayed softly, "You love me. Do you know I love you? Can you even tell? I don't understand what all this is about; I just need to know what you want me to do about it. Did I pick the right path, God? I've got to do this your way or a lot of people could get hurt, including me." Not that that mattered so much . . .

A thought slapped her, *"Love others as I have loved you. You're an 'other.' Treat your self the way you want to be treated."*

Collin whispered, "I'm not worth it and I don't deserve it."

"You don't deserve love, either, but I gave it to you. My Son died for you. That makes you worth far more than you know."

Collin let that thought percolate in her brain. Worth? As a tool to be used, maybe? But of real value? That needed more time to consider than she had right now. Now there was a river, Mitch and a major monster to deal with. Maybe when Jeff got back they could discuss love. God's love, that is. Anything else was too painful to hope for.

Collin arrived at the dock and found Robbie lounging around trying to look cool. She walked up to him keeping her head down and said, "Hey, dude."

Robbie took one look at her and just stared. After a moment he asked, "What did you run into, a '57 Chevy?"

"'49 Ford, actually. Does it look that bad?"

"With that gunk you got on? You should be wearing a sign says, 'I got the snot beat out of me.'"

Collin sagged. "Give me a break, man. What am I supposed to do?"

Robbie led her to the side of the dock, dipped her towel in the water and instructed, "People as don't wear makeup don't wear it to hide nothing, neither. Wash all that garbage off but don't rub it. You ain't wanting to look any redder than you is." As Collin complied, Robbie continued to instruct her in the fine art of abuse-camouflage; an art Collin had gradually forgotten over the past twelve years. "Lose the glasses. You never wear them. It makes people look at your face when you got something different on. Pull your hair out on the sides like you was too late to comb it or something."

Robbie stepped back and looked at the finished product. He shrugged and said, "I guess you pass." He studied her hand, her face and her awkward stance and asked, "Know who done it?"

Collin said quietly, "He didn't leave his name. Dressed all in black, boots, gloves, mask . . ."

Robbie said dryly, "White guy, huh?"

"Yeah. White guy. Rob, this is serious, man. Let's get to class and I'll explain on first break." They started walking and Collin continued, "Work with me, dude. The Man's gonna be in the hills with us today: in the trees, the bushes, playing commando. Don't let it spook you, and if anyone else says anything, divert them, okay? Got it?"

Rob's eyes clouded with concern but he said, "I got it." To his credit he asked no questions. Yet.

Collin said, "Go nowhere unless it's with a group. And I mean nowhere, Rob. As in absolutely nowhere. The bigger the group the better it is. Got it?" Rob took this silently but nodded. "Last thing. Do you remember battle code red?"

"You Xena, I'm Ares? I remember it. Dumbest code we ever did."

Collin smiled wryly. "Yeah, but no one ever guessed it, did they? They might guess you was the god of war, but . . ."

Rob finished the justification, ". . . no one ever gonna suspect you was no Warrior Princess. I got it, I got it. You ain't near as strong as she is. Ain't near as ugly, neither."

Collin grinned. "Why, Rob, that's the nicest thing you've ever said. Especially now."

Rob kept his head down. "Yeah, well, look like you could use some nice things about now." He looked up at her and said, "You better have one good explanation for all this, case worker lady."

"I will." She had all morning to think of one. They arrived at the dock and found all members of the crew present and accounted for except Mitch. Collin leaned against a piling and said evenly, "Morning, crew." It was her standard opening. If Robbie was right, the more routine she followed, the less attention she'd garner.

Niles grumbled, "Teacher be late. Teachers ain't supposed to be late. Kids supposed to be late, not teachers."

Nyla sniped, "You'd be knowing about being late. You ain't been on time since you was born."

Collin smiled inside. That sounded so familiar it hurt. She said, "The rule in college was if the professor hadn't shown up in twenty minutes, class was cancelled. We can wait that long then go back to the lodge and see if anyone knows what's happened to him. No one knows, we go back to bed or back for another breakfast." Collin wasn't sure which alternative the cheers were for. She knew which got her vote.

They waited another ten minutes and excitement began to stir about whether Mitch would make it or not, and whether there would be anything different for breakfast the second time around. But to the chagrin of the majority, Mitch suddenly came pounding down the path yelling, "I'm here, I'm here! I'm coming."

Boos and jeers greeted him but he just waved and bowed. Collin said "We were contemplating mutiny."

Mitch grinned and looked around. "Not my crew. You'd wait for me forever, wouldn't you?"

In chorus the kids answered, "No way!!"

Mitch smiled. "That's what I like. Solidarity. Come on, people. Let's go find a river we can practice on. Show me you got it together and tomorrow we do the real thing."

That won him approval and support of the vocal kind. Collin studied the man's eyes and saw something different in them: a spark of energy, maybe, or a light of enthusiasm that hadn't been there before. A cold tingle that started in her gut raced through her and just as quickly died. What had Sheriff Bo said about paranoia? If she was to start suspecting everyone she might as well cut off her own hands now. We're talking about Mitch, here. Pompous, obnoxious, lecherous, maybe . . . okay, no maybe. But a talker not a doer. And unless the monster from last night was wearing elevator shoes, Mitch did not fit the profile.

As Mitch grabbed supplies from the shed, Collin and crew slid into position. Collin experimented with the paddle, trying to find a hold that she could manage, could still paddle, and not end up screaming in pain with each stroke. None was completely satisfactory and all were going to be intense. She finally settled on a variation of the original and left it at that. She'd have to be tough, that's all.

Collin realized Nyla was watching her closely but saying nothing. Collin shrugged and said, "It'll work."

Nyla asked, "You want to switch sides?"

"Thanks, Nyla. I really appreciate the offer. If Mitch says we can."

Nyla hesitated then asked, "What you do?"

Collin definitely needed to work on an answer for that one. An honest but not-too-involved answer. She knew Nyla was waiting and said finally, "My hand got stepped on."

"Stepped on? How?"

Guess that wasn't the one to use. "I was playing hoops . . ." true enough; or was going to play, anyhow, ". . . things got intense. I got knocked down and stepped on."

Nyla's eyes narrowed slightly and she said, "You saying the truth?"

Collin lowered her voice and said, "All that I can."

That seemed to satisfy Nyla. It told the girl that Collin didn't think she was stupid enough to believe that was all that happened, and that Nyla would eventually be party to the rest of the story. Nyla looked at Collin a moment longer then said, "Guess your face got stepped on, too, huh."

"Yeah. Something like that."

Mitch came back with a cooler and a load of supplies, secured them in the boat and said brightly, "Well, are we all ready to rock and roll?"

Nyla's hand shot up quickly. "Mitch, me and the lady here wants to try switching sides."

Mitch asked curiously, "Why?"

Nyla continued to take the lead. "Cause she ain't worth nothing on her side. We got to pull even and she can't pull near as good as I can on the right."

Mitch seemed uncertain. "I don't know. We've been practicing it this way and doing pretty good. What about it, Collin?"

Collin did not turn to address him but shrugged. "Fine by me. I think Nyla's just jealous. All the cute guys on the shore have been on my side of the boat." She grinned at Nyla; the girl threatened her with her paddle.

Mitch said, "Well, that settles it, then. We must by all means keep you from ogling any cute guys but me."

There were hoots from the male contingent and Mitch smiled broadly. Collin and Nyla switched sides without further ado. Again, Collin whispered to Nyla, "Thanks. I owe you one."

Nyla shrugged. "Twins got to stick together. Even if they ain't same blood." She looked at Collin and asked, "How you live, your brother being gone?"

So that was what had struck the nerve in Nyla. Contemplation of life should she lose Niles. Collin said softly, "I almost didn't at first." The boat pulled away from the dock at Mitch's command. Paddling on the opposite side was painful but at least on this side she could do it and scream inside, rather than not do it and scream outside anyhow. As they pulled with steady, even strokes, Nyla matching her stroke to Collin's, Collin matching hers to Niles' up front, Collin said quietly, "I lived in hell for two years until I met a Man who could fill the emptiness Erin left behind. A man who knew me better than Erin did. Who knew everything I'd said and done and loved me anyhow. A man who promised to be with me forever; to never leave me no matter what, to stay with me and defend me and help me wherever I was."

Nyla snorted. "Ain't no man can do that."

"One man can. And he has."

"Yeah?" Nyla's voice was rife with disbelief. "Where was he last night when you was being 'stepped on?'"

"He was there, Nyla. I'm not dead, am I? I'm not laid up somewhere in a hospital." She silenced the voices that started to protest she'd been told that's where she should be. "Nothing's broken but the hand and it will heal. I've got the chance to do something good, and I think that's pretty good protection. My friend never promised me nothing bad would happen. He just promised me he would always be there to help me when it did."

They paddled out slowly towards the sister leg of the river, one Mitch had promised was little more exciting than a water slide. Collin had her doubts. She'd seen a few water slides in her day, and tame they weren't. Nyla's conversation was a good distraction from the fear that was starting to mount in her. The girl asked, "This friend got a name?"

"Jesus." Collin decided to lay it out with no apologies and no dressings. Speak the name and let him do the rest.

Nyla snorted again. "Thought so." She hesitated then admitted, "But I ain't seen you religious types so real before. Ain't seen none as cut they hand open to prove a point, neither."

Collin said quickly, "Don't take that as a good example, Nyla. Knowing the Lord doesn't exempt me from being stupid on my own. The Lord did all the bleeding for us. He doesn't ask us to repeat his sacrifice."

Nyla pointed to the look on Mitch's face and said, "He gonna yell at us for talking, we don't quit. Maybe we get a break you answer some more questions for me."

Collin smiled. "I'd be happy to, Nyla." Both females lapsed into silence and Mitch's countenance cleared. Collin focused on her paddling, trying hard to keep up with the young man in front of her. The hand throbbed even though only the fingers and base of the palm were actually contacting the paddle. The brunt of the stroke's force was carried by the left hand and both shoulder joints. But even with that, some contact could not be avoided. The bandages were staining pink. As the morning progressed Collin began to hurt more and more. She forced herself to concentrate, to focus all her attention away from the pain and outward to her paddling. Focus. Focus. Concentrate. Shut out all distractions and focus. Focus hard. Focus harder. If you focus hard enough . . .

You forget where you are and what you're supposed to be doing. Robbie's foot nudged her in the back sharply. Collin came to with a start and looked at him. He hissed sharply, "Wake up, lady. You zoning out and getting Nyla all messed up."

Collin shook her head to clear the cobwebs, mentally swatted at the spider as he jeered at her, then said, "Thanks," to Robbie and, "Sorry," to Nyla. Robbie grunted in response, the male equivalent of "No problem." Nyla only shrugged.

Collin looked around, trying to get some sense of where they were, what time it was and how far they were from a break. The answers were all of the "who knows?" variety. Suck it up, woman. Do the deed and get on with it. Collin let out a sigh then began counting strokes as a diversion. *"Up, forward, dig, pull, retrieve. Up, forward, dig, pull, retrieve. Up, forward, dig . . ."* It became a chant in her head, a mantra to ward off pain. And if you do it hard enough . . .

Robbie's foot in her back wasn't quick enough to save Collin from detection this time. She came to with Mitch literally in her face shouting, "Walker! What do you think you are doing? This isn't nap time!!"

Collin sat up sharply, hoping to redeem herself. She knew better than to say, "I'm sorry," and give him further ammunition to berate her. She said instead, "I was out of line. You're right."

Her tactic took some of the steam out of Mitch's assault. He huffed a couple of times but couldn't think of anything to say. Finally he asked, "Do you want off?"

"No. But I could use a break." She hesitated then admitted, "I hurt my hand last night, and it's killing me right now."

Mitch ordered, "Yeah? Let me see it." Collin unwrapped it slowly and held it out for Mitch to see. He took her hand and cradled it in his own.

Shock waves exploded in Collin's brain. It was *him*. It *was* him. The monster may have been wearing gloves but the touch was the same. Collin's heart leaped in her chest like a hammer crashing against her ribs. She willed herself, begged herself, to remain calm, to not let on that she knew. Mitch was gently poking and prodding her hand, twisting it gently this way and that, moving her fingers around. Collin tried to think of something clever to say but the only things that came to mind were grotesque and maudlin. She swallowed hard, tried to find her voice, coughed then said, "It's not an excuse, I know. But if we're anywhere near a break period, I'd appreciate one."

Mitch ignored her statement and asked, "How did this happen? What were you doing?"

Collin stuck to her story and said, "I was playing out on the basketball court and my hand got stepped on."

"Stepped on?" Mitch looked surprised and concerned. "By who? How? Why?"

Gee, he left out when and where. But he already knew that. Of course, he already knew the who and the how. And he was the only one who could say why. Collin said evenly, "Mitch, it really doesn't matter. But if someone doesn't start paddling we're going to be hitting that hole sideways, and you taught us that's the wrong way to start a run."

Mitch turned and realized they were headed crosswise into a trench. He yelled, "Niles, pull hard starboard. Ta'waan, back stroke. Helmsman, get us out of here!" The crew jumped back to life, and the boat was turned to its proper heading. With Collin's blood and the crew's sweat, they were able to pull away from danger, back up, and hit the trench head on as a proper ship should.

The rest of the morning's trip was spent in silence other than terse commands and even more terse responses. Collin's request for a break was forgotten or ignored and she passed the time in private agony. She returned Nyla's looks of concern with tight-lipped smiles, or when she could manage it, a pain-filled grin. Mostly she spent the time praying and praising and rolling her fear and care over on the Lord. It did a great deal to ease the stress and even lower the pain levels some. Like squeezing the hand of someone bigger and stronger than you when you get a shot or they take out a splinter, or pull a tooth. It somehow just doesn't hurt as much when you share it with someone else.

And eventually they did reach the "beach" Mitch had promised them: a shallow, flat point used as a jumping off spot for river cruises. It was just after midday when they rounded the curve and Mitch ordered the boat run up on shore. The coolers were unloaded, lunch was divided and distributed and everyone spread out to relax. Mitch called, "One hour break. Make good use of it, crew. We've got hard paddling ahead."

Collin found a smooth boulder to lean against, shoved her sandwich back into its bag uneaten and closed her eyes. Maybe she could catch a few winks; however long a wink was. How long was forty winks? Well, let's see. The traditional 40 winks was a full night's sleep, so let's say eight hours. Twenty winks would be four hours, ten winks two hours, five winks one hour. Sixty minutes in an hour, so five winks into sixty equals . . . Collin couldn't get her brain to do the math, and then couldn't get it to stop trying. Not that thinking about math was really diverting her attention from how miserable she felt. She ached everywhere and where she didn't ache, she hurt. Her head was pounding, keeping pace with the throbbing in her hand. She wanted very badly to crawl in a corner and cry but knew that was not an option. First, she couldn't cry. Second, there were no corners in the wilderness. Third, it would hardly be becoming of an adult of her professed strength and maturity. Collin laid her head back against the rock and tried to drain all feeling from her system, starting at the top and working down.

She'd gotten as far as her hair when a hand on her shoulder shook her insistently. She looked up; Robbie stood beside her, looking more concerned than she'd seen before. He asked, "You okay, lady?"

Collin admitted, "I'm beat, Rob."

"Who beat you?"

Collin figured Robbie was too young to know the joke version of that routine. She motioned for him to sit down, looked around to see where Mitch was then said truthfully, "I don't know for sure. I got tagged out on the court last night. I never saw more than his shape."

"But you chased him off, right? I mean, you're here so you must have whipped him good."

Legends die hard. Collin said slowly, "Actually, he let me go, Rob. He's some kind of head case; he's got this thing about women's hands. The Man thinks he'll come back for me."

"Why you still here?"

"No freak's gonna run me off, Rob. I've got to ride this cursed river, first. Bus don't leave until Saturday and neither do I." She looked at Robbie then asked quietly, "You want to leave?"

Robbie snorted, "I ain't got no woman's hands." He thought a moment, trying to put it all together, then asked, "So what was the stuff about staying with the group about?"

"I don't want someone coming at me through you, using you as bait." The more she thought of the potential danger to Robbie, the more uneasy she became with this whole program. Especially if it was Mitch. Which, now that she'd been able to rest awhile, seemed ridiculous. She was getting paranoid, that's all. Surely the sheriff had run a check on all the employees of the camp after the second murder. If Mitch had given them even the slightest reason for suspicion there would have been something in the files.

Collin looked up and saw Robbie studying her. She said, "Stay with the group, Rob. Whatever happens, stay with the group. Or a group. Or any group. Don't get caught alone."

Robbie said, "Yeah? What about you? You being a target, ain't you?"

Collin shook her head. "Not a chance. You don't see me out walking in a field someplace with a sign on saying, 'Come and get me,' now do you?"

Robbie said slowly, "No." He looked at her pointedly and said, "Don't mean you ain't, neither. What's the Man doing about all this? Why ain't he out here looking?"

"Looking for what?" Nyla had joined the discussion. "Who you be talking about?"

Robbie looked at Collin, not sure how much he was allowed to share. Collin said quietly, "Rob wanted to know if the Man was out looking for the guy who 'stepped' on me."

"Is he?"

Collin nodded. "Man's out there. Sheriff said we wouldn't see him but he's there." She looked at Nyla and said, "Sort of like my friend I was telling you about. Can't see him but I know he's there."

Nyla plopped down beside Collin and asked, "How can I ever be knowing him? If I got to clean all up on the outside just to go to church where he ain't, how'm I ever gonna be clean enough on the inside to stand where he is?"

"You can't. No one can. He doesn't expect you to, Nyla. That's what Jesus came to do for us. It's like you're standing there in old dirty threads and God says, 'Nyla, I want you to come be with me. But Nyla, you got to put on a clean shirt, first.' He didn't say 'Take off all the dirty stuff first,' he just said put on a clean shirt. So you look through all you got, but you know you haven't got any shirts that will ever be clean enough for God. And even Niles hasn't got anything good enough to borrow, even if he'd let you."

Nyla snorted. "You know brothers better than that."

Collin smiled slightly. "I remember. Anyhow, you can't find a shirt anywhere. Then Jesus comes along and says, 'Nyla, I've got a shirt for you. You take this one of mine I give you, and you can be with God any time. I'm the only one with a shirt clean enough for him.' When God sees the shirt he says, 'I know that shirt; it belongs to my son. And if my son has given it to Nyla to wear then He must have accepted her so I will, too.' We can't clean ourselves up. God does that after we come to him. We just have to accept the shirt that Christ gives us."

Collin hesitated then continued, "Except it wasn't just some spare shirt Jesus had laying around. It was his blood, Nyla. He died. He gave everything he had because he loved us and wanted us to be with him. His death was the only way that could ever happen. Once we accept him, though, he promises to never leave us alone again."

Nyla considered it, then looked at Robbie. "You been around this lady awhile?"

"Most part of a year." Robbie gave her a half grin. "Longest ten months of my life."

Collin smiled at him sweetly. "Ah, Rob, you remembered."

Nyla ignored the interplay and said, "But you be knowing her, right? She straight on this stuff? You be believing it?"

Ah hah! Let's see how Robbie handles this one. Robbie considered how to answer the question. When he did it was slowly and with thoughtfully chosen words. "Lady be straight on this stuff. She be believing it, she be trying to live it. I seen it make a difference in her. Am I believing it? I be believing it can be; I just ain't accepted the shirt from the man, yet."

Collin nodded, satisfied. Well put, my man. Very well put.

But Nyla wasn't satisfied. "Why ain't you? If it so great and all and make such a difference, why ain't you?"

Collin said quietly, "Nyla, everyone has a reason why not, until they're ready. Taking the shirt means more than just getting to be with God. It means you're gonna start living the way God does, the way God says. Like loving your enemies. You'd have to give up hating the Southside gangs and learn to love them instead."

Nyla's eyes narrowed. "Ain't no way."

"God says there is, and he'll teach it to you when you become one of his. But not until then."

Robbie admitted to Nyla, "Got some enemies what I ain't done hating, yet, neither."

Before anything else could be discussed Mitch stirred from his napping spot: a clear signal that lunch was over. Nyla jumped up and said, "Gotta go wake that good-for-nothing brother of mine. He sleep all day if you let him."

Collin looked at Robbie and said quietly, "Watch out for yourself, my man. I promise I won't put myself in open danger and you promise me you won't be stupid and think you really are Aires. Got it?"

Robbie snorted and said, "I got it. I ain't no fool."

"I know you're not. You're my main man, Rob. You always will be. I don't want anything to happen to you. I'd hate myself forever if something did and I could have prevented it. I don't know what I'd do without you. And I don't want to have to find out."

Robbie stared at her for a long minute then whispered, "You something else, Collin. You know that? You something else. Crazy man out after you and you worried about me. Where they come up with you? And why they give you to me??" He reached out and in one quick motion hugged her, then just as quickly let her go and headed back to the boat.

Collin stared after him then whispered joyfully, "First time. First time he ever called me by name. If that's your reason, Lord, then bring on the muggers. Thank you. Thank you."

"Thank me for what?" Mitch had come up on Collin without her noticing.

"Thank you for the break just now." She flexed her fingers gingerly and said, "I think I can manage the rest of the trip now." Mitch took hold of her hand. Collin stilled the screaming meemeeies inside and asked, "What?"

Mitch stared at her hand then curled it around his own saying, "I think we should give this hand a long break. Why don't you take the point and I'll paddle with Nyla."

Collin retrieved her hand, shuddering with revulsion. He wasn't helping her bid to dismiss him as the monster from the basketball court. She said, "I'd appreciate it but I don't think it's a good idea. I don't know the river like you do. You know where all the rocks and stumps are submerged."

Mitch chuckled. "You mean where all the bodies are buried?"

Inwardly Collin shuddered again. Did Mitch know what she thought? Was this some sick attempt at macabre humor or just the idiot's badly timed joke? Was he jibbing at her fear of the river? Whatever the purpose Collin said evenly, "Something like that. I can paddle left handed."

"Walker, you can't paddle with either hand and you know it. This thing with the river has you so spooked you're practically useless out there. You froze twice this morning. You didn't think I saw it the first time, did you? I did. If I had any sense at all I'd ground you here and now."

Collin counted to ten slowly then asked, "Is that your professional evaluation?"

Mitch nodded. "It certainly is. I should just leave you here and send maintenance back after you when we get to base camp." He stopped then said, "But you'd like that, wouldn't you? Maintenance means Jeff. You'd enjoy a long drive back with him, wouldn't you?"

Mitch's tone and face both were taking on an ugly cast. Collin said evenly, "Jeff is out of town, Mitch. You know that; the notices were posted all over camp that maintenance would be closed for the next few days. And I've already told you Jeff and I are friends. That's all. If I'm not fit to crew, tell me."

What was all this? Why this sudden attack on her abilities? What did he expect from her? What did he want her to do?

Get mad and stay behind. He expected her to say, "Fine, I'll stay here." Which she wouldn't give him. Collin sought her most diplomatic side and said, "Mitch, I don't know what's given you the impression that I can't carry my weight as part of this crew. If you truly believe I'm a detriment then I'll take the lookout point. Or I'll sit in the middle and be ballast. Either way I want to finish this class with my crewmates."

The four older crew members had gathered around, listening to the discussion. Nyla said, "She ain't doing bad. Ain't thrown me off once."

Niles unexpectedly jumped in on the good guy's side. "Yeah. For a white lady she got good rhythm. We might could make a rapper out of her yet."

Collin said dryly, "When pigs fly."

Ta'waan challenged, "You wasn't making no noises about how she was stroking earlier. You always making noise when we off stroke. So what's the deal, here?"

There followed a chorus of, "Yeah, what's the deal? What you trying to pull? What's going down?" from various quarters and voices too varied to distinguish.

Mitch's face broke into a wide grin and he began to laugh and clap his hands. "This is great! This is fantastic!" To the confused and suspicious faces he said, "The 'deal' is you all passed the test with flying colors. A real crew needs to pull together and not just on the water, either. You've got to stand and defend one another. I wanted to know if you had all really learned that, yet." He slapped Ta'waan, Niles and Nyla on the shoulders then said, "Good job, crew. Good job. Now let's get loaded and back on the water."

He moved off jovially taking Niles and Ta'waan with him. Nyla looked at Collin and asked, "You believing him?"

Collin answered truthfully, "I don't know what to believe about him, Nyla."

"I be believing he a snake. I ain't trusting him. What your God got to say about that?"

Collin phrased her answer carefully. "I believe God would say keep your eyes open but treat him like an honest man. He's innocent until we prove him guilty."

"Or he proves hisself guilty."

"Amen." Nyla took herself back to the boat.

Leaving Robbie and Collin alone once again. Robbie looked at her, his face dark with concern. He said, "Collin, lady, you be watching your back." He corrected himself and said, "I be watching your back. I got a bad feeling about him."

So did Collin but she wouldn't admit it. She said softly, "Don't hate a man for being a fool, Rob. He is what he is. But I appreciate the support." She did the unthinkable: she put an arm around his shoulders and hugged him. To her everlasting joy he did not pull away from her, but wrapped his arm around her waist and together they walked to the boat and took their designated places.

The remainder of the trip down the sister leg of the river was by all accounts, "awesome." Collin declined to issue her standard reprimand that only God was awesome. For these street kids, seeing the Creator's handiwork was as close to seeing the Creator as they had ever come. During the three hour trip they spotted deer grazing in the fields, hawk and eagle soaring high overhead, ground hog and squirrel in the rocks and trees. The most awesome sight had to be the mama bear and her two cubs on the edge of the river fishing. All—okay, almost all—of Collin's fear of the river vanished as she watched the city-wise hardness dissolve into small child wonder on the crew's faces when Mama bear flipped a brown trout out of the water into the paws of her cubs. Wonder turned to glee when the baby bears growled and whined as they tried to catch their madly flipping dinner. Not even master monster himself could defile that moment. It was, for Collin, the single defining moment of the whole trip. Second only to Robbie calling her Collin. And giving her the hug. And meeting Jeff . . .

Okay, so this trip had a lot of defining moments and they were all going to be forever precious. This was what life was all about. Collin smiled all over as she paddled. For maybe the first time in who knew how long she could hum a favorite song whose tag line was, "Oh how great it is to be alive."

Nyla was watching her, her face puzzled. She asked, "What you so happy about?"

Robbie cautioned, "Don't be asking no questions. She get like this she be dangerous. She really start talking 'bout that God she serve."

Nyla studied Collin. "You be thinking 'bout God? And that make you happy? You all beat up, got Mitch there hitting on you, then dissing you and you happy?"

Collin grinned. "You got it."

Nyla looked at Robbie. "What she taking?"

Robbie shook his head. "Ain't taking nothing. She like this all on her own. Her and God."

Mitch called back, "Less chatter, more paddle. We've got white water ahead."

Nyla lowered her voice and asked, "White water. You still happy?"

Collin nodded, determination in her eyes. "Yep. I know God is with me. We'll get through it together."

But the rapids proved to be less than her fear made them. Fast, yes. Precarious, yes. Swiftly angling from side to side, pitching the raft back and forth . . . of course. But no one lost their seat and everyone stayed in the boat, so it was a huge success in Collin's estimation.

Mitch seemed pleased with the effort and as the boat ground up on the landing site he shouted, "All right, crew!! Well done! Well done! One more little test and you're all ready for the big run tomorrow."

A crew with a flatbed truck and a van was waiting for them. With expertise they loaded the boat and its contents, but not its occupants, onto the truck and pulled away. Gratefully, the porters left the van behind. As good as Collin had been feeling, she was not prepared to walk back to camp from here. She had no idea how far from the lodge they were, but one mile or twenty, she didn't have the reserves to make it back. Both her head and her hand were throbbing, a sure sign that she had controlled the pain about as long as she could and the threshold had been crossed. Time for rest, sleep, drugs if she could find any. Legal ones, of course. Illegal if not.

Stop that. Pay attention. Mitch was talking, telling the crew, "I promised you a surprise at the end of the run. I don't want you thinking I'd cheat on a promise. We have to hike just a little ways over that rise and we're there."

Groans of gloom, despair and agony met Mitch's pronouncement. "Hike?" "Walk??" "Man, we just paddled 300 miles, and you want us to walk?" "Dude, I can't even feel my legs, how you expect me to walk?"

Ah, youth. Mitch merely laughed and smiled, an overgrown but still annoying sheltie as he herded them along. "Come on, crew! You can make it! You're young, you're strong, you're full of energy . . ."

Pardner whined, "But we're tired!"

Mitch grinned at her. "No you're not. You just think you're tired. If I told you the man himself, MJ was there? You'd all bust a gut to get there, wouldn't you?" He waited expectantly for an answer. "Tell the truth. You'd make it, now, wouldn't you?"

He drove them forward up an overgrown path that could barely be discerned, save for one recent track where the grass had been stomped down. Wherever he was taking them no man had gone before. Or at least not in recent history. Collin struggled along the way and each step became more and more uncomfortable. And although they were leaving the river well behind, she could still hear the faint hint of water rushing. Would this never end?

Mitch dropped back to join her, foregoing his sheep herder duties. Collin waited for him to broach a subject, if he indeed had anything on his mind. She would voluntarily give him nothing on which to feed. After several moments of silence Mitch said, "You did great this afternoon when I was baiting you. I knew I could count on you to play along with me."

"Do you spring that on all your guests without warning?"

"Not usually. It's not often I find someone as sharp as you to play with." Collin got an uneasy sense of his meaning but let it go. No paranoia. Mitch studied her closely a moment, then said, "Whoever you were playing with last night must have been pretty rough. You want to tell me about it?"

Collin said firmly but not rudely, "No, Mitch."

He shrugged. "It's good to talk things out, you know."

"I know, but it's still too . . . close."

"Did he hurt you anywhere else?"

"Just my pride."

Mitch nodded knowingly. "Yes, you're the one that's always in control, aren't you? It must have been terrifying for someone else to have control over you."

Collin's eyes narrowed as her gut squeezed closed abruptly. She kept her voice steady and said, "It happens, Mitch. I'm not always in charge of a situation. You learn to adapt."

"Adapt to being attacked from behind in the dark? I don't think so. No one is that cool, Walker. Not even you."

Mitch's voice was hard with disbelief. And Collin's breath was being slowly squeezed from her as she listened to him. How did he know she'd been attacked from behind? She'd said nothing at all about being attacked, just that she was playing ball. What was the expression, "Just because you're paranoid doesn't mean they're *not* out to get you?" Yeah, right. This day needed to be over, and about half an hour ago, too. She looked at Mitch and said, "It's not a matter of being cool, Mitch. It's a matter of doing what you've got to do. If you're breathing, there's something to be done and you do it."

"Fear never stops you, then? There's nothing you're afraid of?"

"I'm afraid of the river. But I'm doing something about it."

"You still haven't told me what makes you so afraid of it. Is it the fact you almost died? Is that it? You're afraid of death?" Mitch was getting almost excited as he probed.

Collin said evenly, "I'm not afraid of death, Mitch. I know where I'm going when I die, and I'm not afraid at all."

"But the dying part . . . that scares everyone. I've never met anyone that wasn't afraid of the dying. In the most bizarre ways, too. Some people are afraid of cancer. Some of dying in car crashes. Some people are afraid of flying, or being trapped in burning buildings. I know one woman who was afraid of being crushed by snakes. Is that weird or what?" Mitch laughed, and there was an unhealthy and unholy light in his eyes. "Everyone has a fear, Collin. I think yours is drowning."

Collin was saved from having to answer by the kids' excited shouting. They had reached the rise and were pointing down slope at something. Calls of, "Way cool, man!" and "Dude!!" and "Sweet!" indicated to Collin that whatever it was met their approval. Which meant it was probably extreme, hazardous and otherwise radically different. She puffed up the last few feet of the trail, took one look and said breathlessly, "Oh, joy. A water slide."

It looked to be an old mining sluice that had been converted to a slide. It was broader and deeper than an amusement park's wont, however. It dipped and rose and fell in river fashion, curving and meandering along at a pace perhaps slower than the river itself, but moving along crisply enough.

Mitch came up behind her and whispered, "Here it is. Your last test before you reach the Holy Grail. Let's see you handle this one."

Sitting up, eyes open no problem. Collin smiled at Mitch with all the pleasantness she could muster. Or wanted to muster. "This should be fun. I haven't ridden the water slides at the Point in two years. I used to have a pass, you know. Or you don't. You couldn't." She laughed lightly but kept any phoniness out of it. “Another counselor and I would have competitions to see who could ride the most in one day.”

Mitch’s face fell slightly and his eyes darkened. “We’ll see who’s laughing when we’re done.” He hustled down to where the crew was gathering and said, “Okay, crew, here’s the deal. This may look like your ordinary water slide but it has a purpose. A pilot may say any landing you walk away from is a good one, but for a riverman it’s not so simple. If he lands, he lands in the water and there’s only one way to do that correctly. This sluice is to teach you just that: how to ride the river in the unlikely and dreaded event you fall overboard. Some of us may already know that experience, right, Walker?” She merely shrugged. She never said she fell out of a boat. That was Mitch’s fiction and if he preferred to hang with it, who was she to say otherwise?

Failing to get the desired rise out of her, Mitch continued, “Let me demonstrate the proper position. I need a volunteer. Walker, why don’t you come down . . .”

Niles suddenly bounced forward. “Naw, she a grown-up. She already get all the fun. I be the dummy this time.”

And in true sister fashion Nyla quipped, “You be the dummy all the time.” Niles glared at her; she gave him the sister smirk that said, “I love you, too.”

Mitch said cheerily, “We’re losing daylight, people. Do we do this or don’t we?” Niles hustled forward and stood in front of Mitch. Mitch instructed, “You’ve all been taught there’s a right way and a wrong way to get into a boat. But there’s a right way and a wrong way to fall out of a boat, too. The right way is when the river smacks you so hard you get airborne and land feet first in the water. The wrong way is to get airborne and land head first. I know there are some pretty hard heads out there, but none of you, with maybe one exception, has a skull petrified enough to be a match for what the river has in store. Under the surface she has boulders, trees, tree stumps, tree limbs, rocks, and anything else mother nature cares to deposit. And then, of course, there is mankind’s contribution to our river’s ecology: bottles, washing machines, freezers, 69 Mustang . . .”

As Mitch continued listing the submersible hazards found in a river, Collin began to flash back. Weary as she was, there were no reserves left to fight them. She began seeing objects whiz by her . . . or was it she that was whizzing by them? And indeed, she did see car parts, though the make and model escaped her. Ghostly and ghastly trees reached out to snag her, sharp rocks cut and bruised her; a large white appliance of some kind crushed her arm as she flailed in panic . . . the river had her. Once again it had her and it wasn’t letting go. Not this time. This time it won . . .

A strong hand grabbed her arm and shook her sharply. "Walker! Snap out of it!! Did you hear one word I said? Did you?" Mitch's voice was full of disgust. Collin fought her way up from the bottom of the river nearly gasping for air. Still disoriented, she floundered for an apology. "I'm sorry. I'm sorry. I lost it for . . ." she had no idea how long she'd been out so repeated, "I lost it. I'm back now."

Mitch said angrily, "No you're not back, not by a long shot. Not until you tell me and this crew what spooks you so bad you can't function. They deserve to know. You're putting their lives on the line. They need to know they can depend on you, that you're going to be there for them, not off in la la land fighting some private fantasies. I want to know, now."

Collin said evenly but with a tinge of heat, "Mitch, it's been a very long day and last night was a very short night. I'm tired, I'm hurting and I lost it. Tomorrow I'll be rested, a lot less sore and it won't be a problem. Being on the river today was great and I didn't lose it to the river once. Lost it to pain a couple of times, but not to the river. I'll be fine."

"That's not near good enough, Walker. Not even close. Your choice: tell me now or you're grounded. This crew will sail without you."

Collin looked around at her crew mates and asked, "You agree with him?"

Mitch snapped, "Don't ask them. It doesn't matter what they say. They know you can have them punished for speaking up and telling the truth. I'm the one in charge here. I'm the only one that matters."

Collin said tightly, "I think my crew knows me better than that. They've never been afraid to tell me what they thought before. They're not going to start now."

Ta'waan said quickly, "White lady got that right. Ain't afraid of her or nobody else." He glared at Mitch and said, "We done played this game before and you say we passed it. Walker's crew. Rob here, he see her from where he stand. He know if she zoning. Nyla see her, too. She slap a paddle upside her head she get to freaking out."

Collin swallowed a chuckle, knowing Ta'waan's defense would not set well with Mitch. But she did love seeing her crew in action. Her crew, not Mitch's crew. And that was probably what was eating the man most.

Rob stepped up in defense as well. "Case worker lady just trying to demonstrate what happens when we sleeping stead of learning. Ask Niles."

Niles shoved Rob but picked up the baton and ran with it. "Besides, who gonna keep my other half straight to paddle, huh? Nyla go paddling on her own, she ain't never gonna keep in time." He grinned sweetly at his sister and added, "Can't tell time let alone keep time."

Nyla rushed across the clearing and smacked her sibling. He ducked, then the two proceeded to have a hand to nose to wrist to ear to gut . . . you get the picture . . . discussion about the superiority of the sexes. As it looked near to being a draw, however, Collin decided to break it up. Watching the two wrestle brought an ache to her gut and loneliness to her being. But it was a good ache and the loneliness was tempered by the knowing she wasn't truly alone anymore.

As the dust settled Mitch glared at each member of his crew and said with ice in his voice, "She stays on one condition. She has to pass the river test, ride it all the way to the bottom and do it right." He glared in triumph at her. "Otherwise she stays behind."

Collin nodded. "Fair enough."

Then Mitch played his trump card "And you ride it first."

Collin felt her stomach lurch. She'd missed the instructions and had the sure feeling Mitch was not going to repeat them for her private edification. She swallowed hard then nodded. "If that's the way you want it."

"That's the way it is."

Or was. Chonnell and Pardner had been whispering and giggling quietly. Suddenly they took off running towards the head of the slope where the start point was, yelling brightly, "I'm first! I'm first!" "Me next! Me next!"

Mitch yelled furiously but impotently at the scampering sprites, "Get back here! Chonnell! Pardner!!"

Chonnell jumped into the slide position: arms across her chest, feet crossed at the ankles, laid her head back in the water and yelled, "Watch me! Watch me everybody!!"

Beside Collin Ta'waan said softly, "She got it right, lady. Gotta put your head down. Gotta lay down, gotta put your head down."

As the child swooshed by her, totally submerged, Collin felt all the life drain from her. No way. There was no way. A voice deep inside sneered, *"Find a way. Make a way. Fake a way if you have to, but do it. These kids are counting on you. They put it on the line for you. You can't let them down. Do it. Don't say you can't. Never say you can't. You can if you want to. If you really, really want to. If it matters more than your puny existence. But you're too weak, too selfish. You don't want to do it, that's all. Not can't, won't."*

A voice outside her ear buzzed softly with a tone of satisfaction. "You can't, can you? You can't do it. You're terrified of this. Why? What power does it have?" Mitch was standing behind her watching her reactions as Pardner followed Chonnell down the slide.

Collin smiled at Mitch with all the bravado she could muster then said to the teens, "Our turn. And I will go first this time." She grinned. "I refuse to be shown up by a ten year old. Two of them no less."

Nyla chuckled, "Yeah. Little twerps. Think they so smart."

The crowd walked to the top of the slope but Mitch stayed near the landing point waiting for Chonnell and Pardner to climb out and join him. At the starting line Collin stopped and said quietly, but with feeling, "I want to thank you guys for getting me another chance. And I mean it. If anyone wants me off the crew say so. I told Mitch I'd be better tomorrow. I don't know that for a fact. All I can do is try."

Rob said, "You been saying that's all anyone can do, case worker lady. Ain't expecting you to do more than that. Just try."

Collin nodded, looked at the other three. "Anyone?"

Niles said, "Not me, man."

Nyla added, "Nope."

Collin asked, "Ta'waan?"

The boy said slowly, "Used to think it was uncool to be scared, like it made you a coward. But grown up lady like you be scared and still do what scares you . . . that be something to think about. If a little old white lady can beat something like that maybe I can, too."

Collin grinned at him and said, "No maybe, Ta'waan. You can."

Mitch yelled up the hill, "We haven't got all day! Unless you want to walk back to the van in the dark. Move it, Walker!!"

Niles grumbled, "That is one uncool dude, you know?"

Suddenly Robbie stepped in front of Collin and said quickly, "Wait 'til I be half way down then go. I be waiting for you at the bottom. Understand? I be waiting for you." He jumped in the sluice, gave a war hoop then went rocketing down the slide.

Collin shook her head. He was covering all the bases, wasn't he? Friends at the top, friends at the bottom. What more could she want? Collin waited until he was just past midway then slid into position. She exclaimed, "Cold!!" then laid her head back, breathed a thousand silent prayers in a moment in time, and let go.

Her body took off like a rocket down the slide, twisting and turning as it conformed to the contours of the run. It was her mind that went instantly out of control, careening back in time. She was bouncing and skipping along the river bottom, flashing helplessly past the outstretched arms of would be rescuers. Screaming, gagging on water, retching, screaming more, carried endlessly on and on and on . . . Finally she was staring up through the water at the face of an angel, ready to go home, wanting to go home, praying to go home . . . only to have the angel pushed aside by a well-meaning stranger who dragged a half-dead five year old from the river's clutches.

Back in the sluice run Collin felt no sense of panic, just the calm assurance she would die, this time, and he would win. Water splashed across her face and Collin held her breath, knowing that to breathe was to swallow water and to drown. How long the run would last she didn't know. It didn't matter; she would die anyhow. Her defenses were gone; resistance was futile. All she had to do was take that one liquid breath and everything would be over. Just one little breath . . .

Strong hands grabbed her, pulling her out of the water, shaking her, pounding her on the back, yelling at her. Collin drew in a deep, painful breath of air as the present returned to her slowly. Robbie was standing in front of her, his hands on both her shoulders, shaking her sharply and demanding, "Come on, lady, come on. I know you in there. Come on. You did it, Collin. You did it. You made it all the way down."

A large body swooshed past behind them, followed in rapid succession by two more human torpedoes. Ta'waan, Niles and Nyla climbed rapidly out of the water, cheering and hollering. Collin reached out and hugged Robbie. He neither stiffened nor pulled away but returned the hug warmly and tightly. Collin roped in the others for a group hug and said over and over, "You guys did it. It was you guys. I couldn't have done it alone. It's you guys."

Chonnell and Pardner did little victory dances back to the bottom of the sluice leaving Mitch standing by himself. The girls joined the celebration as Collin pointed to each of them. "You two. You two are something else! What am I going to do with you two?" She hugged them individually and corporately then sat back against the sluice to let all the emotion flow.

Nyla said darkly, "Here comes . . ."

Collin said softly, "Whatever else he is, he's still our instructor, Nyla. One more day. Keep it cool one more day." She thought, *"And then we nail his hide to the wall."* How someplace as wonderful as Grace could hire someone as unbalanced as Mitch was a mystery to her. Some serious flaw in their personality profiling. She should speak to the owner about that. Or maybe she should just tell Jeff and he could tell the owner. Jeff seemed to be able to get what he wanted done. Nice that the owner had that much confidence in his maintenance staff.

Mitch walked up to the group, a picture of contented accomplishment. He smiled with delight as he said, "Congratulations to all of you. I knew you could pull together as a crew if I just provided enough pressure. You did great." He looked at Collin and said, "No hard feelings? But this was the final test and you all passed it with no problem."

Robbie started to speak but Collin silenced him with a glance. She eyed Mitch piercingly and said, "No more games, right? No more little tests, no more phony fights. This really was the last test?"

Mitch nodded. "Well, the river itself is the final test. But this was the final test to see if you were ready for the final test. And each of you did marvelous." He looked at Collin and said, "Especially you, Walker. I've never seen anyone so relaxed. It was like you were unconscious. Or dead. Amazing." He paused to let her consider that then clapped his hands together and said with enthusiasm, "Okay, everyone. Back to the van and back to camp. Tomorrow is the big day, the one we've been waiting for." His eyes sparkled as he looked at Collin and said, "I know I've been looking forward to it." He paused, smiled warmly at Collin then said, "We meet at eight thirty sharp on dock two. Everyone get that? Eight-thirty, dock two."

The walk back to the van seemed to take longer than the walk out to the sluice had, or so it seemed to Collin. Maybe it was the weight of the emotional roller coaster she'd been on since yesterday. Or maybe last night's rendezvous was catching up with her. Whatever, she was bone tired. She abdicated her "adults up front" privilege, opting instead for a bench seat in the back that she could stretch out on, sort of. Pardner got shotgun honors by virtue of being the youngest. The kids tried to introduce Mitch and Collin to punk rap but Mitch couldn't get the hang of it and Collin was too tired to even try. She slept most of the hour trip back home but it was fitful and restless, as some sense of unease nagged at her subconscious. It didn't help that every time she woke she found Mitch staring at her, smiling. She cautioned herself against flaming paranoia and tried to sleep again.

It was nearly seven when they arrived back at camp. Collin noted with wry satisfaction that the spring in everyone's step seemed to have sprung a mite. Even the youthfullest of the youths was having a tough time dragging themselves out of the van. Only Mitch seemed unaffected by the day's toils. As the tired crew dragged up the hill to paradise—hot showers, hot food and stationary beds—Mitch called cheerily, "Eight-thirty, dock two. Latecomers walk!!"

Nyla groaned, "Can I stuff him, please? Just one time, I promise."

Collin assured her, "Tomorrow. Tomorrow you can stuff him."

Niles added, "And I get to help."

"I'm in for that."

"Mark it." Ta'waan and Robbie weighed in.

Collin chuckled then said, "Tomorrow."

Suddenly Mitch called out, "Walker, hold up a minute."

As a body the whole group turned to face Mitch. Collin scanned the area and saw at least three other bodies working on the dock area and at least two kayakers coming in to land. She called back, "What, Mitch?"

"I just thought of something that can help your hand. Come back down for five minutes and I'll show you."

Collin checked the area again and it was still crowded. She looked at the crew and said, "Go on up. I'll be along shortly."

Robbie's face was colored with concern. "You sure, lady?"

She nodded. "There's plenty of company. I'm fine. Go on up." She nailed Robbie with a stern glance and said, "Stay with the group, Rob."

She could tell from his face that he didn't like it but he nodded. The crew went on up to the lodge. Collin came back down to where Mitch was standing and asked, "What?"

Mitch's voice and face were friendly as he said, "I've been thinking about it all day and it finally came to me. There is a grip you can use that won't put pressure on your palm. It's awkward, but no more so than that convoluted way you've been holding the paddle."

Mitch held the paddle out to her; she took it gingerly. He instructed her on the manner in which to position her hands but Collin wasn't getting it. She shook her head. "I don't understand, Mitch. It's all backwards."

"Here, let's try it this way." In one smooth motion he swung behind her, holding her between himself and the paddle. Collin stiffened immediately. Mitch said soothingly, "Relax, Collin." He lay his hands on top of hers, moving hers into the proper position. "See? Try it that way." Without taking his hands off hers he began to swing the paddle in its see-saw motion. "Isn't that better? Come on, relax, Collin. You are so uptight." He dropped hold of her hands and began massaging her shoulders. "Loosen up, woman. Stress isn't healthy, you know."

Collin tried to force herself to relax, and at the same time step away from Mitch. But he continued to hold her by her shoulders. He cooed, "Come on, Collin, lighten up. Enjoy the moment." He pulled her closer to himself, wrapping his arms around her.

Collin noted that one or two of the crowd that had been on the docks was leaving without glancing their way. Typical: don't get involved. She kept her voice even as she said, "Mitch, stop. Don't ruin a good friendship."

Mitch nuzzled her neck lightly and whispered, "This only makes it better."

Collin said more forcefully, "Stop, Mitch. Don't make me hurt you."

Mitch lifted his head and began to laugh. He released her from his embrace but did not let go of her hands. He chortled, "That's what I love about you, Collin. You have the strangest sense of humor. You, hurt me? Give me a break, woman."

Collin pretended to laugh along with him. "Yeah, well, we can dream, can't we?"

Mitch looked at her hands and said softly, "It's a shame you had to get hurt. You have beautiful hands." He held them together, examining them.

Collin choked, coughed then said in a strangled voice, "Can I have them back, please? I need them for tomorrow."

Mitch kissed the backs of her hands lightly. Without looking up he said, "Hands like these should be treasured." He began to kiss her knuckles one by one.

The last kayaker passed them, one of Collin's fellow counselors. He gave Collin a questioning look, asking in a sense if all was well. Collin called out joyfully, "Hank! Meet my instructor, Mitch. He's a terrific white water captain, Hank. You should try it next summer."

Hank walked up and said happily, "Great. Mitch, was it? Wonderful."

Mitch had, of course, dropped his hold on Collin's hands as soon as Hank approached. He shook the counselor's hand, reverting to sea captain self and said, "So, you prefer to take the river solo, huh? Dangerous move, my man. Out there unprotected."

Hank grinned. "Oh, I usually have a friend around. And speaking of friends, you two do know the dining room closes in twenty minutes? Collin, have you tried the veal, yet? It's wonderful."

Mitch said "We'll be up in a minute or so."

Collin said swiftly, "Hank, would you mind waiting? I wanted to ask you how Stella and Peale are doing."

"Sure, no problem." He smiled amiably and stood back, prepared to wait as long as necessary.

Collin looked at Mitch and asked, "Are we done here?"

Mitch smiled politely and said, "For now. We may discuss this further tomorrow. I'll see you in the morning. Good night, Collin. Pleasant dreams."

"Night, Mitch." Collin turned to Hank and said, "Let's go. And you can tell me all about Stella and Peale."

They walked up the path together. As soon as they were out of earshot of the docks, Hank said in a low voice, "Boy, you drag out all the old stuff, don't you Walker? You're lucky I remember back that far. Hank and Stella are in protection 101, aren't they?"

Collin let out a long sigh and said, "Yeah, but Gene, you did it perfect. Thank you so much."

Gene, alias Hank, asked, "Do we need to report this guy?"

Collin shuddered then said, "I'm going to. Tonight." She shuddered again. There was absolutely no question. Mitch was master monster, the murderer of two women. Who wanted to make her number three. She shivered yet again.

Gene studied her a moment then said, "I'll go with you if you want, if you're afraid they won't believe your story."

Collin smiled at Gene and said, "Thanks, Gene. I appreciate it. If I need you I know where to get a hold of you."

They reached the lodge entrance; Gene held the door for her. He said, "You really ought to try the veal. I never touch it myself."

Collin grinned. "I know. You're a vegetarian. Thanks again, Gene. You saved my life."

Gene shrugged. "Or just your enjoyment of it. No big deal." He walked jauntily off down the hall, whistling.

Collin watched him go then whispered, "No, Gene. You literally may have saved my life. And it is a big deal." She looked at the dining hall. It seemed disrespectful to call it a cafeteria, and downright insulting to say "chow hall." She debated whether to go in or not. She should let the kids know she was here and safe. Collin went in and found the crew sitting together watching the door. Plates were full but mostly untouched. Either they had just gotten seated or were waiting for her. She waved across the three tables' distance to signal she was fine. A cheer went up and forks and spoons began flailing through the air, making up for lost time.

Collin shook her head and started to leave, but turned back as Robbie's voice yelled, "Collin! Wait there!"

Collin waited while Robbie struggled out from the table, bounced over two chairs, and ran up beside her. "What's up, my man?"

"You can't leave. You ain't ate anything."

Collin shrugged. "I haven't been hungry, Rob."

"Yeah, but Jeff put me in charge of getting you to eat something." Robbie grinned with wicked delight. "He say I should cram it down your throat if you don't. Those were his words, too. Cram it down your throat."

Collin said archly, "He did, did he? And where does he get off thinking . . ."

Robbie held up a hand to stop her protest. "Lady, I'm just saying what is. You want to fight with me or with him?"

Collin snorted. "I'll take you both."

Robbie suddenly grew quiet and said softly, "You couldn't take the monster man."

Collin sobered up immediately. She looked at Robbie and said, "You're right, I couldn't." She let out a slow breath then said in resignation, "Okay, my man. What's good on the menu?" All fight gone, she let Robbie lead her to the line.

Dinner over, Collin went straight to the message center to use the phone to call Bo, then to call Jeff. She wished there was a more private place to do it but these were the only phones available for camper use. She smiled at the receptionist and said, "I'm Collin Walker. I need to make a call."

The woman looked at her desk a minute then said brightly, "No you don't. This was left for you this morning. We tried to reach you before you left on your class but apparently you left before the phone arrived."

Collin looked at the cell phone the woman was handing her and asked in confusion, "From who?" Or whom? Did it really matter? Did she really care? "Any idea who left it?"

"Not a one. There's a phone number on the card, though."

Collin looked at it and was mildly disappointed it wasn't Jeff's. It wouldn't take much for her to believe he'd do something this . . . persistent? Romantic? Crazy? You fill in the blank. Collin thanked the woman then hustled back to her room. She closed the door, locked it securely, checked under her bed—and in the closet for good measure—then sat down to phone Bo.

But before she could punch in the last digit she hesitated. Was she sure? Was she really sure? She was about to accuse a man of murdering two young women. Was she absolutely positive? How did she know?

Collin shuddered, but reviewed both the attack and Mitch's behavior. It all fit together so neatly. Maybe too neatly. It was so obvious it couldn't be real. But maybe he was too crazy to be devious. Yeah, but why wasn't it obvious the last time? Or the time before that? How should she know! She wasn't there, then. She was here, now, and she was convinced Mitch was the attacker. Whether he was tied to the previous two murders wasn't the issue. Maybe it was to Bo, though. Maybe if she couldn't hand him the Handyman on a platter Bo wouldn't be interested. She'd have implicated Mitch, ruined the kids last chance at a river run, and all for nothing. Was she sure?

Collin stared at her hands then said softly, "It's Mitch. I know it's Mitch." She drew in a deep breath, picked up the phone and punched in the numbers.

After two rings a rugged male voice said, "Speak to me."

Collin swallowed hard. "Sheriff Lodi?"

"Ms. Walker, I presume."

"Sheriff, I know who attacked me last night."

"The boating instructor, right?"

There was disbelief and a little sarcasm in the voice. Collin decided to ignore it and said, "Yes."

"And you're absolutely sure about this? You're not by chance implicating him because he was coming on to you this afternoon?"

Collin stared at the phone. A multitude of questions ran through her mind. Chief among them was, "How did he know about that?" She shook off the inquiries and said sharply, "I don't play games with people's lives, Sheriff. And I've been mauled by more than one office letch and handled it on my own. If you don't trust my judgment then pick your phone up at the office." Collin ended the call, wished vainly for the days you could slam a receiver down in someone's ear, and threw the phone sharply on the bed. She would have preferred to dash it against the floor but it wasn't her property. She threw herself on the bed and let out a loud groan of anger, frustration, pain, emptiness . . . all the emotions that rattled inside of her and could not find release. Not for the first- or last-time did she regret not being able to cry. It would have been such sweet release.

The phone began to beep. Collin picked it up, looked at the caller ID and threw it back down. She seethed, "No, Sheriff, I do not want to reconsider." It continued to beep. Collin yelled, "Go away! I'm not answering!" More beeping. Collin stared at the phone, waiting. Beep . . . beep . . . beep . . . Finally she reached out and took the phone. She pressed the send button then said tightly, "Sheriff . . ."

He interrupted her abruptly, "Laura Mars was my niece. I want nothing more than to nail the slime who killed her. So I have to watch my feelings. I question every motive, every hunch, every intuition. You understand?"

As Bo talked Collin grew silent. When he was done she said quietly, "I do understand, Sheriff. I question my own as well. If Mitch were only a jerk I wouldn't have even mentioned him to you. But I know he was the one who attacked me. I don't know if he's your killer or not."

Bo said evenly, "That's fair enough. Don't suppose you could present any evidence to that effect, could you?"

"That would stand up in court? Not much. Some things he said, stuff he knew that no one else does. The way he acted . . . some of the things he did." Kissing her knuckles. Holding her hands. Collin shuddered again. Man, that was annoying. She said, "I don't know how it would play before a jury."

There was silence on the line then Bo said, "We need to talk. Can you come to the station?"

Collin sagged then asked, "How long would it take me to walk?"

Bo chuckled. "How about if a female detective and I come to you? Would that be considered proper?"

"Exceedingly. But civilian clothes. I still don't want to spook anyone needlessly."

Bo said, "We'll be there in half an hour. What room are you in?"

Collin told him the number then the line went dead. Collin tossed the phone on the bed, gently this time. She saw there was another phone message on the floor, from Jeff, no doubt. Four messages now. He really was going to think she'd lost interest. She would call him tonight right after Bo left. No matter what time it was. She lay down and let her whole body relax. Five minutes. No, ten. Ten minutes, that's all she asked. Actually she'd ask for about three days, but would happily settle for ten—maybe fifteen minutes. Twenty tops. Just a little nap. Collin curled up around her pillow and closed her eyes. Bo said half an hour. Maybe she could go twenty five . . .

A loud, incessant pounding on her door woke Collin with a start. Her heart was racing and panic fogged her brain. She sat up quickly and shouted, "Who's there?"

A muffled, irritated voice said, "Bo. Open the door, Walker."

Collin scrambled out of the bed and rushed to the door. The peep hole provided a rather distorted view of the Sheriff in civilian clothes and a female companion similarly dressed. Collin dragged her better hand through her hair then opened the door, apologizing, "I'm sorry. I fell asleep."

Bo merely grunted then handed her a phone message. "Taped on your door. Thought it might be important." He and the female officer came in.

Collin closed the door then folded the message in half and stuffed it in her pocket. Probably from Jeff. Later, dear heart. I promise. "Thank you."

Bo asked gruffly, "What kind of schedule are you on tomorrow?"

Collin looked at the other officer and smiled. "Hi. I'm Collin Walker."

The woman grinned. "Cheryl Nance."

Bo asked, "You two done being social? Can we get to business?" Collin and Cheryl nodded. Bo harrumphed then asked again, "What kind of schedule you on?"

Collin thought then said, "We're to meet at the docks at eight-thirty, portage to the river starting spot, then go from there."

"All of you together?"

"That's the general idea."

"Ever a time anyone goes off by themselves?"

Collin shook her head. "Ideally we all stay together in the boat the entire day. We land at designated locations for rest stops, but then it's boys on one side, girls on the other." Something about the phone message niggled at her. Had the "from" designation said Jeff?

Bo continued his questioning. "At what point could he get the group split up and you off by yourself?"

Collin shook her head. "He can't unless he capsizes the boat. Even then there are no guarantees who would end up with who." She cautioned the internal English teacher, *"Don't even start!!"* The message. What was it about the message? Collin took it out of her pocket and opened it.

Bo began to pace. "Something's wrong. We're missing something. The Handyman was never this patient."

"Maybe he's not." Collin's voice shook only slightly.

Bo looked at her. "What?"

Collin held out the note. It was typed and read, "Collin, meeting time changed to six am, dock five. Rob."

Bo shook his head. "So?"

Collin fought to control her voice. "Rob and I have a code for messages when there's trouble." She colored slightly but admitted, "He's Ares, I'm . . . Xena."

Bo drawled, "Uh huh." He thought a moment then said, "He's a kid. He forgot."

"Rob wouldn't forget." There was heat in her voice but she had to make him understand. "We don't play this game for fun, Sheriff. If we're using codes, it's deadly serious." Poor choice of words, that. Watch it woman. Collin pressed on. "Rob never addresses me as Collin. He calls me 'lady' 'case worker lady' and if he's really mad at me, a few other things I won't mention. But he never calls me Collin." Until today but that was because of duress, and that didn't count. Collin finished, "The note is bogus, Sheriff. Rob didn't send it."

Bo considered her evidence then said slowly, "Okay, Walker, for the sake of argument, what if he didn't send it? Why couldn't it be some other prankster sending you out early for a joke?"

"Only the crew and Mitch know where and when we are meeting. No crew member would do this for a joke. We're all too serious about tomorrow's run. If you could listen to the campers at dinner, no one is pranking anyone tonight. The kids are wired about tomorrow, Sheriff. And there's this: no one else is up at that hour. We've met at that time before, and trust me there is no one around, especially down by the docks. And dock five is the dock furthest from the lodge and closest to the river mouth. If I wanted to make a quick getaway, that's where I'd leave from."

Again Bo considered the evidence. He said, finally, "Makes sense. What do you suggest we do?"

Collin studied the man closely, trying to decide where he was coming from. She chose her words carefully and said, "Sheriff, I am fairly well convinced my attacker and your Handyman are one and the same. I'm absolutely convinced my attacker was Mitch Kellum. But I have no real proof, so tomorrow at 6 am I'm going down to dock five to get that proof. If I'm right I'm determined to see no one else is going to suffer. What you do is entirely up to you."

Bo drawled, "Well, nice you have that all figured out. You mind if me and some of the boys tag along just in case Xena needs a little help? 'Course, being the Warrior Princess she could probably handle it all by herself, now, couldn't she?"

Collin sagged down in a chair, defeated. "What do you want from me?"

Bo said heatedly, "I want you to step out of my investigation and let the professionals handle it. We may be back woods folk but we do know how to handle criminals."

Collin snapped, "Fine! Wonderful!! I'd love not being a target for some perverted killer! But when I don't show up tomorrow he's going to know something's wrong and he'll go underground again."

"Let me worry about that."

Collin leaned forward, her voice urgent. "Listen to me, Sheriff. I'm not stupid. I have no death wish and I'm scared. I'd rather face the river than Mitch, and the river terrifies me. But this is your best shot ever of nailing this guy. He's not going to hurt me and he's certainly not going to kill me. I trust you not to let that happen. It's been handed to me and I'm going to finish it. Let me help."

Bo measured her with that penetrating glare then said softly, "Okay, Walker. But we do it my way, understand?"

Collin nodded and said quickly, "But I have three conditions."

Bo snapped, "Three? What . . ."

"Just listen, all right? They're easy. One: please, the name is Collin. I thought we established that once before. Collin, remember?"

Bo almost smiled. Almost. "Okay, Collin. What's next?"

"I won't wear a wire. I've had two good friends killed because of them. I'm convinced every thug out there suspects his victim is wearing one and always checks. No wires."

Bo nodded and the light in his eyes said he understood. "So we've learned." He added, "Won't need one, anyhow. I plan on having enough men in the field; you won't ever be out of sight, no matter where he goes."

"Will they be out of sight?"

Bo cocked an eyebrow and said, "Young woman, I never put a man in the field that hasn't first stalked and brought down deer, bear, and turkey. If you know anything about hunting you'll know stealth and invisibility are the two most important prerequisites."

"I'll take your word for it. I've never hunted anything more vicious than my car keys."

Bo shook his head then said, "Three."

Collin hesitated then said softly, "Unless there is a real and imminent threat on my life itself, you wait until I signal to come in and get him."

Bo looked confused. "What are you talking about, lady?"

"Unless you know—and I trust your instincts are well-honed enough to be able to tell—that he's actually ready to kill me and not just making threats, I'd prefer no one came storming in to the rescue unnecessarily,"

"Why?" There was an edge to his voice.

Collin's voice grew even softer. "There's a young woman out there that never came home. I'd like to help bring her back. Animals like Mitch can usually be convinced to talk about their conquests. Maybe I can find out where she is."

Bo was silent a long minute. His voice was slightly uneven as he asked, "What kind of signal?"

"How about one very loud prolonged scream?"

"And how are we to tell that from any other scream?"

Collin said icily, "There won't be any others."

"You're so sure about that, are you, now?"

Collin's voice and stare were both dead cold. "Mitch is no different than another animal I lived with for many years. He couldn't make me scream, or cry, or feel anything at all. Neither will Mitch."

Bo eyed her cautiously, as if for the first time considering what he'd gotten himself tangled up with. He said softly, "You are one cold woman."

"When I have to be. Are we agreed?"

Bo studied her a moment longer, then nodded slowly. "All right, Wal . . . Collin. I'll wait—unless my finely honed instincts tell me you've crossed the line." There was only the finest edge of sarcasm in his voice. Collin nodded, acknowledging his authority. His voice hardened again, "But you remember my condition: you do nothing without my permission. You get to the dock and I don't like the looks of it, this whole thing is a bust, you understand?" Again Collin nodded. Bo said, apparently satisfied, "Good. There's not much sense talking real strategy since Mitch will determine where we go from here. He probably has a hide out or something where he can go underground if he gets nervous. Do all you can to stay out in the open but stay out of motorized vehicles if possible. And don't worry too much if he takes you out on the river."

Collin grumbled, "That's easy for you to say."

Bo shook his head his head. "Xena will face a murderer but not a river. Lady, you are something else."

"Everyone keeps telling me that but no one will say what."

Bo shook his head. "Never mind." He thought slowly then said, "It may sound stupid, but be careful out there." He looked at her pointedly and said, "You may think you know his type, but I've learned they all have their quirks that make them unique, and therefore deadly. If Mitch is the Handyman, he's killed twice. He won't hesitate to kill again, even out of pattern. You may never get that opportunity to scream."

Collin nodded. "Understood." She hesitated then admitted, "Sheriff, I'm not under any delusions about who or what I am. I don't think I'm smarter than he is and I know I'm not stronger than he is." She shuddered, but let it pass. She was getting used to the sensation. Collin continued, "It's a chance I'm taking because I think the benefits outweigh the risks. If we nail him, he's gone, case closed. If our court system does its job right. If he kills me, you nail him, and the same case gets closed. Either way a particularly vicious threat to society is taken off the streets. Or the waterways. In my book that makes it all worthwhile."

Bo looked at her a moment then said, "You really believe that." It was not a question.

"I really believe that." Her voice was calm and even.

"Then there's not much else to say but I'll see you in the morning. You won't see me but trust me, we're out there."

Collin smiled. "Sheriff, I've been trusting in one I can't see for several years now. My faith is in him."

Bo nodded. "Keep it there."

Collin walked Bo and Cheryl to the door. She said, "Good night, Sheriff." She looked at the deputy and grinned, "It's been a pleasure talking with you. Maybe we can do it sometime when you actually get to say something."

Cheryl smiled. "I'd enjoy that." She whispered conspiratorially, "Some of those 'men' in the field might be women, too, but don't remind him. He likes to pretend this is still 1960."

Collin nodded. "I see."

Bo growled, "Let's go, Nance."

She whispered one last shot, "I'm still working on bringing down the bear." She motioned towards Bo, grinned then straightened up. "Yes sir, boss." They walked off down the hall.

Collin closed the door then leaned against it for support. That had been delightful. She looked at the clock: it was just after nine. Late, but not too late. She hoped. She pushed off the door, walked to the bed and picked up the phone. She drew a deep breath, let it out slowly then began to punch in numbers. She'd pay Bo for the call when he got the bill. Better yet, she'd leave a few bucks on the counter with the phone in case . . . well, just in case.

The phone began ringing on the other end. Collin felt her whole being tighten up and whispered, "Be there. Please, be there."

A female voice answered, "Faell resdence." The lisp was pronounced though the voice was mature.

Collin swallowed then asked, "May I speak with Jeff Farrell?"

"Jeff nowt vailble now. I take message?"

Collin sagged, bit her lip, then played a hunch. "Is this Leesa?"

"How you know my name?"

"Jeff has told me about you and how proud he is of you. He says you're going to graduate from high school this year."

"Jeff big dummy for little brother. I got big test take tomorrow then know if I g-rad-u-ate." She drew the word out, spacing the syllables as if it was a word she was still learning.

Collin said, "I'm sure you will do fine, Leesa. Jeff tells me you study all the time."

"Jeff help me study. He not too stupid bout some things. Just bout mos things."

Collin grinned and smothered a laugh. She asked, "Is Jeff home and he's busy, or doesn't he want to be bothered with phone calls tonight?"

"Jeff home. He in a shower but I not suppos say that."

Collin said solemnly, "I won't tell." She bit her lip again then said softly, "Will you tell him that Collin Walker called?"

The shock wave was instantaneous. "Collin Walker? Ooooh!!" The phone dropped and Collin could hear the sound of feet pounding up stairs. All the while Leesa was yelling excitedly, "Jeff!! Jeff!! She call!! She call!! Jeff! Jeff!"

Collin stared at the phone in confused amusement. What was that all about? She could hear Leesa's excited chatter in the background combined with a loud pounding on a door. In the foreground, however, a woman's voice was asking calmly, "Now what has gotten in to the child?" The voice came closer to the phone. "Who left this receiver off the hook?" The voice got closer then asked, "Hello? Is anyone there?"

Collin guessed quickly, "Mrs. Farrell? Please don't hang up. I was calling to talk to Jeff, and Leesa answered the phone."

"Oh, well that explains it. Leesa can be somewhat flighty sometimes. A good child but not always stable, as you know." The voice was of an elderly, not quite all there woman. Is that what Jeff had meant about his mom? Like someone floating through life, seeing only the pleasant places . . . Poor man. Poor woman.

Collin said, "No, Leesa was a joy to talk to. But she got excited about something and dropped the phone. I'd like to leave Jeff a message if I could."

A smooth, pleasant male voice approached the phone. "Who is it, Lacey?"

Lacey half covered the receiver and said, "Well, I'm not sure, dear. I haven't asked her yet."

There was a chuckle in the voice as the man said, "If it's that Walker woman, I'd like to speak to her myself. Maybe she can get Jeffrey's head out of the clouds. Though I'm sure she's the one that put it there to begin with. I haven't got a decent hour's work out of him since he came back."

That got Collin's attention. This was better than talking to Jeff himself. She would probably learn a lot more, too. She listened closely as Lacey said, "Now, dear, you were young and in love, once."

Mr. Farrell, the elder, said tenderly, "Yes, I was. And now I'm old and in love." There was the sound of two people kissing and Collin ached for the simple beauty of it. After a moment Mr. Farrell asked, "Shouldn't you ask the woman her name?"

"Oh, dear. I forgot." Lacey came back on the line and asked, "May I tell Jeffrey who is calling?"

"Collin Walker."

The voice broke into smiles. "It is you, young lady. You've had our Jeffrey quite concerned. He'll be very disappointed to have missed your call."

Collin heard the phone change hands and Mr. Farrell instruct his wife gently, "Lacey, my love, instead of running up the woman's phone bill, go hustle your son out of the shower and get him down here. I will not spend another minute with the boy if he misses this call." Collin heard footsteps leaving, then Mr. Farrell came on the line. The voice was pleasant, refined, but not in the negative or phony sense: rich with just the hint of a brogue. "Ms. Walker?"

"Mr. Farrell, sir."

"My son will be down shortly. Could I impose on you to wait for him? I'm sure he will be happy to split the cost of your phone bill."

Collin grinned. Scotch brogue. "That won't be necessary, sir. I'll wait." She couldn't help it; she added, "I'd wait all night if I had to."

There was silence at the other end. Finally Mr. Farrell said softly, "It's worse than I suspected. You both have it. This could be . . . interesting."

Collin looked at the phone, a little confused. "Sir?"

Before she could ask further, yet another voice exploded on the scene. "Dad! That's my phone call!"

Mr. Farrell said, "Jeffrey, calm down. Ms. Walker, it's been a pleasure talking with you. Very informative. I believe my son is available to take this call, now."

Jeff's voice was restrained but urgent. "Dad, please."

"In a moment, son. Ms. Walker, when you return to Oakton you must come out to visit us. Don't wait for Jeffrey to invite you. We're in the book. The only Farrell on Lewiston Road."

Collin projected a quick mental map trying to remember where Lewiston Road was. On the east side, to be sure, divided north and south by the river. North was flashy new money: condos and townhomes and mansions too new to have trees of any size. South was old town: big comfortable houses that had been there before Oakton; that you wouldn't want to heat in winter, nor cool in summer. Homes that developers were always wanting to tear down to make way for more condos and multi-family units. Collin asked, "South of the river, sir?"

Mr. Farrell sounded impressed. "Shrewd guess, Ms. Walker."

Collin could hear a still respectful, but slightly more pressing, "Dad, please may I have the phone? Calls are limited from camp, remember? I'd like to be able to say more than 'hi.' Please?"

Mr. Farrell relented, apparently taking pity on his desperate offspring. He said, "Take it upstairs in our room, Jeff. It will give you some relief from Leesa. Just remember working people need their rest, too." Collin heard the sound of footsteps taking stairs two at a time, a shout of "I've got it," and someone picking up the line. Mr. Farrell said pleasantly, "Have a good evening, Ms. Walker."

"Good night, Mr. Farrell." The downstairs phone clicked off. Collin felt suddenly shy and very uncertain how to proceed from here. Her voice trembled slightly and she said simply, "Hi."

Jeff's voice was soft and there was a vulnerability in it that struck Collin hard. "Hi yourself. I almost thought . . ."

Collin cut him off quickly. "Don't. Don't ever think that. I was always gone when you called and . . ." And why couldn't she call back? Because she'd been mugged? Been sitting in the sheriff's office? Plotting strategy on how to trap a killer? Collin said, "I couldn't get back to you right away."

Collin heard the caution in his voice as he asked, "Any reason why?"

Collin deflected the question with a question. "Are we going to start this with a fight?"

"No." Jeff hesitated then said quietly, "Tell me you wanted to, but you couldn't and I'll let it go."

Collin's throat constricted and she had to swallow hard in order to whisper, "I wanted to, Jeff. I really, really wanted to. I miss you."

He said softly, "That's all I need to know." There was a pause then he asked, "How are the classes going?"

Collin cradled the phone against her shoulder, pulled out a pillow in order to get more comfortable, then curled up on the bed. She said, "I'm . . . surviving. We did the water slide thing today. That was . . . uh, well, I guess 'intense' fits. The kids were great, though. All of them. They're the ones pulling me through this."

There was concerned confusion in Jeff's voice as he asked, "Water slide? We don't have a water slide. You mean the old sluice? Out by Lester's Run?"

"I have no idea where it is, Jeff. Lester had to be running in the middle of nowhere if it was his."

She heard the grin in his voice as he said, "Not that kind of run, dear heart." The concern returned quickly. "How far away from camp were you?"

"I don't know, Jeff. Why is it important?"

"The sluice run I know of was supposed to be closed. I shut it down myself last year for safety reasons. If it's been reopened I need to know about it."

Collin laughed. "You mean maybe the owner made a decision to do something and didn't tell you first? Is that it?"

Jeff laughed but it sounded forced to Collin's ear. "Right. I'm supposed to be his technical consultant on these things. He doesn't make a move without me."

Collin decided this was a much safer vein to pursue rather than having him ask her about her own activities. She said, "He must really value your opinion."

"Second only to God's. And his dad's. He has a very close relationship with his father."

"That gives you something in common. What does his wife think? Does he listen to her advice?"

"He's not married. Says he's never found that one perfect woman."

"Has he looked?"

She heard the grin. "Are you prospecting?"

Insulted, Collin huffed. "No. I was merely asking." She grinned. "Besides rich men can be boring."

"How would you know? Have you ever dated one?"

"Are we digging up bones, here?"

"Depends on whose graveyard is deeper, I guess."

Not the pathway she wanted, folks. Collin adjusted the course sharply and asked, "Why won't you tell me his name? I'd like to write him a letter of thanks but addressing it, 'Dear Occupant' hardly seems appropriate."

"He's received more than a few of those, I'm sure." Jeff's voice became quizzical and he asked, "What would you tell him?"

Collin definitely approved of this new heading. She said, "Oh, I'd tell him . . ."

"No, do it like a letter."

Collin protested, "I can't do letters in my head."

"You can't do anything else in your head but that hasn't stopped you from trying."

Collin growled, "You'll pay for that one, Farrell."

"I'm not worried."

"You'd better be. There's a basketball just waiting for you when you get back here, and it has your name on it."

"I've got several of those in my room. How'd you get hold of one?"

Collin threatened, "Farrell!"

"The letter, Collin. Get back to the letter. What would you write?"

Collin sighed then said, "Dear Occupant, thank you for your gracious hospitality . . ."

Jeff began to make gagging noises. Collin tried again. ". . . for your commitment to young people . . ." More gagging. Collin snapped, "Well, then, you write it!"

Jeff said, "Collin, just be you. What would Collin Walker, case worker lady, say to the man? Pretend I'm him. What would you say?"

Collin was silent then said softly, "Thank you for caring about Rob, and Ta'waan, and Chonnell, and Pardner, and Niles and Nyla and all the kids whose lives you're touching. Thanks for giving them a place that's safe, where they can be kids again, and play and have fun and be challenged. Thanks for giving them a clean place to sleep, and good food to eat . . ."

Jeff added, "None of which you've touched."

Collin snapped back, "I have too. Ask Rob. And we need to have a word about this cramming food down my throat idea."

"The letter, Collin. Stick to the letter. You're doing great."

Collin shook her head but continued, "Thank you for all the changes I've seen in my man Rob since he's been at camp." Her lip quivered and her voice trembled as she whispered, "He called me Collin. First time since we've been together he called me Collin." She paused long enough to still the emotion then said, "Thank you for providing a place where my faith has been challenged, and where I've had to walk the talk more than I knew possible."

Jeff's voice was gentle but he said, "All that in just six days? Amazing."

Collin bit her lip then decided to finish it out. "And finally . . ."

"There's more?"

She ignored him, ". . . finally, thank you for allowing me to meet the most wonderful man I've ever known." She let the silence linger then added, "Even if he can't ref worth a nickel."

Jeff laughed. "And you were doing so well there, too." His voice was quietly pleased as he asked, "You really mean all that?"

"What, about you not being able to ref? Of course."

There was silence then Jeff said, "I'm sure the owner would love to get a letter like that. He'd think it made everything worthwhile."

"So you know what he thinks now? How close are you two?"

Jeff said, "I'd rather not spend my time talking about him. And speaking of time, why hasn't the timer shut this call off? I know you've been on longer 15 minutes."

Collin tiptoed lightly. "I'm not at the message center. A . . . friend loaned me their cell phone and said I could use it. That's got to be redundant. Why would you loan someone something but tell them they can't use it?"

Jeff said patiently, "That simply means we're limited by the life of the battery and I still don't want to waste quality time on meaningless trivia. I want to talk about something interesting. You."

Collin said quickly, "Let's talk about you instead. Your dad seemed to indicate you haven't been much good at work."

Jeff laughed. "Dad says I'm never much good at work."

"Seriously?"

"No, not really. Dad is very supportive of all I've accomplished, or am trying to accomplish. He values my judgment which is why I'm here right now. He won't close a deal until I've inspected it."

"What kind of deals?"

"Property mostly. He's got four parcels and is bidding on a fifth. He's been trying to secure this contract for months but it's been tied up in probate court; something about inheritance issues. We were told it would be December before it got kicked loose. Then Tuesday night Dad's lawyer calls and says it goes to market Friday and we need to be ready to move on it. Thus the semi-frantic phone call to the camp saying, 'Jeffrey, come home.' So home I came."

"Where is all this property?"

Jeff's voice took on an evasive note. "Sort of all over town. One lot's up on the north west corner. Two are south, and one's close to the middle of town. The one he's bidding on is east."

Collin considered Jeff's answers. They were specifically vague, giving her enough information to satisfy the direct question but not volunteering anything more. Collin started to push then stopped. Weren't there more than a few vague areas in her life she preferred would remain vague? Uh huh. Good thought. She asked instead, "So did your inspection prove the place suitable?"

"Not for what they're asking. But it gives Dad some room to negotiate. And he does love to negotiate."

Collin said softly, "I can see that." Pain was beginning to creep in around the corners of her consciousness. Collin shut her eyes and did some deep slow breathing.

Jeff said, "There's opportunity for a final inspection around nine in case I want to look back over something I might have missed the first time. Leesa has her test at noon and I told her I'd try to be there for that. I can leave here by one; be back to camp by three."

"Not legally you can't. Not if you're driving. It took us four hours on the bus."

"Ah, but I don't drive the bus. I drive a jeep. And I know all the short cuts and back roads, so trust me, I can make it in two hours legally. Well . . . two and a half." There was a pause then Jeff asked, "What's wrong? You sound . . . pained."

Collin hesitated then said, "I'm sore. Have you ever paddled for half a day?" After being mugged? Let's not mention that, shall we? Hmmm?

"Not recently. Sort of like playing cutthroat hoops after being sedentary for months, huh?"

"You might say that. You might lose friends but you might say that."

She heard his grin. He said, "Anyhow, I'll be there at the pick-up point to meet you, probably around six. Will that work?"

"If I can't have you in the boat with me, or for me, then I guess it will have to do." She slid down a little on the bed to get more comfortable but caught a rib on a sore spot and gasped slightly.

Jeff said sharply, "What? What's wrong."

Collin said strongly, "Nothing. Will you stop?" She decided another change of venue was required, so said, "I'd love to meet your whole family. They seem like good people."

"Who all did you talk to?"

"Well, Leesa answered the phone, quite professionally I might add, then your mom took it and then your dad. Are there any others I missed?"

"Not at home. I've got two older brothers, both married but not to each other, of course."

"Of course." Collin shook her head.

"Ren has two daughters, ages I don't know, and I don't have a clue. One still sits on her uncle's lap, and the other won't have a thing to do with me unless I come bearing gifts." Collin did a mental tally, and guessed 5 and 13. She loved his descriptions. "Mike has three boys, all in the rug rat stage, a little less than a year apart. He always was a slow learner. After Sammy was born Dad took him aside and explained how these things happen. I think it sank in: it's been almost a year now and no new additions."

"Bad. You are so bad."

"Ain't I though? Then came Leesa who you talked to tonight. Did you have any trouble understanding her?"

Collin sensed something in Jeff's voice, as if it was important how she answered. No doubt protective of his sister. That was . . . sweet? Heartwarming? Gratifying? To the man's credit, anyhow. A man that cared about a handicapped family member was a man of character. Collin answered honestly, "Not at all. I understood her perfectly. She's very bright and she's got a definite personality all her own."

Jeff grumbled but she could tell he was pleased, "Sometimes too much personality. She's never afraid to tell you what she's thinking that's for sure."

"Takes after her brother." Before Jeff could deflect the comment, she added quickly, "Her younger brother. Thought I'd clarify that."

"Oh, by all means. Don't give me any escape for my bruised ego, there."

Collin grit her teeth against the anticipated pain as she tried to lower herself down even further. She said as evenly as possible, "Your folks must have really loved children to have you after Leesa."

"They prayed hard about it, I know. But Dad says they were afraid that if they quit after her, Leesa would somehow think she had frightened them out of having more, and would believe they loved her less. I still think that's kind of a stretch for Leesa to come up with, but hey, who am I to argue? They had me then Dad said absolutely no more children. I always wonder if I scared them."

"Bad. Jeff . . ." She stifled a yawn.

But not fast enough. "Am I keeping you up?"

"No." That came out faster than she intended. Collin said more levelly, "Well, yes, but I don't want to let you go." Ever. Ever, ever, ever. "Keep talking, Jeff. I miss having you to talk to."

"Which is fine but I'm doing all the talking."

"Okay, I miss listening to you. Does that make it any better?"

"No." Jeff's voice took on a serious tone, one that would not be sidetracked. "Collin, what's wrong? I've asked you three times, now, and you still haven't answered me."

Collin hesitated then said, "It's the river, Jeff, and going down it tomorrow."

"Liar."

Collin sat up a little straighter. "I am not lying."

"And you're not telling me the whole truth, either. I grant you the river's got you spooked, for whatever reason you've got tucked away in that convoluted brain of yours."

"At least I have one."

Jeff's voice was sharp. "Knock it off, woman. And no more games. Do I need to come back to camp now?"

Collin said softly, battling back the ragged emotions that were threatening to overrun the place, "Your family needs you, Jeff."

"Do you need me?"

Oh, the question. How to answer? Yes? No? More than you could ever imagine? She stared at the phone, stared at her heart then whispered, "Yes. But your family needs you, too. I don't want to get off on the wrong foot with your dad."

Jeff said heatedly, "I'll take care of my dad. Talk to me. What's happened?"

Collin prayed desperately for wisdom, then chose her words with extreme caution. "I went up to the courts last night and . . ." This was hard.

Jeff coaxed, ". . . and what?"

Collin said tightly, "I got mugged."

Jeff exploded. "What? Are you okay? How . . ."

Collin interrupted the outburst and said quickly, "I'm fine. Shook up, but fine. He didn't hurt me, he just messed with my mind, that's all." With her hand, actually, but she chose to overlook that reality for the present. "Sheriff Lodi took the report and has his men out looking for the guy." True enough. "I've got an escort so I'm being protected." Could be true, though she didn't know that one for certain. Unless you count the heavenly escort, and then it was truer than some might care to admit.

Jeff was silent for a long time. Collin remained silent as well, allowing him to assimilate the information. After a few moments he asked, "Is that what you meant by you wanted to call but you couldn't?"

"I've spent most of my free hours with the Sheriff, yes."

"He have any suspects?"

"Maybe one."

"Maybe?" Jeff's voice was sharp then immediately backed down. "I'm sorry, Collin. I know how Bo is about his investigations."

Collin looked at the phone. "First name basis with the Sheriff?"

"Never mind. Are you sure you're okay?"

"Dr. Wallace checked me out. Bruised but not broken. He said your stitches were fine, too."

There was amused disbelief in Jeff's voice. "He's checking you out for being assaulted, and you ask him about your stitches?"

"I promised you I would."

She could see him shaking his head. "Oh, Collin. Lady . . ." He hesitated then asked, "So how are you?"

"Scared." Collin admitted it. "I'm the one in charge, you know? The control freak. But I felt so vulnerable." Her lip began to tremble, and her voice kept time. "I couldn't even put up a fight. Or much of one, anyhow. All I could do was run."

Jeff said softly, "You survived, lady. That's all that counts." Collin was silent, unable to answer without betraying far more emotion than she wanted to. Jeff asked, his voice gentle, "Do you want me to come back tonight?"

Collin drew in a deep breath, let it out slowly then said, "No. Yes. All of me wants nothing more than a white knight to come racing back here, slay all the dragons and whisk me off my feet to his castle wherever. But I'm not Snow White, or Sleeping Beauty or any of those fairy princesses. I'm Collin Walker, Juvenile Worker, Queen of Oakton."

"Yeah, and I'm George of the Jungle. I can be there in less than an hour."

"Jet pack?"

"Never mind." She heard him moving around, though obviously limited by a phone cord. A household without cordless? How quaint. Jeff was searching for something; she could hear objects being tossed and overturned. He was also muttering, "How many places can you hide an alarm clock? Come on, Dad, you had it this morning. I heard it. So did half the neighborhood. Oh, wait, what's this? What is this? I don't think I want to know." Collin grinned, feeling some of the intensity of the moment draining off. He was so good for her. Jeff continued to mutter, "All right, one more time. If you were an alarm clock where would you hide? Uh . . . bingo. Right here under the mattress. Of course. Where else would it have logically been?" He came back fully to the line and said, "It's 10:00 now. I can be back just after 11."

Collin added, "And curfew is 11 so I won't be able to see you anyhow. Jeff, I'll deal with it. The Lord allowed it so I'm supposed to learn from it and deal with it. You have your responsibilities, I have mine." She hesitated then said softly, "I want you here. But I can't have you here. Take care of your people. I'll take care of my people, then tomorrow, after the river ride, you can pick up all the quivering pieces and put them back together again." Maybe put them back together right this time.

Jeff said reproachfully, "Collin . . ."

She cut him off. "Jeff, I've got to go. This phone is a loaner and I shouldn't run up the bill too much. Come tomorrow like you planned and I'll see you then."

Jeff said urgently, "Collin, don't go, yet. Please. Tell me again you're okay, tell me honestly you're okay and I'll let you go. For tonight."

Collin kept her voice even and said, "Jeff, I'm fine. I will see you tomorrow." She hesitated then said softly, "I miss you, Jeff."

"I miss you, lady."

"I'll see you tomorrow."

"Count on it."

"I am. Night, Jeff."

"Sleep peaceful, milady."

Collin ended the call, smiled sadly at the phone then curled up around her pillow. She did not bother changing to pajamas, turning out the lights, or even closing the closet door, ignoring the bogey man's threat. She simply closed her eyes and slept.

Jeff, meantime, was a little less serene. Agitated was a better word. He tried to digest, analyze and process the preceding conversation, and kept coming up short. She wasn't telling him everything, and what was missing was important. Jeff punched in three digits and listened for the playback of the phone number Collin had used. It rolled around in his head, familiar, but not too. It was the camp area code and local prefix, but he couldn't place the . . . Suddenly the bell rang in his head and Jeff stared at the phone. "My good buddy, Bo. What do you know about all of this?" He corrected himself, "What do you know that you'll be willing to tell me about all of this?"

Lacey's voice floated up the stairs. "Jeffrey, time for bed, son."

Jeff called back, "Five minutes, Mom." He grumbled, "Which is three minutes more than Bo will give me, I'm sure." He dialed a number and got an answering machine. He waited for the beep then said heatedly, "I know you're home, Bo. Pick up or I'll have this phone number on every telemarketer's call sheet from here to Taiwan."

A moment passed then a familiar drawl came on the line. "Well, well, Jeffrey Farrell. What a surprise. I've been wondering when you might call. Didn't figure it would take you this long, though."

Jeff said dryly, "Well, I'm not as informed as I used to be. People aren't telling me everything I need to know."

"Or want to know, either, I suppose."

"That too. What's going on with Collin Walker?"

"Nice young woman, Jeff. Head strong. Gonna take quite a man to keep her in line."

Jeff ignored the comment and said strongly, "No games, Bo. I need to know what's going on. If there's a danger to the camp . . ."

"We would have notified the owner. There is such a thing as privileged information, Mr. Farrell." He made the "mister" sound almost like an insult. "What you are requesting falls under that category. Unless of course it's something you already know. What do you know, Mr. Farrell?"

Jeff explained patiently, "Collin told me she'd been mugged last night; that you have a suspect and will have the guy under wraps shortly. Is that about right?"

Bo drawled, "Your lady friend does know how to condense a story, I'll give her that much."

"What did she leave out? Was she hurt? How bad?"

"She was bruised up pretty bad. Doc Wallace says nothing permanent and she keeps insisting she's fine."

"She would. She's bullheaded."

Bo's voice was dry. "So I'd noticed."

"Got to you too, didn't she?" Bo chuckled but didn't answer. Jeff sighed then said, "So I have your word she's safe?"

"As safe as I can make her. As safe as she'll let me make her."

Jeff heard it, and said quietly, "Those aren't the same, Bo."

"I'm aware of that. And I need to clear this line." Bo hesitated, as if debating, then asked, "Will we be seeing you tomorrow morning, Mr. Farrell?"

Jeff said, "I wasn't planning on being back to camp until the afternoon."

Bo restated the question. "We will be seeing you tomorrow morning, won't we Mr. Farrell?"

Jeff caught on. Slow, but caught on. "Certainly. I seem to have forgotten the time, exactly."

"Five thirty. At my office. Not that I invited you. I have promises to keep myself." Again Bo hesitated then said quietly, "She's going to need a friend, Jeff. Be there." The line went dead.

Jeff stared at the phone in his hand and whispered, "What have you done now, love of my life?"

FRIDAY

At precisely quarter to five in the morning Jeff stood in front of the Sheriff's office trying to look neither anxious, nervous, worried, impatient, nor any combination of the four. Truth be told, he was failing. Not miserably, mind you, but failing. She'd need a friend. That wasn't much to go on. Enough for nightmares and delusions but not enough for reason. As the Sheriff's patrol car pulled in, Jeff began praying, "Lord, direct me. Direct my words, or shut my mouth. Direct my steps, or break my leg. Whatever it takes, Lord. Help me." He walked over to the car and waited for Bo to climb out. As soon as Bo straightened up Jeff said, "Okay, Bo, I'm here. What's going on?"

Bo eyed him closely and said slowly, "Why, Mr. Farrell. What brings you to our little town so early in the morning?"

Jeff was in no mood for theatrics. Hysterics, maybe. But hysterics had never gone over well with Sheriff Bo. Jeff had learned that early on in their relationship. He stayed calm and said, "Oh, I don't know. Something about a mugger and a woman I've grown quite fond of in a very short time."

Bo drawled, "Is that so? Well, Mr. Farrell, step into my office and I'll see if I can help you out." He looked at Jeff's eyes and asked, "How much coffee have you had this morning?"

Jeff admitted darkly, "Not enough."

They passed into the building and Bo deposited Jeff in his office. "I'll get you some real coffee, not that tea you civilians drink."

As he left Jeff shuddered. This was going to be done Bo's way and in Bo's time. Jeff settled into one of the time-worn oak chairs that had been here under the previous administration. That had been longer ago than Jeff could remember—and would probably be here under the next administration as well. Jeff looked casually around the room: a dart board on one wall, a hanging calendar from 1969 on another. Awards won by special units, awards won by little league teams. A bowling trophy. A nice 12 point buck, and a bass little more than legal. First bass, last buck. Bo was a man of many levels. If anyone could keep his lady safe, Bo could. With the Lord's help, of course. Jeff relaxed slightly. She was, after all, in the Lord's care, too. Still, it was nice knowing Bo was the instrument God had chosen to handle it.

Bo returned with a box containing two cups of evil looking coffee and a couple of still-warm muffins. He handed a muffin to Jeff along with a cup of the coffee and said, "Jenny made them this morning. She figured some of the boys might not get to eat before they went out on surveillance."

Jeff took a large swig of the coffee and nearly choked. He swallowed and gasped, "That's awful."

Bo shrugged. "Your lady drank it without any problem."

Jeff shook his head. "My lady has a few screws loose, too, or hadn't you noticed?"

Bo said dryly, "I noticed she was somewhat taken with you."

Jeff tried the coffee again on the off chance it might have improved. Or maybe his taste buds had atrophied. Neither was the case but he swallowed it anyhow. Grimaced, but swallowed it. He said tightly, "Delicious."

Bo said, "Now, Mr. Farrell, before . . ."

Jeff cut him off. "What is with the Mr. Farrell bit? You've known me since I was tall enough to steal gumballs off the candy counter at the theatre. It's Jeff, remember?"

Bo eyed him, measuring him, then drawled, "The Jeff I know would never run off half-cocked no matter what. He'd listen, he'd do what he was told, he'd respect the authorities over him. Am I dealing with that Jeff or with some stranger who might go off on his own thinking he knows better than anyone else what to do, and maybe gets himself, or one of my men, or even someone he's grown fond of, killed. I need to know who I'm dealing with, Mr. Farrell."

There was a very long silence as Jeff absorbed the rebuke, corralled his baser protective instincts and tried to form an answer both he and Bo could live with. At last he said quietly, "It's Jeff, Bo. I'm here."

Bo clapped him on the shoulder and said easily, "I know you are, son. I just wanted you to remember."

Jeff looked at him and said, "This is bigger than a mugging, isn't it." It was not a question.

Bo looked him dead in the eyes and asked, "Do you remember the Handyman?"

Jeff stared back then as it sank in, paled and whispered, "Oh, God." It was a prayer, not an expression.

Bo nodded. "That's about the way I see it. Your lady is convinced the man who attacked her and the Handyman may be one and the same. In the interest of time we won't go into all the details. She's also convinced she knows who he is."

"Who?" Jeff's question came out a lot more forcefully and sharper than he had intended.

Bo said calmly, "We'll get to that later. I'm going to brief the boys in five minutes, so you can listen in and I won't have to do this twice. But Collin got a message from someone telling her to meet them at dock five at six this morning. We intend to be all over that area well before then."

Jeff sat listening. Mostly he was listening to what Bo wasn't saying, and what that could mean. Jeff looked at Bo and said, "She's the bait, isn't she. She's going to walk right down there and think she can single-handedly bring this guy to justice." He shook his head. "Tell me you figured out a way to stop her."

Bo asked softly, "How well do you know your lady friend, Jeff?"

Jeff said angrily, "I know she's a fool! She thinks everything depends on her. The world can't turn unless she's up to help it along!!" He looked at Bo, pleading, "You've got to stop her, Bo."

"What would you suggest?"

"Lock her in her room under guard. Deport her to Michigan. Throw her in jail, even."

Bo seemed interested in that option. "On what charge?"

Jeff threw his hands up in the air. "I don't know what charge! Jay walking. Feeding the pigeons. Wearing blue on Thursday. I don't know! You never had any trouble coming up with charges to throw me in jail."

Bo's eyes danced. "But Jeff, you were always guilty."

"What does that have to do with anything?? You can't tell me you're going to let her walk down to that dock alone and unprotected . . ."

Bo drawled, "If you let me get to my briefing, she won't be either of those things."

Jeff groaned, "Father God, help her."

Bo grasped Jeff's shoulder strongly and said, "He is, Jeff. Hang on to that. Then get the rest of yourself under control. I want you with me for her sake. But only if you're under control. Understand? Only then."

Jeff breathed out slowly and whispered, "'The Lord is my light and my life, whom shall I fear? The Lord is at my right hand, of whom shall I be afraid?'" Jeff prayed silently, *"Watch over her, Lord. Don't let her do anything stupid, please. Keep her safe."* He looked at Bo and said calmly, "I'm ready."

Bo smiled with approval. "I knew you would be. Let's go." Together they went to brief the troops.

At just before six, Collin approached dock five. There was enough light to see by, but it was gray and gave everything a dingy cast. She looked around, trying to spot friend or foe, not sure which one she wanted to see most. The combined voices in her head for once were all in agreement: this was a bad idea. Of all the bad ideas she'd ever had, this was worst. She still had time to back out, tell Sheriff Bo she found her mind, changed it and wanted out. It would make him happy. It would make her happy. It would make her . . .

A coward and she'd never forgive herself if she didn't go through with this. She prayed softly, "Lord, if I'm wrong about this, forgive me, and if it's not presumptuous, help me, please." She could see the dim figure of someone working on a canoe: one of the smaller, two man versions. The raft they had been practicing with was nowhere in sight. Which didn't mean a whole lot; most of the world was still nowhere in sight. Collin took a deep breath, let it out slowly then advanced purposefully towards Mitch. The river man was shifting supplies in the canoe, his hands occupied and out of sight. Collin smiled what she hoped was a friendly smile and said, "Morning, Mitch. Where is everybody? I suppose I am a little early, but I figured . . ."

Mitch turned and looked at her, his eyes wide. He looked as if he was high, or maybe just pumped on adrenaline. He gave her a wide, wild smile and said, "I think you know where the others are." He straightened up and there was a five-inch blade in his hand.

Collin made one more attempt at playing dumb. "What are you talking about? I thought the time was . . ."

Mitch said harshly, "Drop it, Walker. Dumb blonde does not suit you at all." He stepped forward, brandishing the knife.

Collin didn't move, just stared at him with an icy stare. She said coldly, "But that's what I thought you liked, Mitch. Dumb females without enough sense to see through you."

Mitch smiled back evilly. "No, no. That's just a pastime." He drew up close to Collin and let the knife trickle down her cheek. Collin didn't even flinch. Old instincts revived and she stood still as a stone. Mitch cocked his head, slightly unsure of her response. He let the knife drift across her chin then down and across her neck. Collin still didn't move but continued to stare dead at Mitch. He pulled the knife back and said, "You are going to be a challenge, I see. This could be fun."

Collin said tightly, "Get all the pleasure from it you can, little man. It's the last pleasure you'll ever know."

Mitch surprised her with his speed. Before she was finished speaking he lashed out with the knife, slashing her right shoulder. Even then she made no sound. On the backstroke he came across her jaw with the butt of the knife, dropping her to her knees. He grabbed her arms, forced them together and began wrapping duct tape around her wrists.

It took a moment for Collin's head to stop ringing and to clear enough for a reasonable facsimile of thought. She muttered silently to the accusing voice in her head, *"Don't bait the bull. Don't bait the bull. I got it, I got it. Now shut up."* Mitch finished his handiwork, fortunately leaving her arms in front of her rather than behind her back. Not that it was from the goodness of his heart, she was sure.

Mitch muttered darkly as if trying to decide what to do next. He eyed her with a piercing glance then said, "No, I won't tape your mouth. Your conversation can be so enjoyable. You make me laugh. Say something to make me laugh now."

"Did you tape Laura Mars' mouth shut?"

Mitch stared at her dumbfounded then broke into gales of laughter. Collin shrugged to herself and thought, *"And I wasn't even trying."*

Mitch finally got himself under control, tears running down his cheeks. He looked at Collin and said with amazement, "You think you're going to survive, don't you? You honestly think you're going to get away and use this information."

Collin shrugged. "Never hurts to dream."

Suddenly Mitch slashed at Collin's shirt slicing it apart. He grabbed the two halves with his hands, ripped it wide open and began searching for the wire he imagined was there. Collin again went stone cold as the man groped inside her shirt. After he satisfied himself there was nothing to be found he looked up and smiled at her. "Sorry, lady. Nothing personal. I have to be careful, you know."

Collin said coldly, "I hope you're insured. I paid good money for this shirt."

Mitch laughed hysterically again. Collin thought, *"Maybe I can get him to laugh himself to death. Or get hysterical and fall out of the boat."* No, she was the one who got hysterical in boats. That could be her greatest challenge. She could experience her finest hour. Or the agony of utter defeat. Take it as it comes.

Again Mitch got himself under control and said, "You are too much."

"Then throw me back and find something more your size."

"Oh, no. No, no, no. This is going to be a blast."

"Meaning the others weren't?"

Mitch said, "No, they . . ." He stopped and said angrily, "Why are you so concerned about the others? You'll be joining them soon enough."

Collin said evenly, "I'd like to know what kind of performances I'm up against. Who I'm going to be sleeping with. Maybe even where I'm going to be sleeping."

Mitch smiled wickedly. "You'll see that soon enough." He grabbed Collin's arms and shoved her into the front of the canoe. It rocked precariously beneath her and for the first time Collin's emotions betrayed her. Mitch saw, then gloated, "That's right, isn't it? You have a thing about the river. You're terrified of it. Isn't that a kick, huh? Ice lady is afraid of the river."

Collin whipped her fear into submission and said, "Maybe before. But not now."

Mitch leered at her. "Matheson tried that trick. But the way she came unglued when I brought in the snakes—it was a thing of beauty. She screamed for half an hour. It was great."

Collin had two tracks to follow. Matheson? That name had never been mentioned. Was there someone else? Or was Mitch just messing with her? The other track was darker. Was fear the trigger for Mitch's psychoses? He got off on other people's phobias? Time for analysis later, but tuck that thought where it can be reached.

Mitch climbed into the canoe and pushed off. Collin willed her stomach to stop churning, forbid her limbs to begin shaking. Survival meant proving she wasn't afraid. Yeah, right.

The canoe moved swiftly away from the dock as the current caught the, to Collin's mind, far too-fragile craft. Mitch began paddling with strong even strokes, bringing the boat to the center of the river. Collin kept her eyes firmly glued on the gunwales, refusing to look any higher. Mitch laughed wildly and began singing badly, "Row, row, row your boat, underneath the stream . . ."

Collin swallowed, swallowed hard, swallowed a third time, then put all the false bravado into her voice she could and sang out, "Ha, ha, fooled you all, I'm a submarine."

Mitch's levity dropped a notch. His voice grew grim as he said, "We'll see. We'll see. We've got the pressure cooker up ahead. Let's see you sing through that one, my pretty." He began to cackle. "We'll see."

Collin encouraged her heart to remain firmly positioned in her chest rather than trying to crowd out her throat. After all, this was merely a pleasant jaunt down a peaceful rive . . .

The canoe hit a hole and dropped sharply. Collin closed her eyes, bit the inside of her cheeks and held herself steady. She heard Mitch moving around behind her; she looked back. The man was donning a life jacket and helmet in anticipation of the run ahead. He picked up another life jacket and helmet, moved forward as if to put it on Collin, then stopped. He looked at her taped arms, looked at the jacket, then said with mock dismay, "Oh, my. It won't fit this way. Too bad. Don't suppose you'll need the helmet then, either." He cackled then returned to his seat and began paddling.

Collin stared at the swirling white water ahead and whispered angrily, "No flashbacks. No flashbacks. Stay in the now." Mitch was trying to rattle her, she knew. And doing a fine job of it, she might add. But he had to keep her alive in order to win his prize. He would not risk losing her to the river. He wouldn't. The thought gave Collin some sense of security. Not much, but enough. Then there was that calm presence of the Lord, assuring her, *"When you pass through the waters, I will be with you. The rivers will not overwhelm you . . . I am the Lord your God."*

The boat dipped with the first hole, then shot high in the air on the second. Mitch dug hard right as the boat pitched to the left. The bow plowed through the crashing waves, half swamping the little craft. The roar of the river drowned out any possibility of conversation, for which Collin was eternally grateful. It meant she didn't have to pretend anything at this point. Over and over the boat pitched and bucked, tossing Collin from side to side. Unable to steady herself, she repeatedly ended face down in the bottom of the boat swallowing river water. She choked, gagged, got herself under control . . . only to repeat the process with the next hole.

It did little to cheer her that Mitch was being tossed around as well. After all, he was supposed to be the expert, here. Collin cracked her head on the rails but not sharply enough to do more than annoy her. The next meeting with the floor, however, jarred her enough to truly hurt and left her seeing heavenly stars. As the tumult of the rapids receded, Collin could hear Mitch laughing in satisfaction. She decided it was time to administer a little salt. She mustered together what little strength and any courage that might be remaining and sang, "Michael row the boat ashore . . .

The handle end of the paddle smacked her sharply behind the ear. Either Mitch was a music critic or her performance did not amuse him. In either event Collin stopped singing. They were coming out of the rapids into calm water once again. Collin asked from curiosity, "Was this the way you were going to bring the kids?"

Mitch laughed harshly. "You really don't get it, do you? I had no intentions of guiding anyone down the river. I was just looking for someone to play with. How dense can you be, lady?"

Collin started to answer, but a voice in her head cautioned urgently, *"Don't say it! Don't say it! Spare your brain for once."* Collin swallowed the smart-mouth response and asked, "What was Laura Mars afraid of?"

"Which one was she?"

"The second one. Dark hair, pretty brown eyes. Worked at the camp."

"Oh, yeah. Her. But she wasn't the second."

Collin went cold inside. "She wasn't? Who was?"

"I can't remember all their names. Didn't matter. Most of them were runaways; strays nobody cared about. Nobody missed them, either. Except the one girl. I did see her face on a milk carton later. I sent her little finger back. Figured it was the least I could do."

Collin was ready to scream and gag at the same time. But no, so far all she had was talk. She needed proof. Insanity gets him off; insanity with proof gets him locked away for good. She asked as evenly as she could, "How many, Mitch?"

Mitch shrugged. "Maybe ten." He laughed, "Maybe twenty. Maybe a hundred. You'll never know, will you? Not until you're buried with them. What's left of you."

Collin asked, "Oh, are we all sleeping together in one bed?"

Mitch began paddling harder, his face darkening. "This game isn't fun anymore. Let's go find one we can play together." He touched her hair with the paddle, flipping it up playfully then laughed.

Collin locked down all the emotions and fears, and sat unmoving. He would not touch her. Ravage the outside all he may, he would not touch the inside. Her father had taught her that lesson well. She guessed this outing was not going exactly according to plan. Good. The more she could upset him the more he might reveal about his past exploits. Of course, the more dangerous it made him as well. But that was Sheriff Bo's concern. Well, not exactly. It was her concern, too, lest unhappily she signal too late, or not signal at all. Hmm . . . use your head, woman. You want to see Jeff again?

And have to explain all of this to him? Decision, decisions. On the one hand, we have no hand. On the other . . .

Stop it! No insanity!! Keep focused.

Collin tried to relax to take the pressure off her brain. This whole experience was stress enough; being continually hit on the head did not improve the situation. She watched the land flow by and noticed that Mitch appeared to be heading toward the near shore. With only a few more strokes he drove the nose of the canoe up on the bank, grounding it on the muddy shoals.

Mitch climbed out of the boat, grabbed Collin roughly by the arms and said, "Come on, lady. You've got friends to meet."

Collin said lightly, "A party? How nice. But I'm really not dressed . . ."

Mitch's knife made an encore performance. He pushed it up tight against her chin, drawing blood. He hissed, "Keep it up, lady. Keep it up. I love it. It'll make it so much sweeter in the end."

Collin said coldly, "You can't win, Mitch. You won't beat me. I was trained by the best, and there's no fear left in me. You can't do anything that wasn't done before."

Mitch's eyes grew cold, and he snickered, "You still have all your limbs, don't you?" He jerked her savagely forward, dragging her along in his fury.

They kept this pace for what seemed to Collin to be an eternity, but in reality was only half an eternity. Or about twenty minutes, whichever comes first. Collin stumbled repeatedly, twice gashing her knees on rocks half-buried in the dirt. The first blow was painful, but tolerable. The second, however took her breath away sharply. She struggled to maintain her composure and asked easily, "Mitch, can we stop for a minute? I think I've got a rock in my shoe."

Mitch sneered, "You don't feel pain, remember?"

"You're right, I don't. But I could get along much faster if I wasn't stumbling all over the place leaving blood and tissue samples everywhere."

Mitch whirled on her. "What game are you playing, witch? You act like you don't want to leave a trail. As if I was stupid enough to let you." He noticed the blood trickling down her leg, however, and said roughly, "Clean that up. Then get the rock out."

Collin shrugged. "Suits me fine. Could I borrow a rag? Maybe the one you were going to stuff in my mouth?"

Mitch slapped her hard. "Keep it up. Keep it up. We'll see who's laughing. I could change my mind about taping your mouth."

Collin's eyes narrowed. That had to be avoided at all costs. She said softly, "Ah, but Mitch, that would be like admitting I beat you. And you can't have that, can you? You've got to beat me fair and square. Otherwise it doesn't count."

Mitch glared at her but handed her a semi clean cloth. "What do you know?"

Collin dabbed awkwardly at the knee, brushing dirt and leaves away from the wound, leaving just enough of a coating to staunch the blood flow. She looked at him and said, "Oh, I think I can guess. You were an under achiever that your folks—at least one of them, anyhow—knew could do better. Nothing was ever right, nothing was ever good enough. You could win, but never within the rules. If you succeeded, it was because someone else just didn't try. Or your chief opponent was having a bad day. Or was sick. Or the teachers felt sorry for you or hated the other guy. But you never won on your own merit, according to your parent."

Mitch yanked her to her feet and began pulling her along again but at a greatly reduced speed. He said, "Keep talking. This is fascinating. You really believe this trash?"

Collin shrugged and said, "It's either believe this, or believe you're just an evil man who likes to torture women. And that would mean there are bad people in the world. But we can't believe that, now can we?"

Mitch laughed coldly, "Why can't we?"

Collin acted surprised. "Mitch, if people can be good or bad then they are responsible for their own choices. Good heavens, man, we can't have that! There has to be a reason why you did what you did. It can't be as simple as you like maiming and killing beautiful young women. Though your choice of me as victim tends to negate the beautiful part. I'm hardly on a par with Laura Mars."

"How would you know?"

"I saw her picture. She was gorgeous."

Mitch said reflectively, "Yeah, she was. Pity."

Collin chose her next words very carefully. "Why did you pick me, Mitch?"

Mitch shrugged. "You just looked like fun. I watched you every night since you got here. Watched you playing ball with that kid." His voice grew harder. "Watched you talking with the janitor. I'll never understand how you could choose him over me. He's a nothing; a nobody. Who cares about a janitor?"

Collin said softly, "I do."

Mitch snarled, "Maybe I should have brought him along on this trip. It would have been fun watching the two of you trying to sacrifice for each other. Maybe next time I'll try that."

Collin fell silent trying to gather strength for the ordeal ahead, whatever it was. She should just put an end to all of this. Surely Bo had enough evidence to close the book on Mitch permanently. There was plenty of premeditation, plenty of intent, plenty of motive . . . there just weren't plenty of bodies. She had to at least get him back to ground zero, wherever that was. And she really hoped it was nearby. Her knee was throbbing, her head was throbbing and she was still feeling nauseous. Not a good combination for appearing cool, calm, and collected.

Another twenty minutes passed before they came upon a corrugated metal shack, or its remains anyhow. Little was left more than a lean-to, a cement fire pit and the remnants of an old still. The area was fairly clear as if it had once been a much-used meeting place. Collin looked around and remarked, "Quaint. Picturesque, even. You can almost smell the moonshine cooking." She looked at Mitch and asked, "Isn't this a little exposed, though? You couldn't really keep someone here for long. Sound carries, I know."

Mitch laughed again. "You really do think you're going to get out of this, don't you? That you're going to find out all my secrets and then somehow escape and tell the Sheriff."

Collin said evenly, "You have your fantasies, I have mine."

Mitch took a ceramic jug from the corner of the shed and poured a long swig in his mouth. He swallowed then held it up for Collin to drink. She declined politely, "Thank you, no. I never drink before breakfast. Or after breakfast, either. I have no tolerance for alcohol."

Mitch leered, "That's even better." He forced it to her mouth and poured it over her face. "I never drink alone, lady."

Collin sputtered but managed to keep the majority of the liquor outside her mouth. She asked, "Is that how you keep your women quiet?"

Mitch stared at her, slack jawed. "What is it with you?" Suddenly his face changed as a light dawned on him. "I know what it is! I got you figured out now. You think you can handle the fear as long as you know what's coming. Well, lady, ask all you want because it won't do you a bit of good. Every one of them has been different." He drank again from the jug and again tried to force it down Collin's throat. She ended up swallowing more this time but managed not to react to it. Mitch watched her closely for a response. Getting none, he continued, "One I hung here in the shed. Took her too long to die so I cut off her hands to hurry the process. Didn't take long after that." He drank again, then pulled out his knife and began circling Collin's face, leaving only a tiny mark of red here and there to prove who held the power. "There was one girl who was kind of cute. You remind me a little of her. She didn't have your fire, though. But I still liked having her around. She lived longer than most. Well, a little longer. She was always trying to scream. Every time I untaped her mouth, she'd scream."

Collin said dryly, "Imagine that."

Mitch laughed. "Yeah. But not you, huh, Walker?" The knife pierced the skin on her neck; Collin merely stared hard at Mitch. He held the pressure on for a moment or two then backed off. "You are good, woman. Who trained you?"

Collin said, "You tell me your secrets, I'll tell you mine. Where did you bury everyone? Tough digging around here. And I can't see you carrying them far. You just dump your toys when you're done with them, don't you?"

Mitch sneered, "Oh, yeah. Like the screamer. As long as she was strong enough to play I kept her around. But since she couldn't eat or drink with her mouth taped she wasted away pretty quick. I cut her wrists and got rid of her."

"Where? Are they all together, or did you scatter them?"

Mitch grinned. "What do you think I did?"

Collin thought hard then said, "You like trophies which is why you keep their hands. You can play with those; use them for reminders. But the rest is just a waste so you'd probably just dump them somewhere. But somewhere nearby." She looked at him and asked, "Good guess, bad guess?"

Mitch cackled, grabbed Collin's head and forced it to his. He kissed her long and hard, then threw his head back, and swigged another drink. He gasped, "Man I love you, woman! You are so unique! It took me awhile but I think I've finally figured you out. As long as you're talking I'm not touching you. That's it, isn't it? If you can keep me talking you figure I won't hurt you!"

Collin shrugged. "It's one strategy. I have others."

Up in the hills, not fifty yards from the clearing, Sheriff Bo whispered into his radio, "All units, be ready. My signal or hers, whichever comes first."

Jeff was near to convulsions. He was facing away from the circle, unable to see what was going on. Bo had him watching a portion of the trail opposite the shed, "in case Mitch has a partner." They both knew better, but Jeff had promised to obey the Sheriff no matter what. Inside he was dying, knowing Collin was out there, and imagining what she was going through. It might be worse, however, to really know. Could he handle it? Considering the way he was dealing with the imaginary, probably not. He breathed a silent prayer, *"Father, be merciful. I know you are, but please, be even more so, now."*

Mitch kissed her hard again; Collin remained stone. He shoved her away and said, "You are cold, witch. You need something to warm you up." He grabbed the jug and began pouring it, not stopping until Collin was forced to choke and gag down a liberal quantity of the shine. She shook her head then stared coldly at Mitch and asked, "So where did you bury them, Mitch?"

Mitch reached up and slapped her hard, screaming, "Shut up! Shut up!"

Jeff heard the sound of flesh on flesh, and curled up in pain inside. He whispered in agony, "Listen to him, Collin. Shut up. Let it go. Please."

Collin repeated the question. "Where, Mitch?"

In frustration he screamed, "Under the floor! It opens on an old storm cellar!! Are you happy now? You want to see them? Will that let you die in peace?"

Collin asked, "Is Laura Mars there, too?"

He grabbed her, ripped the tape from her arms and sneered, "I dumped her there like I'm going to dump you. But first, you need to be brought down, woman." In one swift motion he dragged her to a rain barrel and shoved her head under water. Collin jerked back with incredible force and let out the longest, loudest, angriest scream mankind had ever heard. Or at least the mankind in the immediate vicinity.

Simultaneously Bo shouted in his radio, "Go! Go!"

But Collin wasn't waiting for rescue. Years of repressed rage and humiliation, capped by the ordeal of the past few days, gave her a strength in fury she never knew she had—nor would want to have again. She lashed out at Mitch with her fists doubled, using them as a club to strike him full in the face. Mitch went for his knife; Collin savagely kicked it from him. Mitch struck back, punching her in the stomach, but she didn't feel the blow. She was beyond feeling, beyond caring, beyond reason. She clubbed at him again knocking him back off his feet.

The rescue party reached her, but held back as Collin continued to beat and pummel her assailant. Jeff and Bo came racing up. Jeff moved forward to catch Collin but was stopped short as Bo said sharply, "Jeff. Wait."

Bound by his promise Jeff watched helplessly as Collin delivered blow after blow, kicking and hitting the hapless monster who now lay curled up in defense, trying only to ward off as many blows as he could and failing. A woman possessed, oblivious to everything but the pain and anger inside, Collin kicked and kicked and kicked . . .

Jeff said urgently, "She'll kill him, Bo. She won't know she's done it, but she'll kill him."

Bo nodded. "Go get her, son."

Collin felt someone grab her from behind She screamed in rage, thrashing back from this new attack. But the force of the grip was stronger and held her tight. A voice whispered in her ear, "It's over, milady. It's over. You got him. You did it. Now it's over. Come on, lady. It's over."

Slowly she began to lose steam and quit fighting. Whoever it was turned her around to face him. She looked in his face, looked in his eyes, trying to make something, anything, come together. Finally she whispered in confusion, "Jeff? Jeff?"

Jeff hugged her hard and his voice shook. "I'm here, Collin. You're safe. It's over."

Collin couldn't understand. "Over?" She looked at Mitch being dragged away none too gently or sympathetically by the deputies. She shook her head, still not making connections. "He killed them. He killed all of them." Her voice began to tremble, keeping time with the rest of her body. She whispered hollowly, "He wanted to kill me. He wanted . . ."

Jeff hugged her even tighter and said softly, "I know. I know. It's okay."

Collin stared at him a moment then asked, "It's okay that he wanted to kill me? That's a . . . ." her voice shook hard. Collin swallowed, said again, "That's a terrible . . ." A single tear trickled down her cheek." She wiped it on Jeff's chest angrily, but still couldn't get the retort out. She looked at Jeff, looked into those eyes, and lost it. Collin sobbed. And with the first sob, the flood walls broke, the defenses fell, and Collin began to cry brokenly, unable to stop.

Jeff rocked her tenderly, protectively, and crooned, "Go on and cry, case worker lady. It's okay now. Everything is okay, now." He picked her up and carried her to a wooden bench tucked away under the trees, all the while trying to comfort and quiet her. "It's okay, Collin. It's okay." He kissed the top of her head, cradling her in his arms.

Sheriff Bo walked over to a deputy wearing headphones and carrying a parabolic listening device. He waited as the man listened to the recording then asked gruffly, "Did we get him?"

"We got him, Sheriff. Got him dead."

Bo slapped the man on the shoulder and said, "Good man. You may sell me on that gadget yet." The man nodded then began packing up his gear. Bo walked over quietly to where Jeff was rocking Collin slowly. Bo looked at Collin, shook his head slightly and said, "She's a keeper, all right." He looked at Jeff wryly and added, "If you can."

Jeff hugged her gently and said, "She's not going anywhere."

Bo knelt beside the bench and lay a gentle hand on Collin's shoulder. Her head was buried in Jeff's chest, and she would not, or could not, look up. Bo said quietly, "You did good, woman. You did real good. You've answered the prayers of a lot of folk around here." He started to add more but decided against it. He squeezed her shoulder carefully then looked at Jeff and said, "There's a medic on his way up. We'll take good care of her."

Jeff nodded. "Thanks, Bo. For everything."

Bo shook his head. "She did all the hard work; I'm just here for the clean-up." Bo walked away from Jeff and spoke into his radio. "I want both forensic teams up here. And the excavator. No, not the big one. We're looking for fragile bones, not boulders. As quick as you can get them here. Right. Right. Uh huh. Just do it, Kelby. Right." Bo dropped the radio to his side and walked slowly to the shed. He peered through a dust covered window, stared a long time in to the blackness inside then said softly, "I'm going to bring you home, princess. And then I'm going to see him burn." He turned away and addressed the men standing around. "Come on, deputies." He stressed the word with an edge of familiar sarcasm. "Doesn't anyone know how to investigate a crime scene? But if one piece of evidence gets tampered with and we lose this guy, so help me, I'll have their head on my wall next to Bambi. Now move!"

The medic arrived followed closely by a two man chopper. Collin was trussed and stuffed into the tiny chopper, flown to County General, IV'd, examined, x-rayed, cleaned, stitched, bandaged, and finally deposited in a room of her own. It was going on six pm when she heard a young, familiar voice say reproachfully from the hall, "This what you get, case worker lady, trying to play Xena for real. You ain't got the muscle for it, and you know it."

Rob slipped his head around the corner; Collin held up a hand for Rob to grasp. He came in and took it; she muttered, "Can't fill the short skirts, either."

Robbie squeezed it tightly. His voice was rocky as he said, "I thought you was dead, Collin. When they brought you back I thought Mitch had killed you." Tears slipped from his eyes and splashed without apology on her arm.

Collin squeezed his hand and said softly, "Want to know a secret? I thought he had, too." She shivered slightly then rolled her eyes in frustration.

Robbie laughed then wiped his face furiously. "You owe me a dollar, lady. You roll your eyes, you owe me a buck. That was the deal, remember?"

He reached out and hugged Collin whispering, "Don't ever leave me alone like that, please? Promise? Never."

Collin rubbed his head tenderly and said, "I promise I'll try. That's the best I can do, Rob. I never really meant to go off to begin with. It sort of just happened." She looked at him and asked, "Did you guys ever get to ride the river?"

"Naw. When Mitch didn't show up, and you didn't show up I got scared. I called Jeff. I ain't real sure why 'cause I knew he wasn't nowhere where he could do nothing. I told him what was going down, how you weren't acting like yourself. He said something 'bout counting my blessings, whatever that meant." He looked at her and asked, "What he talking about?"

Collin said dryly, "Let's ask him next time we see him."

Robbie shrugged. "Whatever. Then 'bout half an hour later he shows up with this big deputy and they takes us all downtown, or, well, down to the sheriff's office. This town ain't big enough to got a downtown. Jeff explained what was happening: how you was the bait in a trap for some psycho dude, and the psycho dude was Mitch. He didn't talk like he was real happy with the idea, neither."

"That would be one way of putting it."

"Yeah, well, he had a few things to say about bullheaded females that I didn't catch. We was all real worried 'bout you. They asked us a bunch of questions 'bout Mitch then let us go. Jeff rode with us back to camp and told us that the camp owner felt so bad about how Mitch turned out that he called all our guardians and got permission for us to stay another day. An' he's bringing in a real professional river guide and we still get to ride the river and do all the cool stuff we were gonna do." Robbie's voice accelerated a notch as he said, "And you know the other really cool part? We ain't gotta ride the bus home! The owner dude is gonna fly us home in his company jet! Ain't that too cool? Collin, we get to fly! Nyla 'bout fainted when she heard that. I thought riding the river would be the coolest thing but we get to fly!"

Robbie's enthusiasm was hard to take at present but Collin didn't try to tone him down. Her head throbbed; her shoulders and neck and leg throbbed; but she asked, "That's great, Rob. What time is the crew meeting tomorrow?"

"'Bout ten. That way we can say good bye to all the brothers and sisters who have to go back the slow way. Buses leave at nine-thirty."

Collin took a deep breath, let it out slowly, then said, "Well, then, I need to get myself together." She began trying to sit up, all the while trying to locate the kid in her head with the gong. If she found him he was dead meat.

A strong male voice said sharply, "What do you think you are doing? Lay back down. Now." There was a seriousness in his tone she hadn't heard before. Jeff gently eased her back to a horizontal position, then asked in frustration, "What is your problem? Accommodations not to your liking? Bed too soft? Pillows too hard? Not enough light in here? What?"

Collin explained, "Hospitals are for sick people. I can heal just as well back at the camp." Collin studied him a moment as confusion began to cloud some of her thinking. A few of the details of the past twelve hours were jumbled. Okay, most of the details of the past twelve hours were jumbled and she wasn't sure but what it was best they stay that way. But Jeff . . . She looked at Robbie and asked, "What time did you call Jeff?"

"Must have been 'bout nine-thirty."

She turned to Jeff. "And you got here when?"

Jeff said evenly, "Let it go, Collin. It doesn't matter."

"Yeah, it does. I've got you in too many places at once and I can't figure it out."

Jeff shrugged, "Well, that's me all over. Now let it go."

Collin groaned and said, "Rob, throw something at him. And make it heavy."

Robbie laughed. "Not a chance, case worker lady. Me an' him, we partners."

Collin looked at Jeff, still trying to make it make sense. "Why are you even here? You were supposed to be helping your dad. And what about Leesa?"

Jeff explained patiently, "Dad got a call late last night, and I do mean late, that the deal had fallen through and the property had been withdrawn from the market. And at three this morning Leesa came down with a severe case of the flu, so severe she wasn't going to be able to test at all. Or that's what she told Mom. It's her usual stage-fright syndrome; happens everytime she takes a major test. We all recognize it but we keep hoping she'll work through it. And Mom keeps scheduling make-up dates." He smiled with smug satisfaction and said, "So the family is well taken care of, courtesy your heavenly Father who covers all the bases. Happy now?"

"No. Why are you here?"

He said reproachfully, "Collin . . ."

"Okay, okay. What does Rob mean by you being partners? In what?" She paused then asked, "Or do I want to know?"

Robbie said excitedly, "Jeff's gonna fix it with the owner so as I can come up here and work next summer. He says I'd get my room and board free and get paid, too. I told him I'd rather get food than a board and for some reason he threatened to throw me out. Something about being too much like a lady friend he knew."

Collin closed her eyes. "I think that's a great idea." After a moment she added, "This camp has some great owner. I'd really like to meet him before I leave."

Jeff shrugged. "We might be able to arrange that. But I told Rob, before he comes up he's got to prove himself. No trouble at home, school or anywhere else. And he's got to keep his grades up. He tells me he's a C/D student. Is that about right?"

Collin answered, "He could do better. He does better when he applies himself." Maybe she should apply herself to sleep. Maybe when she woke the kid with the gong would have finished his solo and she would feel better.

Robbie said, "You know me, lady. I don't always understand it the way the books say it. But once you explain it, I got it. Ain't that how it is?"

Collin did not respond. Jeff and Robbie looked at her closely; Jeff touched her cheek lightly and called softly, "Collin . . . Collin." There was no answer. Jeff looked at Robbie and said, "Guess the conversation was too much for her."

Robbie asked worriedly, "She be okay, won't she? She be back to herself, right?"

Jeff smiled a little sadly and said, "I'm sure she will be. You have to give her some time." He thought in frustration, *"She has to give herself time. Why can't she see that? Lord, what drives her so hard? I know she loves you. Why doesn't she understand?"* Jeff looked at Robbie and asked quietly, "Are you hungry? They told me you and the crew didn't eat lunch today. Brought the whole cafeteria crew to tears."

Robbie grinned slightly then shrugged. "Maybe a little. You want something from the kitchen?"

Jeff looked shocked. "Eat hospital food? Are you out of your mind? Don't you know how they keep people here as long as they do? They poison them with hospital food." Jeff dropped the theatrics and said, "Besides, I was thinking more like Mickie Dees. You want anything?"

Robbie shrugged again. "I don't know, man. What do you want me to bring you?"

Jeff shook his head. "Doesn't work that way, my man. I'm going if I can get you to agree to sit with our lady, there. Someone needs to keep her from trying to go over the wall again. Now, what do you want?"

Robbie protested, "That ain't how it work, dude. You the man. You supposed to tell me what to do, where to go an' then expect me to just do it whether I want to or not."

Jeff hesitated a moment, then asked, "Is that how you want it to be?"

Robbie said sharply, "No. Just the way it is."

"It doesn't have to be. I don't like being ordered around so I won't order anyone else around, either. There are times when, as a boss, I have to tell people what their jobs are, but that's different. When it comes to just people a wise man said it best: treat others the way you want to be treated."

Robbie thought a moment then said slowly, "The lady tried to teach me something like that. She called it the, uh . . . the . . . some kind of rule. The golden rule. That was it." Robbie was pleased with his recalling and instinctively looked to Collin for approval. But she was deep in sleep, breathing shallow, her face flushed. Robbie turned back to Jeff and admitted, "I always thought it was something she made up to try and make me walk straight."

"She didn't make it up, Rob. It's very real."

Rob was silent for a long time studying the floor pattern. Jeff waited, knowing there was something deep going on in the boy's heart and head. After several minutes Rob looked up and said, "You a man, right, Jeff?"

"Last time I checked."

Rob shook his head slightly then said, "You tell me straight. All them stories she be telling me 'bout God and love and loving your neighbor and about some carpenter's son. They be the truth? I mean, how could some dude tell me to love the punk that stole my ride and is trying to make a hooker out of my little sister? How you gonna love Mitch after what he done to the lady? Ain't no way. Man say that don't know the streets."

"He knew the streets, Rob. The streets he walked weren't much different than ours. He got beat up, spit on, mocked, cursed, you name it. In the end his enemies had him killed by whipping him, then nailing him to a cross and hanging him up there to die a slow death from suffocation and loss of blood. They even drove a spear in his side just to make sure the deed was done."

Rob shook his head sharply. "Don't make sense, Jeff. Lady told me all that and it don't make sense. She told me as how he had the power to come storming down and fry every one of them what was in the crowd—in the whole place, even—but he never raised a finger. Why? Why not fry them all?"

Jeff asked carefully, "Did the lady tell you who all was in that crowd?"

"Yeah. She said they was a bunch of murderers, and thieves, and liars and pushers and cheaters and people as what hate other folks and . . ." Rob's list grew and became inclusive. Suddenly he stopped. He looked at Collin, then looked at the floor, then looked back at Jeff. "People like me."

Jeff nodded. "And me. And the lady. And Ta'waan and Nyla and Niles and even Mitch. The Bible says there wasn't a single person ever born that was good enough not to be in that crowd. God wanted to come storming down, and one day he will. See, God knows that anyone who breaks his law will die. He told us that from the very beginning of time. 'Whoever sins, dies.' And the only way not to die is for someone else to take your place. But not just anyone. It has to be someone perfect; someone who hasn't done anything wrong. And there wasn't anyone. Never has been; never will be. So God sent Jesus to live and die and take our place. Jesus is the only one that can. And when we accept him—when we believe that he did take our place and we give him our lives—then God's law is satisfied and we're given a new life. We're given Jesus' life. That's how we can learn to love our enemies and forgive those who hurt us and hate us." He finished by saying, "The lady did it, and that's why she can call on God to help her when she's in trouble. I did it and I know now I'm never alone. I've always got a friend to talk to, and who talks to me."

Robbie asked, "But how you know that? How you know God ain't still mad at you? Or this friend you can't see be talking with you?"

"Because Jesus didn't stay dead, Rob. They buried him but he didn't stay there."

Robbie said very slowly, sounding out the unfamiliar syllables, "The Resurrection? Him coming back from the dead? Lady told me 'bout that, but I ain't believing. Ain't no one comes back."

"Jesus did. The people that were closest to him had a hard time believing, too, until he let them touch his hands and feet where the soldiers put the spikes in him. And he ate food with them, too, to prove it was really him. If God hadn't been satisfied—hadn't accepted what Jesus did—Jesus would never have come back to life. But God was satisfied. He let Jesus take the rap so that anyone who wants to can trust in Jesus and never have to worry about God turning away from them. Even when we mess up, and mess up big time, he still loves us because of what Jesus did. The Bible says Jesus is our mediator, or lawyer. He stands between us and God and says, "Look, Dad, I know Farrell screwed up again and he really does deserve to be blasted out of existence. But Dad, he's one of my friends and I promised I'd take care of him. So for my sake let him go again. I'll deal with him. And I know exactly how to do it. I'll send that hard headed Collin Walker to him. She'll make his life so miserable he won't ever stop talking to you."

Robbie grinned. "She gonna bust you for that, you know."

Jeff grinned in return. "Yeah, but truth hurts."

Robbie studied the floor again, then said, "I seen the lady get through some mean times an' always give the credit to God, like he was some real friend. You talking 'bout him the same." Robbie hesitated a long time then asked, his voice quiet, "Can I be knowing him like that, too?"

Jeff nodded, his voice soft, "Anytime you want to, you can. The Bible says that if you confess with your mouth the Lord Jesus—that means that you're committed to following him and are not ashamed of him—and you believe in your heart that God raised him from the dead—that you really believe what God said and did is true—then you will be saved. And that means when you accept God, he accepts you." Again Jeff prayed silently, *"If I'm leaving anything out, Lord, fill in the blanks for him."* Aloud, Jeff said, "Look, man, I'm about to starve. You want anything?" Robbie shook his head silently. Jeff nodded. "Okay, then, man. Keep an eye on our lady." He got up and walked out the door.

Outside in the corridor Jeff leaned against the door and prayed softly, "He's all yours, Father. He always has been, I know. Maybe Collin planted. I hope I've watered a little and not just drowned him. But you're the one who'll make him grow. It's you and him now. If I'd said any more it would've been me and him, and that's not what it's supposed to be. Take care of him, Lord." Jeff pushed off from the wall and headed down the corridor to the exit.

He was gone about forty minutes and smuggled back two cheeseburgers, large fries, and a chocolate milkshake. He knocked softly on the door to Collin's room and heard Robbie's, "Come in." Jeff kept his back to the boy as he downloaded his contraband, afraid to look in the boy's face. But you can only hide for so long in an eight by ten foot room. Jeff said lightly, "I brought you something anyhow, Rob. Hope you don't mind chocolate." He looked Rob in the eyes and saw there the reflection of a young man newly born again. Jeff broke into a grin and gave Robbie a huge bear hug. Robbie hugged him back. Neither said a word; there was no need.

From the bed a weak voice croaked, "If he doesn't want it, I'll take it. I love chocolate."

Robbie laughed and turned to look at Collin. "You so bad, lady. That be my supper. They be bringing you yours later."

Collin groaned. "Is that any way to treat the wounded?" She sat up slowly. "If you're not going to feed me then take me back to camp."

Jeff said with all the patience he could muster, "Collin, the doctor hasn't been in yet this evening."

Collin sniped, "Jeff, I don't care. I want out of here. You've got to take Rob back sooner or later, so you may as well drop me off, too. Please?" She pushed her head against his hand and repeated, "Please?" Jeff shook his head; she stuck out her lower lip in a little girl pout and said again, "Please?"

Jeff groaned and said, "Lady, what am I going to do with you?"

"Take me back to camp, send me to my room, and ground me from chocolate for a week?"

Jeff looked to Robbie for support. "What do you do with her when she's like this? How do you put up with her?"

Robbie just grinned. "Hey, man, I ain't never had this problem with her. Ain't never tried to tell her what to do. I be knowing better than that."

Collin started to say something, Jeff cut her off. "Just hush, woman. Lie back there and at least pretend you want to get better until the doctor gets here. We'll let him decide."

Collin lay back down, the little girl pout still on her face, but the pain, physical and emotional, still shadowed her face. Jeff wondered silently, *"Lord, what are you dealing with in her? And how do I help?"*

Before any answers could come, or maybe it was the answer itself, a knock sounded at the door and Doctor Wallace stuck his head in. "Am I interrupting? I can come back later."

Jeff said, "No interruption."

Collin added, "These gentlemen were just leaving for some fresh air."

Robbie sniped, "And a quiet place to eat. My dinner getting cold."

Jeff put an arm around his shoulders and said, "I know when I'm not wanted. Let's go, Rob."

Robbie gathered up his food and drink and the two men walked down the hall to the waiting room. After both cheeseburgers and half the fries were consumed—or inhaled, as the case may be—Robbie asked, "What you gonna do about the lady wanting to leave? You can't make her stay, can you?"

Jeff admitted, "I've been trying to figure that out, Rob. If I know her the way I think I do, I could probably convince her to stay. But it could put a tremendous dent in the long term relationship I'd like to have with this woman." He hesitated, then said softly, "Still, if I was convinced her life was in danger I'd do it anyhow."

Robbie finished the fries then downed the now-melted milk shake. "You be loving the case worker lady, ain't you?"

Jeff looked at him and said honestly, "I be trying, my man. I be trying."

Collin's door eventually opened and Dr. Wallace came out. He walked down the hall and up to Jeff and Robbie. He looked at Robbie and asked pointedly, "Are you family?"

Jeff answered for him. "He's as close as you're going to get in this state."

Wallace said only, "I see." He hesitated a moment, then said, "I think she's out of any immediate danger." He looked at Jeff and said, "I don't like the fact that the left eye is dilated more than the right but she insists it's been that way for some time. Seems to me I noticed a slight difference when I examined her Wednesday night but it wasn't this pronounced." He shrugged and said, "Not that it's a major problem. It's more like a shadow, one that you think might be there, but then again might not be. Something to keep an eye on, so to speak." He must have realized he was losing his audience because he suddenly switched gears and said, "The knee is cracked, but with physical therapy and a good long time off of it, should regain full mobility." He looked pointedly at Jeff and said, "I'm going to let you tell her about the time off part. But overall I'd say she was a very lucky lady."

Jeff didn't try to correct Wallace's impression. Instead he stated, "She really wants to go back to the camp."

Wallace said dryly, "Yes, she made that abundantly clear while I was examining her. Emphatically clear."

Robbie quipped, "The lady like to be understood."

"And I did, I did. I can't see any reason she has to stay here if some specific guidelines are followed."

Jeff looked at him in disbelief. "After what she's been through? Are you nuts?"

Wallace shrugged. "It's because of what she's been through, Jeff. Think, man. She fought all morning just to survive. She wants a nice, quiet, safe hole to hide in so she can lick her wounds and digest all of this. A hospital does not fit that bill. The camp does. So take her back there, post a 24 hour guard on her so she doesn't try to escape and do something stupid like tackle America's Most Wanted top ten list and let her heal up."

Jeff took a few moments to digest that then asked, "What guidelines? What does she need?"

"Sleep and all she can get. But someone needs to be with her for the next twelve hours just as a precaution."

"Looking for . . ." Jeff prompted.

"Listening for slurred speech, for unusual word patterns. Watching for stumbling, or swaying . . . no, check that. She's not to be on her feet any more than absolutely necessary. I'll check you out some crutches and a wheel chair." He grinned at Jeff. "Good luck."

"Anything else?" Jeff refused to see the humor in all this. Wallace was a good doctor; he knew that. But was the man really sure about letting Collin out? Just to keep her happy?

Wallace must have sensed Jeff's misgivings for he said soothingly, "Jeff, if I thought for one minute you'd see any of this I wouldn't let her go no matter how much she begged. These are the mandatory worst case scenarios I have to present. Like complaining of double vision."

Robbie said, "That ain't no big deal. She complain 'bout that all the time."

Wallace was suddenly concerned. "Really?"

Robbie backed down. "Ain't really complaining. But sometime she tired, more tired than usual, and she say she be seeing two of me which be one more than she need, so then she go home." Robbie hesitated then added, "Say she go home. I seen her sleeping in her car couple times like that. But she don't stay long then she drive off."

Jeff and Wallace exchanged knowing glances. Jeff said, "I'll keep a close eye on her."

"Bring her back to my office tomorrow at one for a recheck then. Otherwise she's free to go." He added, "I've got rounds. Believe it or not, I've got patients that look forward to seeing me and actually appreciate being here." He set off down the hall.

Jeff looked at Robbie and said, "Let's go take our lady home."

Within an hour the threesome was back at Camp Grace. Robbie was sent off to his room with instructions to relax, rest and be ready for the morrow's river run. Jeff planted Collin firmly but gently in a room off the main corridor, having shifted responsibility for Jill and Chenille to another counselor's ministrations. Collin changed with difficulty but equal determination from the hospital clothes into her own pajamas. Getting under the covers while she was lying on them was tough but she refused to wait for help to come. There were some things she would do alone, thank you. She couldn't reach the light but knew Jeff would be coming back to make sure she was settled and hadn't run off to save the earth or something. It was going to take some doing to live down this super-girl image. Collin sighed. You do what you do because it's what you're handed, and you just gotta do it. Why couldn't she make him understand that? Especially when the Lord told you to.

But had he? Had he really? Where was it written . . . Collin silenced the accusing thought. Didn't matter now. Over. It was over. Collin whispered, "I did it to please you, Lord. Whatever it takes, all that matters is that you're happy with me. That you know I love you. All I want to hear is 'well done.'"

A knock at her door interrupted Collin's prayer. She called, "Come in."

Jeff poked his head around the door and asked, "You doing okay?"

"I will be."

She motioned for Jeff to come in; Jeff did but, not surprisingly, left the door open. He sat down hesitantly beside the bed then asked carefully, "You want to talk about it?"

"About what happened? No."

"I was thinking more about why it happened. Why you thought for one moment that you had to go out there the way you did."

Collin sighed in frustration. "Someone had to. And the Lord . . ."

Jeff said firmly, "The Lord has sheriffs and deputies and all manner of law enforcement people that could have gone."

Collin snapped, "But the Lord handed it to me. I was in the right place at the right time and I wasn't about to let him down."

Jeff studied her a moment. A long moment. Collin waited, not sure what she had said that brought on this much confusion in the man. Finally he asked, "You really think you could 'let him down?' That he doesn't already know your heart?"

Collin scowled at him. "My life is about pleasing the Lord, Jeff. Finding his will and doing it. It's all that matters."

Jeff's voice was gentle as he asked, "And you really believed it was his will for you to go out there and single-handedly take on Mitch?"

Irritated, Collin snapped, "Yes." She closed her eyes against the sudden sadness that welled up in her. Collin bit her lip then admitted, "I want him to be proud of me. I want him to love me. I want him to know I love him." She opened her eyes and quoted, "'If you love me, keep my commandments.'"

Jeff shook his head slightly. "You're twisting it, Collin. Or someone has twisted it for you. We don't have to prove to God we love him. And we certainly don't have to earn his love. He loves us because he is God, because that's who he is."

Collin said quickly, "I know he loves me, Jeff. I know that, okay? I've taught it over and over. It's the message of the Gospel: God loved the world. He loved me and accepted me when I accepted Jesus. But after—now—I need to prove that I love him. That I really am grateful for all he does for me. I need to show him."

Jeff shook his head again. "Like he doesn't know?"

Collin ground her teeth in frustration. Her head began to throb. She waited for the pounding to lessen then said, "Okay, listen. Let's fight this out tomorrow after I get done riding the river. We'll have plenty of time I'm sure. Okay? I can't think straight right now. I need to sleep and be rested up."

Jeff's voice was incredulous. "Ride the river? Are you out of your mind? You can't ride the river! Look at yourself!"

Collin said strongly, "I am going to ride that river, Jeff. If nothing else, I know that was why I came up here. I have to face it. I have to get that much of my life back in control. I'm riding it. Period."

Jeff eyed her a long moment then said softly, "We'll see how you are in the morning."

"I will ride it, Jeff. If it kills me, I will ride it."

Jeff stood up slowly and said only, "I'll see you in the morning, Collin. Sleep, lady." He walked out and carefully closed the door behind him.

Collin felt tears sting her eyes. She whispered tightly, "I will ride it. You brought me up here for this, and I will make you proud. You'll see." Collin settled down in the bed, closed her eyes, and slept.

Jeff stopped outside the door and sagged against the wall, shaking his head. He whispered, "What can I do, Lord? She's not mine to command. Watch over her, please? Whatever it is you're doing with her, keep her in the center of it. It's the only place she can be safe from herself." What was it she was trying to prove? Maybe who was she trying to prove it to was a better question. Jeff shook his head and moved off down the hall.

Even though it was well past curfew the sounds of elated and wired campers were still very much in evidence. Today most of them had reached the Holy Grail, of sorts. Jeff checked the bulletin board for the lists and noted with deep satisfaction that only one other class, hang gliding, had failed to meet its goal. Well, not true. Not necessarily true, anyhow. First, wind conditions had prevented a safe landing so take off was cancelled. But if the kids had learned from the experience, then the class met its goal anyhow. Camp Grace would offer to bring the class back so they could fly. Or maybe they could take the kids to a site nearer to home . . . but where family and friends could watch. Jeff would suggest something to the owner in the morning so the kids could go home knowing these dreams, at least, were still alive. No one walked away from a Grace Challenge camp feeling cheated or unsatisfied, except by personal choice.

Two of the instructors passed Jeff in the corridor. Nan Crouse was the riding instructor; Peter Vance handled the street luge. Both stopped as they recognized Jeff in the dim corridor. Peter grinned, "Jeffman! Where were you all day? You missed some great racing."

Jeff nodded. "That's what I heard. You've got some candidates for the X games, I hear."

"For anything they want to do, trust me. I had my doubts when this class started but the kids proved me wrong. Again. I love it."

Jeff grinned. "You got it." He looked at Nan and asked, "How did your group do?"

"For kids that have never seen a horse, much less ridden one, they did great. I've got two, the little ones, Beth and Avery, that could make professional jumpers given half a chance." She eyed Jeff closely and asked, "You think our good owner could be enticed to help foot the bill to continue this dream? Beth is a great kid. She's only ten but there is potential in her. Do you know anything about her background? Family?"

"Hunt up her counselor."

Nan snorted. "That one. She disappeared on day one and didn't come back until tonight, after the shouting was done."

Peter agreed. "As great as these kids were I've never seen a more dead beat bunch of counselors. Not one of them participated."

Jeff said quickly, "Not true. Three of them did."

Peter challenged, "Who? What'd they do?"

Jeff had to think hard for the names. "Um . . . Mr. Tremont went with the rappellers. And . . . uh, Mr. Lawler was it? He did the street skiing."

Beth added, "And that woman, Walker, she went with the white water group."

Peter nodded, "Yeah, that's right. I forgot about them. What happened to the white water group? I didn't see their class posted."

Jeff hesitated then said, "They didn't raft. They won a stay over and will shoot for it tomorrow."

Peter whistled low. "A stay over? Someone must be very impressed with those kids."

Beth's eyes twinkled slightly as she said knowingly, "Well, Peter, when you work here long enough you come to realize our owner is a push over for kids. And their counselors."

Jeff was suddenly uncomfortable. What did Beth know? Or was she simply of a suspicious nature? He cleared his throat and said, "Look, people, this is fun, but it's past my bedtime. I need my beauty sleep."

Peter grinned. "And all you can get. See you in the morning, Jeff."

Beth continued to smile that knowing smile and said, "Good night, Jeff."

Jeff made his way to his maintenance shack and checked his messages. Thankfully, none of the animals were complaining about anything. Jeff undressed then knelt beside his bunk. He quieted his mind and heart then prayed, "Lord, thank you. Thank you for being you, for loving me, for dying for me. Thank you for never giving up on me. I was not a model of faith and trust today, I know. I was scared, I was angry, I was frustrated . . . I probably murdered Mitch a dozen times in my heart . . ." Jeff trailed off as the emotions of the day's ordeal did an instant replay in his head. He waited for them to subside then continued, his voice almost broken, "I could justify all of it, Lord. All of it and probably more. But what really eats at me, what really tears at my gut is that it was on my recommendation that Grace hired him in the first place. I vouched for him. Lord, is this my fault?"

Jeff sat back on his heels, determined to go no further in this discussion until that much was settled. He'd vouched for Mitch, true. Had met him a few years back and though he thought him a bit pompous, found him to be an expert on the river. Any misgivings Jeff had felt he dismissed as personal bias: Mitch had taken to dating a young woman Jeff had seen once or twice. Rather than being accused of holding it against the man, Jeff had recommended Mitch apply for the job at Grace. And he had passed all the background checks, psychological testing, etc. There was nothing whatsoever to indicate Mitch Kellum would turn out to be a mass murderer. So no, he had no responsibility for Mitch, nor consequently for what happened to Collin. He could manufacture some guilt with very little effort, but what purpose would it serve? Deal with reality, folks. Jeff continued softly, "Thank you, Father. Now tell me where we go from here. How do I help her? What do I say? What don't I say? Lord, I've never been more convinced that this is the woman I want to marry, and more important, that you have for me. Don't let me mess this up, Father. Show me how to bring glory to your holy name." Jeff crawled into bed and under the covers, turned out the light and finished with, "Thanks, Dad. In Jesus' most precious name, amen." Then one very tired maintenance man closed his eyes and slept.

SATURDAY

The alarm went off at six, but Jeff didn't need it. He'd been awake since four; not tossing and turning but simply awake, reviewing, forecasting, planning, and generally mapping out what came next with the camp, the campers, the river rafters, and with a certain young woman he'd grown rather fond of in a short time. First things first, however. Jeff reversed the nighttime process, climbed out of bed and hit his knees. He prayed, "Good morning, Lord. It's your day, your plan. Help the campers put this week in perspective. And for Collin's crew, Lord, let their day be extra special." His voice became more gentle as he said, "Help her, Lord. Help her work through whatever it is she's dealing with. You want honesty, Father, so I'm giving it to you. I love her, Lord. I haven't quite figured out all the reasons, but I do. I want to make her my wife. You're the only one who can prevent that. Your will, your glory, Lord. That's all I want. Thanks for listening. In Jesus' name, amen."

Jeff rose and said, "Okay, first things first. The lady needs sustenance. The lady's servant needs lots of sustenance." Jeff dressed, checked his message board one last time, then headed out the door.

Twenty minutes later, Jeff returned to Collin's sick room with a tray loaded with covered plates, a carafe of coffee, and a single dandelion in a Dixie cup. He lightly and carefully knocked on the door, then opened it slowly.

Collin stirred slightly, moaned slightly, blinked several times. Jeff guessed she was trying to put time and space back in proper perspective, and having a hard time doing it. She looked at him, looked at the room, looked back at him and stated, "You're Jeff, this is Camp Grace. I'm in my room, and it's . . ." this one was hardest of all. "it's . . . Saturday. And I get to ride the river today."

Jeff grinned. "Wrong on all counts." She looked at him sharply; Jeff relented. "Okay, wrong on one count. I'll let you decide which one."

Collin said defiantly, "I do get to ride the river today."

Jeff deflected her comment. "I brought your breakfast." There was going to be a battle, he could tell, and he wanted to be well prepared for it. Jeff began uncovering plates and bowls, setting them out on the table.

Collin's voice was horrified. "Jeff, I haven't eaten that much food in a month! You can't be expecting me to eat all that!"

Jeff looked at the table and said, "That's my breakfast. Yours is on the tray." He set out a small plate that he carried to Collin. On it were two pieces of bread, toasted and lightly buttered, a glass of orange juice and a cup of coffee with sugar. It also had the dandelion.

Collin looked at it and said softly but with delight, "That's so sweet."

Jeff shrugged. "Roses are hard to come by this time of year but dandelions I can find anywhere."

Collin smiled. "Thanks."

Collin nibbled at her toast while Jeff attacked his breakfast. He saw the look of amused disbelief in her eyes as she noted the quantity of vittles he was putting away. Defensively he said, "Look, I haven't eaten since . . ."

Collin interjected, "Last night?"

"Night before last, actually."

"Didn't you eat when Rob did?"

Jeff shrugged self-consciously. "No, I forgot my wallet. The manager turned out to be a friend from summer school a few years back. He let me take something for Rob."

Collin looked at him curiously. "Did you grow up here?"

"Summers, yes. My family spent every summer up here since I was old enough to form memories. Working at Grace is just carrying on a family tradition for me." Collin pushed her plate away; Jeff noted she had only eaten one of the four pieces of toast. He said sternly, "Eat. You can do better than that." Collin frowned at him but tackled another slice. Jeff resumed eating, then asked, "How's the head this morning?"

"It's fine. The knee is fine. I'm fine. And I'm going to ride the river."

Jeff looked at her and said, "Collin, be reasonable. You're hurt, woman. You don't need . . . ."

Collin cut him off, determination in her voice. "I am going to ride the river, Jeff. I have to."

Jeff finished his breakfast silently then said quietly, "Have it your way, lady. Boat leaves at ten. I'll see you when you're done. I drive the truck to meet the boat at the base of the river." He paused then added softly, "I hope you beat your demons, Collin. Whoever they are." He put her crutches where she could reach them, then walked out.

Jeff returned to the maintenance shack. There he puttered around, straightened up the work bench, put the books and manuals away. He was really only killing time. It all had to be done sooner or later, though. May as well be now. All the bright and happy visions of the future that he'd been letting creep into his thoughts of late seemed far less tangible. Jeff whispered, "Watch over her, Lord. Please."

By ten he'd done all he could do to take his mind off Collin, and none of it had worked. If he walked to the dock, she'd be gone. Unless she had gained some sort of insight between the time he'd left her and now. It could happen. Not likely, he admitted, but it was within the realm of possibilities. Or maybe the instructors would refuse to take her. Also not likely. Maybe he should walk down there, just in case. It wasn't like he had anything important to do. Other than overhaul the camp from Kidsworld to Adultland by Monday. Catch and relocate the herd of horses from the north pasture to the south. Dismantle the sluice run once and for all. Order supplies . . . Jeff grimaced. Ah, well, all in good time. If nothing else he could talk to the owner about hiring more help for the maintenance crew. Not that the owner was fond of spending money, mind you. But it wouldn't take much to convince him that Jeff needed more help so he could spend more time with Collin. The owner was such a softy about these things. Jeff began to smile slightly, and walked towards the dock.

From the distance he could see a single fragile figure sitting alone on the dock, leaning forlornly against the pilings. Jeff's heart surged as he approached cautiously, trying to assess Collin's mood. Had she gained some wisdom in the past hour? From the tear tracks on her face he guessed not. She did not look up, but tossed a pebble dejectedly into the river. Jeff sat down carefully beside her. He studied her a moment then asked softly, "Couldn't catch them?"

Collin continued to look down, tossed another pebble then said lowly, "They wouldn't take me."

"The instructors?"

"My crew." Her voice was incredibly sad as she said, "My crew—my crew—took a vote. Rob insisted they vote and they voted against me. Said

I wasn't in shape to go." She looked at Jeff and asked sorrowfully, "What kind of crew is that?"

Jeff said carefully, "One that cares about you more than you know." He wanted to add, "More than you care about yourself," but didn't. Discretion didn't come naturally to him, but he was learning. He did add, "There was no way Rob was going to let you go on that trip. He's growing up, Collin. You've taught him well."

Collin dropped her head again and whispered, "Too well." She stared out over the river then whispered, "I really, really wanted to ride it, Jeff. I needed to ride it. Just once."

Jeff slipped his arms around her shoulders and asked, "Why? Can you tell me?"

There was a very long silence. Finally Collin asked, "Can I tell you a story? It's about a girl I know."

"A friend?"

"I'm never quite sure."

Jeff nodded. "Sure. I like stories."

"You might not like this one. It's not a very happy story."

Jeff said quietly, "Even bad stories can have happy endings, Collin."

She shivered slightly; Jeff hugged her to himself carefully. Collin stared out over the river and began. "Once upon a time there was this man. He was a rich man and had the rich man's disease. Whatever he had it wasn't enough. 'More' was his favorite word. More money, more power, more more. His parents were even richer than he was, and since he was the first born of three boys he looked to inherit it all. But his parents followed an old family tradition in their choice of who got the money. Fortunes were passed to grandchild, not child. First born of the first born, so to speak. If the first born had no progeny, then the first son to produce an heir got it. There was, of course, plenty of money to spread around for everyone so no one was left out, but the lion's share and control of the resources went to that first born's first born.

"Well, this man was nothing if not determined. Everything he did, he did with determination. He determined to win the family fortune so he determined to find a wife. And he did: a beautiful, patient, woman who adored him. He actually cared little for her; he was mostly interested in her ability to have that son he wanted." Collin looked at Jeff and repeated, "Son, mind you. Not child. Son. Females were pretty useless as far as he was concerned. Besides, a girl would get married and the family fortune would pass into a stranger's hand. That was unthinkable. No, no girls. A son. A son was the answer."

Collin turned back to the river. Jeff felt a lump growing in his throat. He hugged her closer as she continued, "Well, the first two pregnancies ended in miscarriages after four months. The man was actually grateful, for both had been girls."

Jeff closed his eyes and whispered, "Collin . . ."

"You want me to stop?"

He grit his teeth and said, "No. Go on." If she had endured the living, he could endure the telling.

Collin continued, "Finally, though, the woman had a pregnancy go into the third trimester. She was watched and monitored and cared for with all the finest medical treatment available twenty plus some years ago. Just shy of nine months the woman went into labor and delivered two four-pound twins."

Jeff said, "The man must have been very happy."

"He should have been. He could have been. But he wasn't. He was furious. The whole thing was a disaster and it was his wife's fault. See, the twins were a boy and a girl. But because the little girl could never stand to be late for anything, well, she was born first." Collin closed her eyes but a tear trickled down her cheek anyhow. "The babies needed medical attention, of course. The man demanded the best care money could buy for the tiny little boy, but would not allow anything beyond the minimum legally required for the hated girl. Fortunately for her, there were good doctors and nurses who cared nothing for money, but kept her alive, and made sure she and her brother both thrived.

"In the end he had to take them both home. The doctors refused to be bribed into altering the birth order and the nurses remained witnesses as well. The father's parents, the twins' grandparents, recognized the little girl as the family heir and life went on. Or so it seemed. The father never got over the fact that the girl had beaten her brother out of his rightful inheritance. He set about to make sure she never beat him out of anything else that is a 'man's due.' Whatever she did, it was never as good as her brother. Mysteriously her arm was broken so she couldn't crawl first. An ankle broke just about the time she was learning to walk. She developed a fear of talking . . ." Collin smiled sadly," . . . if you can believe that . . . after she scalded her throat on hot coffee, accidently left where she could reach it." Collin looked down and said quietly, "She was never allowed to win games, play sports or do anything that would outshine her brother."

Jeff swallowed hard, feeling the twisting in his gut. He pulled Collin even closer, trying to shield her from a past he could not change. Collin smiled sadly and leaned against his chest. She said, "I told you it's not a happy story. My friend has a real hard time telling people about it. Mostly she doesn't. People don't like sad stories."

Jeff's throat was tight as he said, "Don't stop. I want to know how it ends."

Collin said softly, "It hasn't. Not yet."

"Maybe we can bring it to an end. We'll write our own ending."

Collin ducked her head slightly. "Maybe." She fell silent, took a deep breath then continued, "When the twins were about five the father decided to take them on a picnic. He packed his wife, the twins, a basket of lunch, even a ball to play with. He took them down to the park by the river. The river was pretty high and fast because there had been a lot of rain that spring. There were even signs posted with warnings about the danger.

"The father played with the twins for several hours until they were tired. They all ate lunch, then the children lay down for a nap. Even the mom fell asleep. But after a little while the father woke up the little girl and told her he wanted to show her something special. She became very excited because her father wanted to spend time with her, and show her something he wasn't showing her brother. She began to skip and dance beside her father . . ."

Jeff's voice strangled. "Don't, Collin. Don't call him a father. No father would ever treat his child like that. He was a man, nothing more."

Collin eyed him closely then said, "Okay. The man started swinging her along, laughing and teasing. He'd swing her high in the air, let her drop, then catch her at the last moment. She thought it was a great game and squealed with delight. Her fath . . . the man took her down by the river where he knew it was deserted. He made sure no one was around to see and continued to swing the girl high in the air. She laughed and shrieked . . ." Collin's eyes closed and all life drained from her face. Her voice was hollow as she continued, ". . . and then the man swung her out one last time, out high over the river, out where she could do nothing but scream in terror until she plunged into the racing waters beneath her."

Jeff groaned, "Collin . . ."

Tears began flowing. His or hers, it didn't really matter. One size fits all. Collin continued her story, unable to stop the flow of memory short of its conclusion. "There were several fishermen around the bend in the river who saw the little girl struggling in the torrent. Someone shouted and two of them dived in to try to rescue her. Their yelling alerted the man and he feared being discovered. So he ran down the banks yelling in despair for someone to save his baby. She was swept past her would-be rescuers but finally was washed into the shallows, where she was rescued from the bottom of the river. CPR was performed and she was revived at about the time the man arrived. He grabbed the little girl from her benefactors, refused their offer of transport to the nearest hospital, and took her back to where her mother and brother were waiting. He proceeded to punish her for sneaking off and playing by the river, telling her that falling in was God's punishment for being a wicked and disobedient little girl."

Jeff closed his eyes and shook his head, trying to reason it out. How? How could anyone be so twisted? He rocked Collin slowly, aching without any means of release. Collin continued her story, "The girl developed pneumonia but the man wouldn't let her go to the doctor until the man's mother paid a visit. She informed him of a little known clause in the family code of inheritance. If the first born's first born should die before inheriting, then the heir became the next son's first born. Meaning if the little girl died, the first born of any of his brothers would get the money. In plain words, the man's son would never, ever, inherit the family fortune. And if anything did happen to the little girl, the man could be sure his mother and father would be first in line to accuse him of foul play."

Collin let out a long, slow breath then said, "Her words at least stopped any more attempts on the girl's life. It didn't stop the hatred or the abuse and her life was little more than misery. She was . . . relocated to Oakton when she was fourteen and lived mostly on the streets for a couple of years. But the Lord had plans for her. She ran into a street preacher with a homeless mission. He took her in, introduced her to the Lord, got her to finish high school, then sent her on to college. She graduated and has done pretty well since then. She has a good job working with kids, volunteers at the street missions and is diligently waiting for God to bring that one good man into her life. But she can't handle running rivers."

Story complete, Collin sagged back against Jeff's chest and fell silent. Jeff continued to hold her tightly, rocking slowly back and forth, unable to find words that would make it right or make it go away. They sat like that for several minutes unwilling to break the tableau that bound them together. Jeff's mind raced as he prayed, *"That's it isn't it, Father? She never pleased him so she's trying to please you instead. She doesn't realize you're already pleased with her. She doesn't have to work to prove anything. Show me how to help her."*

Before Jeff could say anything more Collin hiccuped slightly then said quietly, "I'm going to miss you, Jeff."

Confused, Jeff said, "What are you talking about? I'm not going anywhere. I live and work in Oakton just like you do. I assume you have a phone and an address where you can be reached. Are you trying to get rid of me?"

Collin looked down then whispered, "You've seen the real Collin Walker. She's a fake. She's not wise, or witty, or bright, or strong or tough. She's a scared little girl who doesn't know what real love is like. That's more truth than most men are willing to handle." She laughed without mirth. "I've seen them run away screaming."

Jeff said firmly, "I'm not running."

"No, you're sitting down. Wait until you get to your feet."

Jeff pulled her chin up gently and kissed her warmly. He repeated, "I'm not running, lady. You're stuck with me. You may be the one running away screaming, when you uncover all my deep dark secrets." He realized too late that his phrasing left a great deal to be desired. He tried to reverse his field and said quickly, "That's not what I meant, Collin. I meant . . ."

Collin smiled sadly at him. "It's okay, Jeff. I know what you meant."

Jeff stood up abruptly and said, "Come with me."

As he pulled her carefully to her feet she asked in confusion, "Where?"

"Just come on. I'll explain later." Jeff handed Collin her crutches then unceremoniously picked her and them up together and started back up the hill. He ignored her startled protests and said, "Faster this way. But don't think this is going to become a habit. Not unless you lose five pounds. The way you eat . . ."

Collin growled at him, "You are rotten! You hear me? Rotten!"

Jeff simply grinned and carried her to the administration building. He made sure no one was around then carried Collin inside. He set her down outside the door marked, "President" and said, "Okay, you've been wanting to meet the owner. It's time you did."

Collin looked skeptical. "Now? Right now? Jeff, I'm a mess."

Jeff kissed her lightly on the forehead and said, "You're always a mess. That's one of the things I love about you. You take casual to a new height." Collin scowled hard. Jeff said quickly, "Wait five minutes then knock on this door."

"Where will you be?"

"I've got some things to check on. Just give it five minutes."

"Jeff, I can't just barge into the man's office unannounced and uninvited. What if he's busy? What if it's not a good time? I'm going to look like a fool."

Jeff said patiently, "You could never look like a fool, milady. And trust me, I know the owner. He loves being interrupted at work. Breaks up his day. Makes it go faster or something. I don't know. Just do it."

Collin objected one last time, "At least stay with me and introduce us, please? I won't feel so stupid."

Jeff smiled at her, kissed her lightly and said, "Please do this my way, okay? Wait five minutes then knock on the door. Everything will be fine. Trust me." He laid his hands on her shoulders and looked her in the eyes until she nodded. He smiled and said, "Good. I'll see you in a little bit." He kissed her again on the forehead then took off down the hall.

Collin sighed as she watched him disappear around a corner. She felt totally out of control of the situation. What happened? They were talking about her past, about running away screaming, about his deep, dark secrets . . . and then here she was about to meet the owner of the camp. Made sense to her. Uh huh. Natural progression . . . or was it? Collin stared at the door and noted a very small plate underneath the President sign. There was a name engraved on it but you had to look very close to read it. Collin leaned forward and read, "Geoffrey McFaell." She sounded it out slowly, "Joffrey . . . Jeffrey?" A light began to dawn in the denseness that was her brain. "McFaell. Mac means son of. Son of Faell." Faell? What kind of name was Faell? Faell. But it did have a familiar sound . . . like she'd heard it before. From a voice with a lisp? Wasn't that how Jeff's sister Leesa had answered the phone? Faell residence?

Collin groaned but stopped just short of smacking herself in the head for stupidity. A review of all Jeff's comments about the owner allowed chinks and chunks to fall in place. She shook her head in disgust at her own obtuseness. Dumb and dumber had nothing on her. How was she going to pull this one out?

And what did it mean? Jeff was trying to tell her that he was more than he appeared. Why? Because he wanted her to know the real him. But who was the real Jeff? Maintenance man or owner? Rich man, poor man? Who was he? The answer was behind that door if she had the courage to knock.

Collin guessed Jeff had had enough time to "check on some things," reached up and knocked on the door. A deep male voice called, "Come in."

Collin awkwardly pushed the door open on a spartan office. There was a medium-size oak desk, three leather upholstered chairs and two filing cabinets. The walls were basically empty with the exception of a hand carved plaque reading "Camp Grace." Carved by a camper, no doubt. The office had the look and feel of a place not often occupied, as if the president did not spend a great deal of time in his office. No doubt true.

The high-backed chair behind the desk was turned away from the door. Collin could tell someone was sitting there but shielded from view. Collin smiled slightly then composed herself and said, "Mr. President? I'm Collin Walker, a guest at your camp. I've got to tell you, sir, I love this place. It is the most special, wonderful camp I've ever been to. But I think you've heard all that before. What I really want to talk to you about is your maintenance man, Jeff Farrell." The chair squeaked as Mr. President shifted his weight in the chair. No doubt uncomfortably. Collin said quickly, "Please don't interrupt until I'm finished. Whatever you're paying him it isn't enough. The man practically runs this place. I think you work him too hard, myself, but you'd know that better than anyone I suppose." Again the chair creaked; Collin hurried on. "I've gotten to know him just a little. He's warm, and caring, and gentle . . ." her voice cracked slightly, but she regained control, ". . . and strong and loving . . . there's a lot more there I'd like to get to know if I could. He's got secrets I need to know about if we're going to make this relationship work."

Jeff stood up and walked towards her, a look of guilt on his face. Collin finished quickly as if not seeing him, "Though I admit if I wasn't so wrapped up in my own fear I would have figured it out a long time ago. It's not like he didn't give me enough hints." Jeff stood in front of her; Collin wrapped her arms around his neck and said softly, "So, Mr. President, do you think you might let the man of my dreams have a little more time off so we can really get to know each other?"

Jeff kissed her warmly then hugged her in relief. Collin laughed lightly then asked, "Why? Why the charade?"

Jeff helped her over to a chair, sat her down carefully then sat down on the floor beside her. He said, "Jeff Farrell can go places and do things McFaell can't. McFaell is a stuffed shirt. Well, that's not fair, not exactly. But he has to entertain sponsors and deal with banks and legislators and federal regulators. Jeff gets to get down with the real people: the workers and the kids themselves. He gets to see the camp from their perspective to see if it's doing what it's supposed to be doing. Janitors go places no one else gets to go. He sees real people, not people acting for some rich owner they want to impress."

Collin hesitated then asked slowly, "And who is the real you?"

Jeff said quietly, "I am. My name really is Jeffrey with a J Farrell. McFaell only exists in business connections. Anyone that wants to know the truth knows it. And there aren't that many that really care."

"So how did you buy the camp?"

He held up his callused hands. "With these. And plenty of sweat and tears for interest. And maybe a little blood thrown in but not enough to amount to anything. Mostly it was by the grace of the Lord. My family used to come to camp here every summer. When the owner decided to sell out I asked permission to buy it for sweat equity. It's taken a few years to get it to where it is now but it's worth it. I think it is, anyhow."

Collin leaned forward and kissed him on the top of the head. "I love you, Jeff."

Jeff turned to face her and his expression was solemn. "Do you mean that?"

Collin hesitated only slightly then nodded. "I mean that."

"But you had to think about it." His eyes twinkled slightly.

Now it was Collin's turn to be serious. "A lot. And long and hard. I never say that lightly."

"No, I don't expect you would." Jeff twisted around on his knees and took her hands in his. "Collin Walker . . ."

Collin pulled back abruptly and said, "Don't. Don't ask. Not yet." Jeff sat back on his haunches, a confused look on his face. Collin saw hurt in his eyes but said, "Jeff, you don't know me. I'm not what you think. That girl that lived on the streets . . . she . . ."

Jeff held his hand up carefully to stop her and said, "It doesn't matter, Collin. If God has forgiven you who am I to say anything at all? What went before doesn't matter."

"That's easy to say."

"Easy to do when you remember where you came from. And I don't mean you, I mean the person doing the accusing. We've all done things we're not proud of. But you know what? That's why we all need a savior. I know I did."

Collin looked deep into his eyes, knowing full well it was a mistake then sighed slightly. She noted a new look of pain in Jeff's eyes and guessed it wasn't from mental angst. She said, "Get up before you get stuck like that."

Jeff gave out an exaggerated moan then climbed painfully to his feet. He offered Collin his hand, she took it and stood up awkwardly herself. She sensed that they were moving on, literally and figuratively. But where? Jeff seemed to be leading so Collin leaned on him as they left the admin building. Jeff locked the door behind him then grinned. "The other benefit of being the janitor: you always have keys for everything."

"Including my heart." It sounded too corny to say so Collin didn't. Wanted to, but didn't. They hobbled down the trail—well, Collin hobbled, Jeff walked—back to the lodge. Collin asked carefully, "Where do we go from here?" not sure which meaning he'd take.

But being the pragmatist that he was, Jeff said, "Well, I've got a few things that need my attention."

"A few?"

"Okay more than a few. You've got an appointment with Dr. Wallace at one but I'll see if I can convince him to make a house call instead of dragging you out. We're supposed to meet the river cruisers at six at the base of the run. It takes about an hour to get there, so we should leave here no later than four-thirty."

"We, meaning you and me?"

"I sort of thought you'd want to go."

"You sort of thought right. I'd better be able to go or so help me, I'll start walking now."

"That's what I thought. We'll make it easy on both of us and I'll drive you down with me. I get to haul the boat back." He looked at her and said, "Seriously, you might want to ride back with the kids."

Collin thought about it then said, "No, let them savor the ride. They're going to want to live it over and over. I'll wait until they've calmed down just a little." She admitted, "I'm not sure I could handle all the enthusiasm right now."

"Headache again?"

"Still. I could use a nap until it's time to go. Would that be permissible?"

"I think we can allow it." Jeff smiled. "I'll send someone to get you up for Dr. Wallace and then again when it's time to head to the river."

"Sounds like a plan."

The two walked back to Collin's room. As Jeff left he said carefully, "Before you go to sleep think about this." Collin waited; Jeff continued slowly, "God is your Father. But he's not your *father.* Your biological father. You don't have to win God's love, Collin. We obey him because we love him; not because we're trying to prove anything. He knows, Collin. He already knows."

Collin studied Jeff, considered his words, nodded her head. "I'll think about it. Good night, Jeff."

"Sleep peaceful, milady."

Collin closed the door, hobbled to her bed then sat down. She whispered, "I don't have to prove anything." She paused. "I don't have to prove anything?" Collin gathered her Bible then stretched out on the bed, closed her eyes and prayed, "Lord, do I have to prove anything?"

The sweet verses echoed in her memory: *"Lord, You have searched me and known me . . . You know my thoughts . . . before I speak a word you already know it." "Nothing is hidden from you . . ." "Man looks on the outside, but God looks on the heart."* What could she prove to God? And if the answer was "nothing" then why was she trying so hard? Why was she trying at all?

Collin let the thoughts roll around in her head. She whispered, "Is that what I'm supposed to be learning, Lord? Was that what this trip was all about? Learning to let go—not of my fear of the river—but of disappointing you? Of making you into him? Lord, help me. Teach me. Show me. Let me understand. Make me understand." Collin settled down in the bed, opened the Bible and whispered, "Speak, Lord, for your servant hears." Then she prepared to listen.

She was interrupted a few hours later when Dr. Wallace came to check on her. He gave her instructions to see her own physician when she returned to Oakton, as well as a medical pass for extended time off from work. Collin tucked it away for future reference then went back to her reading. She read and prayed and slept and read and slept and slept and read until a knock at the door sounded, and an unfamiliar but concerned face looked in her door.

Collin asked, "Can I help you?"

"Jeffrey says it's time to go if you're up to it."

"Thank you. You can tell Mr. Farrell I'll be out in a couple of minutes." She tried to move then modified her assessment. "Tell him five minutes. I'll be there in five minutes." The woman disappeared. Collin groaned, tried desperately to swing her leg over the edge of the bed, and was met with total defiance. *"Move? Are you out of your mind?? We're not going anywhere!"*

The woman returned and asked, "Is there anything you need? Anything I can help you with?"

Collin smiled tightly. "No, thank you. I'm fine. Really."

"It's not a problem, Ms. Any friend of Jeffrey's probably needs all the help they can get."

Ah hah! Maybe a chance for some past history. Collin recanted, "I could use some help getting up. My knee is pretty stiff. If you can help me straighten it out . . ." She showed the woman what she needed done then slowly and carefully swung around to place it on the floor. There was obviously going to be no weight borne here, yet. Collin asked, "Could you hand me my brace? We haven't been introduced."

"Trilby Shane. I work in the kitchen." And as if to prevent any misconceptions she added, "I'm a dietitian."

Collin said, "Thank you. Have you worked here long?"

Trilby smiled. "I worked as a dishwasher here for five years. Then I went to school, interned last summer, and this is my first year as a registered dietician.

Collin was impressed. "That's quite an achievement."

"Yes, it is." The woman smiled. "And it's Jeffrey's fault."

Collin applied the brace to her knee, and had to loosen it considerably from before. The knee had obviously swollen during her nap. Which did not bode well for sleeping through the night without the brace on. Or with it on, either. Drat. She asked, "How is it his fault?"

"Jeffrey 'adopted me' as his surrogate mom up here. He knew I had dropped out of school years ago when times were hard and that's why I was working here. He kept telling me I needed to do more with my life than sit around and watch it go by. That I needed to go to school, get my diploma, and get a career of some kind." She smiled, "He can be a nag."

Collin said wryly. "I'm beginning to see that." She finished adjusting the brace, and had Trilby help her to the sink in order to wash up anything that needed it. She looked in the mirror and groaned. "The whole thing's got to go. Trash it all and start over." She looked at Trilby and said, "So he nagged. Then what?"

Trilby continued. "Out of nowhere Camp Grace began a scholarship program. Any employee that wanted to go back to school, or to go to school, could sign up for classes. If the classes could benefit the Camp, say, in animal husbandry, or water resource management, or food preparation, or nutrition or whatever, then the person would have their tuition paid for and be paid half salary while they actually attended the classes. If you graduated and stayed on at least another season you got the rest of your wages reimbursed along with your normal salary. How could I pass that up? Several of us took advantage of it. I'm certain Jeffrey talked to Mr. McFaell and convinced him to set up the scholarships. He won't admit it. He won't admit a lot of the things he does around here, but we know." She smiled. "His friends know."

Collin knew better than to ask, knew just how catty it was going to sound, could even guess what Trilby was going to think of her for asking but asked it anyhow. "Does he have a lot of female friends?"

Trilby laughed lightly. "Girlfriends, you mean." It was a statement, not a question. "I've never seen him with one." She smiled. "Not that all of us mothers with eligible daughters haven't tried at least once to turn his heart." The sparkle in the woman's eyes told plenty. "Think of it: the Prince of the valley and my Katie, together."

Collin repeated, bemused, "Prince of the Valley?"

"Our secret name for Jeffrey. Finding a proper wife for him has been a regular cottage industry around these parts." Trilby laughed again. "There has been a regular parade of young women come to work at the camp just to try their hand at heart stealing. And not a one of them has been successful."

Collin finished washing up and said, "You never know. He might wake up one day and realize what he's been missing."

Trilby shook her head. "Not with Jeffrey. Besides, I think he has found someone, finally."

Collin asked softly, "Oh? What makes you say that?"

Trilby grinned. "You have to understand our Jeffery. He can play the clown, but when he gets serious about something, believe me, there is no question but what he is serious. You learn which is which after a while. Since this morning he's been inviting people to his wedding, telling them he wasn't sure about the date, yet, but to plan on coming. The man is in love."

Collin combed out her hair gingerly, avoiding stitches and bruises and blooded clots. She finally lay the comb down in defeat and said, "This is as good as it gets. Which is pathetic, but hey, that's life." She refused to comment on Jeff's wedding announcements, preferring to process the information over time. She looked at Trilby and said, "Thank you for helping me. I do appreciate it."

Trilby shrugged. "As I said, if you're a friend of Jeff's I'll give you all the help you need."

Which would probably be a good thing. Collin threw the thought back into the recycle bin, let Trilby bring her the crutches, then hobbled out and down the corridor, and out to the lobby.

Jeff was standing at the entrance glancing at his watch and grinning. He said sternly, "Ten minutes late. My, my."

Trilby quipped archly, "And when did you learn to tell time, boy?" She added, "Be nice to Ms. Walker. I've never seen one of our guests this badly battered before." She looked at Collin with concern and asked, "What were you trying, anyhow?"

Collin quipped, "Needlepoint. And hey, I passed. Thanks again, Trilby."

Trilby grinned at Collin, then shook a finger at Jeff and said as she walked past him, "Behave."

Jeff nodded obediently, "Yes, ma'am." He grinned as she walked off down the hall, then turned to Collin and asked, "So how are you feeling?"

"Isn't there a don't ask, don't tell policy around here somewhere? You don't ask me how I feel, and I don't have to lie about how bad it is. Deal?"

"Collin . . ."

"Jeff, I hurt, okay? I hurt everywhere. But I have to go see the kids come in. Please let's not start a fight here in the lobby. We can fight in the truck while you're driving to the base camp. Okay?"

Jeff studied her a minute, then softened and said, "Okay. I'll drive and we'll skip the fighting. Come on, lady." He turned her around then stood back out of the way as she propelled herself out to the waiting truck and trailer rig. Jeff carefully lifted her into the cab, put her crutches in the back seat, ran around to the driver's side and climbed in. He started the engine, pulled it into gear and headed out the driveway towards the river.

It took the full hour Jeff had predicted to reach a spot at the river where there was room to park the double rig. Jeff pulled to a stop and said, "They should pull up near here if the current's right, and if they handle the boat properly. We'll wait here for them."

Collin said firmly, "No, I want to go down to the water." She looked at Jeff and said softly, "I want to touch it."

Jeff studied her but did not challenge her. He led her down the ramp to a point where the water was calm, providing some relief for tired boaters trying to come ashore. A natural reef had been expanded to provide a safe haven of calm water. Collin and Jeff walked past two kayakers buttoning up their boats after a day on the river.

Out at the end of the jetty the river still roared and rushed past, boiling in its fury. Collin stood silently watching for several minutes then indicated to Jeff that she wanted to go out to the point. Conversation was limited as the thunder of the river squelched all noise but its own.

Jeff shouted in her ear, "You can't use the crutches out there. Too slippery. I could carry you."

Collin shook her head and shouted back, "No. Too dangerous. Can you just support me? I can make it with help."

"You sure?"

She nodded. She'd never been more sure. Carefully and slowly they made their way out to the point where the water splashed and danced against the rocks and boulders. Collin stopped about five feet from the bank letting the spray soak her thoroughly. Jeff stayed right beside her, not impeding her progress but not advancing it any, either. He let her do that at her own pace. Collin stepped forward down to the edge of the bank. She stopped just shy of the water, staring deep into its depths. She expected old memories to come flooding back, to drown her again in their icy grasp. But what lay before her was simply an expanse of water: a swiftly moving expanse of water, to be sure. But there was no small child screaming noiselessly beneath the surface, no valiant fishermen struggling vainly to rescue her. There was only hydrogenated oxygen.

Collin turned to Jeff, a look of relief on her face. She shouted, "It's just water! No monsters!"

Jeff hugged her. "No monsters!"

"Can you help me get down? I want to get my feet in it."

"It's slick, Collin."

"Please? I'll be careful."

Jeff hesitated then reluctantly nodded. He helped her ease down to a sitting position so she could put her feet into the rushing foam. Collin shouted with delight, "Cold! Fast, too!" She eased in farther to just below her knees. The iciness stripped her knees of feeling, which was a good feeling all in and of itself. A perverse thought urged her to go in a little deeper: just a little deeper. Jeff was there. He'd pull her back if she got in trouble. You'll never know if you've beaten it until you go in all the way, you know. Not truly beaten it.

Collin stared hard at the river mesmerized. Slowly, almost without will of her own, she began to inch forward, her mind a blur of thoughts and emotions and memories and . . .

Strong arms lifted her out of the water and back on to the gravel bank. Jeff turned her to face himself; she stared into his eyes, unable to speak, to defend or deny or explain her actions. They stood thus for several moments, reading each other, measuring each other. Finally, Collin leaned forward against Jeff's chest in surrender; he gathered her in his arms in a tight embrace.

A shout from up river startled them apart: the river rafters had returned in triumph. Paddles were raised high in the air, being shaken in victory salutes. Someone spotted Collin and Jeff and the cry went up of "Lady! Hey, lady! Case worker lady!!" "Jeff! Hey, janitor!! We made it!"

Collin grinned at the exuberance they could still muster after a long day on the river. She waved at them though they were still a good distance from the landing point. Excited shouts continued; the boat began to bounce up and down with the force of the crew's excitement. Without warning, Robbie jumped to his feet and let out a warhoop. At the same instant the boat hit a hole and dropped out beneath him, leaving him no landing place but the river itself. He plunged in with a cry and disappeared below the surface of the water.

Collin screamed, "Robbie!!" and with no thought, no brain, and only blind instinct, dove into the river after him. She fought her way out to the center then turned back to see Robbie surface, buoyed up by his life jacket. His face was pale with terror as he grabbed helplessly at twigs and branches for assistance. Collin could hear yelling from the beach as the two kayakers they had passed earlier launched their crafts in an attempt to help. Collin let the river carry her towards a petrified tree trunk she had seen. It jutted out far enough that if she could reach it and get anchored, she just might be able to grab Robbie as he went by—provided he could be convinced to turn backwards in the water. If not, she'd have to wait until he was actually past her before attempting to grab him. And that was not a scenario she was comfortable with. Either way she would have one shot at getting him, and one shot only. She prayed fervently, "Lord, help me, please. For once, I'm not trying to prove anything . . ." she bumped hard against the tree trunk, grabbed hold and inched her way out to the end, ". . . but please help me. Help me save Robbie. Oh, Father . . ." Collin anchored herself between sunken limbs. She saw Robbie caught in an eddy, slowly twisting him around and around, him fighting all the way. Collin risked a glance at the shore. The boat had landed and the rest of the crew was on dry ground. Jeff was with them keeping them calm, trying to keep them in one place. The first of the kayakers was mid-river and closing fast, but not fast enough. The second was aiming more towards Collin's perch. Collin turned back to where the eddy had finally released Robbie, praise the Lord, sending him backwards down the river towards the crashing falls. He was so, so close . . . if she would just let go and reach . . . but Collin waited. No heroics. She was not out here to die with Robbie, but to catch him if she could. Collin waited, and waited, and waited . . . and waited one more moment . . . and one more . . . then reached out and snagged the boy seconds before Robbie shot past her. She dug her heels into the muck, grabbed at a stub of a tree limb and held on with all the might the Lord would give her.

And in his ineffable wisdom it was enough. The river swept Robbie past the trunk but she held fast onto his straps. And then it was a tug of war between Collin and the river, and Collin wasn't about to let go. Like reeling in a giant fish, Collin worked her way up his tether until she could reach Robbie's jacket itself. She clutched at it desperately, then pulled him around to face her.

Robbie's eyes were wide with a mixture of terror and elation. He yelled, "Ain't it great!! Ain't it great! Case worker lady, this is so sweet!"

Collin screamed in frustration and rage, now released from fear. "Sweet!! Sweet!! You moron, you could have been killed!" She grabbed him and shook him as hard as she could. "Idiot! Isn't that the first thing they teach you? Never stand up in a boat! I hate boats and I know better than that!! What were you thinking? You weren't thinking! You never think!" She was running out of steam and Robbie was just grinning at her. Collin shoved him back very slightly and moaned, "What am I going to do with you?"

Robbie suggested, his eyes dancing, "Love me?"

Collin let out a loud groan, grabbed what she could reach of him and hugged him. "Robbie, I always have. What would I do without you?"

"Pick on some other poor brother."

Collin growled and snarled, "What are you grinning about?"

"You. You terrified of rivers yet you out here in the midst of one, no life jacket, no helmet and you yelling at me about being stupid? Case worker lady, you something else."

Kayaker number two arrived before Collin could decide to drown Robbie herself and finish what the river hadn't. The kayaker shouted, "Everyone okay out here?" He handed a life jacket to Collin along with a rope harness to go over her shoulders. He tossed a second harness to Rob then directed, "I'm going to tow you back to shore. It'll be further downstream but there's another site we can use. Your job is to float still and quiet at the end of the harness. Got it?"

Collin yelled, "Take Rob first. He's been in the water longest."

"You sure?"

"Yeah. Get him out of here before I throttle him." She made sure the harness was secure, handed it to the man, watched him secure it to his craft then watched them shoot off down the river out of sight beyond the bend. Collin sighed and looked back towards shore. The boat was securely tied down on the trailer, all equipment stowed and ready to rumble. The crew had been loaded into the van and was headed down the river to meet the kayak at its landing point. Jeff was standing off by himself looking out at her; a strange, dejected, almost mournful look on his face. He was too far away for Collin to read his eyes. She couldn't even begin to guess what he was thinking. Accurately. She could guess all sorts of things he might be thinking but none of them would be right. Her best guess would be that he was upset with her, again, and rethinking his marriage plans. Too impulsive, this one. Too irresponsible. Never stops to think. Never thinks. Walker, will you never learn?

She stopped ruminating and prayed softly, "Thank you, Lord. Thank you for loving me enough to die for me and loving me enough to let Robbie live. I didn't do this to prove anything, you know. Not this time." She smiled slightly and added, "You do know, don't you? I love you, Lord." As she finished the first kayaker bumped into her tree. He shouted, "Ready to go home?"

Collin shivered but nodded. "Yeah. I've had all the fun and excitement I want for today." And tomorrow and the next day and the next day and the . . . She tossed her tow strap to the man, stepped away from the tree and swirled into the waters once again. She was instantly spun around backwards then jerked hard as the kayak caught the current and shot ahead. Collin closed her eyes but felt no terror. It was almost pleasant: like drifting backwards on a pillowy cloud. Or might have been but for those nasty holes she kept dropping in. She was mindful not to kick and splash when that happened but tried to merely wipe the water from her face, choke out the river she swallowed and stay relaxed. Yeah right.

How long it took, Collin didn't know, and didn't care. All that mattered was that finally, blessedly, there was a crunch of fiberglass on gravel and someone's strong hands were pulling her out of the water. Someone else stripped the life jacket off and a third someone—or maybe the first someone over again—wrapped a blanket around her. Then several someones of varying heights, ages and vocal timbres threw their arms around her, cheering and shouting. Collin couldn't get the ice cubes out of her brain long enough to take it all in and make sense of it too, so just let the sounds flow around her. Good stimulation for the brain, anyhow.

At last Jeff's voice broke the madness, saying, "Okay, ladies and gentlemen, let's give her some air to breathe and a little space to rest. Everyone back on the bus." The cheering stopped, and the polite, respectful jeering started. Jeff gave them a no-nonsense, "Back!" and they quit.

Collin's teeth chattered as she pleaded, "Don't send them away. They're warm!" She noted that Robbie was on the bus wrapped in blankets, and being warmed, no doubt, by the tongue lashing he was receiving from guide and crewmates alike. All was well. There. Here, there was still Jeff to contend with. Again. Collin looked at him and said softly, "I'm sorry."

Wordless, he helped her to a small tree stump stool and set her down carefully. He began to rub her arms and shoulders, trying to restore warmth and circulation. He neither spoke nor looked her in the face. Collin repeated more strongly, "Jeff, I'm sorry. I didn't plan that. I didn't even think that. I didn't think, I know. I reacted. I reacted badly. All I saw was Rob out there in trouble and I did what seemed right at the time. You would have done the same thing." Why hadn't he done the same thing? *"Because he has more sense than that, stupid. Why do you think he's so mad at you? He knows what's right and you don't. It's that simple."*

Jeff kept his head down but said softly, "You're right, I would have." *"See?!"* "But I couldn't. I should have been the one out there not you. I couldn't help him."

Collin asked gently but confused, "Why?"

Jeff shrugged, still looking down. "Can't swim."

Collin studied him a long moment trying to determine if this was one of his jokes or not. But as he looked up the guilt and embarrassment in his eyes looked very real.

A tremendous sense of relief swept over Collin. She felt a smile coming on, tried to smother it but couldn't. She snickered slightly, covered her mouth, then grinned and laughed, throwing her arms around him.

Jeff looked at her critically. "It's not funny."

Collin hugged him and sighed happily. "Yes it is, Jeff. It's wonderful. It's the best thing you've ever told me about yourself."

From the look in his eyes Collin guessed he was rethinking those plans. Did he really want to marry a lunatic? He asked almost angrily, "How do you figure?"

"Superman has no flaws, right? Jeff Farrell, man of my dreams, has a flaw. He's not perfect. He's human. Just like me he's human."

"So?"

"So I can't marry Superman. I'd never be good enough for him. I'd try but I'd never make it. But another imperfect human . . . that—or him—I can marry."

Jeff took this all under consideration then said slowly, "So knowing I have a fault means you can love me?"

Jeff stood in front of her facing her. Collin nodded solemnly, "Uh huh."

Jeff kissed her tenderly and said, "Well, then, love of my life, let me help you love me even more." With each revelation he kissed her lightly. "I never hang my coat up. I drink straight from the milk carton when no one is looking. I'm terrible at answering mail. And I never put the cap back on the toothpaste."

Collin said softly, "Jeff . . ."

"Yes?"

"Shut up."

There followed one long embrace, then Jeff helped Collin back into the truck, still warmly bundled in her blanket, and they headed back for camp. They drove along in silence for several miles then Collin said, "Six months."

Jeff looked over at her, obviously not thinking the same jumbled thoughts she was. "Excuse me?"

"Six months."

"I heard that. What about six months?"

"I want six months before you officially ask me to marry you. If you still want to by then."

"You're twenty-six years old, Collin. You think you'd change that much in six months? I know I haven't changed in years. Which is why I'm still single, so I'm told."

Collin explained, "I know we're not going to change who we are . . ."

Jeff interrupted, "Though there are a few areas you could work on, you know." She sneered at him playfully. "Your temper, for one thing."

Collin ignored him and continued, "But we need time to see if this is real."

Jeff said seriously, "You know it's real, Collin. I know it's real. I have a feeling we've both seen the counterfeit enough to know the difference."

Collin tried again. "We both know it's what we want. But is it what God wants?"

Jeff stared at her, aghast. "What does he have to do with this?" Collin looked aghast. Jeff grinned and said, "Okay, try this. You want to know whether it's God's will or not? Flip a coin. If it lands on the ground you'll know God is saying yes, marry the idiot. If it suspends itself half way down you could get a pretty good idea that he's not in favor of this arrangement. But you might want to do a two out of three trial, for safety's sake."

Collin glared at him in frustration. Jeff grinned, "Okay, okay, how about if you read the word and pray about it and ask the Lord to show you very clearly whether this is his will or not. And at the end of six months, if you can't come up with an honest reason why you can't marry me then we get married. Agreed?"

Collin asked, slightly suspicious, "And how will you know?"

"I already had my talk with him about this. He said yes."

"Oh? And when was this?"

"The first night I met you. When a lofty case worker from Oakton wasn't too good to sit and talk to the lowly maintenance man. My being the janitor, greasy hands and all, didn't bother you in the least. And then when you set the Lord before your pride and prayed in front of a total stranger," Jeff's eyes shone, ". . . that's when I knew you were a lady worth loving."

Collin laid her head on his shoulder and said quietly, "That's so sweet."

"So we can make it tomorrow?"

Collin groaned, "You are so bad."

"But you've got to love me, don't you?" He looked down at her and asked, "You do, don't you?"

Collin closed her eyes, leaned against him and said firmly, "Five months." Jeff dropped his arm around her and whistled happily all the way back to camp.

Once they arrived Collin asked, "Jeff, what schedule are we on now? When do we have to leave?"

The maintenance man drawled, "Well, as pumped as the kids are I don't know whether it will do any good to feed them now or not. Flight's not long enough to serve anything but peanuts and I have the feeling even those would become airborne missiles."

Collin added dryly, "Good guess."

Jeff nodded, then continued, "So, the prudent thing to do is give them a couple of hours to unwind, or vent, or download, or whatever you professionals call it these days."

Collin said primly, "We call it relaxing."

"Kids this age don't know how. They just think of more active things to do to take up the time."

"Until they collapse from exhaustion," Collin added drily. "Which is fine, but hasn't answered my question. When do we have to leave?"

Again Jeff seemed to be stalling. "Well, I know the owner and he wouldn't have any objections if you all decided to stay overnight and go home in the morning."

Collin shook her head. "Nice thought, but no can do. I know the parents and the fact you reached all the guardians at all is a minor miracle." She added quickly, "And another evidence of God's hand in all of this, yes. But having told them all the kids would be in tonight we need to get them in tonight. Chances that you can get hold of parents twice in the same forty eight hour period are pretty slim."

Jeff shrugged. "We could try."

Collin touched his cheek softly. "Let it go, Jeff. We have to leave sometime. Even you can't stay here forever."

Jeff turned her to face him, and studied her eyes long and deep. After an immeasurable silence he said quietly and firmly, "I am going to marry you, woman. I will not say good bye, now, or ever. I'm not a stalker, I'm not a masher, I'm not possessive or obsessive but I do know I'm going to marry you. Five months or five years it doesn't matter." He stopped, thought a moment then added, "Of course, if you plan on having those five kids it would be nice to start early enough so no one thinks 'grandpa' is coming for Parents Day."

Collin could do nothing but look at him slack-jawed. "Five kids? Five?"

Jeff turned her towards the lodge and began walking her back to her room. He asked, "You want more? Okay, I think we can afford that. Just means I'll have to take on some extra work here and there. Bo is always looking for extra deputies. Not that he pays much but I could probably pick up a few hours while I'm here. And . . ."

Collin cut him off. "What time do we need to leave for the airport?"

"Eight."

"Fine. We will be assembled at the front of the lodge at eight. I suppose you will be driving the bus, since you do everything else around here." A sudden thought hit her and she said with horror, "Don't tell me. You're flying the plane, right?"

Jeff laughed. "No. That I don't do. I'm not rated for anything that large, yet." Collin groaned; Jeff said defensively, "I have a lot of interests."

"And too much free time. That's obvious."

"My time is never free, Collin. 'Private amusement' is not a phrase in my father's vocabulary."

There was a note of seriousness in Jeff's voice that Collin recognized, yet not one of bitterness or anger. Collin sobered up slightly. "I'm sorry. We really do need this time, Jeff. There's so much about you I don't know." A battle began raging in her head, *"Are you really ready for this?" "What about those five kids he wants?" "What about his family?" "What about* your *family?"* That one last shadow that was still out there . . . Collin dropped her head and said quietly, "There's so much about me you don't know."

Jeff lifted her chin, kissed her oh, so gently and said softly, "I know I love you. I know you love the Lord. Anything else, we can work out." He smiled slightly and said, "Go get your things packed and I'll see you later. I love you, Collin Walker."

Her heart ached, and her eyes stung with tears. *"'I love you, Collin Walker.' He loves a lie. There is no Collin Walker. Not in reality."* Collin closed her eyes and marched to her room to pack. "Lord, help me."

At last Collin and crew gathered in the foyer of the lodge. Collin noted that everyone seemed a little muted, a little contemplative. It should be a quiet ride home. As the silent group shuffled on board the waiting bus (which Jeff was *not* driving) Collin decided enough was enough. She waited until everyone was seated then asked, "Everyone ready to go home?"

General murmurs and grunts were her only reply. Only Robbie's face was shining as he said, "You got it, case worker lady. Time to get working."

Ta'waan stared at him in some confusion. "What you talking 'bout?"

Robbie nodded seriously. "This place ain't just about here. It supposed to teach us about living at home. Ain't no sense learning all this stuff if we can't put it to something."

Collin nodded, pleased and a little proud. "Straight truth, my man."

Pardner seemed to have caught on as well. "Yeah. Place is fun an' all but I can't stay here forever. Got things to do."

Collin grinned. "Like what? What did you learn up here, Pardner?"

The youngster was quiet, thinking it over before answering. Finally she said, "Guess it's like the man said. Learned I can. Put my mind to it, work hard, work long and hard . . ." she drew it out for emphasis, ". . . looong and haaaard . . ."

Chonnell threw a pillow at her. "We got it, we got it. You ain't worked no harder than the rest of us, you know."

Pardner said quickly, "But I was the littlest so I had to work hardest. Thing is, I did it." She looked around and corrected herself, "We did it. All of us."

Niles chimed in. "Know what you mean. If someone a told me I'd been working together with a Southsider . . ." the boy looked at Ta'waan then looked at Collin in almost an apology, ". . . and a white lady, or got to be friends with little kids . . ." Chonnell stuck her tongue out at him; Niles grinned, returned the favor then finished, "I'd of probly killed 'em. Ain't no way. But now . . . now it don't seem like it should ever been a big deal."

Nyla said quietly, "Maybe I learned something, too. Like maybe I'm not in control of my own life like I been thinking. Like maybe things can happen that we ain't planning on. And then it's what we do that counts. People say anything they want don't make 'em real. What they do, that makes 'em real."

There were general nods in quiet consensus. Collin waited to see if anyone else had anything to offer then said, "I'm sure the owner of the camp will be very pleased to hear all your glowing reports. Think about writing to him and telling him." Groans and moans met the suggestion; protests of "School work!!" "Write letters?" "Write???" echoed from around the bus. Collin stuck to her guns. "I think it would be a good thing. Don't you think if it were you, you'd want to hear from the people you helped out? I can give you his name and address . . ."

Snickers, howls and catcalls began all over the bus. Collin looked around, confused and a little lost. "What? What'd I say?"

Nyla sniped, "'I'll give you his name and address.' Like we don't know who he is. Get real, woman."

Ta'waan shook his head. "You aren't for real gonna sit there and tell us you don't know who the owner really is? That you never figured it out?"

Collin's face began to burn ever so slightly. "I'm a little slow . . ."

Robbie laughed. "A little? Case worker lady, we had it figured out the first night! Whole camp knew it."

"How?" Now Collin was suspicious. What was it she'd missed? Besides everything?

"The way he looked; how he dressed." Nyla began explaining, "When Mr. Parks introduced all the staff we all figured the owner would have to be there just to see what he was getting."

Collin asked for clarification, "Who's 'we'?"

"All of us; all the campers. We talked about it on the way up, trying to figure out who was paying so's maybe we could get him to pay for other stuff, too."

Ta'waan added as in jest, but probably with more truth than he meant to share, "Or so as we could sue if things didn't work out the way they was promised."

Nyla shrugged it off. "Yeah, well, some kids talked like that. Rest of us, we just wanted to know who it was. So anyhow, we get to the introductions. Mr. Parks, he looks like a director. Mr. Ted, he got on the warm-up suit; he dress the part of a coach. Ms. LeeAnn, she got on the secretary stuff, so she right where she should be. Only one as wasn't right was 'Dr. Wallace.'" The young woman said the name with almost total sarcasm. "You ever seen a doctor in cowboy boots? Or with a ponytail? Didn't even stand up when they called his name. Jus' lounged around sitting on the desk. Only someone as owns the place be that lazy. And did anyone ever see him do any doctoring the whole week we was there? I heard word someone saw you an' Jeff and Ms LeeAnn up at his office after you cut your hand. Why they be there if there be a doctor, huh?" She looked at Collin quizzically and asked, "Why did they be there?"

Collin said simply, "Jeff put stitches in my hand and LeeAnn was there to chaperone." She waited for the catcalls but got only silent stares. Collin waited a moment then said, "Even adults need chaperones sometimes. If LeeAnn hadn't been there, what kind of talk would have been going around?"

There was contemplative silence then Pardner offered, "That you was hitting on the maintenance man?"

Collin looked shocked. "Me? Why would it be my fault?"

Pardner grinned. "Jeff too nice a guy for that. Anyone talk to him know that."

Collin shook her head. "Thanks a bunch, crewmate." She looked at Robbie and asked, "Were you in on this round of thinking?"

"Nah. You too busy to be thinking 'bout hitting on guys. Got your nose stuck in your work." Collin launched a pillow at him. A five minute free-for-all broke out as adrenaline, anxieties, aggressions and various other left over emotions erupted. They did, however, remain in enough control not to bring any missile close to the driver.

Who almost too soon shouted, "War's over. We're here." Everyone looked out the windows to see that they had arrived at the small field which served as the county airport. A private executive-type jet was waiting, engines running, prepared to take them home. As the camp van approached the aircraft Jeff could be seen waiting at the bottom of the steps. Collin snorted. He probably pre-flighted the thing himself. Was there nothing the man couldn't do?

Swim. And hang up his coat. Collin grinned. Nyla saw and asked playfully, "Where you be, lady? Or maybe I need to be asking who you be with?"

The pillow fight had probably done Collin the most good of all of them. She felt incredibly relaxed, and finally, finally hopeful once again. She took one last glance at the man of her dreams then with mock sternness said, "Never you mind, woman. You got your secrets I got mine."

Niles heard her and hooted in derision. "Secrets? What you talking about secrets? The man asked us all to the wedding. Said we could be ushers and maids if we kept our act straight."

Nyla corrected him, "Bridesmaids, you moron. Bridesmaids. Don't you know nothing 'bout weddings?"

"Don't want to know nothing. I ain't never getting married. That be for old folk like Jeff. He old and he crazy."

Collin muttered, "Amen."

Robbie jumped in the conversation. "Yeah. Dude kept saying he got to come get my permission to marry you, lady. Say he be 'round in 'bout four months. That make sense to you?"

Collin reached in her pocket, handed Robbie a dollar without comment, then rolled her eyes heavenward. She shook her head and said, "Unreal. The man is unreal."

The van rolled to a stop and everyone disembarked with Collin hobbling along in the rear. Jeff high-fived, low-fived, slapped fists, and generally said good bye to one and all in the current body language of the planet. Robbie, though, he pulled aside and hugged. He said quietly—or as quietly as you can say anything and still be heard over the roar of jet engines—"You made the start, man. Follow it through. The case worker lady can help you with the reading if you're serious about learning. She can help you with all of it, you know."

Robbie nodded but said, "I want her to see it, not just hear me say it, man. I want her to know it be real in me."

Jeff clapped him on the shoulder then hugged him again. "I want to see you up here next summer. Maybe we can work out something over Christmas break. We have ski camp, too. You ever ski?"

"You see any hills in Oakton?"

"Good point. We'll work on it." He released the boy and Robbie scrambled up the steps.

Collin bit her lip to stop the trembling. This wasn't forever. It wasn't. It wasn't even good bye. It was simply "see you later." It was. It was. It was . . . she stomped her crutches on the tarmac in frustration. She smiled politely and said, "I'll see you."

Jeff must have known but was having none of it. He put his arms around her, ignoring the hoots and whistles of Collin's more juvenile crewmates and kissed her warmly. Then he released her but not from his arms. He said softly, "I'll call you when I get back in town. Be about four days."

Collin bit her lip then asked, "Can I call you before then?"

Jeff shook his head. "Don't. I'm two days behind the changeover now and I won't be where anyone can find me for more than five—well—fifteen minutes at a time. I love you, milady, but I've got work to do."

Collin quoted, "'I could not love you half so much, loved I not honor more.' I understand."

Jeff nodded. "Good thing because I have no idea what you're talking about. You're to get that knee checked on Monday, no question, no debate."

"I have the number in my backpack."

"And the stitches come out a week from tomorrow."

Collin nodded. "And I'll pull them, unless there's a problem, yes, sir."

"And you're calling your boss tomorrow first thing and extending your vacation another two weeks . . ."

Collin interrupted, "I don't have two weeks. I've only got five days."

Jeff continued as if she hadn't spoken, ". . . five days so you can recover. Bo is sending him a fax with all the particulars of your help in bringing Mitch down. He'll have you sainted if he gets his way."

Collin said darkly, "If Mitch stands trial and gets put away then we'll celebrate."

Jeff said soothingly, "Count on it, milady. Count on it." He lifted her chin gently, kissed her one almost last time and whispered, "I love you, Collin Walker."

Collin hesitated only slightly. The words hurt, the fear was intense, but she answered softly, "I love you, Jeff Farrell." Yet another last kiss followed.

And then a burly and brusque voice shouted sternly, "Farrell! We only have so much fuel, you know, and it burns at the rate of many dollars per minute. McFaell makes me account for ounces, man. Let the lady go!"

Jeff grinned, waved the pilot off then looked at Collin and said, "I'll call you. Be careful, milady. I love you."

Collin turned and worked her way up the steps, blind for the tears in her eyes. He had not said good bye. Gratefully, he had not said good bye. Collin made her way to an unoccupied seat and collapsed in it. No good bye. It was a point of hope, a glimmer of light to hold on to. Maybe this time, finally, it would be different. Maybe this time the ghost of the past would leave her alone. Granted, if he were a ghost, it wouldn't be a problem. But since he was all too real flesh and blood . . . But maybe he had forgotten her. Maybe he would let Jeff live in peace. Maybe he would let *her* live in peace. Maybe. She whispered softly, "I love you, Jeff. I'll talk to you later."

Robbie slid into the seat beside her, buckled his seat belt, buckled her seat belt then said encouragingly, "He be crazy 'bout you, Collin. He be crazy, period, but he be more crazy 'bout you. You be seeing him again."

Collin nodded, not trusting her voice. It was going to take some doing to retrain all her emotions back to their proper places and restraints. Robbie said, "I like the dude, you know? Ain't never put much stock in no white man before but Jeff be different. Be the Lord what make him different, ain't it?"

Collin nodded and was able to say, "Yeah. It's knowing the Lord that makes him different."

Robbie looked at Collin and said quietly, "I gonna be different, too, lady. You watch. You see." He reached out and awkwardly took Collin's hand then squeezed it carefully. "I got me a family an' I'm gonna make them proud."

Collin smiled and sighed. She squeezed his hand back and said, "I already am, Rob. I already am." She let her head fall back, closed her eyes and let the tears fall. Dreams come true. God answers prayer even when you've given up asking. Could anything be better than this? Could it? Could it?

Ask her again in four days . . .

CPSIA information can be obtained at www.ICGtesting.com
Printed in the USA
BVOW071232040613

322403BV00002B/126/P

9 781462 726394